Child of Paradise
Listen to your Dreams

Pratibha R DH

Published by Flugel Publishing House

Copyright © Pratibha R DH, 2017

First Edition, April 2017

ISBN: 8192592855
ISBN-13: 978-8192592855

ACKNOWLEDGMENTS

I am extremely grateful to the following persons who have helped me more than they know in the writing of this book.

Bibekananda Das For helping me understand police procedures, strategies, and investigations, nature of police work, classification of crimes, knowledge about mental states required for certain crimes, criminal procedures and other aspects of criminology. He helped me greatly in my research. Bibekananda Das is Additional Deputy Commissioner of Police (APS), East Police District, Dispur.

Anamika Tewari For connecting me with the right police personnel who helped me in my queries on police procedures, crime investigations, cyber crimes and cyber laws. She helped me greatly in my research. Anamika Tewari is currently the Deputy Secretary to Govt. of Assam's Tourism & Fishery Department.

Antara Buragohain For answering my queries on cyber crimes, cyber laws and police investigation procedures. Antara Buragohain is an ACS (Assam Civil Service) Officer.

My friend, *Dr. Ankita Saikia,* and my cousin, *Dr. Jyotirmoy Das*, for helping me with medical terminologies and procedures and in editing those parts, along with my cousin, *Dr. Jahnabi Das*, for patiently answering all my medical queries on the same.

My friend, *Anil Singh,* for giving me inputs on corporate procedures and laws and guiding me to people (especially his good friend *Manoj Sharma*, who provided me many useful insights for which I am so grateful) with knowledge on the same.

Mishti (Arundhati Ghosh), my buddy, for our endless discussions on crime and detective resources that stimulated my 'mental Wikipedia' and provided me tremendous inspiration. She is a true detective buff and a great buddy to discuss stuff on crime and detectives.

Psychics **Peg Torbert**, **Marla Valentini**, **Sally** *aka* **Unicorn** and **Kelly Callaghan** whose work I closely watched and from whom I learnt a lot on after-life. They inspired me at various points while writing my novel.

To Wicca practitioners **TipToe Chick (Dolores Chapman)** and **Charming Pixie Flora (Flora Sage)**, both of whom I followed on YouTube and their social media pages. All the Wicca resources I used in the book are pearls I learnt from them. Both TipToe Chic and Charming Pixie Flora have also hugely inspired my children book series, *Magical Ventures of Loli and Lenny*, in which I have used a lot of magical spells, talismans and magical stuff based on resources provided by them.

My buddies, **Lakshmi (Srilakshmi Ramachandran)** & **Sowmya Sharma**, as well as my brother-in-law **Madhurjya Phukan** for providing me a lot of information about the beautiful city of Bengaluru, in which my novel is based. I owe the city a lot and consider it my second home as it was kind to me at a very crucial time in my life. I survived all my life challenges with the amazing love and support from some awesome friends in Bengaluru who still remain the best of friends to this day.

My niece **Rhea (Nayanika Saikia)** with whom I share a common passion for reading, writing and books. We always tend to take the contributions of our family members for granted. So today let me take this opportunity to appreciate the fact that, through the years, my long and stimulating conversations with her has given me a lot of feedback on the pulse of the younger generation – their revelations as well as the current trends. This has helped me immensely in writing the expressions and feelings of my characters, especially the younger crowd.

My super-duper editor, **Tulip (Rhinusmita Lahkar)**, whose encouragement and support goes a long way back in my work as an author. Her easygoing rapport makes it less of a professional relationship and more of a cool friendship. Words fail to express the awesome boost and wisdom she has bestowed on me through all my years as an author.

Listen to Your Dreams

Child of Paradise

Child of Paradise

Listen to your dreams

Chapter 1

May 21, 2015
Bengaluru

"How did she get out of the car?"

"Must have got thrown out...I saw a car rush by – it didn't stop. Gosh! Look at all the blood..."

"Do you think she is dead?" asked an anxious voice.

There were a lot of vague noises and scuffling around as Tia sensed an unbearable pain in her stomach and her back. Everything was hazy. The world seemed to be moving round in circles as she felt herself being lifted and rushed somewhere. She was enveloped by the sounds of sirens, vehicles and people's voices. Somebody was calling out her name and crying in anguish. Then suddenly she was drifting into darkness as she lost all consciousness.

"Someone call a code!"

"I will start the CPR!"

"Ok, do compression..."

"Give me epinephrine, please!"

"Epinephrine – given at ten...continue CPR for two minutes and then we'll check for pulse..."

"Let's listen for breath sound..."

"Let's stop and check for pulse and check the rhythm."

"I have no pulse..."

"Give me another epinephrine please..."

"Let's give another epinephrine."

"Ok, that's number two."

"Continue CPR for two more minutes and then we will check the pulse again."

"IV fluids are up!"

"IV fluids are open...any other causes of this unresponsiveness in this rhythm? Anything happening, nurse? Check for pulse...do we have a pulse?"

"I have a pulse...now check for blood pressure."

"Oh, you have a pulse..."

"I have a pulse..."

"Check the blood pressure."

"Blood pressure 86/60...we can give more fluids..."

"I am losing the pulse now!"

"We are losing the pulse!?"

"Yes..."

"What is the rhythm!?"

Tia felt herself sucked out of her body and was overwhelmed by a strange sensation. She looked down to see doctors and nurses working frantically all over her body while she lay plastered with tubes and tapes on a hospital bed.

Was this a dream? Or was she already dead?

"No, you aren't dead." Somebody seemed to have read her thoughts. She turned and saw a beautiful, luminous lady with dark hair standing by her side, a soft smile hovering around her lips.

"Who are you?" Tia said, quite blatant and sounding a little rude. She was feeling quite out of sorts actually.

"I am Meena."

"And who is that?" Tia pointed at the lifeless form on the operating table.

"That's you, of course, my dear."

When Tia looked confused, Meena gently said, "They are trying to revive you."

"Am I dead or something?"

To that, Meena smiled again and held her hand. "Come with me. Your mother's waiting."

Tia felt herself being sucked away again in a white tunnel with Meena holding her. There seemed to be orbs of light rushing past her and sometimes even people. Everything happened much too fast as she felt herself sucked into a golden white light.

Then their flight seemed to slow down as they approached a beautiful, green, hilly meadow with flowers blooming everywhere the eye could see.

There were people gathered in small groups here and there as if they were having a picnic while some wandered around in solitude casually. They all looked relaxed and happy with children playing or running around the trees. Everyone seemed to know her and they smiled at her as she walked past them.

"Look, there is your mother." Meena nudged her softly towards the opposite direction.

Tia felt her heart would burst as her mom descended slowly down the stone steps of a hill.

Her beautiful mom looked even younger now. Her dark hair was tied in a bun as she had always seen her. Tia rushed towards her and held her mother tight as tears streamed down her cheeks like floodgates breaking forth.

She felt that unexplainable sense of love and bliss as her mom embraced her back. Was this really happening? Oh God! If this is a dream, let me never wake up, she thought.

"My darling daughter, my Podgy, how I have missed you!!" Her mom's voice was overflowing with emotion.

As Tia walked by a beautiful brook with her mother, she felt like a child again. She kept looking at her mother over and over again, a sense of déjà vu completely overwhelming her.

Now that she was with her mother, she never wanted to leave her again.

Again, as if her mother read her thoughts, she looked at her gently and said, "It's not your time yet, Podgy, my love. You must go back." Her mom looked a little sad too.

"Am I not dead then? Must I go back?" Tia could feel a tightness in her chest at the thought of leaving her mother again.

"No, Podgy. You were brought here just for a short while. You must go back now. There is a lot of life ahead of you, darling."

"But why!?" Tia sounded outrageous. "I don't want to go back. I want to be with you here. There is nothing for me back there anyway. Let me be with you..."

"No, honey. One day you will be here. But not now. Now is not the time. You have a long life to live. Show your gifts to the world. Be an angel, spreading love and happiness to others like you did to me. The world needs more people like you in this world."

"Mom, I'd rather be here. It's lonely out there."

"No darling, your sister – Nysa, your brother – Dev, they all are waiting for you down there. And they love you a lot."

"No, they do not! My absence will be hardly felt," Tia sighed.

Her mother smiled again as she pointed at two little chubby boys who looked utterly cute and angelic.

"See, your children are waiting too. They can get a chance only if you give them."

As the two toddlers flashed their mischievous smiles at her, she looked quite taken aback.

"My children!?"

Her mother nodded, amused.

Her mom must have developed a wacky sense of humour, Tia thought.

"Mom, I miss you. I don't want to go back!" Tia knew in her heart it was a losing battle.

Her mom kissed her forehead and held her shoulders as she said, "I have never left you, darling. I have always been by your side in your every waking hour and even when you sleep. You just weren't aware of it."

At that moment a shadow fell across her face and she gasped at the smiling face of her dad.

Her happiness knew no bounds as her father hugged her emotionally.

"Mom, where is sis?"

Her mom's face immediately took on a haunted look. Tia was surprised to see her fleeting emotions from happiness to loss and then sadness. Her father and mother exchanged worried glances.

"Where is Rianna, Mom?" Tia's voice sounded agitated.

She noticed a sadness mar her dad's face too as she darted glances from one to the other.

At that precise moment, Tia felt herself being pulled back into a vacuum while there was a white noise humming in the background. She returned to her body in the hospital as the nurses and doctors hustled around her. Most of them looked anxious and tense as they hurriedly worked round the monitors and machines of the ICU room.

She could feel pain all over her body as she heard a female voice exclaiming frantically,

"I can feel some pulse, doc!"

"You do!? Check her blood pressure..."

And then she was overtaken by numbness as she lost consciousness again.

Chapter 2

"Tia?" Tia heard a familiar voice calling her name hesitantly. She tried opening her eyes and feeling groggy and heavy in her head. She sat up to release that numb feeling in her body.

"Whoa, whoa...slow down. Not so fast!" It was Yuvi, her childhood friend.

"Podgy, don't get up so fast...it will make you dizzy...." Her sister was by her side in an instant, trying to make her comfortable. Nysa looked older than her years as Tia gazed at her sister's beautiful face.

"How long have I been here?" asked Tia. Her voice sounded croaky.

"Almost a week, Tia. You have been pulling off that sleeping beauty stunt very well, while giving us sleepless nights," said Yuvi, tongue-in-cheek.

"Have I?" she asked, her tone teasing him back.

"But I am glad you are alright, Tia." He sounded greatly relieved as he looked at her with fond affection. Very close as kids, they had lost all contact in their teenage years. But once they started working together, their relationship picked up right where they left off.

Nysa ran her fingers lightly across her sister's brow in a loving caress as Yuvi continued, "Do you remember anything? We found you on the roadside and it looked like your car fell off the slope of the hilly road..."

"Yuvi, is she ready for this?" asked Nysa in concern.

"I know, Nysa," Yuvi sighed. "I am just preparing her in case the police question her..."

"It's okay, Nysa. Yuvi, I do remember avoiding a car which came out

7

of nowhere. I tried to avoid the collision...maybe my mind was elsewhere..."

"Hmm...some local people did see your car rolling down the hill from afar and called the police. The police said there was no sign of any other car. At least they didn't find anything as nobody came forward. And then your condition was too serious – a matter of life and death. Your head badly hit on the dashboard and you lost a lot of blood," he said.

"Luckily, the doctors managed to stop the hemorrhage in the nick of time." Nysa heaved a deep sigh of relief.

"Whoever it was you tried to avoid was a mean bastard!" Yuvi muttered angrily.

Tia sensed flashes of memory – vague memory of her car being hit several times. The intense fear of trying to save herself from being killed made her grimace in pain. But maybe she was not hit after all. Maybe it was just the impact of her car skidding down and rolling off the slope. She was not at all sure which though.

"I can't remember anything much actually..." Her face lost colour and sweat beaded her brow as she looked at them with confused eyes. Nysa immediately held her, caressing and soothing her at the same time. "That's enough. Stop thinking too much and drink some water." Her sister made her drink some cool water to get over the shock.

"But I do remember having a beautiful dream, Nysa, maybe while I was in the OT..."

Nysa looked relieved to see the smile on her sister's face. She kept the glass of water back on the table and was immediately at her sister's side.

"You do?" Her voice was gentle and encouraging so that Tia could quickly come out of her dismal mood.

"Yes. At first it wasn't good. I could see myself lying on a hospital bed and the team of doctors and nurses working on me. I was in pain..."

Yuvi too quickly pulled a chair next to her as she recalled slowly.

"A beautiful woman by the name of Meena took me by hand and we hurtled through infinite white space. It was actually like a long, white tunnel. Then there was this gorgeous meadow with people all around – happy, smiling...and then I saw Mom walking towards me..."

"Mom?" Nysa smiled, a questioning look in her eyes.

"Yes! We hugged and embraced each other!! I don't remember being so happy in a long time. Then there was dad too. Mom said I had to get back...but I wasn't so happy about it. I told her I wanted to be with them..."

Nysa and Yuvi exchanged looks, their eyes sympathetic, as Tia found herself going back to that space and time.

"It felt so real, Nysa..."

Yuvi petted her hand as he said, "We know you miss her a lot, Tia. But that's exactly what your mom wants – you to be back on your feet and charging with that super energy that you are known for."

Yuvi always made her feel good. He was that true-blue friend everyone should have by their side in difficult times. He was quite good looking and well built too. She heard that many girls fell for him, back in school, but he was the quiet, detached type that drove the girls even crazier.

He quickly looked at his watch as he said, "I need to get back for a board meeting, Tia. I will be back later." He pressed her hand warmly as he bid her goodbye and left quickly.

The next couple of days were a rushed round of calls from the police, doctors and nurses. Her sister took time to visit and bring her tasty meals while she recovered. Tia felt better in a week and was raring to leave the hospital as she was going crazy with boredom. She wanted to get back to the comfort of her cozy little home. The police never found anything about the car that supposedly hit her and, eventually, their visits stopped too.

Her brother, Dev, and his wife, Maya, came to pick her up from the hospital on the day of her discharge. She lived on the ground floor of their family home in Indranagar while the first floor and second floor were used by her brother and his wife.

Her apartment looked quite neat as Maya must have taken care of it while she was away. She knew it was very thoughtful and caring of her sister-in-law, despite Tia being at odds with her brother in more ways than one. Her relationship with her brother was no longer comfortable as it was in their childhood. Maybe because he was the oldest and there was a twelve-year gap with Tia, who would be turning twenty-five soon. Now as he got more and more busy with his business and his own family, she felt that they had somehow drifted quite far apart.

Tia had never felt so alone in her apartment. Nysa had quickly visited her and once she made sure her sister was comfortable, she had to leave to make arrangements for her daughter's upcoming birthday. Her sister was also the managing director of a software company along with her husband and was quite the busy lady with hardly any time in her hands.

Tia missed the company of her sisters and her mom, now more than ever. They had always been a huge happy family and her mom had always been there for them. She too, like her mom, was a total homebody and missed not having her large family that she grew up with. Her parents always had guests, mostly relatives, coming and going any time of the year. That also included a great deal of sleepovers and vacation visits, especially from their cousins. Her mom came from a large family and her sisters often stayed over at weekends or vacations. Tia's adolescent years were spent amidst a lot of chatter, cooking, noises and stories. These days, however, she found it very difficult to make new friends or have any kind of new relationships.

Alone now in her huge apartment, she put on some music while wandering into the kitchen to feed on the noodles that her sister had left her. Maya had come along with her daughter once to check on her, but she had to leave quickly for her daughter's music classes. Tia's twelve-year-old niece, Alisha, was preparing for an upcoming school concert and so Maya was quite busy with that. Not that Alisha herself didn't want to spend a little more time with her aunt.

"Maybe I will skip practice today and spend some time with Aunt Tia, Mom," she said. "We already played for straight two hours in school...I'm tired." Tia smiled when she heard her niece protesting.

"No, Lisha. Deepali Ma'am will be really upset if you skip your practice at this crucial time."

"Aunt Tia, why don't you spend the night with us?" Alisha said excitedly. "You are just back from the hospital and you mustn't be alone – isn't it? And it's been a quite a long time since we've had a sleepover together!"

"You have a test tomorrow, Lisha," her mother reminded. "So, no sleeping late tonight..."

Tia anyway declined and promised her niece that she would try to make it some other time when her concert and tests were over. Her niece left soon after, not without a sullen pout, though. Tia threw her a flying kiss coupled with an apologetic pout.

Uncle Neal had called and asked her to get back to work only when she felt better. The company was doing very well without her interference, he jovially added. Tia knew that it wasn't true. He couldn't afford to give any of his employees time off, what with the company not yet completely recovered from the financial disaster that took place some time back. But of course, he didn't want Tia feeling guilty and thereby cut short her recuperation period. Neal Arya was a widower with no children. Age was catching up with him and he really looked to his favourite niece, Tia, for running his business. Especially during the last couple of years, when it was facing major downswings.

Tia had no idea when she drifted off to sleep with a book in hand. When she woke up, she saw a light streaming from under her closed bedroom door. Her bedroom lights must be all on. As she groggily sat up on her living room couch, she noticed it was still dark outside.

She turned on the living room lights and slowly walked to her bedroom. Opening the door of her bedroom, she could not see any light. How strange! There was a rustling noise, however, and the beaded curtains in her bedroom moved as if somebody had just touched them. Tia's heart beat very loud, fearing it might be an intruder. But their neighbourhood had always been one of the safest in the area.

The light was actually creeping in below the outer door of her bedroom that opened out to the garden lawn. She armed herself with a tennis racket and slowly walked to the door. She still could not see the source of light after peering through the peephole. She quickly unlocked the door and stepped outside. The midnight air that touched her skin was cool as she walked down the steps.

Was that a shape of a person below the gulmohar trees, she wondered. Tia told herself that she should have got a torch, although the street lights left a reasonable amount of visibility around. She slowly ran towards the figure that seemed to be walking away very fast. But when she neared the trees that stood at the edge of the lawn, there was absolutely no sign of anyone around. A scarf was dangling from one of the tree branches. Must be the shadows playing tricks, Tia thought, as she made her way back to the house.

Lying on the bed, she kept tossing around. After a while, realizing she couldn't go off to sleep, Tia walked back to the living room. She took out her family album and lounged cosily on the couch. She loved the photograph of hers on the first day of school, when she had just turned six. It was taken on the school grounds. They all studied in the same school and her brother, Dev, at eighteen was a handsome young man. He was totally into body building those days. Rianna, who was eight years her senior and in the ninth grade, was quite the poised lady. She was holding Tia piggyback on her shoulders while Nysa, the tomboy at twelve, was doing a stunt on her cycle. She must have been in the seventh grade. They all looked so happy. Her mom had one of her hands latched at her waist while her other hand was pointing at them as if admonishing them about something. Dad must have taken this picture, Tia thought tenderly.

Then there was another one where her mom was combing her hair and she was crying. She must have been fussing about going to school. She hated school when she was young. Another set of pictures at a very happy time in their lives was at Diwali during her brother's wedding with Maya. Her brother made a handsome groom with her equally beautiful sister-in-law. Rianna and Nysa looked gorgeous in their silk saris.

The next one was with her sisters Rianna and Nysa during Nysa's first day at NIT, Kurukshetra, where she would be studying for an engineering degree in computers. Her dad looked so happy and proud that Nysa had got into one of the most prestigious colleges in the country.

The picture of her mom in a wheelchair was the one which hurt most. It was the time her parents had met with the car accident that took away her dad's life. Someone must have taken the picture on their way back from the hospital. She was only fifteen. Her sister Nysa had to be back at the campus for her studies and Dev was on tour for his business. All the responsibility of their family, especially her mom, had fallen on Rianna's shoulders. Rianna had just completed her diploma in animation in a college nearby. In spite of a hectic schedule what with a part-time job as a web designer in Uncle Neal's company as well as running her own animation freelancing business, she handled everything stoically and gracefully. She was the rock of the family taking care of her and their mom as well as the household finances quite remarkably. Her business had blossomed pretty well in a short time all because of her hard work and her graceful nature. Her clients were quite taken with her charming personality and sincere attitude.

Then there was the picture of her along with her mom and sisters – when she got admission in the same college where Nysa had studied for her engineering degree the previous couple of years. Her mother, although in frail health, looked very proud and happy. This was at their home just before Tia left for college. Who would know a year later when she was just about to come home for her vacations, their mom would pass away. Tia felt that familiar pang in her heart again. She wished she had stayed close to her mom and studied nearby in one of the local colleges. Rianna had to manage everything alone, especially as their mom's health was deteriorating day by day. But her sister was adamant that Tia completed her college and not miss the golden opportunity of a lifetime. She could always help later once she completed her degree in computers according to Rianna. What made her feel guilty was that she too had wanted to complete her degree in that college so badly. She wished she had insisted a little more on staying back.

The picture of Rianna engaged to Jeff Bailey was one of the last pictures Tia had of her. Rianna looked so happy and utterly blissful – so full of life. And then six months later, her sudden tragic death shocked everybody, and left her whole family devastated. Tia felt she would never recover from the loss of her sister. Nysa had dropped her prestigious job in New York to return to her family home and a job nearby. But nothing could fill up the void of Rianna.

To help her overcome the darkness in her life, Tia had emerged headlong into her studies and managed to perform quite brilliantly in her engineering exams. Not wanting to be back home to face the emptiness again, she got into one of the top companies in Singapore and worked there for a while.

The pictures of Nysa's wedding with Jeff Bailey a year later were amongst the few that Tia could never enjoy happily. Nysa was hurt that Tia managed to only make a brief appearance at their wedding.

After working in Singapore for a year and a half, Tia felt somewhat homesick and wanted to work close by home. Whether or not it was a good decision to return home, she was not sure. Her twenty-fifth birthday soon was something she was not looking forward to at all.

Chapter 3

"She slept off on the couch?" asked Nysa, amazed.

"Looks like she has been going through the old albums again," said Dev, an impatient sigh escaping his lips.

Nysa gave Dev a dark look to which he shrugged and looked suitably chastised.

"Podgy...wake up." Nysa shook her sister gently.

Tia blinked to the bright sunshine flooding into the room. "What's the time?"

"Almost midday," Nysa smiled. "Did you sleep well?"

Tia blinked as she sat up.

"I think I had a nightmare." She grimaced tiredly.

"Nightmare!?" asked Nysa.

"Hmm...felt somebody about last night...not sure."

"Must be due to a disturbed sleep," said Dev as he sat near her. He looked into Tia's eyes and said slowly, "What's with all this, Tia?"

He took the albums in hand as he questioned her. "Staying up and looking through old albums won't get you through life, you know?"

A hint of tears welled up in her eyes as she turned her head away.

Dev sighed as he got up to go. "And, Podgy, the doctor wants you to collect your final reports. Let me know when you are ready and I will take you. Uncle Neal too called in while you were asleep but he didn't want to disturb you. Maya's left you some soup and chicken rolls. You might want to heat it before you have it. You left your door unlocked too, so please be careful next time. See ya later."

Tia murmured a quiet thanks as her brother left shortly while her sister got her some tea and toast.

"What's your plan for the day?" her sister asked as she poured her a cup.

"I think I will drop by office. Check on Yuvi and find out what's been happening while I was away."

"So soon? You were just released from the hospital yesterday. Must you not rest a while?" asked Nysa, concerned.

"Nothing left to do here. Might just as well..." Tia shrugged. "What about you? You are usually very busy at this time of the day?"

"Yes, but I can make some time for my little sister who is just out of the hospital, can't I?" She ruffled Tia's hair lightly just like when they were young.

Did her youngest baby sister realize how pretty she was, mused Nysa, as she looked at her lovingly. Her feminine features were more than attractive what with her high cheekbones, angular jaw, sharp nose and olive skin against wavy raven hair. Her hair was long and shiny matching her dark long eyelashes. Her shapely full lips and bold brow arches enhanced her delicate bone structure while her almond shaped dark eyes gleamed with an intelligent brilliance.

"How is Lola?" Tia broke into her reverie.

"Lola is behaving terribly as she will be soon jumping into her terrible twos. Keeps her granny on her toes." Nysa smiled.

"You are lucky. Jeff's mom is really handy with my niece and you can still keep your job – meaning run your company."

"I won't disagree, Tia," said Nysa as she took in the tea tray and rushed to the kitchen. "You want me to give you a lift? I have to rush back to office before lunchtime."

"No, I will manage. Carry on."

Tia was glad to be back in the daily grind at her office near Ulsoor lake. With a staff of fifty people it was quite a busy office running a software business. It kept her happy and busy. Her uncle, Neal Arya, was a great boss and they had a great working relationship. After a year and a half in Singapore, she joined her uncle's firm at twenty-three. Her uncle's company, however, was running at a great loss then, especially from the time around Rianna's death. Rianna had been someone her uncle could trust, but with her no more, things were falling apart left and right. Yuvi was good at the technical side of things but otherwise the financial side of the business was running haywire.

From a staff of two hundred people, the company had come down to thirty people. Soon after Tia joined, in a very short amount of time, she had helped her uncle bring the company back to its feet somewhat. Even now it had a staff of only fifty people but it was making reasonable profits. They had found the main culprit behind the embezzlement of funds and once Jai Biswas was fired, everything seemed to be getting back in shape, albeit slowly.

Her family and friends questioned her when she left her lucrative job in Singapore. Tia had better career prospects there and could do better. Yet, Tia had the satisfaction that she brought a loss-making company back on its feet, besides helping her uncle – one of her favourite persons in the world. After her parents and Rianna, he was one person whom she looked up to and who in turn really had her interests at heart.

The day passed off in a flurry of activities. Yuvi dropped in once to check after her and also to discuss some upcoming proposals with a few foreign clients.

Back in her apartment, after a bath and a hot dinner, she flipped through the TV channels but finally switched it off as she couldn't find anything that interested her. She felt incredibly drowsy as she tried to keep up with the pages of the new book that her sister had got her.

Strangely, there were still a lot of cars buzzing round the neighbourhood and she felt disturbed. Then after a while everything went quiet when she heard footsteps at her door. When she looked up, she saw her door open. She felt herself gliding down the steps. There was a car waiting for her outside. It was a brown Xylo used by one of her friends. But she couldn't remember whose it was. She felt something make her get in and drive the car. He was waiting for her. She was already running late. Could she deliver whatever he had expected of her? Would the lighting be good enough for her shoot today? Anyway she would have added a new collection to her portfolio and killed two birds with a stone.

She stopped and looked down at the waterfall running down the rocky side of the hill. Luckily the waterfall was heavy due to the rainy season and she could get some good shots of the valley. Otherwise there was only scanty water during the dry seasons. As she moved around taking scenic shots of the beautiful flora around, she saw somebody waiting a little further away with the back turned on her. She walked towards the person who looked like a young lady in her twenties. Tia called out to her. She was about to tap on her shoulders when the person turned around. She couldn't believe her eyes as she found herself looking into her sister's face. Tia gasped and was about to hug her in relief when she saw blood oozing out of her sister's mouth and her eyes dilated. There were scars sprouting abruptly all across her body and blood was pouring everywhere. Tia couldn't take it anymore and she turned back to run towards her car. She stopped in her tracks when Rianna called out, "Tia, don't leave me, please...help me be free...Tia, you must!"

Her sister was crying out woefully in a hoarse voice. Tia was shocked to see Rianna in this state but she didn't look back and rushed to the car. The colour of the car had turned from brown to red all over. She felt nausea overwhelming her once she sat inside the car. There was blood all over the car – on the steering wheel, on the seats and on the floor. Tia didn't know how long she was screaming when she felt warm hands holding her.

"Tia, Tia...it's alright, it's alright...shhh..." It was her brother holding her. He was sitting on the side of the sofa and holding her while Maya got her a glass of cool water.

"How did you get in? Was my door open?" she asked once she felt calm.

"Fortunately you left the inner door connecting our staircase open," said Maya as she sat down close by. "Are you okay? We heard loud screams."

"Yes, better..." She found herself trembling.

"You are shaking." Her brother shook his head in concern. "What was it?"

"I had a dream." She shuddered thinking about it. "And Rianna, Rianna..." Her voice broke out in sobs.

"Looks like the nightmares have started again..." Her brother looked at her worriedly.

Tia looked away, not meeting his eyes. Her brother had never understood this side of her emotions. He always said that she was living in the past and entangled in a web of unnecessary regrets. She was not letting go and that was not healthy for her. It was also the cause of her nightmares and intermittent depression.

"Tia, I think you should not be alone tonight," said Maya, her eyes clouded.

"No, I am perfectly fine...I..." she started but her brother interrupted. "Don't argue, Tia. You just had an accident and your emotions are raw. We have two extra bedrooms. You can use either one for a few days."

Dev took her by her hand as if he would hear no more. The rest of the night, Tia spent in her brother's apartment on the first floor. The next morning dawned out bright and beautiful with Nysa sitting on an armchair nearby. She had a mug of coffee beside her and a book in hand.

"You are just in time for coffee and toast. Maya made some mouthwatering *uttapam** too."

"What are you doing here?" said Tia, her voice grumpy. "Shouldn't you be in office?"

"It's a Saturday in case it has escaped your notice," said Nysa, her voice chirpy as she hastily got up. "Freshen up. I will get you fresh coffee and breakfast."

Alisha was more than excited to find Tia in their apartment, early morning. She left for school only after extricating a promise from her aunt that she would spend the night at their place again.

"So what was that about last night?" asked Nysa as she laid down the coffee tray, her face masking the concern that Tia could instantly read in her eyes. Tia sighed as she sipped her coffee. She felt bad for worrying her brother and sister but sometimes it upset her that they never did get this part of her.

She massaged her forehead as she said, "I dreamt of Rianna. She was drenched in blood all over..."

"Oh, my gosh!" Nysa cringed at that. "Hadn't it stopped a long time back? You weren't having them for quite a long time now, were you?"

Tia bit her lip as she moved her head from side to side.

"Maybe the shock of the accident has triggered it all over again. I don't think you should be alone for a few days. Stay here or come to live with me...what do you say?"

"It's okay. I don't want to cramp your routine..."

"Of course, you won't! You are our Podgy...our little sister...you know we are always there for you, hon?" Nysa's voice changed to a softer tone. "I am sorry I haven't been very understanding the past few years and we have had our differences. And I know you miss Rianna a lot...but I care for you a lot...because you will always be my little sister." She paused and her eyes looked watchful. "You know that, don't you, Podgy?"

Nysa looked quite emotional and showed the side of her which Tia rarely got to see. She couldn't take that easily and held Nysa's hand while trying to smile hard. "I know Nysa, I do! But I think I will be okay. I will let you know in case I feel otherwise. Meanwhile, I really need to get back to my work – get busy! Idleness drives me crazy. And then I'm sure I will be okay." She tried to infuse some enthusiasm in her words.

Tia did not return to her apartment for a few days. She stayed for a night with Alisha, who excitedly shifted her pillows and covers to share her aunt's bed. Tia was more than amused to hear her prattle nine to dozen all night. She humoured her with infinite patience but moved to Nysa's place the next day. She didn't want her niece to be too distracted from her studies, especially on a school day.

She knew Maya was very particular about Alisha keeping her grades consistent and even though her sister-in-law had not shown her any displeasure, Tia worried that her recuperation might unnecessarily cause hiccups in their carefully planned routines. What with Dev being a very busy man, Maya had to manage everything on her own at the home front. Tia didn't want to add any hassle to her schedule by coming in her way.

After a week with Nysa, she immersed herself headlong at work keeping late hours in the office. But her dreams didn't seem to cease as she tossed and turned restlessly at night. They were all dreams of Rianna crying or seeking Tia's help. "Tia, I need you to help me," she would often plead. But luckily they weren't as gory as the first one she had.

Finally, she returned to her apartment. Once back, she felt a strange sense of desolation inside her. Insomnia hit her hard the following week. It was just like her days in engineering college after Rianna had passed away and she had gone through a massive depression. Her grades had sunk steeply and she would cry all night. In fact she didn't remember sleeping at all. The doctor had prescribed her sleeping pills. But they didn't seem to have worked too.

Tia didn't want to go back on medication. Maybe I should hit the gym, she thought, as she tossed on the bed restlessly. Finally it was in the early morning hours that she fell asleep. She dreamt of her mom this time. She was looking really beautiful in a mauve chiffon sari. Both she and her mom were walking through a beautiful paved pathway with flowers growing in the sidewalks. It was a beautiful moonlit night and it looked like they were in a beautiful town with cute cottages and lanterns lighting the bricked pavement.

"Happy Birthday, sweetheart. Can't believe you are twenty-five now! My little girl's all grown up..."

"I know, Mom. I still feel younger, like when I was in school and you used to be behind me for every little thing. Gosh! How time flies!"

Then her mom, Pooja Arya, turned to her and said carefully, "Podgy, I am not happy with the way you have been getting on with life. Is that what I have taught you to do...break down like this? Tia, I am really upset with you!"

She looked displeased in a loving way but not angry at all.

"But why, Mama?"

"You are not the brave girl I thought you to be!"

"What makes you think that?" she asked, puzzled.

"You are lapsing back into your depression phase – especially for Rianna. You had put that all behind you, didn't you? But now it's starting all over again..."

"You know she is my sister...and I can't forget her easily. Just like I can't forget you, of course. And after this accident I am feeling out of sorts, actually. Some kind of empty hole burning in my heart, leaving me desolate. Maybe once I am emerged in my work and my projects, this will fade away slowly as it did before...."

"But life has to go on, Podgy. Nothing must deter you..."

Tia sighed at that. She didn't have the strength anymore, she sometimes felt.

"But it isn't easy...and I miss you..."

Pooja interrupted her softly, "I miss you too, honey. And that's why I am always by your side." She continued slowly but earnestly, "Now I want you to promise me something. You will take care of yourself and do everything as I say?"

"What do you want me to do?" said Tia, her voice was low with dejection. "I am working my head off..."

"What about trying some holistic practices? Maybe that might work out..."

"Holistic practices!?"

"Yes, like yoga and meditation. It helps calm the mind, fight depression, brings inner peace...you will find good teachers if you look around you."

"Okay, Mom. I will do that."

"Check in the lake area – on the northern side of your company campus..."

"I will do that. But Mom, what's up with Rianna...she looks so sad...so unhappy..."

Her mom shifted her eyes and looked away at that. "We are all trying to help Rianna."

"We?" she asked puzzled.

Her mom seemed uneasy at this subject, "You should not concern yourself with all these matters, honey. Leave Rianna to me. In fact she shouldn't have contacted you in the first place. I have told her not to..."

"What do you mean? Why shouldn't she contact me...why is she so unhappy...Mom? Mom!?"

Tia woke up to a bright sunshine flooding her room and a sound of the doorbell.

It was her friend Krystal who rushed in with her peppy energy.

"Hey! How you doing, Kitkat?" Krystal quickly thumped her shoulders and squeezed in a tight hug. "Sorry, got back late last night. Totally jetlagged with this whirlwind tour. Howz you? Back to being the 'tears' queen, is it?"

"I am sure Nysa's filled you in with all the trivia." Tia smiled dryly. This was her friend, Krystal, who was a straight talker but she never seemed to mind. They had been childhood friends – seen each other through highs and lows.

"By the way, Happy Birthday!" said Krystal as she handed her a gift from her bag.

"You remembered?" Tia smiled as she opened up the gift. It was a beautiful blue floral dress – just apt for the summers. "It's beautiful. Thanks, Poppins!"

"Glad you like it. Let me get the cake. It's in the car."

"Oh, you shouldn't have bothered..."

"Come on, it's your birthday, Kitkat! And with all of us in our mid-twenties, that calls for a celebration too. What say?"

Krystal filled her in with the local gossip and all that she had missed while both of them had a quick breakfast of toast and eggs. She ran a fitness clinic and was a nutritionist. She met a lot of people every day. It was never boring to be with Krystal. But beneath her peppy and infectious exterior was a sensitive and a down-to-earth girl who was compatible with Tia's quiet nature. No wonder they got along so well even in the years apart while at college and when she was working.

"Are there any yoga centres nearby?"

"Yes, there's a new one coming up. Why do you ask?"

"Thinking of joining one."

Krystal narrowed her eyes as she said slowly, "You can always join the gym or take up a dance class at my fitness centre. Why do you need to look elsewhere?"

"Mom's orders, Poppins."

"What?!" exclaimed Krystal as the toast fell off her mouth.

"She told me in my dreams to try yoga and meditation...and check out teachers in the lake area."

Krystal's mouth fell further. "Holy moly, did she? I have heard of a certain Natasha Abraham recently in our locality...but dunno where exactly."

"She said to check in lake area, northern side of my office."

"She is again coming in your dreams? It had stopped, hadn't it?"

"No, just twice. Once in the hospital. And then again yesterday." She felt strange as she recalled back the dream. She thought about discussing Rianna but quickly changed her mind.

"So that's why you have decided to practise yoga?" asked Krystal, her voice laced with curiosity.

"I don't know...never liked it that much. Too slow for me. I was thinking about the gym or swimming. Let me think about it." Tia shrugged.

"Hmm..." Krystal nodded slowly as she buttered another toast.

"And how's your love life been, Poppins, while I was away?" Tia asked smoothly.

"You want to know about my love life? Now that's new..." Krystal said meaningfully.

"Sometimes I do have human thoughts and feelings too, you know."

Tia's tone was dry, although her lips curved into a smile.

"I know, Kitkat. Just kidding. All I can say is I am sick of men. I prefer my single status for some time." Krystal released a huge sigh. She looked at Tia meaningfully. "But you, my dear, better see someone quick. It's been almost two years here and folks are questioning. This is not Singapore you know."

"Questioning what?" Tia gushed out.

"Hmm...usual for us single girls of marriageable ages...what's with this Tia...isn't she getting married...are there no boyfriends in scene...is she a lesbian...something in those lines..."

"Oh, really? They can think what they want. I am sooo not worried, you know!" Her voice was lowered in a conspiratorial tone.

"You know what?" Krystal lowered her voice in a meaningful way. "There is this new guy at our centre who..."

"I don't wanna know!" Tia's hands quickly moved to her ears.

"Friends like me don't come easy, Kitkat...who is single and still lets an opportunity free for God's sake!?"

"He must be your cousin or your ex – or just fat?"

"None of the above. He is simply not-my-type!" They bantered awhile about Krystal's love life as Tia locked her door and each headed their own way.

After a long day at the office, Tia had a quick bath at home, changed and then drove for a while around the Ulsoor lake area. She came across a cafe and thought of stepping in to ask if they had heard of any good yoga centres nearby. There was only a guy sitting in the cafe reading the paper and sipping fresh coffee. The coffee fumes teased her nose and she felt like having some too.

A lady in her fifties ran the cafe and she was quite friendly. "Well, I did hear of a new yoga centre that had come up with a certain Natasha running it. But I'm not so sure where is the exact location," she said.

"Maybe I can help?" It was the man sitting with the paper who had approached her from behind. And it looked like he was quite tall.

"Yes, I..." Tia was at a loss for words when she realized who he was. He was even more handsome than ever and leaner with chiselled good looks.

"Tia!"

He looked zapped too.

"Ron..." Tia said softly. There was a loud thumping noise close to her ears or was it her heart bursting out?

"Well, well..." He smiled lazily. "Who would have thought...where have you been and how have you been?"

She mustn't blush like this, she thought. What was wrong with her for heaven's sake? At least she had always imagined she would be a little more poised if ever in life they met again.

"I'm good." She smiled shyly. "What about you...you live here?" She managed to catch her composure somehow.

"No, no, no...just around for a short visit," he said as he moved his hands vaguely and gave her a keen look.

She was not at her best today, especially with her faded jeans and an old t-shirt. Her hair was roughly tied up too.

A phone buzzed and she jumped to check hers.

"It's mine." He smiled in amusement.

"Oh!"

He raised his forefinger and his tone was that of apology as he said, "One minute?"

Somebody called her from behind, "Ma'am, your car is parked at the wrong place."

Tia wanted to catch Ron's attention but it seemed like the call was important as he looked distracted.

"I gotta go," she mouthed as the restaurant manager looked at her impatiently.

"What?" Ron asked while leaning his head towards her.

"My car is on the wrong side," she mouthed again softly. He looked undecided but she quickly made her way out as the restaurant owner too came and requested her urgently.

She wasn't at her best anyway and she didn't know why she felt she needed some distance away from the full impact of meeting him.

Uttapam* - Uttapam is dish from South India made by cooking ingredients in a batter. It is like a thick pancake, made from fermented rice and white lentils with toppings such as chopped veggies cooked right into the batter.

Chapter 4

"How is she?" asked Krystal as she chopped away the onions neatly.

"Awesome, Krystal," said Tia. "It's been a week and a half and I feel so good already. I think you should try it too."

"How long is a class?" asked Krystal.

"Well, Tasha makes us do yoga for forty-five minutes. And then we have around twenty-five minutes of meditation. It feels so good. My body is relaxed and keeps me geared for the day. The meditation classes have been awesome. I feel so much at peace. Just talking to her makes you feel so good, so peaceful."

"Who – Tasha?" asked Krystal.

"Yes. You will love her. Strangely the dreams have stopped too, Krystal," said Tia. It was great to have Krystal back in town. Just like old times.

"Dreams about Rianna?" When Tia nodded, Krystal shuddered. "Well I am glad. Some were quite gory, I remember. They had come to you long back around the time of Rianna's death and then they stopped, didn't they? Why did they resurface again? Was it because of the accident?"

Tia shrugged at that. "I really don't know what could be the trigger."

"When Rianna passed away you were in your third year of engineering, right?"

"Yes, Poppins, just after my twenty-first birthday."

"Those gory dreams of her – how did they stop?"

"I don't know. Maybe because I immersed myself in my studies day and night to forget the pain," said Tia.

"And then Aunt Pooja had come in your dreams too, you had once mentioned?" she asked.

"Yes, good that you reminded me. She told me to keep the book of Hanuman Chalisa or the Bible near my bed always with a rosary. Then she asked me to say a prayer that she often used during our childhood. After the prayer she asked me to use the rosary and chant a Buddhist mantra around 108 times every night."

"But how did you know the mantra?" asked Krystal.

"It was one she had in her diary and used it often. She asked me to check there."

"The dreams stopped after that?" she asked.

"Yes, completely. Although my depression lingered for a long time. But then with my projects and exams I could somehow get through it."

"Your mom always manages to come to you during your difficult times, doesn't she? Almost as if she is hovering beside you, like a guardian angel. How moving is that!"

"I know, Krystal. But it's only the dreams about Rianna that disturbs me. Wherever she is, it must not be a happy place...that's what I sometimes feel."

"I understand, Tia." Krystal sighed. "But at the time of her death her face was totally disfigured as well as her body. Maybe that is the reason why you get those bad dreams. Subconsciously, it did affect you in a bad way at that time, didn't it? In fact, all of us."

The atmosphere was strained as both Tia and Krystal were lost in their thoughts of Rianna. Krystal wished she had not broached up the topic. Tia had just managed to settle herself.

"I will put on some music," said Krystal as she walked towards the music system. The door bell rang right at that moment and she went to see who's come.

"I have a surprise for you!" said an excited Krystal bursting into the kitchen where Tia was busy preparing a fruit salad.

When Tia looked around, she saw Krystal's eyes brimming with excitement.

From right behind her jumped out a cute petite brunette.

"Nina!" Tia looked astonished.

Tia was at a loss for words as Nina hugged her tightly. She was overwhelmed to see her other childhood best friend standing next to her.

"I am back for good!" Nina exclaimed.

"Back for good? How? Why?"

"She has been hiding her cookies pretty well..." Krystal's smile was smug.

"Oh, come on Poppins!" Nina smiled happily. There was an aura of happiness surrounding her, in fact a radiant glow.

"What have you been up to? How come you're here without notice? Did your boss let you out so easily?" Tia was full of questions.

"I have left my job!"

"What!?" Tia never knew Nina to be so rash in her entire life.

"I have been thinking about it for some time. And now I have totally decided to start up a consulting business here. My fiance's also supportive of my decision."

"Nina?" Tia looked at Krystal who looked absolutely zapped too. "I am totally lost here. Fiancé?"

"Yes! I am engaged!" She flashed her ring, her face brimming with excitement.

"When, how...?"

"You sneaky devil!" exclaimed Krystal. "When did this come up, Eclairs?"

"I am sorry, guys. It was a whirlwind affair. I am totally in this state of disbelief myself!"

"Alright, calm down. Now sit here and begin from the start." Krystal commanded as she pulled Nina to the sofa while Tia followed slowly behind, amused.

"Remember Ryan from high school?" said Nina.

"Jina Taneja's brother?" asked Krystal.

"He is the one!" Nina piped in happily.

"OMG! Forget Ryan. Are you sure you can handle Jina?" Krystal winked.

"I am so happy for you, Eclairs. I remember he was three years senior to us in class. How did you meet him? You did have a crush on him in school," said Tia.

"Yes, he was too busy dating the hotties then. But this little girl blossomed in time too." Nina batted her eyelashes flirtatiously.

"And?" Tia could hardly contain her curiosity. She felt cosy and happy as she hugged her friend. It was like old times, almost like being back in school.

"And one day we bumped into each other in an art exhibition in London."

"He recognized you?" asked Krystal

"Well yes! Why not?" She acted wounded.

"Stop that! You clown!" Tia threw a cushion at her friend.

"Then?" asked Krystal impatiently.

"He asked me for coffee and we hit it off immediately, reminiscing about the bygone days. He asked me for dinner the next day and one month later he proposed."

Krystal whistled to that.

"That's quite fast, isn't it?" Tia looked surprised.

"Yes, but I am ready to settle down, Tia. Enough of trotting around the world. I am past twenty-five, ready for babies and cooking at home. I need a break from all that corporate life and staying away from home." Nina sighed. "And we know each other since ages, grew up in the same town...so again that's familiar territory..."

"That's so beautiful..." Krystal said softly.

"Poppins, I can't believe you have tears in your eyes," Tia said, amused. Krystal was the hardnosed cynic among the three.

"I better check on my cake..." Krystal disappeared into the kitchen.

"I am so happy for you, Nina." Tia hugged her warmly as Nina showed her pictures of herself and Ryan on her iPhone. They looked so good together. Ryan didn't have that boyish look anymore. In its place was the picture of a mature man.

"Coffee with freshly baked cake for the immortal gang of Kitkat, Eclairs and Poppins!" Krystal breezed in happily.

"Hey, I picked up some chicken sandwiches on the way." Nina bent down to retrieve the sandwiches from her bag.

"Umm...the sandwiches are good!" Tia gushed as she finished one and sat down with her coffee and cake.

"Talk about a blast from the past, hmm," Krystal murmured thoughtfully, her eyes crinkling with amusement. "Life's strange, isn't it?"

"Absolutely!" Nina said. "After Manav broke up with me, I thought I'd never recover. And when I met Ryan, I was like, not another fling in life...and then it all instantly clicked – right away!"

Krystal and Tia exchanged looks. Nina looked so much at bliss. Even they could feel a part of her happiness rubbing off on them.

"Actually, I met someone from the past too," said Tia casually as Krystal and Nina looked at her with keen interest.

"Remember Ron Garg?"

Both their mouths fell open.

"Of course I remember, Kitkat," Krystal answered. "He had a thing for you and the same went for you too. And I thought you two would have been an item if you were not distracted by persuasive Arjun in high school."

"Oh, come on he never did have anything for me!" protested Tia.

"Tia, of course he did. I noticed too. He was in final year of school and we were in the ninth grade," said Nina.

"Yes, he was three years older. We knew him as a senior only for a year and then he had gone for college." Tia relished the taste of latte that Krystal had made so well. "We met him later only because of his sister, Tanya."

"Come on, you did look for him a lot when we reached our ninth grade and so did I," said Nina coyly.

"Did we, Eclairs?" asked Tia innocently.

"Yes, I stopped when I thought he looked interested in you," said Nina with a sad sigh.

"Oh, stop it Nina!" Tia couldn't help laughing as Krystal and Nina shared meaningful looks.

"Actually, I remember in school he would come and chat with us, especially you, on the pretext of talking to Tanya." Krystal winked.

"Oh really?" said Tia, raising an eyebrow. They were not going to drop it quick, so Tia decided to play along.

"Yes, really!" They chorused naughtily.

"Come on! Siblings do meet for a chat at school," Tia explained patiently.

"But not that frequently. And I remember whenever we used to drop at Tanya's place for group study, he would keep dropping in the living room at one pretext or the other. Even Tanya started picking up the signals." Nina's eyes darted from one to the other meaningfully.

"He was quite the genius in Math, I remember. Helped me at times with my Math homework," said Tia, thoughtfully.

Krystal and Nina exchanged mischievous glances at that.

"He would, wouldn't he?" Nina teased.

"How very convenient!" said Krystal, tongue-in-cheek. "And it's called subtle flirting, by the way."

Tia acted as if she never heard them. "Wonder where Tanya is?" she mused. "I totally lost touch!"

"You lost touch with all of us, didn't you?" Nina's voice had a hint of accusation.

"I am sorry, guys." Tia sighed. "With mom's passing away and then Rianna, everything was so overwhelming for me."

"But we would have been there for you, Tia. You needn't have cut us off, you know. Please remember we are always there for you, Kitkat," said Nina softly.

"I know, I know...." Tia held Nina's hand. "I have been damn lucky to have you two in my life. And it sure feels good to have you guys back in my life again."

"It sure does." Krystal smiled happily while tucking in her legs cosily on the sofa.

"I wonder how's Tanya. She was the whiz kid amongst all of us," said Tia curiously.

"I don't know, Tia," said Krystal. "She never tried to keep in touch. Never replied to my mails too. I heard she holds a good position at Biogen in Massachusetts."

"Maybe some part of her mom rubbed on her, after all. I remember Aunt Nita was quite reserved and a snob at times," said Nina.

"Ron was planning to do business management, I remember," said Tia vaguely.

"Yes, he is one of the top young financial consultants in Delhi I heard," said Nina.

"Hmm, why doesn't that surprise me," said Krystal happily. "They were quite the geek stars in our school."

"Aunt Nita must be in another cloud altogether what with both her children doing so well."

"And what about their other sister? Royna? Remember her?" asked Tia, grimacing at the same time.

"Who can forget! She was older to Ron and took after her mother completely. She was even more snobbish than her mom. Heard she filed for divorce too. Who would want to spend their lives with someone so full of themselves anyway? I don't know how Tanya and Ron turned out so well," said Krystal.

"Maybe because of their dad," said Tia. "Sahil Uncle was very nice, my mom told me. And a genius to boot. Both parents of Ron were so different in their personalities. Mom always wondered how they got along so well. Nita Aunty was the society butterfly while Sahil Uncle was a down-to-earth guy, dedicated to his work. Ron and Tanya spent the major part of their childhood with Uncle Sahil's mother and his sister while both their parents had to travel on business. Royna was in a boarding school, though. Mom used to meet their grandmother and aunt during their parties and other local events. They were very nice and down-to-earth just like Sahil Uncle. But tragically he passed off when Ron passed his twelfth."

"Yes, I remember that too," said Nina. "In fact, they had just moved into Bengaluru when Tanya had taken her admissions in the ninth grade and Ron was in the twelfth grade. Everyone in school, including the teachers, knew him only for a year but they were quite taken with him as he soon became a school topper in studies as well as sports."

"I heard Tanya isn't that friendly these days. Some of my friends have got in touch with her in New York but she is not too keen to reunite," said Krystal.

They all went silent at that. Strange how life changes people and the people who you grew up with turn to be somebody else.

"Anyway, back to the topic of Tia and Ron..." said Krystal interestedly.

Tia threw a cushion at Krystal and showed her tongue.

"Yes, let's not divert, shall we? I was sure something would have come up if golden boy, Arjun, didn't make an appearance in between," said Nina. "I am positive about that!"

"Arjun – the superstar! All the girls in school were mad about him. I think I was the only one who never understood why," mused Krystal.

"He was very good looking and a great cricket player at that," mused Nina. "I remember Tia was confused as to which one she liked more –

Arjun or Ron."

"Arjun was always following me around, gifting me chocolates and flowers. How could a sixteen-year-old me resist?" said Tia. "Quite flattering for my ego what with Ron making me wait years for a sign and then never around, eventually. And don't you forget that Ron was always going around in school with someone or the other."

"Those were rumours. Tanya said that it was the other way round. Girls fell for Ron but he never gave a damn," said Krystal. "She never knew him to be serious about any of them."

"When he first came to school he was with this gorgeous girl from Shimla – Priya. And then there was Sonia..."

"Wow!" Krystal and Nina looked at each other with exaggerated surprise. "You even know their names!"

Tia continued coolly as if she was never interrupted, "Then he went to college and with Arjun paying me so much attention, I was thrilled. In my eleventh, I remember, Ron lessened his visits back here. He was never around and Arjun seemed to distract me a bit as he turned his attention full frontal on me. We went around for three months. Who was to know that he was trying to make Sanjana jealous?" said Tia slowly.

"What a bastard! He had the gall to tell you that!" said Nina in sheer annoyance.

"Can't blame him. That was nine years back. We were all so young and I was the dewy-eyed girl pining for the great unattainable Ron," said Tia, shrugging her shoulders.

"So you admit to that!" Krystal winked.

"Guilty!" Tia lightly shrugged her shoulders.

"Arjun was a total jerk. I was appalled when I came to know he tried to force you," said Nina with contempt.

"I know. We planned to work on a school project at his home and he did come on strong. Thankfully his brother had turned up with his friends at the house. They were planning to watch a cricket match together. It was a sudden plan and Arjun wasn't aware. His brother was quite nice always. And not a rogue like Arjun. But then I am still not sure how far he would have gone..."

"But to everyone in school he was the golden boy!" muttered Krystal in disgust.

"Then you never met Ron again?" asked Nina curiously.

"No, they moved to Delhi, remember? Because their mom had to handle the family business. Tanya took a transfer midway in her eleventh and that way Ron never had any reason to visit Bengaluru again."

"Do I hear a regret there?" Nina smiled mischievously.

"Oh, stop it, will you, Eclairs!" Both Nina and Krystal had decided to rake up her past that day for some reason. But she was not sure if it was only them because lately she had been dreaming of Ron a lot. Not that she would reveal that fact to her friends.

"Was there anyone else later, Tia? You never told me about anyone else except for Raj Shavik." Nina's eyes were watchful as she looked at her friend.

"Yes, you know that turned out to be a disaster too. Me and my stupid heart." Tia mocked at herself.

"Come on, you were young...and that too right after your mom passed away. Raj provided you a comforting shoulder and you gave in..." said Krystal.

"It was a year into the affair, wasn't it, when you found out he was gay?" asked Nina sympathetically.

"Yes!" She sighed. "He wanted to hide his secret behind me and fool his family."

"All jerks!" Krystal ranted.

"And then there was no one," remarked Nina, with a question in her eyes.

"None!" said Tia happily. "And I am happy that way." She suddenly saw Ron's face in her mind's eye.

Nina seemed to be thinking on the same lines too as she said, "But who knows with Mr. Ron Garg in town..."

"He might just be passing town, for all we know," Tia protested. "It's almost a month now, come on. I never did meet him again..."

"But do I see a blush there..." Nina's smile was impish and Tia couldn't help laughing. She shrugged indifferently though in her heart she did wonder about him and hoped to see him again.

"It sure feels good to catch up on old times. Coffee, anyone?" asked Krystal happily.

Chapter 5

"Tia, go there..."

"Where, Mom?"

"The coffee shop," she replied.

"Alright," said Tia and went inside. She found it was the familiar coffee shop she had visited the other day. But it was empty.

There was a table there with a beautiful jar lying on the table. The liquid inside shimmered with orange gold. Miraculously, a glass appeared on the table. A beautifully designed glass.

Tia walked to the table and looked at the inviting drink in it. Somehow she felt very thirsty and wanted to gulp that liquid down her throat.

Her mother was behind her. "Drink it," she said, nudging her, her smile beamed with encouragement.

Tia poured the liquid in the glass and started drinking it. It tasted delicious and cooled her dry throat. As soon as she finished drinking, she felt a strange happiness overwhelming her. She felt euphoric and wanted to do something joyful such as dance and sing or maybe fly.

She hugged her mom and said, "It's awesome, Mom. I feel so good – so happy and energetic. I haven't felt this in a long time."

"I know." Her mom smiled. "Now I want you to come here tomorrow morning before office and maybe order a drink."

"Before office?" she asked puzzled. "Mom, you know it's a rush hour in the morning, what with my yoga, meditation, then a quick breakfast and..."

"But I want you to come here before you go to office..."

Tia woke up to bright sunshine, chirping of birds and the ringing of the door bell.

"Hey, haven't you woken up as yet?" It was not the bell but Nina on the phone.

"Yes...I just did...I missed my yoga classes today!"

"It's ok, Kitkat. Skipping classes once in a while will not ruin your peace of mind. I called you to remind you that we are going shopping today evening. I will pick you up."

"Yes, I remember...hey Nina...one more thing..."

"What hon?"

"Are you free now?"

"Yes, for another hour. Why?"

"Wanna go for a quick coffee nearby?"

"Right now?" Nina sounded quite surprised. "Won't you be late?"

"Yes, but I have my reasons. I will tell you on the way."

"Okay, I will reach you in another twenty minutes."

Tia had a quick bath and was dressed up by the time Nina came.

"Treating you to coffee today!" Tia winked at her friend as she got into the car.

"Alright, but what's the occasion and where is this cafe?" asked Nina, amused.

"It's a new one. I had gone there a month back. I will guide you. Take the left?" she instructed her friend.

"Is the coffee good there?" she asked curiously.

"I don't know. MOM asked me to go there!"

"What?" Nina's jaws almost dropped open.

Tia smiled at that. "Still the sentimental fool, you must be thinking."

"Of course not, Kitkat! I always loved you for the person you are – emotional, romantic...whatever. Although these days you are more closed about it. And Poppins tells me you always take your Mom's dreams seriously. No harm in that. And I get a free coffee too!" Nina chirped cheerfully.

Tia smiled back, drawn in by her friend's effervescent vibes. Nina was always the bubbly one amongst them. She was just the kind of friend one needed on a depressing day.

"That's the one, Eclairs," Tia said after they drove for fifteen minutes.

"You go and place the order while I park this one and join you," said Nina.

Tia walked in the cafe and saw the restaurant to be empty except for the waiter and the manager. Tia took one of the window seats and quietly sat there looking at the menu, waiting for Nina. Questioning her sanity for following some silly dream, she shrugged her shoulders and got busy browsing the menu.

The restaurant door opened and Tia looked up to beckon Nina to her table. The sun streamed in through the door making a halo around the person coming in and it was not Nina. Tia felt a sudden jolt in her stomach and the wind knocked the breath out of her at the sight of none other than Ron.

Ron seemed to notice her too. He waved at her and coolly walked to the cashier. After probably placing an order, he slowly walked to her table. Tia felt her heartbeat race and she hoped her emotions didn't show as she schooled her face to look calm.

"Hi, we meet again, Tia." His smile was cool and his eyes impassive.

Tia felt a little let down as she said, "Yes, it's a small world."

Hope I don't sound breathless, she thought. She didn't want him to continue carrying that schoolgirl impression of her, of the time when she was awkward and silly over him.

"Visiting home?" he asked with a polite interest.

Why did he think she left this place or how did he know, she wondered.

"No, I live here." She tried to sound as nonchalant as possible. "What about you?"

"Visiting on business."

There was a silence as Tia didn't understand why she felt so tongue-tied and at a loss for words. The silence would have stretched awkwardly if not for Nina's chirpy voice who sounded almost excited.

"Ron!?"

Ron quickly turned to see Nina standing close by with a warm smile.

"Why isn't this pretty little Nina now?"

"Oh, Ron you're still the same," said Nina as she easily hugged him. Tia couldn't help feeling the wee bit of jealousy at the ease between them.

"It's like being back in school again, isn't it?" he said, turning on the old charm that he was known for.

"I know! Amazing, isn't it?" gushed Nina. "Why don't you join us for coffee or are you running late?"

"Well..." He quickly looked at his watch as he said, "I am a little early for my appointment. I do have another free hour, actually."

He took the empty chair beside them.

"That's just awesome," said Nina as she sneakily winked back at Tia.

"The coffee's on me though." He raised his hand when Tia was about to protest.

"We don't mind. Chivalry is truly a novelty these days." Nina was at her flirtatious best but Ron didn't seem to mind either, Tia thought. She raised her eyebrow at Nina but she coolly shrugged her shoulders while Ron ordered coffee and doughnuts for all of them.

"So how come in this part of the world?" asked Nina once he finished with the orders.

"Well, as I was telling Tia, I am here on business. I am working on a few financial portfolios for clients of mine based here."

"Are you here for some time?" she asked.

"Yes. I have rented an apartment here. Initially I was planning to stay for two months as per my clients' requirements. Now let me see...getting a few tempting offers. So might set up another branch office here in Bengaluru. Still in the nascent stages of planning though..." He shrugged.

"Oh, then you must come for my wedding to be held within the next few months. I'm right in the middle of choosing the wedding date," she said excitedly while passing a quick glance at Tia.

"Oh really? Who is the lucky guy?" His eyes sparkled with interest as he leaned forward.

"I think you might know him," said Nina, her smile a hint of coyness.

"Who is it?" Ron's eyebrows tweaked with curiosity.

"Ryan Taneja?" Nina suggested.

"Why that....Didn't I meet him yesterday now..." Ron looked stunned but happy.

"You guys are in touch?" asked Nina as she darted a stunned glance at Tia.

"I got in touch with a few of my school pals once I got settled here. I and Ryan had some awesome time yesterday with few of our school mates. Now he owes me one – that sneaky brat!" Ron winked. "But congratulations, Nina. I can't think of a better girl in his life. Lucky fella."

Ron kept the conversation rolling as they switched topics from their lives to their mutual friends and acquaintances while Nina was her usual chatty self, enjoying herself. After a while he turned his gaze at Tia, giving her a deep look, yet curious."What about you, Tia...what have you been up to?" asked Ron. He finally did take an interest in her, thought Tia petulantly.

"Nothing much, working in my uncle's company," said Tia quietly.

"Tia is quite the business magnate these days. After a degree in engineering at NIT, Kurukshetra, she had an enviable job in Singapore. But she left after a year to come here and help her uncle. She paints a lot too in her free time...her paintings are quite out of the world..." Nina quickly rushed through the last part as Tia glowered at her.

Ron looked amused as he saw the exchange between the two old friends.

"I do remember Tia used to paint a lot for the local competitions here. Tanya often told me how busy you'd get with your sketches whenever you could snatch some free time between classes."

"Oh, did she?" Tia was not good at taking compliments, that too from Ron, so she quickly diverted the topic. "How is Tanya? Haven't met her since school."

"She is good. Busy with her job in the microbiology department. Lots of research, study – never has the time for any of us." His smile was of pure charm as he looked deeply into her eyes or was she just imagining that.

Tia quickly glanced away at Nina, not knowing what to say.

"It's time I got back..." she said as she looked at Nina meaningfully who seemed to be amused, a naughty smile hovering on her lips. She must have guessed Tia's escaping tactics and she quickly chirped in, "Ron, I am hosting a small dinner party at my place tomorrow evening. Ryan will be there with few of our friends. Some of them from school whom you might already know. Would you like to join us?"

"Why not! I'd love to socialize...evenings are boring anyway." His smile showed he was more than keen.

As soon as they got in the car, Tia and Nina looked at each other zapped. They both burst out laughing almost unable to control themselves. It was quite some time before they could calm themselves down from their hysterical fit.

"Your mom...Tia," burst out Nina in a stunned manner, "is behind this. Do you think she is playing cupid now?"

"Oh, come on Nina, he might be married for all we know!" gushed Tia, shaking her head in disbelief. But she couldn't deny the feeling of hope she carried in the past few days of seeing Ron again. Maybe subconsciously she had willed destiny to make their paths cross again.

"Uh uh, didn't see any wedding ring!" Nina shook her head vehemently while biting her lip suspiciously.

Tia rolled her eyes at her friend. "Or engaged for god's sake...or maybe there's a girlfriend that he is utterly besotted with!"

"I can get that information right away." Nina lost no time in dialling a phone number.

"What do you think you are doing?" Tia almost made for the phone.

"Finding information!" Nina batted her eyelashes while moving deftly away at the same time.

"Is Ron Garg engaged? No?" she squeaked into her iphone. "Any girlfriends...? Just asking! Yes, yes...bumped into him here...invited him for the party...alright hon...love u...cya later." Her smile was like that of a cat who got the cream.

"Ryan says he is not married or engaged...though not sure of any girlfriend."

"Nina...what would Ryan think...what makes you think if any of that matters, you Eclairs, you *Kaddoo**..." Tia almost squealed.

"Just for info...just for info...calm down now, Kitkat." Nina smiled mischievously. "Now, Tia, tell me the truth – I could see a spark there."

"No!" Tia denied but she couldn't hide her smile.

"I know there is," Nina smiled at Tia's evident blush. "And we could spend some more time with him. What was the rush?"

"I don't know, Nina. I just felt like I was back in school...so tongue-tied, so awkward, so shy..."

"Oh, honey! That's something I must say," said Nina, dancing her head like a bell. "We have got something going here, ding dong!" She winked.

"Nina...I don't know...I..." Tia looked at Nina with a vulnerability which tugged at her heart.

"I know, Kitkat, but please, please, don't let this chance just pass you by? Don't close your heart, for once...give it a chance. Life is never the same, you know...good things do happen in life. Do let in the trust, please! I am sure that's what Aunt Pooja wants too..."

Tia looked at her friend for a while and simply nodded.

"Promise me?" Nina asked her friend earnestly.

"I promise," she said softly as she let out a huge sigh.

Kaddoo – Pumpkin in Hindi

Chapter 6

"So what was his reaction like...did he look keen?" asked Krystal looking into her friend's eyes.

"I don't think so. I didn't see an ounce of interest in him," Tia replied in a dry tone, although deep inside she couldn't deny feeling butterflies in her stomach at the thought of seeing Ron again.

"Oh Tia, why are you jumping to conclusions? You weren't quite the social guy either. You hardly spoke!" Nina protested.

"He was keener on Eclairs, in fact." Tia raised her eyebrow while folding her arms across her chest. "Are you sure you don't wanna think once more before settling down?"

Nina smiled meaningfully. "Now I can smell something burn from a mile...am I right, Kitkat?"

"No, Nina, will you stop and listen to me?" muttered Tia. "I am just happy with my own life the way it is. It may look less appealing to you but frankly I am happy discovering myself. Some of us like it alone, you know. Now I'd like to go out for a breath of fresh air."

Tia abruptly walked out dismissing the amused glances of both her friends, but she did hear Krystal murmuring, "Some call it nerves, you know. And fresh air does work wonders when we are too excited and nervous about something..."

Tia didn't deign to answer as she marched away and almost blindly bumped into someone.

"Hey, hey, hey..." Warm hands descended on her and she looked up to see it was none other than Ron. Her heart skipped a beat when she realized that he still had those strong athletic arms and his eyes changed to a beautiful brown at times.

She stopped short of staring when she found Ron looking down at her with an amused expression on his face.

"Sorry about that," she said and quickly sidetracked her way out.

But Ron held her elbow as he said, "Don't we say hello here?"

Tia realized he was laughing at her and not wanting to look as if she was escaping, she smiled wryly, "Yes...hello...sorry...my mind was elsewhere actually."

"Apology accepted. Going out?" he asked.

"Just taking a walk. Guests are yet to arrive," she shrugged.

"Then hang on there while I hand over this champagne to Nina. I need to stretch my legs a bit too." He winked at that. He seemed to be the old Ron that she knew with his blatant charm.

"Alright." Tia smiled tightly as he hurried back inside.

He seemed to be a little different today, she thought. But what on heavens would they talk? She quickly texted Nina and Krystal simultaneously on their WhatsApp group chat.

Ron is coming with me for a walk!

She got replies from both of them.

"Yay!" – Nina

"Wow!" – Krystal

"What am I supposed to say?" – Tia

"Lol! He just passed me the wine...all the best!" – Nina

"Don't say anything...just bat your eyelashes!" ;) – Krystal

"Ready?" he asked softly as she chucked her mobile inside the pocket of her jeans.

"Yes. What had you in mind?" she asked, looking away.

"Didn't have anything in mind. Following you around."

Tia quickly looked at him from under her eyelashes.

But he simply walked by her and turned on his lethal smile as he said, "Lead the way."

Had nothing changed? Would she always be like that school girl, walking on egg shells and measuring her every word, whenever she was with him?

"There is a beautiful sidewalk behind Nina's house running towards the lake," she said in a rush, her voice soft. "I often come here alone or with them in the evenings."

"Yes, it's been a long time since I visited these old haunts around Ulsoor Lake and Indranagar. It would be really nice walking by these old lanes again."

"Have you visited back here after you left?"

"Yes, a couple of times I think, but I don't think you were here. I found out about your mom and sister. Sorry about that."

Tia nodded although she felt quite surprised to learn that he was well aware about her family.

The sun had gone down and, far in the horizon, the moon was slowly finding its way up in the evening sky. The breeze brought the fresh fragrance of the jasmine as well as a sweet mixture of many others.

They walked in silence for a while and she strangely enjoyed the silence.

"The lake looks gorgeous," Tia sighed happily.

"Wanna sit for a while?" asked Ron as he beckoned towards the bench.

"Don't mind." She smiled.

"You have grown your hair," he said as he picked up a strand.

Tia couldn't help blushing as she swept her hair away.

"My sisters interfered with my hair a lot. They liked to keep it short back then so that their youngest looked younger and they not too old." She smiled at the memory.

"Yeah, the baby of the family." He was teasing her and she couldn't help blushing.

"Yes, but I have had enough of the bob and the pageboy cuts," She smiled. "Long hair it is for me."

"In school, you looked good any day." He touched her hair playfully again.

"I didn't!" She protested although she couldn't help feeling a slight tingle at his touch. "We were the quiet ones, nobody noticed us."

"They didn't? I remember I did!" He slightly tilted his head towards her side. His eyes crinkled at the corners. He still could fascinate her like he always did.

"And what about Priya, Sonia, Naina...weren't they the hotties in school? Their followers were a legion."

"Their followers were crazy. I knew the star right away." He winked.

"And who was that?" She didn't know if she was holding her breath or it refused to start.

Ron took her hand in his as he looked into her eyes. "You know it was you, Tia," he said softly.

He was flirting and he was not hiding his interest in her at all. She took her hand away deftly as she turned to look at the distant waters of the lake.

"And what about your harem of other girlfriends who were always at your beck and call?" she teased.

51

He waved his hand at that. "They were not serious. You know that."

"I do?" she asked, raising her eyebrow. He was about to hold her hand but she quickly moved away in the pretext of walking. He fell in step beside her. He was teasing her, just like the old times.

"You hardly spoke to me yesterday," she said almost like an accusation and could have bit her tongue. *Did she just say that?*

"So, did you?" He raised his eyebrow at that. "But we can always rectify that..." This time he held her hand more successfully.

"I..." She blushed and looked away.

"I was quite taken aback seeing you again, Tia. Not that I wasn't pleased. It knocked the breath out of me. You always did that to me, even back in school..."

She was quite surprised at this blatant admission. She didn't know what to make of it.

"We are getting late...others might be wondering..."

"Would they?"

Tia didn't answer to that but he laughed silently as he walked by her side.

He did not let go of her hand this time. Tia didn't protest any more. She stopped resisting and simply gave in to the warm and euphoric sensations that blew her mind away. When they walked into Nina's beautifully decorated garden, her friends were sending her questioning looks. Besides Ryan, there were two other couples and three of Ryan's school friends. They all took the garden chairs and sat relaxed with drinks in hand. Nina and Ryan were busy with the barbecue while Krystal and Tia helped with the salad and starters.

"Tell me! How did it go?" asked an excited Krystal.

"What do you mean?" asked Tia.

"Now don't give me that, Tiala! I can see that blush all over..." Krystal sounded outraged but in an amused way.

"I don't know what to make of it, Krystal. He was flirting with me outright..."

"That's great news. So why are you so confused...be happy...enjoy the moment!"

She shrugged at that when Krystal said dryly, "You always were confused at his attraction towards you although we could see through it right away, even back in school."

Tia smiled wryly as she looked away, her tone light, "Too many good looking girls to stand out."

Krystal shook her head disbelievingly when she saw Nina beckoning her and she left. When Tia turned her attention back to the salad, her glance fell on Ron. He seemed to be staring at her unabashed. Tia pretended to be busy as she pushed a stray lock of hair behind her ears.

He might be just looking, stop it, she told herself. He might have a steady girlfriend for all she knew. Her life was just getting settled after a long time. She didn't want to be led falsely and again let down. They had all changed from what they were back then. Heart breaks, failures, egos had all come in. Situations or people don't remain the same always, she mused.

The evening passed in a flurry. Most of Nina and Ryan's friends seemed to know each other since childhood. They chatted, sang, drank and brought up old stories. Tia found herself next to Ron more than once. But their conversations were very casual and mostly about old times.

"Have you got your car?" asked Ron.

"No, but Krystal's going to drop me," Tia said quickly. She guessed he wanted to drop her, but was she ready to be alone with him, she thought, as her heart skipped a bit.

Krystal seemed to have overheard and quickly suggested, "I'll be a little late, Tia. Ness wants to take me for a ride. Ron, can you drop Tia?"

Tia looked mutinously at Krystal who seemed oblivious to her reaction. But when Ron turned to look at her questioningly she kept her face bland.

"I..."

"Come on, you don't have to panic. It's just a ride." He quickly winked at Krystal who giggled naughtily and gave him a thumbs up.

Except for looking daggers at both of them, Tia had no option but to follow Ron.

The car felt small as soon as Tia got in beside him. She jumped abruptly when Ron moved and his breath fanned on her cheeks.

"What?! Relax...." He laughed. "Just helping you with your seat belt."

"I will do it." She felt self-conscious and blushed. When she looked up he seemed to be smiling tongue-in-cheek. She felt even more mortified thinking Ron might have guessed her feelings for him and she asked tersely, "Are you laughing at me?"

"Why should I? You just amuse me. You always did." He laughed.

"Nice to know I am a source of amusement for you." Ron grinned again at her sullen face.

"Every expression of yours has always been beautiful to me...beautiful and innocent...like a child of paradise..." His eyes sparkled and his voice was soft. Tia was at a loss for words and she looked down at her hands.

Ron seemed to sense her shyness as he started the car and said quietly, "You still need to show me the way, Tia."

"Yes, uh...you have to go straight and then take a left."

"You still live at your parent's house in Indranagar?"

"Well, mom left the downstairs wing in my name. The first floor was for Rianna and second floor to Dev. Dev now uses the first floor as Rianna is no more. Not that she ever lived there as we both lived with mom downstairs after Dev got married. The other house in Koramangala was bequeathed in Nysa's name which she uses for her work."

"That's quite some property your parents left and a nice arrangement as it still keeps you siblings close as a family."

"Yes. It was Dad's idea to keep us close but of course bro is too busy these days and so is Nysa. We hardly get to meet nowadays."

Once he halted the car where Tia showed him, he turned to her, his eyes intense and searching.

"I am here for some time, Tia. I'd like us to go out sometimes. Would you mind if I call you?"

Tia felt her heartbeat racing as she looked up at him. His eyes changed colour as he leaned towards her.

"Yes, but I can't promise you when I'll be free," she said and quickly moved away. "Evenings are busy at office what with appraisals and estimate time drawing close."

She felt this was moving all too fast and she needed to maintain a distance.

"But you need to eat some time," he said as he backed his car and winked at her. He threw her a flying kiss as he drove off.

Tia couldn't help feeling weak in her knees while her heart soared. Was this truly happening?! There was a time in her life when she wanted this to happen very badly. But that was just a teenage crush for Ron. Now they were adults and she wasn't a lovesick teenager any more. She had to think practically. What if Ron was only looking for a good time or just passing his time in the city while he was on business?

In spite of all the rational thinking she couldn't help putting on some music while she glided away for a shower. She felt so light, a sense of euphoria enveloped her and she sang merrily while releasing herself completely into the joy of those moments. After the shower, as she made a fresh cup of coffee, she heard her doorbell ring.

"Poppins!"

"Hey babe!" Krystal smiled as she sat with a tired sigh.

"I thought you wouldn't make it. How was your date with Ness?"

"Not bad!" She sounded happy. "How was yours?"

"Everything is going too fast, Krystal. I am not so sure."

Krystal smiled mischievously. "Oh! That way...."

"Yes...this is not the Ron I knew in school..." Tia slowly admitted. "Have some coffee."

"Cheers to new beginnings, then," said Krystal as her eyes sparkled with meaning.

Chapter 7

The sunrays beamed on her flawless skin and silky hair as she walked towards the rocky edge. She dazzled in her floral, halter-neck dress that simply looked like it was made for her. Tia felt like a silent spectator as she watched her sister from above. Rianna seemed so happy and full of life as she spoke animatedly to someone. As she looked closer, she saw a guy standing next to her. Rianna was talking passionately, her hands making a lot of gestures and pointing at something afar. Suddenly the guy grabbed at her neck. Rianna was startled and she pulled at his hands to break free as the guy tried to strangle her without mercy. Tia couldn't see the man's face as his back was turned. The muscles below his blue sleeves rippled as he used all his strength on his victim – her sister Rianna. At that moment Rianna's voice croaked almost weakly, "Tia, Tia help me...save me...don't trust this man...he will destroy you too..."

As Tia tried to grab at the man's shoulder she felt her hands passing through empty air. She couldn't seem to grab at him.

At that moment, she turned to see Rianna falling down beside her. Her body was soaked in blood and her face distorted in the most grotesque manner. Her head was swimming as she saw Rianna's body fall off the rocky hill. She was about to jump after her. But somebody stopped her.

She turned to look and she was shocked to see it was Ron! He was gently holding her. She couldn't believe that the man who had just killed her sister was Ron.

Ron looked agonized as he pleaded, "Trust me, Tia. You have to trust me..."

Strangely she saw Ron was dressed all in white now and a strange glow emanated from him. He was the devil in angel's disguise, she thought, as darkness overwhelmed her at that very moment.

When she opened her eyes she found Krystal at the side of her bed. Krystal gently shook her as she said, "Hush Tia! Have some water."

Tia quickly gulped the water as Krystal wiped her brow. "You were calling out for Rianna. Did you dream about her?" Tia nodded tiredly while gulping the water hurriedly down her dry throat. Krystal left her alone for some time. It was already early morning and she quickly took a warm shower.

By the time Krystal was dressed, Tia had loaded the kettle and said in a rush, "I need to hurry for my yoga classes."

Krystal didn't pursue the matter as she quietly watched her friend's face looking strained and haggard. They talked on mundane matters as both friends got ready for their day out.

Yuvi was waiting for her as soon as she reached her cabin. "Neptune Technologies asked to send them a proposal. Did you get a chance to look at the specs?"

"I think we have to let that go, Yuvi. Unless of course, Mr. Sharma completes all their pending payments. Uncle Neal is not to keen on doing business with them anymore."

"But they are sending some of the big businesses our way! We need to keep that in mind too, Tia. One of Sharma's friends, CEO of Ebony Software, is most likely going to sign a deal with us for a huge game project this week. In fact the client has asked to arrange for a meeting on Wednesday. We can't afford to annoy him now."

"But that won't cover up the losses if they don't send us the checks soon, Yuvi. We will find better clients. Uncle Neal believes that and so do I."

"Alright." Yuvi shrugged. "How's your head now? Any more headaches?"

"Much better! Thanks Yuvi." She smiled at Yuvi's concern.

"Wanna grab a bite tonight?" he asked as he leaned by the edge of her table.

"I don't think so, Yuvi. Krystal and Nina have planned something for tonight," she lied. Lately she felt a difference in Yuvi. She always took Yuvi for an old pal and she didn't want their relationship to develop any other way. This was because she couldn't risk losing Yuvi for anything in the world.

"So all you school friends back together, isn't it? Now where is the time for good old Yuvi!"

Tia quickly looked up but Yuvi seemed to be in good cheer and she shrugged lightly instead.

The day passed off quickly as she supervised the ongoing projects, wrote proposals, answered emails, perused project specs and handed assignments to her team. By evening the phone rang and she instinctively knew who it was.

"Hi, Tia." His voice sounded even sexier on phone.

"Hello, Ron," she answered breathlessly.

"How was your day?" he asked interestedly.

"Not bad. I have been busy. What about you?"

"Yeah, same here – too many meetings..." As Ron spoke, Tia got the flashes of her dream. She tried to push away the nagging uneasiness from her mind.

"Tia?"

"Sorry, Ron. You were saying...?"

Ron gave a soft chuckle. "You were elsewhere. Not good for my ego, though."

"Well...I...bit of work pending...so..." She spluttered awkwardly.

"That's okay. How about dinner at the Polo Club tonight? Or you'd prefer some other place?"

Tia felt this peculiar kind of sinking feeling. It was only a dream after all. But why did that disturb her so much?

"Tia?"

"I'd like to go, Ron."

"Awesome! I'll be there by seven."

At home after a quick shower and deliberating which dress to wear, her phone rang. It was Nina and she was sounding quite excited when she came to know about her date with Ron.

"I want to find out more about the dream, Nina. That's the only reason I have decided to go."

"What!?" Nina sounded shocked. "Yeah, Krystal told me about the dream you had this morning. But are you taking this seriously? It was just a dream after all..."

"I know, Nina. But I don't know why I am not able to let it go...I just keep thinking about it again and again. And you know Mom has always brought some meaning to my dreams...what if Rianna is trying to tell me something too?"

"But you did have nightmares of Rianna years back, didn't you? Was there any meaning, then?"

"I know...but this is the first time I saw someone else in the dream too."

"Maybe you have been giving a great deal of thought to Ron and that's why he came in your dreams too. You know dreams are nothing but what you think about the whole day," said Nina jovially, as if to lighten her mood.

"That's true, Nina..." said Tia slowly.

"So, cheer up, will you? Ron looks keen. Don't spoil the moment by living in your past, Kitkat. All your mom and sister would want is for you to be happy *today*. And it's time you are. You have been alone for far too long now. Remember all the babies we dreamed about? You wanted four, remember?"

"And you wanted three." Tia smiled fondly.

She pulled up the zip of her raspberry-red, sleeveless, scoop-necked dress that had a graceful flared skirt ending right above her knees. The satin belt cinched around her waist coupled with her maroon heels accentuated the feminine curves of her beautiful slender figure.

The doorbell rang and Tia quickly picked up her purse.

Ron gave her a slow appreciative look from head to toe and she felt herself blush.

"Hello, gorgeous."

"Hi." He definitely looked very handsome himself in his grey silk shirt and dark slacks and Tia's heart missed a beat.

"Ready?"

"Yes," she said as she turned to lock her door.

The ride to the restaurant passed mostly in monosyllables on Tia's part. Tia was aware of Ron's baffled looks once or twice as she quietly gazed at the passing scenes outside his car window.

"What's the matter, Tia? Upset about something?"

Tia shrugged her shoulders weakly and shook her head. "Nothing. Just tired."

Of course, she couldn't really say that she was feeling more than alive just being with him or that her heart was in an odd rhythm many a time. So instead she smiled lightly saying, "And I have never been much of a talkative person either."

"Really! I remember what chatterboxes all of you were in school. Dad and Mom always used to wonder what the heck was there for four young teenagers to yap about all day as nonstop chatter filled the house. You want me to believe this now?" His eyes teased her.

Tia simply smiled in answer and turned to look outside the car window. He was right. How different life was then.

Once they were in the restaurant, Ron ordered for both of them.

"Have you come here before?" he asked.

"No, I don't eat out much, you know."

"How did you survive in this boring old city the last two years?" he questioned with more than a little curiosity. It was as if he wanted to know what made her tick.

"Boring for a Delhite, maybe. Some of us love an easy laidback life." She said lightly.

"Touché!" He smiled, his face oozing with charm and she lightened up. She knew he didn't mean to be judgemental.

"Anyway, Krystal moved in a few months back and now Nina too. So maybe we will try out some new places. Before it was mostly work and maybe eat-outs with my sister, once in a while. But Nysa is pretty busy with her family – her hubby and my niece, so that has been rare too." She sighed as she looked at him quietly. "Helping out my uncle to stabilize his company took most of my time which was almost on the brink of closing off two years back. Weekends maybe I would read or paint a bit. Sometimes I go out in the wooded areas in the outskirts of Bengaluru to paint the scenery or take photographs around the areas. There are many beautiful places around Bengaluru filled with natural beauty and solitude which some of us love."

"It is. But that's quite a hectic schedule with a nil social life." His lips slanted slightly in a smile as he looked deeply into her eyes. He took her hands in his as he said, "Now you will have a hard time staying home what with Krystal, Nina – and me around." He added the last bit softly.

"I am not the same person you knew in school, Ron," she said slowly as she looked at him from beneath her lashes.

"No one is." Ron agreed as he searched her eyes, his face watchful.

"I have my moods and some time back I had major depression issues too. I am not an easy person to be with, you know." The restaurant was buzzing with activity as she looked at the happy couples around.

"It happens...different kind of things...unpleasant...to many of us. You are not alone." He took her hand in his. "How do you feel now? Your depression I mean. Does it still bother you?"

"It is much better now. I find ways to be at peace with myself. My yoga and meditation routines helps to keep me grounded although at times it gets harder. I am just a simple girl, Ron, trying to live my life. So if you have some other expectations from me you will be truly disappointed – I am serious."

Her eyes were pools of vulnerability and almost pleading as if she didn't want him to start something which could have no future. But Ron smiled as he caressed his finger lightly around the inner corner of her wrist.

"I want to get to know you more, Tia. Be with you, know you...let's give us a chance, Tia." His voice was husky and her heart skipped a beat as he looked into her eyes, meaning every word. His eyes turned a shade darker and were mesmerizing in their intensity as she felt drawn into them.

The meal was delicious and Tia felt sated. She declined dessert and Ron held her hand as they lingered around the restaurant lawn for some time. When they reached her place, Ron walked her to her door.

Before she knew it, he lightly brushed her lips with his and her heart beat a staccato rhythm as she leaned heavily against the door. Her senses felt acutely alive in the stark darkness of the night. The sound of the traffic seemed to fade away at a distance and her ears felt numb. She wanted this moment to last forever in her mind.

"Wanna catch a coffee later in the evening, tomorrow?" he asked. His fragrance enveloped her as his face drew closer and she felt herself go weak in the knees. Tia felt this was all moving very fast but she couldn't help nodding her head. Ron quickly covered her lips with his own a second time and he left before she could react to anything.

That night she dreamt of Ron taking her for a walk near a beautiful brook in the woods. They went inside a chalet nearby and her mom opened the door. She invited them for a coffee and sandwiches. After they had their meal, her mom gave Ron a beautiful diamond ring and he was about to slip the ring on her finger. But another person from the corner of her eye caught her attention.

It was Rianna looking at them from the doorway and she looked very sad. She shook her finger at Tia as if asking her not to do it. Tia looked confused as she looked at her sister while Ron slipped the ring and kissed her hand softly.

Tia woke up to the ringtone of her mobile.

"Hello..."

"Good morning, sweetheart." Ron's voice was a sensuous caress. "Did you know I dreamt about you last night?"

Tia felt a warmth spreading all over her body which was suddenly replaced by a sinking feeling as last night's dreams came flooding in her mind. She was wide awake in an instant.

"Really?" Tia responded after a while.

"You don't believe me?" There was a smile in his voice. "You want me to be more graphic?"

"Ron!" she exclaimed. She couldn't hide the smile in her voice as her mind resorted to different images – not entirely innocent.

"See you in the evening, sweetheart. I'll pick you up at your office." His voice was gentle as he hung up.

Tia hid her face in her hands. What was happening? Why was she having these strange dreams? Why was Ron hovering in her dreams this way?

She got up and quickly splashed her face with cold water. Once she wiped her face with a towel she could hear the splash of running water. Hadn't she just closed the tap, she wondered. She turned it off with a firmer hand and walked back to the kitchen, quickly gulped a glass of lemon juice and rushed for her yoga classes.

Yuvi had arranged a series of meetings to be held with their clients that day. The whole day passed off in a jiffy as Tia attended the meetings one after the other.

Evening, Ron waited for her in the sidewalk as she descended down the stairs of her office. His eyes watched her lazily as she got into his car. She suddenly felt conscious in her lemon-yellow, petal-sleeved chiffon blouse and white pencil skirt. But Ron always seemed to have a knack to make her feel that way.

"We'll come back for your car later?" he asked.

"That won't be necessary. Suresh, our office chauffeur, offered to drive it home with the duplicate key."

As she got in, Ron leaned to give her a quick peck but Tia quickly avoided him. There was a questioning look in his eyes as he slowly closed her car door. He kept the conversation going though Tia kept mostly quiet the entire time. After their coffee and a light snack, they took a walk by the lake.

Ron took her hand and asked quietly, "Something on your mind, Tia?"

"Nothing, nothing at all..." She shrugged as she turned to him. Ron resumed his walk as he slid his warm fingers through hers. There was a beautiful breeze blowing and the waters of the lake glistened with what looked like a million stars against the beautiful evening sky.

"You can trust me you know, Tia," he said after a while and he looked deeply into her eyes.

Tia shifted her eyes while her heart raced wildly. She folded her hands and rubbed her arm as her eyes sought refuge in the gentle waves of the lake.

Ron took her chin in his hand as he lightly tilted her head.

"You take my breath away, Tia."

His voice was gruff as he covered her lips with his own. His hands slid possessively over her back and she felt warm all over. Tia couldn't resist his touch as she felt her body tingle with wild sensations. His deep languorous kiss shot an explosion through every nerve ending of her body, making her dizzy and mindless in a different space altogether. He swept deep, drugging kisses on her mouth as he kissed her again and again. As her body swayed towards him, she could feel his heartbeats race against her through the clothes that separated them. His fingers threaded through the thick silky strands of her hair to clutch at the nape of her neck while his breathing grew hard and ragged. His other hand wrapped around her waist drawing her closer. Her legs quivered and she felt a wild flutter in the pit of her stomach as he nibbled the tender skin of her earlobe. He explored every inch of her sweet mouth and trailed hungry kisses down the graceful line of her neck to the hollow of her throat.

Her blood was on fire as her body arched towards him unbidden, her insides melting at the grasp of his strong arms. His face buried in her hair as she clutched his shoulders, her soft curves begging for his touch. Tia couldn't resist any longer as her hands entwined behind his head and she gave into his long sensuous kiss. His hands moved urgently as they caressed her hips, the narrowness of her ribcage and her flat belly while their mouths grew hungrier by the second. His hot breath fanned her flushed skin as he fitted her body into his and she could feel every inch of his muscular body. His hands pressed at her back and pulled her in roughly as he kissed her till she couldn't breathe anymore. A whistle broke into their trance and they stared at the young cyclist showing them a thumbs up while riding away.

"We gotta go," she said as her breath grew steady. She broke away but Ron pulled her back in his arms again.

"Don't fight this, Tia. I know you want this as much as I do..."

He cupped her face in his palm and possessed her mouth again. Tia never knew anything could feel this good but suddenly her sister's face flashed in her mind and she pulled away. "No, Ron...I am not ready for this." She gasped while trying to catch her breath. "We hardly know each other..."

He didn't let go her hand as he said, "How can you say that Tia? I have known you since school..."

"That's different Ron," she cried. "I told you. Things have changed. I can't give you what you are looking for...I gotta go." She broke into a run as she tried to get away from him as fast as she could.

Chapter 8

The drive back was silent and Ron looked austere as his skin stretched tightly across his face. She quietly got off with a clipped goodbye. Ron slightly nodded at her almost giving her a passing glance. His eyes looked cold and steely as if he had reached the end of his tether.

Tia returned to her empty home and flung her bag while crashing into the sofa like a zombie. She didn't know how long she lay there. The phone rang and reluctantly she picked it up. It was Krystal. Tia didn't know if she had the energy to face up to her questions. But Krystal fortunately didn't pester her except for, "Tia, would you like me to come over for the night?"

"No, I am okay," she said simply.

"Ron called me up and wanted to know some stuff about you. He is keen about you, Tia. But I know it's best you take things slowly. And I told him just that. Call me if you need me."

She hung up after that. As she sat in the partial darkness of her lamp shade she felt as if somebody was looking at her from the corner of the doorway. But when she turned round there was nobody. She shook her head in resignation and then walked into her bathroom to brush her teeth. She quickly massaged her face with a night cream and got under the bed covers. It was a long day and she was tired mentally and physically.

They were walking through the rocky banks, barefoot. Her sister made her climb one of the hills that held one of their favourite trees. At seven, she was far too clumsy to climb the rocks as effortlessly as her sister could. Her sister always took her for these outdoor adventures and they explored all the rocks and crevices around the woods. At fifteen, Rianna was tall and lanky and very good at outdoor sports like mountain climbing, trekking and athletics.

Rianna crouched near a tree calling for her at the same time. She sat next to Rianna as she started to dig through the sand with her bare hands. After a few minutes of digging, her sister showed her one of her muddy hands. There was something shining within the mud. Rianna rubbed the mud and pebbles away and there, lying in her hand, was a chain with a beautiful locket. The locket was oval in shape and Tia took it in her hands. The engraving was that of a pentacle and it glittered in her hands as Tia closely observed it.

As soon as Tia took her car out of the garage the next morning, she met Krystal who just drove in.

"Hop in," she said and together they drove off to Pearl Valley.

"Pearl Valley? What for?"

"We need to search for something, just a hunch," she said. She looked and sounded enigmatic and Krystal didn't question her any further.

As soon as they got off their car, they made their way through Pearl Valley. The bank of the stream was rocky as they walked towards the small waterfall.

"Remember that tree over there?"

Krystal looked over at the gulmohur tree pointed by Tia.

"How can I not? We had countless picnics there and remember how we used to swing on its branches."

"I saw it in my dream last night."

"You did?" Krystal tilted her head, her eyes curious.

"Yes. Rianna showed me a shiny piece of jewel – a chain with locket – which she unearthed from near that tree.

Krystal raised her eyebrows at that. "Oh!"

"Come, help me dig this up." Tia handed Krystal a small garden shovel while she started digging with the other. They dug round the tree for a while when Tia sat tiredly on a rock nearby.

"I guess it was only a dream after all. Sorry, Krystal for tiring you..."

"I am sorry I do have to agree with you, Tia. Anyway, childhood dreams never ever leave us. And this was one of the best spots we spent time with our sisters." Krystal's sister, Grace, was one of Rianna's good friends. But now Grace had moved to the northeast with her husband and Tia hadn't met her in a long time.

As Tia rubbed the mud off her hands, she heard Krystal exclaim in a startled voice. "Look...there is actually something here!"

Tia quickly reached Krystal's side as she tried pulling at something that was gleaming in the mud. It was a slim, silver chain that had a locket hanging from it.

"This was what I saw in my dream!" Tia said slowly. She turned the locket over and over. It had a pentacle engraved over it. "How amazing!"

"Was that Rianna's?" asked Krystal.

"No, I don't think so. I don't remember Rianna having a thing for jewellery, ever."

"It's made of silver...but the design looks more like a man's chain than a woman's, actually," said Krystal as she peered at it again. "Could Rianna be telling you something?"

"I really don't know...nothing makes sense, actually." She pushed the locket back inside a trouser pocket and headed for her car.

Later in the evening, after a shower, she sat in the quiet of her room with a glass of orange juice in hand. After a long, hot day in office, she felt quite relaxed in her light-blue tank top and white cotton shorts. She tied her wet curls on the top of her head although a few of the tendrils escaped and lay down her bare shoulders. She studied the locket over and over when the door bell rang.

It was Nina at the door with Ron behind her. Nina looked guilty as she hurriedly got in and placed a casserole on her dining table. "I just wanted to squeak in for a few minutes to hand you this chocolate cake – freshly baked! Ron had dropped in to meet Ryan who isn't home yet...so he said he'd give me a lift." Nina shrugged her shoulders, though not without an expression of guilt.

Ron stood behind, looking at Tia but not saying anything. "I'd like some juice too," he said all of a sudden, his face brazen as he glanced at her glass.

Tia raised an eyebrow and went to the kitchen.

"What about you, Nina?" her voice was colder than usual.

"Don't you worry your head off about me," Nina smiled brightly. "I've got to complete some errands in the neighbourhood. I'll take a cab – so Ron, don't bother." She tried to ignore Tia's dagger looks as she quickly made her way out.

"Don't be hard on Nina. It's not her fault. I was more than persuasive."

Tia kept quiet as she got the juice ready. "Either way it doesn't matter."

"Doesn't it? You are lying, Tia."

"What do you want me to do, Ron?"

"I want you to stop shutting me off? Talk to me, Tia!"

Tia tried to make herself out of the kitchen door but Ron took her by the shoulders and stopped her.

"Leave me...you are hurting me!"

"I am sorry, honey." He apologized quickly while rubbing her shoulders at the same time.

She trembled as she made to walk away, trying not to meet his eyes. But Ron pulled her back as he hugged her from behind. Tia closed her eyes as they stood silently that way for a few seconds. Ron rubbed his face in her hair while he breathed in deeply, taking in her fragrance.

"Give us a chance, Tia," he said softly, his breath warm in her ears. "I'd really like us to make this work."

He slowly turned her to face him. Tia felt drawn to him like a moth to a flame as her breathing slightly quickened. He was the man of her girlhood dreams. He was the man she had so badly wanted to be hers in school. So why did she resist him so much now? Because of a few dreams which weren't the reality? Dreams are only what we think about all day, she tried to reason herself. There couldn't be any truth in it. A life based on dreams was like living in a fool's paradise.

"Tia?" Ron slowly tilted her face to look into her eyes as his face drew near.

When he possessed her mouth with his, she felt sucked into the passion of his hot kiss, her defences altogether down. Her breathing quickened as he gathered her in his sinewy arms while his kisses grew deeper and deeper. His hands swept over her gentle curves in a possessive caress as he moulded her delicate body to his. Her fingers dug into his hair as she surrendered her lips to his smothering mouth. She kissed the pulse at his throat and felt his pulses quicken as he pulled her tightly against him.

She felt wanton and wild as his mouth crushed into hers. Her skin burnt wherever he touched her, stirring flames of desire as she writhed wildly in his hungry embrace. His kisses were urgent as his mouth explored every inch of her face, neck and further down her soft crevices. She was mindless as she yielded into his lean hard strength. Fire burnt in her belly fiercely as he rasped her name almost in a muffled desire. His lips nibbled her silky skin sending shivers down the length of her spine. Her blood pulsed and pooled like hot lava all throughout her veins. She felt her breath coming out in short gasps as his lips moved against her with a bruising pressure.

Her eyes were still closed when Ron stopped. She slowly opened her eyes and stared into his which were as mesmerized as hers. She was in a daze and suddenly realized that she was sitting on his lap in the living room couch.

"Ron?" her voice was a plea almost as if she didn't want him to stop.

"I want you so badly, Tia." Ron swallowed thickly and his eyes burnt with a passion that shook her to her core. Her lips were swollen and her skin felt vulnerable from the onslaught of his arduous – almost rough passion for her. She quickly broke away from him and went into the kitchen. Ron followed her but she stopped him as she silently raised her hand.

"Tia, I don't want to rush you." He took her raised hand in his as he lightly pulled her in his arms.

"So, then let's have some juice." She tried to smile lightly but her lips shook tremulously. Ron was a force into himself and she could not fight this rage of passion between them that was volatile and beyond her control.

His eyes too seemed to look relieved and his face lightened in good humour. Tia felt like a woman truly desired with him next to her. They had juice and cake while browsing some movies on a channel. They finally decided on the "Beauty and the Briefcase," – one of Tia's favourites. Ron helped her cook tomato spaghetti and crispy chicken. It was almost midnight when he left. Except for a light peck he didn't try to get any closer and Tia felt quite relieved. Everything between them was just too overwhelming at the moment for her to take it all in.

Chapter 9

Ron didn't call her for the next few days. Tia couldn't help hoping to bump into him somewhere or hear her phone ring. The evenings felt a little desolate and she was really looking forward to spending some time outdoors over the weekend.

Saturday morning at first light, she and Krystal were on their way to trek around Nandi hills, which was about 65 km away from the city.

"You sleep better now? Any more dreams?" asked Krystal as she sat on one of the rocks to catch her breath. The trekking trail they had taken to Nandi Hills was quite invigorating, accompanied by magnificent scenic views all around. Tia soaked in the feeling of lightness and calm as she sat next to Krystal.

"You mean dreams of Rianna?"

"Yes?"

"Didn't get any in the last few days. But strangely Krystal, these days I get the fragrance of one of her favourite perfumes in the evenings. It would last for some time, maybe say about...thirty minutes."

"Did you check for any perfume bottles that might have been left around open somewhere?" asked Krystal.

"I did! I checked across the corners of the room, under the furniture...everywhere, but there weren't any..."

"Hmm..." Krystal looked into the hills, lost in thought. She was never a superstitious person but lately she felt there was something very mysterious about Tia's place.

"It is not as if it's happened only now. In the past too I would sometimes get a sudden whiff of her perfume. And I had put it down to my own yearnings to feel and touch her once again. But it's at an increasing frequency now. One more strange phenomenon that I'd never mentioned is about her portrait in my house. I often find it tilted from its position for no reason. That usually occurs once I come home from my office in the evenings."

"The one near the dining table?"

"Yes."

"I remember. She looks so beautiful and happy in that one..."

"I know."

"Could it be the wind or something?"

"I don't think so...my doors and windows are locked from every side after I leave home. Nor can it be a stray cat jumping at it or something, as the portrait is placed far too high for it to reach it."

"Does it frighten you?"

"Actually no, Krystal. Strangely no. Except for the dreams that unsettle me, I am quite comfortable in my house otherwise."

"There is one thing I too have felt lately, Tia. But I never mentioned it as I didn't want to unnerve you."

"No, you can tell me. Go ahead."

"I can't exactly place it. But I get this weird feeling that someone is watching me in your house..."

"I have felt that too...right from the time I came back home from Singapore – almost two years back."

"Do you think it's Rianna...maybe she watches over the place?"

"I really don't know, Krystal..."

"Or, maybe we miss her a lot...especially you. Maybe that's why we tend to still feel her essence around the house. She grew up there, didn't she?"

Next week passed in a breeze what with helping Nina with her wedding shopping and hanging around with both the girls. Nina didn't mention anything about Ron and she too didn't betray her curiosity at Ron's absence as much as she wanted to.

Friday came soon and there was Ron standing in the driveway with a happy smile and flowers in hand. Tia could feel her heart racing as she walked towards him. She almost hastened her steps as she couldn't deny the happiness of seeing him any longer. Once they were inside the car, she raised her face as he reached forward but was strangely disappointed when he only gave a peck on her cheek.

"I missed you!" he whispered as he handed the flowers and she breathed in the scent of the beautiful white roses.

"Care for a movie?" he asked lightly.

"Why not?" She smiled happily.

Ron spoke generally about his work and his life back in Delhi during the ride to the theatre. It was a romantic comedy and she enjoyed it every bit. The restaurant he took her later had a cosy, romantic feel about it and Tia never felt so loved in her life.

"I thought I'd let some distance between us so as to give you some time. And also to make you miss me. Did you miss me?" His voice was like a caress in her ears as she felt tiny butterflies in her stomach.

"I did, Ron," she said softly.

"Can you be a little louder?" he asked, his eyes turned a shade darker while his lips curved into a sensuous half-smile.

"I did," she spoke a little louder and blushed as she saw the teasing glint in his eyes.

The next day dawned bright and beautiful. Tia looked forward to a walk in the woods and a picnic by a beautiful waterfall with Ron. As they took pictures all around the woods, Tia was overwhelmed by a feeling of complete bliss. Later, after a lunch comprising of sandwiches, burgers and fresh juice, they lay on the mat lazily, talking about their common friends in school.

"Do you remember Sanjay Kothari – the mathematical genius?"

"Yes. He had these thick glasses and buck teeth...and had his nose in a school book every time I saw him." She grinned.

"Yes. Ryan used to send him love letters in his own hand. And then he would sign them off, pretending it to be from the head turner of our batch." Ron chortled in amusement.

"How mean!" Tia laughed out. "How did he respond to them?"

"He used to come to us asking for suggestions on how to answer them."

"And you helped him?" Tia sounded shocked.

"For a while..." He winked at that.

"Ron!"

"It diverted him from algorithms and algebra for a while. Don't you think that's good progress?"

"Oh Ron! Where is he now? Still got those thick glasses?"

"Nah...no more glasses. Looks very muscled and well toned with all that working out and all. President of a music company with one or two tattoos on his chest."

"Tattoos! I sure can't imagine good old Sanjay with tattoos!"

The conversation changed to his family. Tanya, his younger sister, had no plans of getting married for a while. His mom was busy running his dad's business and his elder sister, Royna was reaping the benefits of her hard work by living the high life and attending high socialite parties. She was also engaged for the second time. Tia felt a certain rift between him and his sister. That was no surprise to her for she always wondered how two siblings in the same family could be so different in the first place.

It was a lazy day and Tia almost closed her eyes as Ron talked about his friends and families. The afternoon sun was not too hot and the beautiful cool breeze lulled her to sleep. She never felt so good in a long while. She woke up to the taste of hot lips and a warm body lightly leaning on her. It was Ron and her pulses raced high as he took his time to savour the taste of her lips. He cupped her mouth while teasing her lips with his tongue and making her gasp.

She kissed him back as she took in his heavy weight and ran her hands over his rugged back. The muscles on his back tensed as he deepened his kiss and then his lips bit into her neck and shoulders. His mouth scorched her skin everywhere it touched and she closed her eyes again giving herself into the delicious sensations. Her body tingled all over and she pressed against him in abandon wanting nothing more than the feel of his body pressed against her, his hands, his kisses and much more. Tia ran her fingers through his nape as he alternately licked and kissed her neck passionately. Sensations of pleasure made her feel dizzy and spasm uncontrollably with desire. He ran his hands all over her hips and her soft curves. She didn't stop him when he ran his hands under her blouse and caressed her bare skin inside. Tia felt her desire would explode like molten fire as he moved lower and lower from her neck to her cleavage.

Her body became inflamed with heat as he unbuttoned her shirt and breathed into her bare skin. His hands ran passionately over her hips, waists and gentle contours while he bestowed hungry kisses all over her smooth skin. She clutched at his shirt and whimpered as she felt herself on fire while he explored the softer parts of her body. Tia dug her fingers into his shoulders as he drove her into a frenzied passion. He met her mouth again as they felt lost in each other's clinch and ravenously kissed while they shuddered in intense passion. It felt like an age before they finally separated. Ron didn't go any further than that and Tia was glad that he didn't.

She was not sure if she could control her desires if it had progressed more than that. After a walk around the woods, they headed for home and it was quite dark when they reached home. Ron refused coffee and left her after another smothering kiss on her mouth which left Tia weak in her knees.

The next couple of weeks they often went out for a coffee after office or for dinner at Tia's place. Weekends were mostly movies or a hike in the woods while Tia painted or photographed and Ron worked on his laptop. Sometimes Krystal, Nina and Ryan accompanied them to the movies or around the beautiful trekking and cycling trails at the outskirts of Bengaluru.

Her days were always full as on the remaining days without Ron, she would accompany her girl friends for coffee or walks by the lake. Life was looking good as weeks turned into months and Tia felt more than happy in her life.

One Sunday, Ron wanted to spend the whole day at her house and Tia felt more than excited as she prepared lemon and pepper chicken, Thai fried rice and a chocolate mousse. Ron kept distracting her and she couldn't stop his hands from running over her curves or his lips from dropping passionate kisses on her face and neck. Once they lay on the couch after lunch to enjoy a movie on television, they found themselves carried away in the heat of passion.

Her body arched into him as Ron's hands moved urgently over her body while kissing her ravenously all over.

"I love you, Tia." His voice was thick as he looked into her eyes and said earnestly, "Marry me."

"What?" she said and felt her body go stiff with tension as she looked into his eyes.

"Marry me."

"Are you serious?"

"With all my heart."

She was silent for a while as he nudged her again and kissed her hard. "So what's your answer?"

"I will," she softly nodded as he shivered. He pulled her tightly in his arms moulding her body to his, every part of their bodies fitting perfectly to each other. His hands and mouth were hungry as he pulled her down below him and moved his hungry mouth all across her delicate curves. He would stop to ask her if he had hurt her but Tia for the life of her couldn't stop herself. She dug her nails into his shoulders and clutched him tightly as he nibbled her at the most desirable places. Their physical need took them into a sea of emotions as they felt almost violent towards each other. Soon they got lost in an avalanche of emotion which was like a raging whirlwind in a restless sea of passion.

Chapter 10

They had a small party with Uncle Neal, Krystal, Nina, Ryan, Dev, Maya, Alisha, Nysa, Jeff and little Lola around. Nysa and Dev were quite surprised but happy as they had known Ron from old times. Ron's mom came down for the engagement too along with a lot of gifts for her.

"I am happy that you made my Ron finally settle down. I had almost given up hopes," she said while giving her a warm hug. "And was I surprised and happy to know that it was somebody I already knew!"

Ron slid the most exotic ring on her finger but that mattered less as she had the most amazing man in her life. Then again, somewhere deep down in her heart, something was nagging her and she didn't know what. She pushed those thoughts aside and tried not to ruin her happy moments as her friends Krystal and Nina would keep advising her from time to time.

"I am so happy for you, Tia." Krystal hugged her.

"Wish it was a double wedding," remarked Nina as she poured more mocktails into their glasses. "Ron's mom looks quite mellowed from the time we last saw her. What about Tanya and the other sister – what was her name? Ah yes, Royna."

"They are out of the country it seems. But I haven't spoken to any of them yet. I still am having second thoughts. Isn't this all too fast?" Tia sounded vulnerable and unsure as Nina and Krystal exchanged careful glances. But they were the only people that Tia could open her heart to without being judged. If Nysa had an inkling of this, she would worry even more. So Tia was hesitant to seek her advice.

"If your heart says so, then yes." Nina assured her. "And Ron is a good, steady guy. Why should you worry?"

"Yes, rich and successful too." Krystal winked but added with a more serious note, "Guys like him don't come in easily, Tia. He is the real deal!" Krystal made a circle with her index finger and thumb to stress her point further. "We all know him from ages back. He is the stable, trustworthy kind – trust me!"

"Look, he's got the young ones wrapped round his little finger too," said Nina with a smile, seeing Ron taking Lola by his hand and chatting up with Alisha at the same time. "Looks like Alisha is blushing with all the attention from Ron..."

Later after they left, Tia rested her head on Ron's shoulder as they lay cosily on the couch. She was abundantly happy with her life, having no regrets at all. He caressed her hair and both lay silent, loving each other's company.

"I wish Dad, Mom and Rianna were around too."

"I know sweetheart. But I am there for you now. I love you so much and I will try to make it all up for you."

"I know," she said as she kissed his hand lingeringly. "I remember Rianna's engagement to Jeff. She was so happy. And you know what she told me?"

"What?" he asked as he gave a light kiss on her forehead.

"Hope you find the same kind of love and happiness that I have found with Jeff. She..."

"Now wait a minute...Jeff? Did you say Jeff? Did he have the same name as Nysa's husband?"

Tia shifted slightly and Ron could feel her body tense in his arms. She sighed after a while as she said, "No, he is the same Jeff that Rianna was engaged to. I thought you knew."

"What!?"

He looked baffled and she answered slowly, "After Rianna died, I guess Nysa and Jeff's grief drew them close together. Although I hadn't taken the news easily when I came to know about it. I gave Nysa quite a hard time because of it. Our relations had been quite strained for some time. I am not too proud of that. Nysa has always been a very good sister to me."

"It's okay. Don't blame yourself. Grief makes us do strange things...happens to the best of us." As they lay silent for some time, Ron continued. "You know we had a huge crush on Rianna at one time. She was quite older but there in lay the fascination."

"Really?! How come I never knew that!" She turned to look at him. "Where did you meet her? I never knew you had known her."

"Just saw her around the neighbourhood, you know - when we used to hang around in the malls or the cricket playground and sometimes at the local club events. She was very pretty. But of course that was before I laid my eyes on you and everything changed."

"But you never proposed!" She sounded sulky at that.

"You were this young innocent babe and my sister's friend. I thought you were too young, innocent – never been with a boyfriend and all. I was not sure you were ready for a fling or whatever else you might have called it," he said with a naughty wink. "Guess I realized too late that I missed my chance when Tanya told me about you seeing a guy by the name of Arjun. After we moved, I did come later to Bengaluru on Mom's business but mostly on the pretext of finding you – subconsciously maybe. Somehow our paths never crossed. Later when I came, you were away at college. I met your sister a couple of times, though. But I figured you might have moved on and met new boys at college...so why would you bother with the brother of your school friend."

"Everyone thought I was going around with Arjun. But it lasted only three months. He almost tried force on me..."

"What! That bastard..."

"It's okay Ron..." She lay her palm on his cheek gently. "I was saved by the bell. His brother's friends walked in as soon as he tried to manhandle me and then he didn't dare. I threatened to tell on him so he never had the guts to come close."

After Ron calmed down, she said, "Rianna never mentioned to me that she knew you."

"She knew me as Tanya's brother, of course. Yuvi was the one with a major crush on her. He would stand for miles near the coffee shop just to have a glimpse of her..."

"Yuvi? You knew Yuvi too! Why is this all news to me now?"

"Of course, I knew him. We used to hang around with the same friend circle at our neighbourhood or play at the Indranagar cricket club whenever he came for his vacations from boarding school. Later, we were in the same college and we caught up like old times."

"But you haven't met him now? He has never mentioned anything about you..."

"Oh, we are no longer the best of friends. Had a business deal that went wrong. I was not happy with his handling of funds."

"Oh!"

"I got the news of your sister passing away very late, you know..."

"Who told you?" she asked curiously.

"It was Ryan who told me, when I dropped in town. I was shocked, you know. Surprisingly, Yuvi never mentioned about that too."

When Tia looked puzzled, he explained, "I mean we had a business fallout much later. The times I called him, although it was not too often, he could have mentioned but he never did."

Tia sighed. "Yes, Yuvi was upset when my sister passed away. He was very fond of her."

"Yes, what a charming lady she was. You know she offered to help me out by photographing some shots for a perspective client of mine. She was a reputed photographer around this area it seemed and had freelanced some major projects."

"She did?" Tia asked. "She never mentioned. But I knew that she was a good photographer and often pursued photography as a hobby."

"Yes. Last time I met her was at one of my client's, Mr. Lyon's, charity event. She was always very friendly and happy to meet me knowing I was one of your friend's brother. A very warm person Rianna was...she loved to talk about you, her little baby sister, I noticed. And I never did mind." He winked at that. "We were speaking about old times and mutual acquaintances when the conversation turned to her photographs. I was looking for a good photographer at that time and she pitched in to help. I asked her to meet me at Pearl Valley the next day and she agreed. But later I had an emergency call so I had to leave...what? Tia? What's the matter?"

Her face had changed colour and she looked shocked.

"Pearl Valley?!"

"Yes, a client of mine wanted some shots of that area...but why, what's the matter?"

"That is where she died, Ron! How could you not tell me?"

"What was there to tell, Tia?! I never did meet her. I had somehow managed to book the earliest flight back home because of the news of Mom's ill health. As far as I remember I left a message for Rianna, saying I couldn't meet."

"So you never met her again?"

"No, I didn't. Mom had a sudden heart attack back home. It was almost a near miss. Her left side was paralyzed for almost a year. Through sheer grit and determination she got back on her feet. I don't remember much. It was years back. I was busy with mom and her business and lost all touch with everyone in Bengaluru except for Yuvi. My relationship with Yuvi was deteriorating by the day. We hardly were on good terms. Our online business together incurred heavy losses and so I was pissed off with him. However, I did visit one year later and they told me that Rianna passed away and everyone suspected it was suicide. I dropped in at Dev's place. He was not around and Maya, your sister-in-law, hardly knew me so it was awkward asking her too many questions. I did hear about her body being found near a waterfall but I never correlated it with the Pearl Valley as there are so many waterfalls here. Maybe that's why Ryan too never mentioned as he had only overheard about the death of Rianna Arya and not all the details. I am sorry, Tia."

They both fell into silence for a while. Ron tactfully let her alone for some time as he cleared their dishes and brought in some coffee.

"Tia?"

All kinds of thoughts were raging inside Tia's mind. Why was Rianna showing her dreams about Ron? And why was Ron telling her all this only now?

"You could have told me all this before," remarked Tia, as she searched his face.

"What was there to tell, Tia? I was hardly around. And this meeting wasn't that important to me. That's why I never thought about it much."

"Okay." Tia nodded slowly but her eyes remained fixed on Ron as her thoughts took a new turn now.

"When were you supposed to meet Rianna?"

"Meaning?"

"I mean the time of the year – which day, month and year?"

"You expect me to remember that? It was years back!"

"But I am sure you remember the number of times you came to Bengaluru?" Her eyes looked pleading although her face was tense. She wanted to remove whatever doubts were springing in her mind like poisonous algae as quickly as she could.

"I have been to Bengaluru a couple of times. Dropped in and out on business...wait. Let me check my mails..." He opened up his laptop. "But what is all this leading to, Tia?"

Tia didn't meet his eyes and her heart was beating very hard. She was having a bad feeling that the floodgates of a dam would suddenly open up and swallow her in its raging waters. And even Ron couldn't save her from that.

"I just want to know..." Her voice sounded listless but she couldn't help herself shutting away from him.

"Okay, I have the mails of that particular invitation. It was a charity event of Mr. Lyons and was held in the evening from 6 pm. It was on the sixth of August, 2012."

Tia felt she would have fainted hadn't Ron caught hold of her. She closed her eyes as dizziness overwhelmed her. He quickly handed her a glass of water. Tia drank the water after she felt a little steady.

"Tia, open your eyes, what is it, tell me?" he asked, his face weathered with concern.

"That was the day before she passed away..." she finished breathlessly.

"What an amazing coincidence...!" Ron was taken aback and sat speechless for a while. He half closed his eyes as he said slowly, "Now, wait a minute, Tia...you think her death is somehow related to me?"

Tia kept silent as she looked at him, her eyes agonized in pain.

Ron shook his head. "I don't believe this," he muttered as he got up and paced about the room restlessly. He ran his fingers through his hair and quickly turned to look at her. His eyes looked perplexed as he searched her face.

"I am totally lost here, Tia...am I missing something?!"

Her voice shook as she mumbled, not meeting his eyes, "I don't know...I mean we have come so close...as much as two human beings could possibly be – almost to be married soon, Ron! And until now you haven't told me about knowing someone or something that I care most in the world...why?"

He looked flabbergasted as he stared at her speechlessly for a few seconds. "But what is there to tell, Tia!" Ron shook his head disbelievingly, "I mean...I really don't understand what you are trying to say..."

Every line of his face looked strained as he looked at her carefully, his eyes intense.

"This is all so crazy...what is running in your mind, Tia!? This is just so...absurd...totally absurd...."

He pushed his hands into his pockets and released his breath slowly.

"Ok, we will talk later. I gotta go."

Tia cried the whole night. When she finally fell asleep, she saw herself when she was six years old. Her puppy had died and Rianna was holding her in her arms and caressing her hair.

"It's best that way, Tia. Some things don't last forever." She consoled. *"The puppy had to die. Things would have only got worse for him and for you too."*

Chapter 11

"It might all be a coincidence, Tia." Nina's face was full of concern as she gazed at Krystal over Tia's head.

"But it's strange he never knew about Rianna's passing away till much later or the fact that he never mentioned to you about his supposed meeting with Rianna." Krystal sounded puzzled.

"That's because he was not around when she passed away," protested Nina. "He was in another town, another city. He messaged Rianna and left and then he didn't think of it much. And that's because Rianna was only a passing acquaintance to him and not a close friend to keep in touch. Like have we kept in touch with most of our classmates? Take the example of Tanya – his sister – we don't even know where she is, how she is and we have not bothered to contact her for whatever reason it might be. So is the case with all the people we have grown up with. So who can blame him?"

"I guess we are all kind of agitated because of Tia's dreams. Or else we wouldn't have given a second thought to it. And those dreams do have a meaning or else why would we get this locket from the very place that Tia dreamt of," said Krystal as her eyebrows tweaked in confusion.

"So what did happen with Rianna's case? No evidence was found right? Or anything else to indicate a murder?" asked Nina.

"No." Tia sighed. "The police said it was a suicide as per the circumstances of death, background check and facts evaluated. There was no other evidence of murder found. The medical coroner too came up with the same verdict. And hence the case was closed. But of course none of us believed it to be a suicide."

"Have you thought of showing the locket to the police?" asked Krystal.

"No. Because what would I say? It might be anyone's locket as a matter of fact – travellers, children, lovers. They would say it might simply be a coincidence after all. Dreams like that happen all the time. They might even laugh for all I know and ask me to check up with the shrink."

"Yes, that's true," said Krystal. "Did Ron call up?"

"Not yet."

"What will you tell him?" asked Nina.

Tia shook her head as she looked at the locket and then yonder. "I don't know. What would I say, for heaven's sake? Rianna comes in my dreams and tells me not to trust you, Ron? It doesn't make sense. I don't know what to do or think?"

Nina and Krystal looked at each other helplessly.

"Don't fret so much, Tia. Give it some time. Time resolves everything – even the most difficult answers." Nina consoled.

Krystal sat near her and took her hand. "Look, Tia, don't say anything. Just say you got cold feet and need more time."

Tia's eyes were vulnerable as she looked at her nails distractedly. "He would keep questioning till he finds out the root of the matter..."

"Tell him the truth then," said Nina. "We believe you, then why wouldn't he?"

"Come on Nina, she can't do that. What if...what if..." Krystal continued slowly, "and I am not saying I am right, what if Ron has something to do with Rianna's murder?"

They were all silent as they looked at each other troubled. Nobody spoke about the elephant in the room.

Tia breathed in as she said slowly. "I need to find out more about Rianna's death. It's not suicide – it never can be. It has always been nagging in my mind the past four years, even before the dreams came or Ron made an appearance. It's as if something keeps prodding me and telling me that there is more to this than what it looks like. I need to find out more about this. I think the locket would be a good start. I kept pushing it away as I didn't want to ruin my feelings for Ron. But denial will only drive us apart what with the dagger of suspicion and mistrust always hovering in my mind. And deep down I must face the fact that there is more to Ron than meets the eye."

She could feel the ache in her heart as she said that. But she must face reality. Her life had always been challenging and she had faced every challenge head on. She must not be defeated by her feelings for Ron.

"I am with you, Tia. But you need not tell Ron anything right now. Behave coolly. Act as if nothing has happened – while you keep getting deeper and deeper into the matter." Nina advised.

"Yes, you are right, Nina. I need not reveal anything to Ron. And act as if nothing has happened."

Later in the day, after Nina and Krystal left, Tia headed for the local market to a small jewellery store of one of her mother's school friends.

"Hey, Tia." Mrs Nilakshi Rao greeted warmly. "Nice to see you after so long. What makes you remember this old lady today?"

"It's nice to see you too," Tia said as she gave her a huge hug. "Most of the time it's office or home for me, Nilu Aunty. Hardly get out these days."

"Oh! You young people should learn to relax, make time to smell the roses...too much work – you know what they say."

"I know, Nilu Aunty, I do."

"Ok, now before I bore another young person with an old lady's lectures, tell me how can I help you. Would you like me to show you anything specific?"

"Actually, Nilu Aunty, I found this old piece of jewellery the other day and was wondering if this was from your shop."

Mrs Rao wore her spectacles while turning the locket over and over, "I am not so sure, Tia. Did you get it as a present?"

"No, no, not as a present. Just found it in an unusual place, so I wanted to know more about its history..."

Mrs Rao looked surprised but luckily didn't push it any further.

"Well, it's got a design of a pentacle. This kind of jewellery was quite a fad at one time. Lot of young people from school bought trinkets like this but mostly from Jenny's shop, I think. You can drop in at her shop. She moved it closer to the lake area. You can check this out there."

"Alright, I'll do that." She smiled. "Thanks."

"My pleasure, Tia. Do visit this old lady at home sometimes. Pooja and I had some lovely times. How I miss her! You are turning out to be so much like her every day."

Tia parked her car near the lake. There was a restaurant and a few shops around the area and Tia quickly located Mrs Jenny Varghese's shop.

Mrs Varghese was another of her mother's acquaintances. She was always dressed up with heavy makeup and a lot of ornaments.

When Tia showed her the locket, she studied it and said, "This is a pentacle design. Mostly somebody from the Wicca community would be purchasing it. But you never can say as many young people do love this kind of jazzy stuff even if they might not be a Wiccan. It's a very old one, Tia. I had lots of this stuff when you were young, maybe in school. But I stopped getting them once the fad died down. Not much market in our side of the town. Hardly anyone from the Wiccan community. Frankly, I am not sure you will be able to even trace out its owner."

"I know," said Tia as she put it back in her purse. "Just thought I would find out about it as it lay amongst my sister's belongings. And she never wore much of jewellery, of any kind whatsoever." She lied as Mrs Varghese looked at her curiously.

As soon as Tia got back in the car, her mobile buzzed. It was Ron. She slowly picked up the phone and answered, "Hello Ron." She couldn't help the breathlessness in her voice.

"Hi, Tia." He sounded quiet. "Where are you?"

"Just driving around for a bit of shopping," she answered.

"Alright," he said. "Would you like to meet for lunch? At my place?"

Tia checked the time. It was early afternoon. Somewhere in her heart she was missing Ron a lot. They hadn't met or called for the past three days. This was going to be very difficult, she thought. *Was she madly in love with...with her sister's killer?* A shudder ran through her body.

"Tia? Are you there?" His voice sounded unsure and had a strange kind of vulnerability in it. Something that she couldn't associate with Ron. Was it likely that she was wrong in doubting him then?

"Alright. I'll come."

"Ok great!" He sounded relieved. "Will I order pizzas and juice?"

"I don't mind," she said softly as she hung up. She must give Ron a chance. Her mom always said that it was wrong to judge someone without finding everything about the truth. Always give a person, even one's enemy the benefit of doubt, she had advised. And deep in her heart she couldn't believe that Ron would do something like this.

"Mom, what do I do?" she mumbled. Tears of frustration welled in her eyes as she drove to Ron's place.

"Ron is good. Trust him Podgy, trust him." She felt her mom's voice echo in her ears.

"But what if he is the killer?" Another voice seemed to drone in her ears.

She shrugged to shake off the voices. She switched on the radio instead to drown out the heavy thoughts running in her mind like a whirlpool. There was one of her favourite numbers on the FM channel, "You can't hurry love." Somehow, the song seemed as if it was her Mom talking to her and she felt light – strangely light and more alive. She gave in to singing it loud as she drove her way to Ron's place.

He had taken a bungalow with a beautiful lawn at a quiet residential area in Koramangala. She could feel her heart skipping in an erratic manner and she couldn't curb her excitement as she walked down the garden path to meet him.

Ron opened the door as soon as she rang the bell. He looked freshly shaved and showered. The water drops on his chiselled, handsome face glistened and his musky deo made her senses come alive.

"Tia!" he said softly and his eyes searched her face intently as if to gauge her feelings. He drew her in his arms and kissed her fervently. He hugged her tight for a couple of seconds and then kissed the top of her head. "I missed you!" He sighed deeply. She felt so safe and secure in Ron's arms, almost as if she was back home after a long time.

He didn't wait for her reaction and walked her slowly to the living room and made her sit. He kneeled in front of her and taking her hands in his, he asked, "What would you like - tea, coffee, juice?"

"Ron, come on – you don't need to be so formal." She laughingly pushed him away.

"Of course, I have to for my princess." He smiled with an avalanche of love in his eyes. And true to his words, he treated her like a queen. The table was arranged in flowers. He put on some music. He then lifted her in his arms and carried her to the table as she shrieked. He had ordered pizzas, chicken tacos and a sumptuous looking banoffee pie topped with caramel sauce. Tia was already full halfway.

After they finished their food, they relaxed with a glass of fresh juice in hand. Ron switched on a game of football on TV.

"Tia, we have to talk," he said slowly. Tia tensed as he turned to look at her. "Tell me what was bothering you so much about Rianna talking to me a day before the unfortunate tragedy happened?'

"I don't know, Ron! I am sorry about that. I don't know...maybe it was the shock...and the fact that you never told me..."

His eyes seemed to almost penetrate her soul as he listened to her hysteric outburst although he didn't say anything for a while. The silence was unnerving and she felt this was a different Ron altogether – one she had never seen – serious and business like.

Ron got up and paced the living room for a while as he ran his hands over his face and hair almost distractedly. He sighed as he sat next to her and held her hands. He looked deeply into her eyes and explained slowly, stressing every word, "I have never mentioned about Rianna because I thought it might upset you. I didn't want to trigger sad memories. I have dealt with death too when my father passed away. I am okay with it now. But Tanya is still sensitive about it. No one talks about dad much when she is around."

"I am sorry Ron for jumping on you like that. Just a shock after all...I am sorry?"

Ron immediately pulled her to his arms and his body shuddered as if in relief.

"I am so glad, Tia, that the problem's resolved, although I have no clue as to what it was. I am sorry I didn't mention about this before. It was wrong on my part. Now that I found you again I never want to let you go," he said with a promise and a look very earnest. "Do you know how priceless you are to me? I wouldn't want to hurt you for anything in the world. So that makes me doubly cautious about whatever I do...whether I am doing the right thing or not when I am with you."

Tia felt torn as she looked into his soulful eyes. They were pools of vulnerability and she felt no one with eyes like that could even hurt a fly. No man in her life had bared his soul to her like this or wanted her this much. She was tortured by this strange dilemma that reared its ugly head whenever she got close to him.

When Ron took her in his arms, she clutched her arms round his shoulders very tightly as if to block those bad thoughts away. They remained like that for a few minutes.

"Are we still engaged?" His voice was unsure and tentative.

"Yes, yes, yes..." She shivered as Ron took her mouth in a hungry kiss. They had been apart for three days but it felt like years as Tia gave into his passion. He carried her in his arms and he laid her gently in his bed as he bestowed lingering, heated kisses all the while. The whole world seemed to stop as they felt swept into a storm of passion. Ron muttered over and over about how much he loved her, his voice hoarse with desire as he tossed her urgently beside him.

When his kisses got hungrier and his hands unrestrained, she moved her mouth away.

"Tia?" He looked puzzled.

"Ron...everything is happening just too fast. Maybe, that's why I get cold feet at times. I...I have never been so good with relationships and the two guys I have gone around with have been a total disaster. I want us to wait."

She looked down at her fingers nervously at the sound of the almost shattered silence stretched between them. Once she raised her eyes at him slowly, she bit her lip and then tremulously said, "Wait till our marriage."

"You want us to wait – after we have...but why?" he asked puzzled.

"I...I...just want to know more of each other." She looked into his eyes as if begging him to understand. "I want us to have more time to understand each other...on an emotional level...learn about each other...we have a lifetime together, don't we?"

"Then let's get married soon...what about next Saturday?"

She laughed at that. "Are you crazy? What will your family say?"

"My family readily accepts all my decisions." He sounded shamelessly autocratic.

"Your mother too?" she asked, raising her eyebrow.

"Especially my mother." He grinned.

"I know, but I am not ready. I want to settle some stuff in our company and be free of it completely. Then I can have some more time with you once we are married. So let's wait for...for another nine-ten months."

"What! That long! Why?" He looked bewildered, in fact shocked as he searched her face.

But she looked back resolutely, determined not to give into Ron's persuasion, although her heart was beating in a fast rhythm. The fear of losing Ron was shaking her inside. He sighed after a few minutes of the terse silence between them.

"That's too long. Six months?" His eyes were ardent but his face determined as he waited for her answer.

Tia looked surprised but she masked her face as she smiled and said, "Alright!"

"Six months is way too long, Tia," his voice was a groan, "...and tough. Especially with all your conditions!"

He pulled her in his arms again and possessed her mouth in a long lingering kiss.

Chapter 12

"Heard you are engaged? To Ron Garg?"

Tia looked up from her design to see Yuvi looking at her with curious eyes. The day was drawing to an end and everyone else had almost left.

"Well, yes, Yuvi."

He sighed.

"Guess you never cared to tell me, huh?" His voice had a hint of accusation.

She shrugged her shoulders apologetically as she said, "Well, it all happened so fast. Nobody else knows except for my family and my two friends – Krystal and Nina."

Yuvi took the chair facing hers, his eyes looking serious. "But news flies fast. Are you sure you're making the right decision?"

She felt a little taken aback when he said that outright.

"Well, of course I..."

"But how long have you known him, Tia? Don't you think you are being hasty?"

"I think I know him enough," she said in an abrupt quiet voice that sounded cooler than usual.

Yuvi looked away as if to try and gain composure. His voice was quite serious when he turned to her and said, "Knowing someone in school is quite different from how they turn out to be in their adulthood, Tia."

"I think you are going too far now, Yuvi." Her glance could almost freeze over the deserts of Sahara.

Yuvi looked away. They were both silent for a while. The atmosphere was tense and it looked like they both needed to cool down.

Yuvi slowly turned and took hold of her hand in his, but Tia refused to look at him. "I know this is your personal life. But I worry about you, you know. I don't know how you see me but for me you have always been more than a friend. And I don't want to see you hurt."

"But why do you think Ron would hurt me?" She looked him in the eye as she waited for his answer. Her face looked remote and quite disappointed as she looked at him.

"Because you don't know the kind of guy he is! I know! We were best buddies in college, Tia!" he protested. "In fact, he was my best friend."

"What?" she sounded shocked.

"Yes! He never mentioned that, did he?"

"No," Tia answered slowly. Ron did mention offhandedly that he was a friend but not in the category of a best friend by far, she mused. There was a lot of stuff Ron had omitted intentionally. He knew that she met Yuvi almost every day – in fact worked closely with him too.

"Tia..." His voice sounded soft as he looked at her with a touching vulnerability. "I have never had the courage to tell you this. And I don't know if this is the right time. But I have been holding this for far too long and I can't help but say it. I love you very much and have done so from a very long time now."

Tia felt a sea of explosion ringing in her ears as she looked at Yuvi. It was as if she had never seen him before or known him before – her childhood friend, her play mate, and her best pal.

"Yes, Tia, I love you. And now if I can't have you...I don't want to see you destroyed by somebody who will make you very unhappy one day." Yuvi spoke to her in a very tender voice as he stressed out each word slowly. "You are somebody I care about very deeply, Tia. And if I can't have you, it's okay; I will accept my fate however hard it might be. But you deserve a better man and not a guy like Garg. He will eat you inside out. He is an outright self-centered bastard!"

Tia looked shocked at the sheer venom in Yuvi's voice. Her voice trembled as she said, "Yuvi, this is all a shock to me. I have never thought of you as more than a dear friend. But I will not have you talk about my Ron in that derogatory manner. He is the man I love. And we are going to get married very soon."

Yuvi went to his knees as he took her hands in his. "I am sorry, Tia. I should not have brought up the enmity between Ron and me like this. It was ages back. All I want from you is to think the matter over carefully. And I want you to give me a chance...once..."

The phone buzzed at that very moment. She was in an uncomfortable position with Yuvi holding her hands. He slowly released her and got to his feet while she answered her phone.

It was Ron. "Hey, sweetheart what's taking you so long. I have been waiting here at the car park since ages. What's keeping you up there? Looks like everyone else has left too."

"Ok, darling. Give me another five minutes." She kept the phone and looked at Yuvi, undecided what to say. Yuvi looked all flushed and vulnerable from their recent exchange. She almost couldn't meet his eyes. The moment was somewhat awkward as Tia packed up her stuff.

"I am sorry, Tia, if it all came as a shock to you. But I do want you to think it over. Can I walk you downstairs if you don't mind?"

She nodded at that and they walked in an almost frozen silence. They saw Ron alone at the sidewalk busy speaking on his mobile, totally distracted. Only when they drew near did he hang up. His smile was all warm as she reached his side but he looked a little startled to see Yuvi with her. Both men looked tense and the atmosphere was quite strained.

"Ron," said Yuvi in a clipped voice.

"Hey, Yuvi!" Ron's voice was not close to warm either as he pushed his hands in his pockets and leaned on his heels.

Once he disappeared from the sidewalk, Ron held her close and kissed her on the mouth.

"How was your day, hon?"

"Good." She sighed as she leaned into his comforting arms and closed her eyes, feeling quite relaxed.

"Would you like to go out for a coffee or maybe a meal," he asked.

"Let's not." She smiled. "I am in the need to cook today."

"Alright! As my lady wishes." He chirped happily in spite of her sullen mood although his eyes remained watchful.

Once they were back at Tia's place, Ron helped her cut the vegetables while she made the chicken ready. Everything was peaceful if it wasn't for what Yuvi had said today evening. Why was everything so perfect and then suddenly, bang! There was a flash of lightning, and everything was all messed up. Or maybe she was just fretting over nothing. People did fight, especially business partners and that didn't mean someone was bad or good. But why did Yuvi speak so badly of Ron? After all, from the time she knew Yuvi, she never heard him speak ill or slander anybody. Everyone in her office knew Yuvi to be a person of high integrity who minded his own business.

"Tia?" She broke away from her thoughts as Ron drew close to her.

"Yes?"

"I have been calling out to you for about four-five times now. What's the matter? You look distracted? Something troubling you?"

"Not at all." She smiled but Ron didn't looked convinced as her smile appeared forced.

"What is it honey? You can tell me. Did Yuvi upset you? Did he say something?"

He looked deep into her eyes searching for an answer and waited patiently.

Tia sighed. "Well, yes. He is not happy that I am engaged to you."

"That's obvious! What else could you expect from him? We were adversaries in business and do not see eye to eye anymore."

"Were you best friends in college too?"

Ron didn't reply immediately. His eyebrows furrowed as he seemed to recollect something. He slowly tried to explain it as if he was trying to understand it himself. "That's what he thought. Yuvi has been kind of passionate about things, people – very cautious as well as an introvert. He was a quiet kind, the silent – deep one. Maybe losing his parents very young added to that part of his personality. I always tried to make him understand that he needed to come out and mix up more. But that was another reason for our rifts in college. We would go for days not talking and then we would forgive each other. Guess with time we became more and more incompatible. And I had other things that kept my mind distracted...he too in his way was very hardworking and focused about his work...and slowly we drifted apart..."

"Other girls you mean..." Tia raised her eyebrows meaningfully.

"Sheath your claws, my tigress." He quickly kissed her and then continued, "Anyway we went our own ways."

"Ok," said Tia quietly.

"And as we grew up, our differences grew bigger and bigger. We met again once, I think two-three years after we left college and we seemed to hit it off again. And then later I realized it was a bad idea to have become business partners in the first place. Both of us had different perceptions and our visions were moons apart. But anyway it is all in the past and I wish him well. We have gone our different ways and that's how it should have always been."

He seemed to shake off the heaviness that hung in the air and his smile seemed to lighten her mood. But now that Yuvi confessed his feelings for her, Tia was not sure how to deal with it.

She didn't know why she couldn't bring herself to tell Ron about Yuvi proposing to her. Maybe subconsciously she was afraid that it would bring in further complications in their lives what with her meeting Yuvi every day. If it was anybody else, it was fine. But this was a sensitive matter as Yuvi was a good friend of hers while Ron and Yuvi were friends who couldn't see eye to eye any more. Over and above all, Yuvi still resented Ron while she still had to work with him every day. How would she face Yuvi now? It would be awkward, she mused. It was all too much and she abruptly decided to push all the bad stuff away and concentrate on the present. She would cross that bridge when she came to it.

Ron wanted to take her out for a long drive and she badly wanted to enjoy that beautiful evening with him. She flung her thoughts aside. Now was not the time to delve into all that, she decided. She simply wanted to be happy and nothing would stop her any more.

Chapter 13

The atmosphere with Yuvi was a bit strained in the next few days and she tried to avoid meeting him as much as possible. But life was good and she was happy after a long time. She had an amazing time with Ron. They went on long drives, walked in the woods, went out for movies, dined out, and had barbecues – sometimes with Ron's friends and sometimes with hers. Ron wined and dined her in the most romantic way. Every day he would bring the most awesome flowers and gifts for her. He cared for her every gesture; the slightest frown would have him by her side, in a matter of seconds in fact. That brought about merciless teasing from Krystal and Nina.

"I am sure you guys will beat us to the altar!" Ryan teased.

"I wish!" Ron would wear a petulant look at that, sending a meaningful glance her way. Tia tried not to understand and look away.

Life was like a dream and she would stop once in a while just to pinch herself and believe all this was true. The nightmares had stopped haunting her for some time now. Maybe because she was so busy and happy with Ron. She didn't miss the emptiness of her Mom and Rianna anymore. Ron fulfilled her in every way.

A month passed away and soon Nina and Ryan's wedding kept them all busy and in a festive mood. There were laughter and jokes all the time and festive flurry in the air. The wedding was a gorgeous affair with most of Nina's relatives who had come to attend from different corners of the country and the world. Everyone danced and rejoiced to the music playing in the background. There were a lot of love songs sung by Nina's relatives besides a local music band. The food was delicious and Ron made Tia taste all the exotic dishes that she had never tasted in her life.

Krystal was having a great time dancing with one of Ryan's friends – Ness Mehra – a software consultant. Once she caught up with Tia at the buffet table, both couldn't help giggling at the way Ron was cornered by one of Nina's drunken old aunts and not letting him go. Ron was making all kinds of faces when the aunt was not looking. Tia often found herself admiring his gorgeous boyish looks and his amazing smile. But was there anything ever that she disliked about him?

She saw that many of the girls at the party had eyes for him and more than one gave her envious looks. She realized this quite early in their relationship, once she started going out with Ron, as he always drew glances wherever he went. Even guys seemed to admire his charismatic good looks. Uncle Neal too had once teased her asking whether he worked in the movies. Her sister and Krystal did question her once or twice whether she realized how good looking Ron was and if she kept a close watch or not, but of course in a teasing manner.

But Ron was totally devoted to her and that made her no less than thrilled. There were moments he would look at her with an intensity which left her insides shaking. Sometimes he would jokingly tell her that his celibacy was taking a toll on him although his eyes were dead serious. But Tia felt that was the only way to have some semblance to the mystery of her dreams of Rianna as well as her death. Otherwise she knew that her suspicions would be hovering like a dagger on their relationship forever and ultimately destroy both of them. She wanted everything to be clear and herself to be completely sure. But how? She didn't know. She didn't want to lose herself totally into Ron, if life decided to take another turn. And she knew that she was partly protecting herself if life or Ron ever let her down.

She shuddered and mentally shook herself. What was she thinking? She was so happy with Ron. Why was she spoiling everything now? It was as if she was cutting off her own legs with an axe while trying to find her way through the dense woods. Why was she ruining her life? There would never be anybody in her life who would love her as much as Ron, she mused.

"Hey honey, where are you?"

Ron was smiling at her but he had a question in his eyes. "Nothing," she said as he drew her near and kissed the top of her head.

"Hope we are not interrupting anything here?" Both of them looked up to see Uncle Neal at their side.

"No, Uncle Neal." Tia smiled at his cheery old face and took his arm fondly. "Please join us for some coffee?"

"No, dear. I've had enough. Lovely wedding party, isn't it? Nina and Ryan have arranged everything so beautifully!" He looked at them from afar, smiling appreciatively.

"Yes, Uncle Neal." Ron agreed as he looked about the hall. "Great arrangements! The food and wine are great too."

Tia noticed another tall guy next to him who looked familiar. Her uncle caught her attention as he said, "Meet Dhruv Rana. He will be heading our animation department, Tia, from tomorrow."

The man was quite tall and well-built although he was older. Must be in his mid-thirties, thought Tia. He had a strong jaw line and quite a pleasing face although in a rugged way.

Both Ron and Tia exchanged pleasantries as her uncle continued talking. "Dhruv was a good friend of Rianna, Tia. He grew up here in Indranagar, studied in the same school as you all but guess you wouldn't know him as he was a year senior to Rianna."

"Oh!" said Tia softly. "Somehow you looked familiar, I thought." Dhruv nodded his head in affirmation.

"Actually I worked with your sister for a while when she started her animation firm two years before she passed away."

"Animation firm?"

"Yes, Tia," answered her uncle. "Rianna had started her own animation firm which was doing tremendously well. Of course that's when she met Jeff with whom she became partners. But guess after she died, Jeff closed off that firm altogether."

They were all silent for a while.

"Ron, I wanted you to meet a person in the real estate business..." saying that Uncle Neal took Ron with him and Tia was left alone with Dhruv.

Dhruv looked at her quietly from his impressive height. He was even taller than Ron.

"I had heard a lot about you from your sister, Tia. She loved you the most I guess, her baby sister."

Tia warmed at that as she looked up at him. There was a quiet air about him. Although he looked austere at first sight, he seemed kinder now.

"How long did you know her?"

"She was a year junior to me. But we often met in our art classes. She was crazy about art then, just like I am. Of course, later her interests turned towards photography. After school, years later, we met again when she put an ad in the paper that she needed someone for her animation business. I joined her as a designer. Quite a brilliant businesswoman she was. Far intelligent for her age."

"Yes, she was. She was very good at academics too. Wanted to pursue her post graduation but other things came in the way and she didn't pursue."

"Other things?" he asked interestedly.

Tia sighed. "She took care of us all. Dad had passed away and mom was unwell. Took on the responsibility for all of us. So she joined Uncle Neal as a part-time consultant, worked with him for a few years and later started her own freelancing work. I didn't know that she had also started her own animation firm, though."

"Yes, animation as well as photography. She was such a good photographer," he answered.

"Hey, Podgy!" Her sister had her niece in her arms as she walked a little breathlessly towards her.

"Can you look after Lola for a while? I need to help Nina's mom with the buffet..." She looked startled to see Dhruv with her.

"Hello." Nysa nodded at Dhruv. Tia was surprised to see Nysa quite stiff in her greeting. Dhruv merely inclined his head.

"Ti...Ti...?" Lola pointed at Tia's earring while trying to grab at it.

"No, Lola baby. Take this!" She plucked a balloon decorated on a side wall and handed it over to her.

Lola was excited and she clapped her hands and gave Tia a kiss. She wriggled to get down from Tia's arms. "Lola lubh Ti..." she said in her cutest baby voice. Tia hugged her niece and answered in a baby voice too, "Tia loves Lola too!"

Lola was busy bouncing the balloon on the thread.

"Nysa's girl – takes after Jeff, doesn't she?" said Dhruv, as he pushed his hands in his pockets. "None of you in her."

"Yes, you are right. Jeff really dotes on her...even more than Nysa." Tia smiled fondly looking at her niece.

"Nysa – is she happy with Jeff?"

Tia was taken aback by Dhruv's blatant question.

She shrugged. "Why wouldn't she be?"

Dhruv's smile was twisted as he looked away.

At that moment Jeff walked by, kneeling right next to Lola at the same time, "What is my little baby up to?"

"Daddy, balloo...balloo..."

"Hope you are not troubling your Tia aunty?"

"Ti give balloo..." she said as Jeff picked her up. Only then did he notice Dhruv and his smile looked strained.

"Dhruv." He nodded in acknowledgement though not too warmly. Not wasting time he turned his glance at his daughter. "Now let us take our little Lola for a walk. Granny wants to meet our Lola."

Jeff turned to Tia and said quickly, "Her granny's asked to get her for a change of dress, Tia. Hope you don't mind."

"Not at all, Jeff, go ahead."

As both father and daughter walked off, they met Nysa on the way. Jeff looked serious as he spoke to Nysa while she immediately gave a sideways glance at Tia and Dhruv.

Dhruv smiled but it didn't reach his eyes. "Looks like they are not too happy to see you with me."

"Why not? I hardly know you." Wasn't he being a little rude now, thought Tia in bewilderment.

"Never got along with Jeff even when I worked with Rianna," he shrugged.

There was an awkward silence between them – at least from her side as they both gazed at Jeff, Nysa and Lola enjoying a happy family moment. Nysa and Jeff were an animated audience to something Lola was saying.

"All happy families," remarked Dhruv with a crooked smile.

"Of course, they are. Why wouldn't they be?" She quipped back.

"Do you think Rianna would be happy too?" He nudged his head towards their side. "Seeing this?"

Tia was speechless at that. *The gall of this man – how dare he?*

"I am sorry, Tia. I do not bother to mince my words like most people. Honesty is all you will get from me. I guess sometimes it does get out of hand." He sighed. "Ok, little one, go enjoy your friend's party. Your boyfriend's on the way too." He patted at her back in what seemed like a brotherly way and then left.

"What happened to you?" Ron touched her nose with his finger playfully. "Seen a ghost?"

"Strange!" She shook her head as if she couldn't believe herself. Krystal joined them at that moment.

"What's strange?" Ron asked quickly while looking at the receding figure of Dhruv.

"He made some strange remarks about Jeff! And Rianna too," she said, looking at them both.

"Who? Dhruv Rana?" asked Krystal.

"Yes," said Tia looking at Krystal with raised eyebrows. "You know him?"

"I have met him a couple of times at Nina's. He has always been a bit weird, Tia. Nina had some tough times with him and it's been unavoidable as they are first cousins."

"You feel like he doesn't like Jeff?" asked Ron curiously.

"That's what I deduced. He said about Rianna not being too happy to see Jeff and Nysa today."

"Tia," said Krystal, her voice soft, "that's understandable. According to the grapevine and some friends I know, they are of the opinion that Dhruv loved Rianna. And that is the reason why he never took Jeff and Rianna's relationship really too well."

Chapter 14

Once the wedding was over, Nina and Ryan left for a week to Switzerland while Ron had to leave for Singapore on an urgent business for a month. Krystal's sister and niece had come down from Guwahati to spend a few days with them and so she was quite busy with her family too.

Tia felt so desolate with Ron away. The evenings back at home were very lonely while nights she tossed and turned and tried hard to sleep. She sometimes visited her sister to spend some time with her and Lola or her other niece, Alisha, when they were around. Ron made it a point to call her every day, sometimes two to three times. At night they routinely talked every day for an hour or more.

Yet, Tia missed Ron a lot. He told her that he might be delayed by another two weeks and that made Tia feel even more low. What was it? It was as if she never had a life without Ron. What did she do till now, she wondered? Ron has entered her life only recently...what had she done all these years, then? How did she pass her time?

All her life she had been very independent, looking after her own. But Ron has changed everything in her life. He had as if awakened the woman inside her and breathed more life into her. Just like Sleeping Beauty in the fairy tale who had been awakened and given another new life by her prince. Tia smiled at that. What was Sleeping Beauty's name – Princess Aurora? Must have been about some real person like her who the author had turned into fiction. Ron has shown her that life can be amazing and even more beautiful with the right person around. They could start a good life together. What a fool to postpone their marriage, she chided herself. Didn't make sense when they loved each other so much.

The sudden buzz of the doorbell broke into the reverie of her thoughts and she set aside the paper and coffee to check who it was. Tia was surprised to see officer Regan leaning against the door. He was

Krystal's cousin and also the police officer handling her sister's case when she had passed away. Regan had worked very hard on this case as Rianna was one of his closest friends in school. He had apologised to Tia when, after months of investigation on Rianna's death, they could find no other evidence and had to close it as a suicide case.

"Hi, Tia. I found a letter belonging to Rianna amongst some files while cleaning up the cabinet. The previous officer hadn't found it important and had tossed it aside. It got misplaced in another case file. I thought you might want to keep it. It was kept inside her purse which she was carrying on her last day. The purse was luckily recovered around the area where her body was found."

"Oh! Let me have a look...but first come inside. I was just making another cup of coffee. Would you like some?"

"Sure!" said Regan as he took off his glasses and sighed. "Had a long day."

"How are Lina and little Donna?" she asked with a keen interest. Lina was Regan's wife and Donna his two-year-old daughter. They all grew up together and even if they didn't meet often, they had an easy bond amongst them that usually came with living in a close locality.

"Lina is having a tough time trying to check Donna's hyper moods. Restless and always running around," he said with a fond smile. "Hey, I am happy to hear you got engaged. Krystal told me. Ron was a nice boy, I remember. My father knew his father very well and often met at club events."

"Thank you, Regan." Tia handed him the coffee while taking a close look at the letter.

"Every little thing of Rianna means so much to me, Regan. Thank you for this," she said as she peered through the letter.

"I know, Tia. Krystal often tells me how much you miss her. And why not! She was the rock of the family. How much she took care of you all!"

"Yes," Tia sighed as she read the letter. It was a love letter to Rianna but there was no name as to who had written it.

Hello my darling Ri,

Time has come for us to meet face to face – to look at each other and feel the love we have for each other. I have loved you from afar for so long...right from the time we were in school. And I know you love me too.

I thought you would have guessed who I am. But that doesn't matter as within a few moments you will see the person who has loved you for so long – with all his heart and a madness that has no logic.

Soon we will meet.

I love you,

From,
The one who loves you most.

"The letter is not dated. We don't know if it was a recent one or an old letter. But she had it in her purse. People do carry some love letters for sentimental reasons. And we know from the handwriting that it is not Jeff," said Regan.

Tia mused for a while looking at the strange symbol at the bottom.

"What is this symbol at the bottom, Regan?"

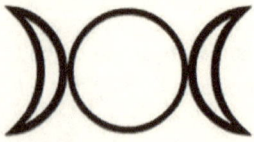

"Well...that one is a symbol of the triple goddess. A Wiccan symbol. It meant whoever had sent the letter was a Wiccan."

"A Wiccan?"

"Wiccans are followers of the Wicca religion. It is a contemporary, neo-pagan and nature-based religion, gaining popularity in US and Europe. There are not many followers in India as of now. Its belief system centres primarily on gods, goddesses, and nature worship. It is characterized mostly by rituals and ceremonies which Wiccans perform to honour their deities. It uses symbols in its ceremonies and follows the calendar in reference to Wiccan festivals. Symbols are a very important part of the Wiccan practice. The pentacle is one of their most distinctive and basic of symbols. Chalice, Cauldron, Athame, and Wand are other primary Wicca symbols besides many others," said Regan as he paused to take a breather. "This religion also has a strong belief in witchcraft, though not all Wiccans are Witches."

"Witches?"

"Witches are people who practise witchcraft, of course. And witchcraft is mainly the use of magic and manipulation of natural energies by invoking spells, casting circles etc."

Tia was quiet for some time. Should she mention about the pentacle locket to Regan?

"Tia?"

"Wait a second, Regan, I want to show you something." Tia went to her bedroom to fetch the chain with the pentacle locket.

"You know what, Regan? This might sound strange to you. But lately I have been having strange dreams about Rianna. Dreams of somebody trying to kill her at that very cliff in Pearl Valley around where her body was found. And the uncanny part is that the other day I dreamt that we were back to being young again. I was my seven-year-old self and she was fifteen. We were picking pebbles near the bank of the stream for a while and then Rianna started digging the sand with her bare hands. It was again in Pearl Valley where Rianna's body was found. In my dream, she unearthed a chain from below the sand which had a locket with a pentacle design on it. Later when I woke up, I went to the same place in Pearl Valley with Krystal. We dug for a while and found the exact chain with a pentacle locket and it was in the exact location as in my dream."

"Wow, that's amazing!" he said as he looked at the chain closely. "Although being a police officer I shouldn't ask this but as a friend I'd like to know if dreams about Rianna have been kind of prophetic till now?"

"Not exactly. Although Mom's has been."

"I see," said Regan, his finger drumming over his mouth thoughtfully.

"But how could you of all people believe it was a suicide, Regan? That's what breaks my heart."

"Falling off that cliff disfigured every part of Rianna's body, Tia. There was no other evidence and we did try hard but found none. No combat weapons or firearms – nothing!"

"I know, Regan...I know! Yet, deep in my heart I just can't believe that Rianna would commit suicide."

Regan sighed at that. "Let me see if I can go through her files again. It's been closed as a suicide case for a long time now. Re-opening a cold case isn't that easy especially with the lack of evidence to substantiate it. And you know police investigations don't run on dreams, the sixth sense or ESP, but on solid, concrete proof."

"You know what kind of person Rianna was, Regan. So full of life – so happy, so confident! We all looked up to her!"

"That's what she showed you, Tia. You were young, in school...her life was a different battle altogether."

Regan's words shook her and she looked at him shocked.

"Calm down, Tia and listen to me."

He came and sat down next to her while taking her coffee cup and handing her a glass of water.

He sighed as he said, "You were very young back then. There are some things she never might have told you. But we knew. Your dad's passing away, mom's sickness, looking after all of you were not easy on her. Dev was busy on tour and Nysa was busy studying. You were too young to lean on. She had to take care of the finances at home and then there was her own career too. It was quite a lot for a young girl like her to handle. Most people didn't know this but she also had a close friendship with Aadi whom we lost to a tragic road accident...in fact he was her very first love."

"Of course! I do remember Aadi – Aaditya Soni. They were best of friends. He passed away very young when you were in college, right?"

"Yes! He passed away a few months before your dad passed away. We saw through all the facade of her laughter and good cheer. It took a greater toll on her than she cared to admit. Rest of us all were having a fun-filled, carefree life at that age. That was not the case with her. She took it all stoically, though. She was very emotional – our Rianna. Always the softie in our friend circle, the agony aunt whatever – the sensitive one. But there was nobody to look after her needs. She shunned all serious relationships after Aadi so that she could concentrate on the family more. There were so many guys ready to lay down their life for her but she told them in no terms that she had other stuff to take care of. And being the good hearted soul she was, she subtly brought me and Lina closer too without our knowing."

Regan stood up and pushed his hands in his pockets as he looked outside the window. "But, after your mom's death and with you away in college, she was a little free of her responsibilities. She worried a lot about you though, since you were very close to your mom and you were very young then. Then she met Jeff in course of her business. They were engaged and she was happy after a long time. But then there were a lot of stuff in their relationship that they were not compatible with. They didn't see eye to eye in their business and that hit their relationship very hard. Rianna had always been taking charge of things in her family and in certain aspects Jeff was equally headstrong. They started to have many differences. Jeff wanted to take a break for a while but she didn't. Anyway, they broke off their engagement and it was mostly from Jeff's side..."

"They broke off!! How come I didn't know about that...no one mentioned...?"

"I know," said Regan. "I was surprised that Jeff didn't tell you that they had broken off their engagement almost a month before Rianna passed away. Jeff also had a fling with someone according to what Rianna told me in her weakest moments. Rianna was going through a depressive phase towards the end of their relationship...the doctor had prescribed her sedatives...not that strong, though. Just some sleeping tablets to overcome her phase of insomnia."

"But so many people take sedatives...that doesn't mean a person is suicidal or depressive!" Tia protested.

"But talking to Rianna's friends and then to her doctor, that's what the investigating team deduced finally and hence closed the case."

"I wish I knew all this."

"Nobody wanted to bring this up as you were already having a hard time coping...so we didn't tell you. Maybe that's the reason Jeff kept quiet too. He felt guilty. And then after a few months we heard Nysa and Jeff getting engaged....how strange life can get..." He sighed.

"Then again, I always thought Rianna never really got over Aadi...she almost looked for Aadi in every guy. Maybe Jeff felt that too. And hence that created a rift in their relationship. Anyway, today Jeff is very happy with Nysa and that is all what matters."

Tia shook her head thoughtfully. "I feel she is not happy wherever she is...Rianna...no wonder..."

"But that's in your mind, Tia. We don't know about the dead. It is a realm – unexplained. We can't forget to live today by living in our past, Tia. Life has to go on. Life needs you today, the people around you here need you now...not the people who are not here anymore, however much we loved them. They have moved on and we should move on too. Jeff has moved on and so has Nysa. They have created their own little world. I hear Ron is a good guy, Tia. Life has again come to you with new opportunities and new relationships. You can have a good life, a family again. And your Mom would want this for you too, Tia. You must move on, sweetheart."

Tia looked away trying to fight her tears.

"Hope you know that we really care a lot about you and worry about you. We just want the best for you."

Regan's phone beeped and Tia got a hold of herself as he answered the call. "I will be right there."

As he hung up he looked concerned.

Tia pushed her hands in her pockets as she said, "I guess you need to be back. Carry on then."

"I will take the chain with me for further investigation. You sure you'll be okay?"

Regan gave her a reassuring pat on her shoulders and asked her to call if she needed anything.

Tia took the letter in her hands and said silently, "What happened to you Ri...I wish I knew..."

There was a sudden gust of wind and the sound of windows rattling. Rianna's wooden photo frame on the designer shelf had fallen and lying precariously at the edge of the shelf. Tia put it back in place and closed all the windows. She looked outside her window and saw the clouds gather. It might rain in a short while, she thought. The phone buzzed at that moment and Tia was happy to see it was Ron. She quickly got under the covers and sighed as she heard his intoxicating voice, "How was your day, honey?"

Chapter 15

"Hello Tia? What are your plans for the weekend?"

Tia looked up from the documents she had neatly arranged in her file bag so that she could take them home.

"Yuvi...umm...I'm not sure..."

"How about some Chinese noodles at The Lantern?" Yuvi sat at the edge of the table waiting for her answer.

"Well, I'm not sure...Nysa..."

"You are still angry with me for making those remarks about Ron? I'm sorry. The news was...well a shock to me and I reacted badly."

"No, that's okay. I haven't thought about it so much."

"Then why don't you join me? It's just dinner after all."

Tia paused for a bit, not knowing what to say.

"Please, Tia!" When she hesitated he insisted with his clasped hands raised in a begging motion. He was the old Yuvi she knew at his charming best and she couldn't refuse.

"Well okay..." She relented with a chuckle.

He playfully slapped her arm as he said, "That's my girl. How about meeting at seven? Is that a good time for you?"

"Fine with me!" She smiled.

"I will pick you up."

Ron called up early that day and she was almost rushed for time.

"Hi, honey. Just to let you know, I will be taking a late flight to

Bangkok tonight. So I won't be able to call you later."

"Is it? No problem. Are you heading to the airport?" she said as she carefully ironed her peacock blue *salwar* suit. It was a delicate material made of taffeta silk and designed with rich embroidery.

"No, no....another hour of meeting and then I will go. You sound breathless, are you going out?" There was more than a hint of curiosity in his voice.

"Yes, just getting dressed up."

"With whom?"

"Some office colleagues..." Tia almost bit her tongue. Why did she lie for heaven's sake!?

"Oh, ok. Have a nice dinner. Miss you so much, honey. Love you!"

As she got dressed, she wondered why she had lied about Yuvi to Ron. Maybe some part of her felt Ron would not be happy about her going out with Yuvi. But on the other hand she didn't want to let Yuvi down too. After all, their friendship went a long way back in time. He had been at her side during their good times and bad times. He would be hurt if she suddenly brought an abrupt distance to their friendship.

The doorbell rang. She quickly took her purse and answered the door.

Yuvi was very chatty on the way back to the restaurant. Although most people complained that Yuvi talked less and was a hard boss, yet with Tia there was always an easy air between them. They talked about their company and some of the funny stuff in the office. Yuvi took her to a beautiful restaurant they had never visited before. They talked for a while and then drifted off to a comfortable silence.

"I am sorry, Tia. That was very nasty of me to talk about Ron in that manner." Yuvi looked contrite and Tia felt guilty for judging him so severely at one time.

She waved her hand as she said, "Don't give it a thought."

"Yes, but just let me explain. It will make me feel a little better – if you get what I mean. I looked up to Ron once and was very proud of our friendship. But he was the star in school as per what I heard in the neighbourhood and later in college too I saw the kind of charisma he exuded. Girls were after him...and all the nerds worshipped him too. He was always the Mr. Popular in school, not in the way of Arjun, of course – your short gig of a boyfriend." He said that almost tongue in cheek and Tia smiled dryly. "He was admired in a different way altogether which also included his abilities in math or the science lab too. He was Einstein and Hugh Jackman rolled into one."

He smiled in a crooked way. "We drifted apart slowly in college and I didn't take that very well. Later, even in business, we had a lot of differences and so we went our different ways. But it was not nice of me to say such things about him. You can put it to envy, I guess. He got the girl too who I had admired for so long."

Tia shifted uncomfortably as his words gave way to silence. "Well, Yuvi, I..."

"Hey, that's okay. You don't have to explain." He held her hand lightly. "It's understandable in fact. Any girl in her right mind wouldn't let Ron go...but I really do want us to continue being friends like we always have been, Tia."

"Well, of course, Yuvi. I wouldn't want it any other way. Your friendship is invaluable to me."

"Same here, Tia. You have always been a very good friend to me. I do not want to lose your friendship at any cost."

His eyes exuded sincerity. The conversation was a little more intense than what Tia could handle, but Yuvi seemed to understand and immediately switched topics. He steered her away from topics that were becoming too personal and touched on lighter subjects instead.

They chatted about some of their common friends. Yuvi could really make anyone laugh when he was in mood, she thought. She laughed her head off as he regaled her with funny stories of younger days and more recent tales from work and office.

After their dinner they took a walk by the lake. Tia felt good after a long time and somehow it assuaged her loneliness for Ron to some extent. It was quite late when Yuvi dropped her home.

Work at office was quite hectic the following couple of days. Yuvi helped her cope with the avalanche of deadlines. She was happy with the amount of work as that kept her busy from missing Ron. Her working relationship with Yuvi was the same as before but now he often took her out to nearby restaurants at lunch break or for coffee after work. Their friendship seemed to have picked up the loose ends and was on the mend. Tia felt as if that bitter conversation between them had never happened. Yuvi was being his old self – a good and considerate friend if ever there was one.

But there were a few raised eyebrows and Nysa was the first one to question. "You and Yuvi are meeting more than often these days?" she asked casually while brewing the coffee.

Tia looked surprised at Nysa's query. She didn't realize that Nysa noticed that much or had the time to mull on her personal life.

"Why do you ask?"

"Maya was filling me in the other day. She told me that Yuvi was dropping in more than often these days and taking you out too."

"Nothing like that. Just business lunches or coffee dates...nothing more. Now that Ron is away for a longer duration, I really feel bored at home. And work has increased too – so what better way to finish than over a coffee break or a luncheon. In fact, he is quite refreshing with all this work pressure."

Nysa nodded slowly although her face showed Tia's answer didn't convince her. She, however, shrugged her shoulders and said, "I am glad you found Ron. I have never seen you so serious in any relationship, ever."

Nysa was truly happy for her sister. She had never seen her sister close to any guy in school or in college. Sometimes, Nysa felt that her sister, although sweet and a very nice girl, was somewhat frozen inside. And she had doubted her ability to love anybody in a passionate way. Jeff too had questioned her about Tia's single state. That wasn't surprising as from the time he knew Tia, he had never seen her with anybody.

 But then again, Nysa knew that Tia kept a part of her life hidden from her and the rest of the world. And even if Tia had anybody how would she know, anyway. As teens they hardly had any time together as Nysa was away at college and then later at the Indian Institute of Management in Mumbai for her management studies. In fact during the last decade they were totally at two different universes altogether. It was not her but Rianna who was Tia's confidante.

Tia laughed silently. What Nysa meant was before Ron came into her life, she never had seen a boyfriend in her life whatsoever – but was too careful to say so. Of course, she kind of overlooked it as she knew Nysa didn't want to hurt her by saying anything out of hand.

But Krystal was point blank altogether as she never believed in mincing her words.

"Does Ron know?" she asked.

"Know what?" asked Tia, although she understood what Krystal meant.

"That you are seeing a little bit more of Yuvi?" asked Krystal, her left eyebrow raised in question. "Overheard some of your office colleagues gossip about both of you at the gym."

"Gosh! How people talk! All they need is a single match stick and they light up the whole town."

"But have you told him?"

"No, I haven't said anything to Ron. Why should I? Yuvi is just my friend. Nothing in particular to say."

"Is he accompanying us to the movies today?"

"Well, he asked me what I was doing on Saturday. And when I said I was going out with you and Ness for a movie, he kind of invited himself along. I agreed as I thought you wouldn't mind." She added as an afterthought, "Do you?"

"No, not at all..." said Krystal slowly. "We have never been on speaking terms although I have known him from afar since a long time – almost from our childhood."

"You know how he is then. He doesn't talk much...has a few friends. But once he opens up he is great company..."

Krystal rolled her eyes at that and went back to the game on her tablet while leaning back lazily on the couch. They were spending a casual Saturday afternoon together.

At that moment her mobile rang.

"Hey, what's my baby up to on a Saturday," Ron drawled in his sexy voice.

"Nothing much...just some paperwork with coffee and Krystal." Krystal waved a hand at her. "And Krystal just said hi."

"Hi her back!" He smiled. "So what plans do you girls have on a Saturday?"

He always seemed to be interested in everything Tia did. He would often ask her what she did the whole day. Even things like doing the dishes, cleaning the room and similar mundane stuff he would want to know. In fact this drove her crazier in love for him and she would feel a flutter in her belly at the things he said. She never knew love could feel this way and be this intense. What she felt for Ron in school was a mild wave compared to the tornado of emotions he raged in her now. He was driving her passionate and crazy for him every day. Missing him was like almost a physical pain as if she was losing some part of her body.

"Well, Krystal just cooked a wonderful lunch for both of us. I am taking care of the dessert – so baking a chocolate cheesecake right now. Then planning to go out with Krystal and two more friends..."

"Who else?" he asked quickly.

"One is Krystal's friend Ness and...?"

"Ness? Good ol' Ness Mehra? Is he her new boyfriend by the way?" he teased.

"Ness? Umm...boyfriend probability is there..." She winked at Krystal who looked up and almost blushed.

"And who else?"

"And Yuvi," she said.

There was a silence as he exclaimed slowly, "Yuvi? Yuvraj Raval?"

"Yes. That Yuvi."

"Alright," he said slowly and there was an awkward silence between them. Tia for the life of her could not fill in the silence.

"Ok. I will catch you later. They just announced my flight. Love you, honey."

"Love you too." Tia felt strange as she hung up her call. Hope Ron didn't take it any other way. Should she stop meeting Yuvi out of work, she pondered, although it looked silly and unnecessary. And she didn't want to hurt Yuvi by ignoring him outright. Maybe once Ron saw that Yuvi didn't hold any grudges and wanted to be friends, he would be okay.

She felt Krystal's eyes on her all the while. But she acted ignorant and rushed to check on her cake.

Chapter 16

"How's the party going? Sorry, I am late. Need any help?" Tia asked her sister over her shoulder.

"Nothing much. Moving the dessert to the buffet table," Nysa said.

"Here, let me take a few," Tia said as she took one of the trays decorated with dessert bowls.

"Alright. Jaya will handle the rest. Jaya?"

"No problems, Ma'am." Her housekeeper smiled while easily manoeuvring two trays in both her hands.

The living room was packed and Tia guessed that the number of guests exceeded hundred. But Nysa had a large patio and a beautiful garden attached to the house and the guests were moving freely in and around with drinks in hand. It was an anniversary party of Jeff and Nysa's software company.

"It seems Dev and Maya cannot make it as they are just back from an afternoon feast at Maya's cousin's place. They are tired," said Tia.

"Oh! Dev could have tried to make it – at least for Jeff! He never seems to bother about certain important things these days...well never mind." Nysa sighed tiredly.

Nysa maintained a beautiful house. Her mother-in-law, Mrs Nandini Bailey, saw Tia and immediately walked towards her with a warm smile. "Hey Tia, long time, no see."

"Hello, Aunty." Tia smiled at her. She was still an attractive woman despite her age. No wonder, combined with the looks from his British father, Jeff had turned out to be quite a handsome man. Nysa often complained about girls trying to flirt with him even with her standing next to him.

"I heard the good news. Nysa tells me Ron is a very attractive young man with a successful consulting business."

"Nysa just exaggerates when it comes to me," she said, smiling back.

"I am sure she doesn't. A beautiful and a nice girl like you deserve a man like that. I am so glad, Tia. Nysa always worries about you, you know."

"Well..." She smiled as she shifted her feet. "She mustn't, you know. I am quite capable of looking after myself."

"I know, I know. Quite an entrepreneur these days, I heard." She smiled sincerely. "But you will always be her little sister. And she loves you a lot."

"Mrs Bailey..." Tia moved away as Mrs Bailey got caught up by some of her other guests.

Jeff came and stood next to her with a drink in hand but she declined. "Comfortable?" he looked around the room.

"Trying to...hardly anyone I know. How is it going?" she asked, looking up at him.

"Most of the guests have turned up. Except for the cake, the caterers have delivered all the food and drinks," he said smoothly.

"Lola's settled?"

"Yes, Mom hired Gita to babysit her. So she is keeping her busy with doll games and of course her favourite dessert. Anyway she is very tired. Will nod off any moment. Had a busy day at the pool with Nysa today."

"Can I have a look once?"

"I am not sure it's a good idea, Tia. If she sees you she would want to come down to the party. She'd be too excited and won't settle down. Hope you don't mind?"

"Of course not, I understand. She is so adorable. I'll just peep in once before I leave."

"Yes, please do that. Her latest fad is to cook. Cooks for me and Nysa as well as her gran – lots of imaginative meals," he said with an adoring look. "And you know today she..."

"Hey Jeff, where have you been hiding?" asked a husky voice. Turning round, Tia saw a beautiful woman in her late twenties. In fact, she was drop-dead gorgeous and her dress flattered her lissome figure which was almost comparable to that of a supermodel.

"Simi! Great to see you. I didn't know you were back in Bengaluru." Jeff smiled at her warmly.

"Yes, came a week back. Good old Rahul told me about the party and gave me a lift. Quite a party you are having here. One of your partners kept me cornered for some time by the way. Couldn't get away easily."

"I am sure you are used to that kind of attention," said Jeff in a teasing manner.

"Oh, you think so? Come on...I know you are never serious." She laid her hand on his arm and looked at him adoringly. Tia found that quite questionable actually, as she tried to skim across the room to see if Krystal and Nina had arrived. Somehow, in a matter of seconds, this lady made her feel quite like an outsider in fact.

"Would you like a drink?" asked Jeff, signaling at a passing waiter.

"Yes, I could do with a drink. Driving this far has made me thirsty." She batted her lashes flirtatiously while her lips pouted sexily to the consternation of Tia. She turned to look at Tia then, her eyes questioning as they darted back at Jeff.

"Oh...meet Tia, my sister-in-law. She is a managing director of a local software company here." Jeff turned to her as he made the introductions. "Tia, this is Simi Panag."

"Nysa's younger sister?" Simi smiled while nodding her head. "Quite a young managing director for her age?"

"Oh, it's just a small company owned by my uncle. I just help him out," said Tia modestly.

"I guess it really helps when you have someone you know or your family members in higher positions, doesn't it? Connections can have you gliding up that ladder easily." Her fingers moved nimbly as it imitated the climbing of a ladder.

Tia was quite taken aback at her cattiness.

"Ahh...it's called nepotism actually when that happens." Tia's lips curved into a slight smile.

"How right you are! You read my mind totally." Simi smiled superiorly at her.

Jeff looked somehow lost at the exchange. "That's not the case with Tia, Simi. She had good offers in Singapore and Australia but left all those big offers..."

"Jeff, nothing like tha..." Tia tried to interrupt him feeling quite embarrassed.

But Jeff continued with that charming smile of his, "You know she is quite a hardworking girl and for this reason she has been able to bring a loss-making company back to its feet today..."

"Hey, Tia!" Krystal appeared and Tia could finally find a way out. "Excuse me, Jeff?"

"Sure. Hey, Krystal! Nice to see you."

"Hi, Jeff. Sorry but I have to get Tia to the kitchen. Nysa's waiting..."

"That's okay, Krystal," said Jeff. Krystal and Tia smiled at both of them apologetically as they both rushed into the kitchen.

"What's the matter...and why are we rushing to the bedroom instead of the kitchen?" asked Tia, perplexed.

"Sorry for that white lie. It's my dress. Can you just help me with this hook?"

Once they were back to the living room, the party had got even busier.

"Who is that hot kitten with Jeff?" asked Krystal as she beckoned towards the French windows.

"That's Simi Panag. Maybe works with Jeff, I don't know. But you were a life saver."

"Hmm...quite a dazzle, isn't she? She is all over Jeff," Krystal remarked as they saw Simi chatting animatedly with Jeff, her hand touching him familiarly every once in a while.

Unwittingly, both the girls were a spellbound audience of Jeff and Simi for a few passing minutes when Tia suddenly remarked, "Where is Nysa by the way?" They both skimmed across the room looking for her when Krystal whispered, "Look, she is walking towards them."

Once Nysa reached Jeff's side, she kissed him on the cheek while holding on to his arm possessively. Simi seemed startled and backed away a little while smiling icily at her.

Krystal raised an eyebrow at Tia as she slowly remarked, "Something's cooking here..."

"I know. I don't feel too good about this...."

"Or, maybe we are reading too much into this," said Krystal lightly. "Let's get some food, Kitkat. I am famished."

"Did you have the chicken roast? It's good!" Krystal was hungrily digging into the food while Tia mostly picked at hers.

"I had a quick snack of noodles after office. So not hungry, unlike you. You enjoy yourself. Must have had a busy day at the fitness centre."

"I can eat a horse," Krystal said, while munching on the food. "Had some dance demonstrations for the upcoming carnival. My muscles are aching!"

"How are my girls doing?" Nysa piped in warmly besides them, both her hands behind their backs. "Are you enjoying yourselves?"

"We are, Nysa. The food's good."

"How about you, Tia? There's nothing on your plate?"

"Not too hungry, Nysa...."

"Missing Ron?" Nysa winked at Krystal meaningfully.

"Aww...now don't start that," Tia protested, pretending to look offended.

Nysa's face abruptly changed expression and she looked distracted. When Krystal and Tia turned to look at the object of her attention, they saw Jeff and Simi making their way towards the buffet table with their plates in hand.

Krystal's eyebrows raised meaningfully at Tia but she simply shrugged. All three stood looking at Jeff and Simi chatting happily as they hoarded their plates with food.

"Hey darling, was looking for you," said Jeff once he caught them staring while making his way out of the buffet queue towards his wife. Simi swayed her hips as she followed him. Most eyes were on her as her dress shimmered over her curvy figure. She was truly a threat to womanhood, thought Tia.

"Were you?" said Nysa in a clipped voice, her smile not reaching her eyes. She looked smoothly at Simi and asked with polite interest. "Hope you are enjoying your food, Simi?"

"I was just telling Jeff that the food was awesome and he told me you had arranged the caterers. So I wanted to get more details." Her eyes were keen with interest while she sent a saccharine smile their way.

"I will be glad to let you know the details. But meanwhile I need to catch up with the bakers. Jeff, can you help me contacting this Manish guy? I can't seem to get his number," said Nysa.

"Well, of course, I have his partner's number."

Simi smiled wryly as Nysa steered Jeff away to the kitchen. Krystal and Tia looked at one other, each trying to read the other's mind. Simi didn't bother to excuse herself as one of Jeff's clients breezed in to catch her attention. Guess she was never lacking in attention, thought Tia. She looked quite preoccupied as she happily chatted away. Tia felt Simi was an egotistic, self-obsessed, ambitious woman with a lack of regard for anyone else. She couldn't help feeling an unusual sympathy for her sister.

"Penny for your thoughts, Tia!" Tia blinked to see Yuvi smiling down at her in amusement. He looked very handsome in his tuxedo which accentuated his angular features and sturdy jaw line. Why wasn't there a girlfriend in the horizon she had sometimes wondered? Or maybe he was very private about his personal life. He was really quite a catch with his boyish good looks, she mused. And although an introvert, once he knew someone personally, he could keep them hooked for hours with his amusing conversations.

"Where were you?" he asked curiously.

"Here and there." She smiled. "Did you arrive just now?"

"Yes, just a few minutes back. Met some old associates. Looks like there are quite a few people I know here."

"Good for you." She playfully punched him on his ribs. "Did you have something?"

"Just a drink," he said.

Nina arrived at that moment with Ryan in a hurried state of affairs. After hugging her and exchanging pleasantries, they made a bee way for the food saying that they had just come down from a long flight. Krystal tagged along trying to catch on all the news, winking at Tia on the way.

"What about dinner, Yuvi?"

"Yes, I'd like to have some. Wanna give me some company?"

"Yes, sure."

Her sister flurried past her and Tia quickly asked her about the status of the bakers.

"Ask your brother-in-law!" Her face was set mutinously as she hustled by. Jeff followed her more quietly behind, with his hands in his pockets looking as if he was trying to appease a sulky wife.

"Anything the matter?" Yuvi quickly asked as he followed her gaze towards her sister and Jeff.

"No, no...nothing at all." She assured him as she looked away.

After Yuvi had his dinner, he sat next to her in the garden with a glass of wine in hand while she opted for some fresh orange juice. It was quieter here. And she also felt she needed a breather for a while. It was just too crowded and noisy inside the house. They chatted for some time and then sat comfortably in the silence. The moon was peacefully gliding across the star-studded sky and the fragrance of the flowers from Nysa's garden made her intoxicatingly content.

"Some wine, Tia?"

"No, just orange juice." She smiled as she finished sipping the last of its remains. Yuvi took it from her hand and laid it on a garden table next to them. He stood and looked around the garden silently, and sighed as he sat down next to her.

"Everything here is so beautiful. Just like you. Do you know how beautiful you are, Tia?" he asked gently. There was a strange look in his eyes that seemed to have a haunting quality about them. A few seconds passed as the humdrum of distant chatter seemed a world away. He ran the back of his fingers gently on her cheek. The crowd seemed so distant as Tia was held captive by his vulnerable eyes and she didn't know what to say. This was Yuvi right, her childhood playmate?

Somehow, she had always sensed a piece of loneliness in him right from the time they were young. As children, she remembered feeling this unexplainable tender spot for him whenever she saw him standing alone in a corner at a birthday party or at club events while she was giddily lost in playing with her other sprightly friends and cousins. She always tried to include him amongst her companions and their playful activities.

Abruptly Yuvi moved his head closer to hers and his breath fanned her cheeks. Tia could feel his head swoon towards her and before he could place his lips on hers, she backed away.

"Yuvi!" She looked stricken and moved her face away. She could hear Yuvi walk a few steps away and take a deep breath as he seemed to calm down. Then he came closer and held one of her hands.

"I am sorry, Tia. Don't know why I behave so oddly whenever I am anywhere close to you. I just do things that embarrass both of us. I apologise, Tia."

"No, it's okay Yuvi," she said quietly as she looked down at her hands.

"Still friends?" His eyes looked regretful and its sincerity tugged at her heart.

"Yes, of course, Yuvi."

"No awkwardness?" He raised his eyebrows as he seemed to almost mock at himself.

"Of course not," said Tia with a slight twist of her lips in a slow smile.

He flashed a broad smile at that, almost in relief.

Tia couldn't help giving into his smile.

"I am glad," he said, his face earnest with sincerity.

"Hey, you two!" The atmosphere changed as Krystal rushed in chirpily with Nina and Ryan.

"Jeff has arranged for a music band that has just arrived. They are calling out for some Karaoke numbers...come along. It will be fun."

The evening was a round of popular karaoke numbers and then some lively dancing. Simi did manage to steal one dance with Jeff but unluckily for her, it was cut short by him due to Nysa's unusually long sulky face, strongly supported by Krystal and Tia standing close by. She pouted seductively as Jeff left her to catch up on his friends. Her smile was sarcastic as she uncaringly turned away. She was quite a bitch, thought Tia, as she looked at her sister's unhappy face. Krystal looked at her helplessly too shaking her head in annoyance.

Tia felt an unusual sinking of her heart. She hoped her sister was happy with Jeff. Did her angry words at her sister during their wedding create bad karma on her sister's life, she wondered. Sometimes negative words and thoughts create bad energy, her yoga guru, Tasha often said. The best way to undo it was to forgive and forget by sending white rays of love through the third eye. She sent a wave of light through her mind's eye at Nysa wishing her happiness and love always.

But still she couldn't shake off the sadness she felt for her sister. She was unusually quiet when Nina and Ryan drove her home later along with Krystal and Ness. Nina asked her more than once if she wasn't feeling well. But she excused herself saying she was tired and sleepy.

Chapter 17

"Did you call for me?" Tia asked her uncle who was busy putting away a few files into the cabinet.

"Come in, Tia. Check this pen drive will you? Dhruv has designed us a few samples for our new gaming project. Can you have a look and see if we can integrate the design with the code? If yes, then we can ask him to sit with the coding team and design a new game for our children's section."

"Alright, I will have a look. Where is he? I didn't see him in the office today."

"Oh, he needs to work on a few landscapes and is working outdoors. He will drop in after lunch. Ample time for you to look at the project and give me a report in the evening."

"Sure, Uncle Neal!" She smiled in agreement. "See you in the evening."

Dhruv confirmed by phone that he would be in office at around two in the afternoon, so after a quick lunch she dropped into his cabin. It was quite an artsy place with easels and sketches all around and the drawing board filled with unusual designs. Dhruv hadn't arrived yet but Tia thought she would sit for while and work on a few projects while waiting for him. She opened her laptop and started answering her emails while attending a few calls at the same time. Once she finished her calls, she continued to work on a few proposals in hand. It was a sunny afternoon and a beautiful breeze carried the fragrance of jasmine flowers nearby. She was distracted by the abrupt sound of wind chimes and when she looked around she saw a beautiful wind chime hanging near one of the window frames.

The design of the wind chime looked familiar and when she drew closer she could not for the life of her recollect where she had seen that unusual design before. She took the different pieces of the chime in her hand and ran her fingers over it as if to remember where she had seen this strange design before. And then it flashed through her mind. She rushed to her cabin and rummaged through her handbag. There was the letter and she rushed back.

She met Yuvi on the way, who raised his eyebrows in question at her hurried gait. But Tia quickly shook her head and hurried back to Dhruv's cabin. Yuvi looked quite puzzled as he glanced away and resumed his work with his designer.

The wind chime had the same design as the one in the letter. There was also a beautiful painting next to the window with a design similar to that of the letter. Tia's heart beat very hard. She looked around Dhruv's cabin slowly. There were a few decorative bronze wall hangers on the wall which looked like the sun. But once she looked closer, she could see that there was a pentacle designed inside the sun. She remembered Regan saying that the pentacle was one of the most distinctive and basic symbols of the Wiccans. Then there was a lampshade at the corner of the room which also had pentacle trinkets hanging inside the corners. Again she noticed a few candle holders on the shelf and each of them were designed intricately. She Googled a search for Wiccan symbols on the internet and saw that they were exactly similar to the carvings on the candle holders.

Her reverie was broken at the sound of the door opening and Tia turned round to see Dhruv standing in the doorway. He was a tall man with waves of curly hair. He was also ruggedly handsome if one liked the rough look.

"Hey, sorry," he said as he breezed in with his windswept hair, "the traffic was really bad today."

He laid his laptop bag on the table and started clearing away the sheets of paper on his desk. "Sorry for the mess." He apologized and smiled wryly. "The crazy artist is the only excuse I can give right now – and eccentric." He tweaked his nose as if in mocking with his own self.

Tia nodded at him silently and waited for him to settle down.

"Anything the matter, Tia?" he asked slowly. "You look pale..."

"No...nothing at all." Her smile was forced.

"Then why don't you take a seat. We don't want us to discuss the new design standing all throughout, do we?" He smiled crookedly.

"No, of course not."

She felt like a zombie as she sat in the chair.

"You need a glass of water?" he asked in concern. "You look quite dazed."

"No, just tired. It's been a long day..." she left the sentence hanging as she looked around waiting for an opportunity to question him about the Wicca symbols.

"Ok..." he said slowly.

"Dhruv, what's that painting on the wall?"

"That's Goddess Brigid," he said slowly.

"Oh..."

Dhruv looked thoughtful as if he was trying to read her mind.

"She is a Wiccan goddess for inspiration and creativity," he explained further.

"You are a...a..."

"No, no...I don't practise Wicca if that's what you're asking. I and Rianna did some design work for a client of ours – Tara Mehta. She is a Wicca practitioner, tarot reader and an astrologer. Designed her website, brochures, apps and similar stuff. She was one of our best clients. She sells a lot of Wiccan stuff through her online shop that we designed for her. I bought some of her stuff too for my home, mostly artifacts and all. You should come and see my home sometimes. Love collecting artifacts wherever I go, especially from different cultures."

Dhruv looked more humane as he spoke about his passion and his eyes lighted up while he showed her pictures of stuff that he collected for his home. His home was beautiful with interiors that were a cross between rustic and vintage design style.

Tia was even more speechless when he bent down a little to take out a few more pictures from his bottom drawer. This was because at that precise moment a chain flashed from around his neck and came out dangling to lie on his chest. And it was the same design as the one she had unearthed from Pearl Valley the other day.

When Tia gasped, Dhruv frowned and sat up alert. "What's the matter, Tia?"

"That chain," she said. Her heart beat violently in her ears.

Dhruv put a finger around his neck, "This one?"

"Yes," she said. "Can I have a look? If you don't mind?"

"Not at all," he said as he gave her the chain to have a look.

She ran her fingers over the chain. It was like the Siamese twin of the one she had.

"My sister had one like this," she said slowly.

"Oh, did she? She gifted me this one on my birthday, right around the time we were working for this client. Maybe she bought one for herself too." Dhruv smiled in remembrance and he went quiet. "Have worn it ever since. Not that she didn't tease me for it."

"Oh..." she said, as all kinds of thoughts raced in her mind. Dhruv was looking at her with half closed eyes as if trying to gauze her every reaction.

"Open the locket...go ahead," he said.

"You mean this locket...this pentacle locket?" she asked surprised.

"Yes, it can be opened. Here, this is the latch." He took the locket and pressed it on the side. The locket burst open and inside was a beautiful oval photograph of Rianna smiling.

"She never knew I carried a photograph of her inside. I guess, I never ever told her how I really felt about her...and damn I didn't! I always do regret that...."

Dhruv's regretful face swam in front of her eyes as the words of the letter flashed in her mind,

But that doesn't matter as within a few moments you will see the person who has loved you for so long - with all his heart and a madness that has no logic.

Soon we will meet.

I love you,

From,
The one who loves you most.

Tia excused herself with a headache and Dhruv looked quite concerned for a moment. But he accepted her excuse and let her go. Her legs shook as she silently returned to her cabin. Once back in her cabin her mind was racing as she sat lost in her chair.

"Anything the matter?" Yuvi popped in through the door.

"No, no, nothing...I just want to be alone for a few minutes if you don't mind, Yuvi."

If he was surprised at being cut short like this, he didn't show it as he quietly said, "Oh, alright. I will be back later."

Once Yuvi left, Tia opened the letter and read it over and over again. She wondered where Dhruv was when Rianna had that unfortunate tragedy. Did he have an alibi?

She decided to ask Regan and quickly dialled his number. Regan picked up at once and chirped in cheerfully, "Hey Tia! How're you?"

"I am good, Regan," she said quietly. "Did you find anything about the locket Regan?"

"Not much Tia except that one of Rianna's clients sells a lot of this stuff online. Maybe this was purchased from her shop?"

"Who was this client?"

"It's a lady – Tara Mehta."

Tia's heart beat loudly as she continued softly, "There's a latch in the locket Regan. Can you check what is inside there?"

"We did. There are two stones there – amethyst I think. I did ask Tara Mehta by the way if she remembers selling it. But she said she doesn't remember as she sells a lot of stuff like that online. It is a kind of an amulet and contains a spell to attract love. It is specially meant for young people who want to attract love in their life."

"Where was Dhruv Rana on that day, Regan? The day when Rianna's body was found."

"Dhruv Rana?" Regan sounded surprised and went quiet for a while. "We checked that too, Tia. It seemed he was attending an art exhibition on the other end of the city. His signature was registered on the guest book and the time mentioned was between those hours the doctors estimated to be the time of Rianna's death."

"He could have slipped later on...or the signature could be forged."

"There were two other guests who swore of his presence there. So that eliminated him from our list of suspects."

"How long did the art exhibition last?"

"All day, of course. I know what you are trying to say, Tia. But take it from me that there was no evidence of Dhruv being present at the scene of death. He had a strong alibi instead to prove him otherwise. And the chain need not be Rianna's, Tia. It might belong to any other sightseer across Pearl Valley who might have lost it while trekking."

Tia put her phone down slowly. This was all going nowhere, she thought. The chain was an exact replica of the one Dhruv was wearing. Was it Rianna's? Why did she see that dream and later find it in the exact place where she had dreamt it. What connection did that chain have with Rianna? Or did it have some connection with Dhruv, then? Was Rianna trying to tell her something here through those dreams? She couldn't resist herself from walking into Dhruv's cabin again.

"Dhruv, I just found this letter amongst Rianna's belongings. Guess I should return it to the rightful owner." She pretended to look distracted as she handed him the letter indifferently.

Dhruv skimmed the letter quickly and his lips twisted in a mocking smile.

"Anonymous love letters? I don't do this kind of sneaky stuff, Tia, if that's what you are getting at."

"Oh!" She acted nonchalant as she took the letter in hand. "Seeing the Wicca symbols in the letter I just thought..."

She left the remaining unsaid as she didn't know what else to say. He leaned back in his chair, his look sardonic.

"Well, you thought wrong..." His mouth curved into a patronizing smile and she left awkwardly.

It was late in the evening by the time Dhruv left. Almost all had left office except for her uncle and Yuvi. She was waiting in her car a little distance away from where Dhruv had parked his car. She followed Dhruv easily all through the busy Ulsoor road. He took a left from the main road to enter another broad road, lined with trees. After driving for another kilometre he turned right again. It was a smaller lane and Tia decided not to follow him down this one as that might put her at the risk of being found out. She parked her car and walked for a considerable distance when she saw a small independent house with a garden. On the nameplate was written, "House No 6, Orchards."

Prior to following him down here, she had checked Dhruv's residential address in the office records and confirmed this to be the one where he lived. His car was parked under the trees too. She waited behind a tree on the opposite side of the road, undecided.

He came out after a while, looking fresh and bathed. Tia hid in the shadows till he left. There was somebody inside. She rang the door bell. It was a middle-aged man and he looked like a cook or a hired help.

"Excuse me, I have come to meet Dhruv. Is he around?"

"He has gone outside, Madam. Would you like to wait for a while?"

"I'll do that. Thank you. Do you live here?"

"No, Madam. I come in the evenings and cook Rana Sir's dinner. I will leave within an hour."

"When will he be back?"

"He said he will be back in a short while."

"Alright. I'll wait, thank you...I didn't get your name."

"Manohar Joshi."

"Thank you, Manohar. I am sure you have been working here for some time with Rana Sir."

"Yes, Madam, from last year. Sahib's a good boss. Let's me do my work in peace. Not too demanding."

"No display of temper?"

"Don't we all have our faults, Madam? It is just a matter of adjustment, isn't it?"

"How very wise, Manohar. What a great philosophy to live by...nice." She looked impressed.

"Thank you, Madam. Would you like a glass of water?"

"No, that's okay."

As the cook turned to go, she called out for him again.

"Can I use the bathroom if you don't mind?"

"Of course not, Madam, you are Sir's guest. Please help yourself."

Tia went into the bathroom next to the dining room and after a few minutes, she called out, "This isn't that clean. Is there another bathroom here?"

The cook looked embarrassed. "You can use the one in the bedroom, Madam, if that's okay with you."

Once Manohar left, she quickly locked the bedroom door and ransacked the drawers and cupboards inside. She took care to keep everything neatly back in place as before. She searched around the room for any clue or something out of ordinary that might hint at anything fishy concerning Dhruv. Her mind was totally restless after she found those Wicca symbols in his cabin as well as the chain with the pentacle locket around his neck. She checked the files at his desk. There was an old file which was named as "Animagic Software". That was her sister's firm, she recalled. Her Uncle had told in detail about it when she had asked him after Nina's wedding party. But the file contained only specs and proposals of different projects they might have done. There were a few photographs of him and Rianna in their office and different locations. She heard the doorbell ringing and then voices. She quickly laid back everything neatly and came out of the bedroom.

Dhruv was no less than flabbergasted to find Tia in his house. Before he could say anything she hurriedly rattled, "Actually, Dhruv, I found myself lost while trying to find my friend's house in this area. And out of nowhere I saw your car whiz by. I followed you here. But by the time I reached, you had already left."

"Is it? Where's your car?"

"I had parked it a few yards ahead and decided to look around for her house by foot. You know how tedious it is to look for a house while driving. Then when I saw you pass by me, I decided to walk here instead."

"But how come I didn't meet you if you followed me. I was here for some time."

"No, I decided I will try a little more on my own before troubling you...hope you didn't mind my using your washroom?"

Dhruv looked at her carefully with half-closed eyes.

"Then let me take you to your friend's place. What's the address?"

"She just rang up to tell me that she'll be late due to an unplanned client visit. So she suggested me to wait a little longer at your place, if possible. But I guess I'm already running late for dinner at Nysa's. I think I'd better skip meeting her today."

She didn't give a chance for Dhruv to answer as she hurried down the stairs. Dhruv had a suspicious look on his face as she waved at him for the last time. Darkness had almost set in and there were a few evening walkers on the road.

She walked fast and was almost shoulder to shoulder with an elderly lady.

"Hello, Aunty. Enjoying your walk?"

"Yes, dear. What about you?"

"Me too."

"Working?"

"Yes, Aunty. I am a software consultant."

"That's nice. You do look like a bright young girl. New to this area?"

"Yes, Aunty. Don't know many folks around here."

"Oh, is it? I live close by – that's my house. You can drop in sometimes," she pointed two houses away from Dhruv.

"So you live close to Mr. Dhruv Rana, is it? I have met him a couple of times."

"Did you? Quite a reserved man he is. Keeps mostly to himself."

"You know him. How is he otherwise?"

"Don't know much, *beta**. Young people these days want to be left alone. They need what they say...'space'."

Tia smiled at that. "You are right, Aunty."

She said bye and drove off.

Tia returned to the same area early next morning and found a few walkers as well as joggers pass by. On some or the other pretext, she asked them about Dhruv. But she didn't get to learn anything out of the ordinary, except for a young jogger whose eyes lit up as she said, "Dishy isn't he – if you kind of like the brooding types? I did chat him up during the time of Diwali festivities in our lane. But..." She sighed with exaggerated emotions.

Beta – Son or daughter. The young in India are addressed in this way by elderly or older people.(Hindi word)

Chapter 18

"I don't believe this, Tia! Are you crazy!?" Krystal asked in a shocked voice. "You might have been caught. And what if Dhruv charges you for theft or maybe illegal trespassing or something?"

"I asked Manohar's permission and I was only using the rest room." Tia smiled cheekily.

"But that's too much risk – and what's with this playing detective? You won't let the matter rest, will you?"

Tia bit her lip as she shrugged her shoulders and looked away.

"Why Tia? Why, when everything is going so well? That chain and locket in your dream might belong to any tourist visiting that area, damn it! Don't push things and try to fabricate problems where they don't exist. Why don't you leave everything as a bad dream, Tia, and move on?!"

"I don't know!" said Tia helplessly. "If only I could quieten my nagging doubts about Ron then everything would be okay...but I can't! I simply can't!"

Krystal raised her eyebrows at that. "Going after Dhruv will get you your answer, you think?"

Tia flushed at that. She felt guilty. She sat down heavily as she said, "I know Krystal. Just to save Ron and my relationship, maybe I am trying to project my suspicions on Dhruv. How very selfish of me!"

Krystal sighed as she looked at her friend looking dejected and totally at a loss. Meanwhile, Tia opened up Dhruv's file that she had picked up from office.

"Don't be so hard on yourself, Tia. It was wrong of me to charge you like this. Maybe I would have done the same too if I was in your place. But I really care about you and want the best for you. Why is it that at a happy time like this these kinds of things happen? What a mess!"

Krystal shook her head, defeated.

Tia buried her chin in her hands. "Why does happiness come with a price?"

"I am sure things will be okay, Tia. Let's quit worrying and have some coffee. Worrying will not get us anywhere, will it?"

Krystal went to the kitchen to pour some coffee. Meanwhile, Tia opened up Dhruv's file that she had picked up from office.

"Why don't you ask Nina if you want to know more about Dhruv? I am sure she will have more accurate information than anyone else," said Krystal as she laid down their coffee.

"I am not sure about that, Krystal. It might go either way. She might be offended that I am suspicious about her cousin. Then again she might never have been so close to him at all to provide any useful insights about him. You know how it is with cousins and relatives...and I don't want to risk losing Nina's friendship at any cost."

"You are right, Tia. Better not risk it." She sipped through her coffee. "Any indicators in the file?"

"Nothing...nothing at all." Tia sighed as she closed the file.

"By the way, Regan asked me to hand over Rianna's chain that you had lent him for the investigation." Krystal handed her a brown packet.

Tia took the chain out and ran her fingers slowly over the locket, lost in thought.

The doorbell rang at that precise moment.

"Who could that be? It's almost eight," said Tia as she opened the door.

Her happiness knew no bounds when she found Ron smiling at her doorstep. "Ron! I can't believe it! You were supposed to come next week!" she cried excitedly.

"Yes, I wrapped up my work as early as I could. I missed you so much," he said between muffled kisses.

"Ahem..." Krystal interrupted them as she collected her shoulder bag and coat in her hand. "You two love birds have a lot of catching up to do. Why don't I leave you two alone...?"

"But Krystal what about the chicken biryani you prepared?"

"Some other time. I have to catch up on some stuff. See you later."

Tia's heart beat loudly as Ron quickly pulled her into his arms. She missed him so much. It was as if she was half dead and felt abruptly awakened again. She slid her hands over his smooth skin and over those familiar lines and angles that she had achingly missed the past few weeks. She took in every detail of his face as he told her about the business trip and things he had done amidst their passionate kisses and hot embraces. Their mouths crushed against one another as they hungrily tasted each other, their hearts hammering and struggling at the same time to get some air into their lungs. After a while they managed to slow down a bit as Ron maneuvered their kisses to softer, more languorous ones.

Before his kisses turned into a full blown seduction, she pulled away hastily and scurried into the kitchen to get their dinner ready. Fortunately she and Krystal had planned an elaborate dinner today and there were lots of stuff to eat. But Ron didn't allow her a second's respite what with a peck here and a peck there till she finally had to push him off. "Stop Ron...we need to eat..."

Her heart sank though when he directly asked her, "You have been seeing a lot of Yuvi I heard..."

"Heard?"

"Well, not exactly. Ryan and Ness mentioned that he accompanied you a couple of times..."

"It's mostly work we take home from office, Ron. There has been a lot of pressure in the office and you know we have been friends for a long time..."

"I know, sweetheart. Just that bit of jealousy creeping in. I trust my girl," he said with another tight squeeze from behind. Her heart gave a lurch when his kisses turned into hungrier nips of his teeth while his palms splayed possessively under her shirt.

"Now don't start that, will you..." She laughed and pushed him away. "When you are not around, Ron, I keep myself busy with office work. Otherwise I just miss you too much. And Yuvi did take me out a couple of times besides our business dinners and luncheons...just filling in my time to fill your void, that's all."

"I know, hon. Just a bit of nagging worry, that's all." His eyes turned a shade darker. "That's because I love you so much and I don't want to lose you to anything or anyone."

His voice almost had a hint of possession as he looked at her with an intensity that quickened her heartbeats. "It's better you keep a bit of distance in your friendship with him, Tia. You never know..."

"I will, darling," she said in an earnest voice. Ron blew her a silent kiss as he got back to helping her lay the dishes.

The next morning was a treat as Ron prepared an appetizing breakfast and dropped her at the office.

The door to her office burst open and she realized it was Dhruv.

"Been snooping around and asking about me, Tia?" he asked point blank, his pose quite threatening.

"Good morning, Dhruv," said Tia pleasantly as she leaned back in her chair. She looked calmer than the quiver she felt inside. She didn't know how she'd answer Dhruv, so she acted nonchalant and cool.

"Drop away the niceties, Tia. That never worked with me. Cut to the chase, will you?" His lips curled in a sneer.

"What do you mean, Dhruv?" she asked, her face a mask of innocence.

"I have friends who tell me things...you have been seen in our lane lately, asking about me. My neighbor got suspicious."

"I was just doing small talk, that's all, while visiting my friend in that area. It's a beautiful tree-lined lane and so I enjoyed walking round a bit." She smiled charmingly. "You hardly come across such nice roads in Bengaluru these days."

Dhruv drew in a sharp breath as he stared at her.

"What's the matter, Dhruv? You look like you have seen a ghost," said Tia.

Dhruv looked around the room and then at her intensely. "You look so much like her. It amazes me at times."

Tia realized that he was talking about Rianna but she didn't know how to react at the vulnerability in his voice.

She shrugged her shoulders casually as she said in a lighter tone, "Siblings do look alike, don't they?"

He sighed at that and said slowly, "Alright, carry on with your investigation, detective. It's a free country after all."

She schooled her face not to show any emotion and said with a smile, "I don't know what you're talking about..."

"A bit of advice, Tia. A detective must check for motives first, isn't it?" he said with a slight slant of his head. His lips curled in an ironic smile. "Why don't you take a closer look at your brother-in-law for a change? I did see a lot of money flowing his way after Rianna's death – the houses, the cars...a point to ponder, isn't it?"

He closed the door softly while leaving Tia shaking like a leaf. She paced the room restlessly.

She felt better by evening when she went out with Ron for a drive and then dinner. At least she could forget her worries for some time. That night after he left she fell on her bed exhausted. As her eyes grew heavy she felt herself being pulled out of bed and standing next to a friend who was helping her dress in a gorgeous backless Anarkali salwar suit. It was made of chiffon and filled with beautiful embroidery. She really felt very beautiful in it. She entered a banquet hall and everyone was busy talking, laughing and drinking – everyone looked so happy. She saw Ron too. He was busy talking to someone. When he saw her, he broke into a smile.

"Hey, I wanted you to meet someone," he said.

It was a lady who turned to face her but she knew her already.

"Mrs Mehta, you know Ron?" she asked in surprise. Mrs Tara Mehta was one of her valuable clients.

"Yes, dear," she said with a smile. "I have been taking his counseling lately on my business. Hope young people like you can put my business right." She winked in a conspiratorial manner and they all smiled.

Tia woke up with a heavy headache. She called in her Uncle to let him know that she would be taking a break from office that day. Maybe she would drive out of the city and spend some time outdoors. She switched off her mobile and then took out her easel and paint. The whole day she kept at her painting as she took in the colours of the changing sky. Changing patterns of the sky just like life – sometimes happy, sometimes monotonous, sometimes dull, sometimes depressing and sometimes murky.

It was dark by the time she reached home. As she was unlocking the door she heard the screech of tires on the gravel of her gateway. It was Ron and he was looking quite frantic and hassled at the same time.

He was about to say something when his mobile rang. "Yes, she is here with me, Krystal. Yes...can you call up Nysa and let her know? She might be worried too."

"Where were you, Tia? And why was your phone switched off..." he asked with disbelief that almost bothered on furiousness.

"It was switched off? Oh...I think I had switched it off by mistake...I don't know…" she replied in a dull voice as she got inside the house.

She tiredly threw the bag on the couch as she heard Ron close the door behind her.

"Where were you, Tia?" he asked softly.

"I went out for a long drive in the outskirts." Her shrug was indifferent as she headed to the kitchen.

He roughly wheeled her around and she saw Ron's face controlled with patience.

"Look at me Tia when I talk to you!"

"What is it, Ron?" she asked in a calm voice.

"How can you just do what you like without letting anyone know about your whereabouts? I was sick with worry…"

"But why should you? I have been on my own, haven't I? Nothing happened to me in my entire twenty-five years before you came. What would happen to me now?"

"Anything! You were out alone…no message, no phone, no nothing…what was I supposed to think…"

"Ron, we are not even married. Quit worrying about me will you?" she quipped back. "Why do I have to inform you about every little second in my life – my every breath…where I go, what I do?"

"What's so wrong about that? Is it so unnatural to worry about the woman I love – the woman who I am going to marry very soon?" he cried out and then closed his eyes for a second. "You have been so distracted ever since I've got back. What is the matter, can you tell me, please? Yes, I am worried…I am worried sick about you!"

She folded her hands defensively, her voice unnaturally calm. "Maybe you shouldn't be."

"Don't pull that act on me, Tia. You have been blowing hot this second and cold another...and I don't have a clue as to what is going on. I can't take this for long...don't play with me like this, will you?"

"I am not..."

"Then tell me what's going on in your mind? Or, is it this Yuvi guy? You have been seeing a lot of him, haven't you? While I was gone...."

Tia's eyes flew in shock and she turned away in disbelief. There were a few moments of strained silence.

Ron walked slowly up to her from behind and started rubbing her arms. "I am sorry, Tia. I have been out of my mind, worried sick about you."

He pulled her quietly to the sofa and they sat silently for some time. He held her and then brushed light kisses over her hair. The tension passed and she felt better. She hugged him back tightly like a woman trying to stop herself from drowning in the quagmire of her own mind.

"Is something bugging you, Tia? Tell me honey, what is it?"

"Ron do you know this lady, Tara Mehta?" She held her breath tightly as she waited for his answer.

"Tara Mehta...let me see..."

He looked into her eyes and scrubbed his chin in thought. "What does she do? Can you give me some more info..."

"She is a Wicca practitioner as well as a tarot reader and astrologer...people go to her for consultations...she has an online shop too where she sells a lot of Wiccan stuff..."

"Why yes...I do know her. She came to me for some financial advice regarding her business...years back of course."

"Oh..." Tia tried to stop her hand from trembling.

"Why Tia...what's this got to..."

"When did you last see her, Ron?"

"Umm...let me see...maybe on the last day when I met your sister...at the event. Yes, I remember clearly now. Mrs Mehta wasn't well and we rushed to get her some water and make her rest on the couch. Your sister was there too...we were all concerned...what's the matter, Tia?"

Tia had turned pale. She clutched her face in her hands as Ron shook her slightly asking what was the matter. She was feeling dizzy as a myriad of thoughts exploded in her ears. Ron rushed to hand her some water.

"Tia, tell me what's the matter. Be honest. There is something that has always come between you and me. What is it?"

Tia looked hesitant and her voice shook as she said, "I..."

"What Tia...say it, Tia, say it!"

He rubbed her arms, encouraging her.

"I keep dreaming about my sister..."

"Ok...that's natural...you miss her and..."

"No, it's not Ron! Because for some reason she keeps showing me that you are involved in her death or maybe...maybe her..."

"Maybe her?"

"Murder!" Tia's voice was a hoarse whisper as she couldn't meet Ron's eyes.

There was a shattering silence as Ron took all of that in.

"What does she show you, Tia?"

He listened expressionlessly as one by one Tia told him all of her dreams. His eyes grew bleaker and his lips thinned into a straight line as he looked with deep concentration at his interlaced fingers. His skin was stretched tightly across his sharp cheekbones.

"You see some random dreams, give them any interpretation you like and make me out to be a murderer?" Ron lashed out as he paced restlessly about the room. "Did I ever hurt you or anyone for that matter to make you believe something so heinous about me!? Did I ever give you any sign of a violent streak in me or any evil vibe for you to even suspect me of murder? Do I look like a person who could ever harm somebody right till the point of murdering someone!?!"

Tia couldn't see Ron's face as her eyes were flooded with hot tears while her throat felt heavy and choked.

"No, Tia...you saw what you wanted to see. You never trusted me and that is what transpired in your dreams. This lack of trust is what has driven us apart. I have tried what I could to make you love me and trust me, but it looks like it is no longer in my hands as you refuse to allow me to help you. Unless you change your mind about your dreams, your past and learn to trust me, there is nothing we can do to save this relationship." He pushed his hands inside the pocket of his jeans as he stressed out his words slowly and meaningfully. "So we better decide now if we want to continue or break up before we hurt ourselves any further. And I leave this decision all up to you. Do you want me to stay or walk away is what I want to know from you right now, Tia?"

The silence could have dragged to eternity as it seemed to pierce sharp knives across every inch of her heart and tear every cell apart. After a while she heard the chink of the ring as Ron lay it on the table. It was the engagement ring that she had placed on his finger a few months back.

"Your silence has given me my answer, Tia. From this moment onwards you are free of me and our relationship," he said quietly when the silence dragged on painfully between them.

Tia didn't know how long she lay on the floor after Ron left. She felt gentle hands on her shoulders and someone help her to her feet. She let herself be led blindly to her bed. It was Krystal who took off her shoes and laid her softly on her bed.

"Ron asked me to check on you, Tia. He told me about your breakup. But he was concerned about you and asked me to take care of you."

The floodgates opened as she hugged Krystal and howled out loud sobs of heartbreak. She cried herself to sleep and didn't remember when Krystal had covered her with a blanket and switched off the lights.

Chapter 19

"Good morning, hon!" Jeff came down to find his pretty wife getting the dishes ready for the breakfast table although she seemed quite preoccupied. He gave her a light peck as he helped her prepare omelets and toast for breakfast.

"Where's Lola?" he asked looking around while taking a seat at the table.

"Mom's taken her for a walk in the park. She was very hyper this morning and almost coerced her granny to take her outdoors," said Nysa with a wry smile.

"She twists Mom around her little finger, doesn't she?" Jeff grinned as he buttered his toast generously.

"Uh huh..." Nysa's eyes were on the morning paper as she hurriedly pushed in her eggs.

"You look like a busy bee early morning. Any special plans?" asked Jeff curiously. "I thought we'd go out for a long drive to Nandi Hills and then check out the Grover Zampa Vineyards. It would be great for Lola too. She'd enjoying seeing the grave vines."

"We can't do that," said Nysa apologetically. Jeff was always thoughtful about giving them ample time in spite of his demanding work at their company and she didn't want to disappoint him. "Mom wants to take Lola out at her best friend's place as her granddaughter is celebrating her birthday today. She is almost the same age as Lola. I too have a meeting two hours from now with the executive members of the Bengaluru Youth Club as we are planning a charity event next month."

"So both of you don't have any time for me on a beautiful Sunday, is it?" he asked, pretending to look hurt. He raised one of his thick brows in question while lazily munching on a piece of toast.

"Yes, that's exactly it," she replied with a teasing glint in her eyes. "Right on every count!"

"You're going to regret this you know."

"Oh, really!" Nysa couldn't help smiling as Jeff kept a serious face and looked like he was too wounded to react. She lightly touched his cheek and pouted playfully.

"Hmm. And then?"

"And then maybe drop at Tia's later after attending the meeting. Just to check on her a bit," she said.

Jeff sighed at that.

"Tia...," he said slowly.

Nysa's brows tweaked defensively as she looked at Jeff. The banter of easy laughter changed to a moment fraught with tension and unease.

She wanted to say something but she changed her mind and got back to the papers.

Jeff cleared his throat at the ensuing silence and said slowly, "Heard from Dev that she and Ron broke off their engagement."

"You heard right." Nysa's voice was cool though she didn't look up from the papers.

"Dev didn't sound too happy about it."

"None of us are...," said Nysa, while looking pointedly at Jeff.

"I was just asking...why the accusatory look, Nysa?" Jeff's look was that of disbelief as he laid his toast on his plate.

"I can feel the hint of sarcasm in your voice, Jeff," said Nysa in a matter-of-fact tone.

"Oh well, Tia's always been so...so..."

"So what, Jeff?"

"I mean she is too sensitive...I always feel like I am walking on egg shells around her. I am sure it wasn't easy for Ron..."

"Jeff, who is Ron to you anyway? You just met him for what...ten – eleven times in your entire life. Whose side are you on...? Tia is your sister-in-law, for heaven's sake!"

"I am not taking sides, Nysa. I was just viewing things objectively which you can't as she is your sister. Sometimes objectivity kinda helps..." Jeff shrugged his shoulders as he looked at her meaningfully.

"We don't need that help, I assure you," said Nysa, her tone mutinous.

"Ok! Quit barking at me! Even Dev thinks Tia is too emotional for her own good. She is living in the past..."

"Dev sees everything in black and white, Jeff. Being the eldest in the family it was easier for him facing the situations than any of us. He didn't have to face the hard knocks that we had to face – especially Tia who was at a very young and vulnerable age. Mom and Dad got him established and gave him a secure future before any of this happened. He was already mature and on his feet when tragedy struck us! Even I was at a better position than Tia was. Busy with my work, my social life to do any grieving. So I don't want to hear what Dev feels about all this right now..."

"Quit pulling the trigger at me, lady...," said Jeff as he lightly held her hand. "I didn't want to upset you...."

Nysa went silent for a while as she tried to calm down.

"It's not that, Jeff. I just feel Tia is judged too much. Especially by Dev and a few others. It hasn't been easy for her you know..." Nysa sighed. "She has always been our little sister, the baby of our family. She always has been so giving and unselfish, and always so happy and cheerful before Mom died – in fact the happiest and most light-hearted amongst the four of us. She wasn't always like this, you know...."

Nysa looked unhappily out of the window.

"When we were young, she always looked up to Rianna as I was too busy with my tomboyish ways...my friends, my drama club and so on. Then later came my college life, my job...we were always on different sides of life. She, a tender young teen while I was carried away by my approaching twenties. She always confided in Rianna most of the time. When we were young, we used to tease her that she was Rianna's little *chamchi**. Somehow I haven't been able to replace Rianna in her life. And she has a lot of Rianna in her. Very loving, emotional while I and Dev have always been the practical ones. But I get all of this – only now. She is lost at times...my little Podgy. I don't how will she manage. This world is so harsh sometimes...only tough ones can survive here...when will she learn that..."

"It's alright...don't worry so much..." He gave her a light peck on her hair and went back to butter his toast.

The silence was broken with a shriek of a little toddler who excitedly ran towards them. "Daddy!"

Mrs Bailey followed her in a flurry as she tiredly sat down. "Quite a bundle of energy, that one," she said with a smile filled with adoration for her grandchild.

They were all an excited audience as Lola described her time in the park and what all she saw in her broken baby voice.

"Come, come we will get little Lola ready for her day at her friend's," crooned Nysa as she got Lola in her arms.

Mrs Bailey too helped herself to a toast while Jeff poured her some coffee.

"You and Nysa looked somewhat peaked when we came in...any problem?" asked Mrs Bailey in concern.

"Nothing, Mom...," said Jeff with a frown. "It's just that Nysa worries a little bit too much about Tia at times..."

"Hmm..." said Mrs Bailey as she poured herself a cup of coffee.

"I don't want her to take undue stress what with our business, little Lola, our family....And now with Tia's problems it's become just a little too heavy for her to handle."

Mrs Bailey thought and said after awhile, "Well, they are siblings...and it's natural that she'd worry, isn't it?"

"Yes, Mom," said Jeff impatiently. "But after a while, it becomes a hindrance to one's life and affects other people..."

"Yes, but in a family each member comprises different personalities, mental make-up, emotional facets and so on. And, at the end of it all, we do have to care for one another, don't we?" said Mrs Bailey lightly with a shrug.

Jeff gave a wary look as if it was all too much to comprehend.

"And I regret that you never had any sibling to fall back on or share your life stories with..." said Mrs Bailey with a sigh. "At least today Nysa has Tia and Dev to fall back upon even if Rianna or their parents are no more. I mean not financially although that is important too but also emotionally. With siblings there is always a bonding in all the special times – the get-togethers, the festivals; even the children have their cousins to bond with..."

"I am really happy with the way you brought me up, Mom – independent and self-reliant. And I am glad I don't have crazy siblings to bear on my shoulders or pull me down," said Jeff, his voice filled with sarcasm.

Mrs Bailey pulled in her breath sharply. Sometimes she felt Jeff was too rational, too pragmatic at times for her to handle. Where did he get that from? Even Dan, her husband wasn't so matter-of-fact or hardboiled as her son, although equally successful and business minded.

"Why are you surprised, Mom? I am glad Nysa isn't so heavy and histrionic like her sisters...and I married the right one."

Mrs Bailey shifted uncomfortably. "I don't know about that, Jeff. It's not easy for Tia what with having so many losses at such a young age. First her father, then her mom and then Rianna so tragically...I was so fond of Rianna. What a lady she was! She was so young to..." Mrs Bailey shook her head as she left her words unsaid. "Anyway may her soul rest in peace wherever she..."

"Well, everyone misses Rianna...who doesn't? Well, I was the bad guy, wasn't I, for betraying her. Everyone made sure I never forgot it, didn't they?" said Jeff in a cold voice that startled Mrs Bailey.

"I didn't mean that, Jeff...she just came in my thoughts..."

"I know, Mom," said Jeff, his lips curved in a tight line. "But I don't want to talk about Rianna or the past anymore. I am glad that part of my life is over!"

Mrs Bailey felt too stunned to react. It was as if this was not the Jeff she knew. He was too cold for her liking and she was not comfortable with this side of him.

He looked into the distance. "And it's time I made Nysa realize that too. Tia is becoming too much of a weight in our lives." His voice was as cold as the Siberian winds, thought Mrs Bailey.

He suddenly seemed to switch off from his reverie and quickly gave a light peck on her cheek as he said, "Enjoy your breakfast, Mom."

Jeff smiled and walked off.

Mrs Bailey sat for a while slowly sipping her tea and looking at the garden. It was nice and relaxing in the house when she was alone. Marigolds, peonies, gerberas and roses were in full bloom amidst the beautiful clump of Gulmohur trees.

The garden was her respite. Nysa and Jeff had built it well. They had invested time and money to make it a haven of peace and beauty. She could spend all day here alone with her thoughts simply talking to the flowers or looking at them.

She thought of her son now – her darling Jeff. She had left her very lucrative career in finance to devote all her time with him while Dan was busy managing their business. Her sacrifice and her hard work had paid off as Jeff had always excelled in academics, sports and whatever he set his mind to. He was the best student in his school and a national tennis player. He had passed with shining medals in IIT and then an MBA from Harvard. They were all so proud of him. His dad always saw that he got the best of the best opportunities. He had to have an 'A plus' in every subject, he had to win the gold medal – nothing less would do. It was as if all his life, Jeff never knew what defeat was like. He was always used to being revered and envied by his peers. All his life he had one victory after another.

But sometimes that could be a setback too, mused Mrs Bailey. Because it was actually the losses, the pain in one's life that made each of us a whole person. Did both Dan and she push Jeff too far? Make him too driven and too ambitious for his own good? She shuddered. Hope they didn't make a mistake here. They always kept Jeff too busy with sports, academics and various other extracurricular activities. There was almost never any time for him to rest or relax. Or learn that life is not only about winning or being the best. Sometimes simple things such as smelling the roses and taking the time for your loved ones were equally important.

At one point in her life, she too had been carried away with the success of Dan's business, what with their exotic travels and high socialite parties. But only after the pain of losing him, when she had turned to spirituality and her guru, did she find a great solace in her heart. She got a sense of spiritual empowerment that she had never found earlier in her entire life. She knew her life hadn't been as whole until she had embraced this new found spirituality.

She hoped that Jeff too one day learnt this vital lesson in his life. She prayed that Jeff soon realized that life was not about winning and amassing a large amount of wealth, but also relishing the simple pleasures as well as sharing them with our loved ones, once in a while.

Although she missed Rianna, God bless her soul, she knew that she was mismatched for her son. Rianna was too gentle, too soft and emotional for her son to handle although she was a successful woman in her own right. It was Nysa who was perfect for Jeff and could always steer him in the right path if the need arose. Nysa with her right bent of practicality and loving nature was well balanced to handle her son. Jeff couldn't get away with any hanky panky where Nysa was concerned. She thought lovingly of her daughter-in-law. Nysa complemented Jeff's hardness and could well knock him off at times with her soft blows. She was truly an exceptional woman, Mrs Bailey thought in relief. If she had made any mistakes with Jeff, Nysa would keep it all in check. She was the real deal – the iron fist in a velvet glove, thought Mrs Bailey, as she happily sipped her coffee and walked towards the garden.

chamchi – Hindi word for fan or an ardent follower.

Chapter 20

"Stop that, Jeff!" Nysa squealed. "You know I am getting late and Lola would be here any minute."

"Yes, that would be perfect as our daughter would know how much her dad is in love with her mom," he said as he nipped her ears and bit her neck while his hands moved enticingly around her slender curves.

"Bye Mama, Daddy..." said Lola as she burst excitedly into the room and was out quickly as soon as she kissed them.

"Lola wait..." But Lola was already gone as she rushed out to the living room and clutched her granny's hand. Both granddaughter and grandmom walked out happily oblivious to anyone except for the exciting day ahead of them. Nysa closed her bedroom door with a sigh. Before she could turn around, Jeff had her in her arms again and didn't give her any time to protest.

Nysa felt herself go weak in her knees as Jeff impatiently pulled her in his arms to resume what had been stalled by an abrupt interruption. Her heartbeats raced at the quick flare of passion his touch always evoked in her. Even after almost five years of marriage, Jeff could do this to her. She had so much stuff to do today. But when didn't she ever have anyway. She felt at times both she and Jeff needed to slow down and spend some quality time with each other. Not that they didn't do it whenever they could.

It was always Jeff who planned out weekend getaways or romantic dinners or simply a day alone completely in an exotic resort. Her mother-in-law also saw to it that they had enough time with themselves taking care of little Lola whenever she could. And luckily the chemistry between them was very strong unlike many of her friends who often complained at the waning passion in their marriage.

"Love you so much..." he murmured in a thick voice as he turned her around and possessed her mouth in a storm of passion while quickly locking the door.

Jeff took his time to caress every inch of her delicate skin until every nerve-end tingled with life. His lips trailed a torturous path across each vulnerable hollow making all her fine body hair tingle in delight. A slow ache started in the region of her stomach and she closed her eyes as her body vibrated with sensations beyond her control.

"Oh Jeff...," said Nysa, her body trembled as he possessed and tantalized every vulnerable curve.

In a dreamlike trance she let her arms slowly encircle his neck. She flailed restlessly when his mouth hungrily devoured the inside contour of her arms, the enticing sweep of her navel, the generous swell of her hips and the slender length of her thighs. The tension in her belly coiled tighter and tighter as whimpers of pleasure left her lips.

She was floating and utterly mindless as he continued to drive her insane with his mouth and hands while laying her not too delicately on their bed. Her responses lacked all inhibition as she clung to him wildly and let herself be consumed by blazing explosion of sensation that ran like quicksilver through her veins. She raked her nails into the smooth muscles of his back, her flesh burning, eager for more as he hoarsely cried out her name. Every inch of her quivered as her body arched into his lean hard frame and she felt sucked into a vortex overloaded with mindless ecstasy. She moved restlessly beneath his touch, impatient and longing, like a wild creature craving fulfillment. Everything else blotted out as she shivered with exquisite – endless torment. The world spun dizzily around her as wave after wave of pleasure spiraled her towards the pinnacle where everything ceased to exist except for her darling husband – her one and only Jeff!

Jeff was lazily looking at her while she got ready for the meeting at the club nearby. She had more than enough time left and she got ready at her own sweet pace. She was undecided about which dress to wear – whether to go for a traditional one or opt for western formals.

She looked at her husband who knew what was coming and answered before she could even ask, "The blue one!"

"You sure?"

"Hundred per cent!"

"You look like the cat's got the cream," she said with her eyebrows raised.

"Or maybe I am just relishing the pleasure of looking at my wife when she dresses up?"

"Or maybe someone's happy to have the wife out of the way for a pleasurable Sunday?" she said with a thoughtful expression.

Jeff threw his head back and laughed. She rolled her eyes at that and then asked, "What are your plans for the day?"

He got up and lifted her hair to kiss the side of her neck. "Now that my wife is too busy for me, I'd have to find a way to pass my time, isn't it?"

"Oh Jeff, stop the drama!" She laughed at his wounded look. "Stop overacting, will you?"

"Hmm. Okay, maybe I will go for a game of golf with Nikhil."

He looked to be in a good mood, thought Nysa, as she looked at him out of the corner of her eye. So she mentioned casually while closing her makeup kit and turning to face him. "You know what, Jeff? Tia's birthday is coming soon and since she is going through a bad time, I have decided to use our Orient account to buy her a cruise ticket. A cruise ticket to the Bahamas. In fact two, so that Krystal can accompany her – if she is willing of course."

Jeff eyes flew with surprise. He took a deep breath and said cautiously, "That's quite an expensive one, isn't it? Are you sure?"

Nysa shrugged her shoulders as she said, "It is expensive but it will do her a load of good, Jeff. A change for her. She hardly gets out any more."

"But there are so many other avenues to gift your sister, darling. Not to mention emergencies or important events like sicknesses, weddings, baby showers etc when we can pitch in to help, isn't it? What is the need to splurge like this? Anyway we are planning to save as much as we can for the new business, remember? You can do this later, can't you?"

Nysa was silent as she looked at Jeff carefully while folding her arms. "Jeff, I don't like it when you try to stop me in matters like this, you know. Tia is my sister and I want to see her happy. And it's not that we can't afford it."

"Yes, I understand. But at a time like this..."

"Jeff," said Nysa as she raised her hand. "Have I ever stopped you at anything where Mummy is concerned? Or compromised whatsoever regarding her expenses?"

Jeff shifted uncomfortably. "No...but..."

"Don't say anything then! I have never made any shortcuts regarding Mummy," said Nysa of her mother-in-law, Mrs Nandini Bailey. "Done the best I can, given the best I could. So please don't try to stop me where my family is concerned. It is my family. I will do what I can or spend whatever I can to take care of them!"

Nysa's heart heaved in short breaths as she turned her back on Jeff but he quietly took her in his arms and kissed the top of her head. "Do what you think best, hon. Your happiness is all that matters to me – always!"

Nysa turned around as she kissed him in relief. Then she gasped as she saw the wall clock and wailed, "Look at the time, I'll never make it to the meeting!" She quickly flew him a kiss as she got her purse and said, "I'll have lunch with Tia. So see you in the evening."

Jeff looked at the closed door as he breathed in slowly. "Tia," he said softly. His eyes took on a hard glint as he looked through the window at the garden and saw his wife quickly get into her blue Chevrolet.

Once the meeting was over, Nysa couldn't wait to meet her sister. What had gotten into Tia, she thought, to break off her engagement with Ron like that. Although she had acted indifferent in front of Jeff a few hours back, yet she herself was reeling with shock. But she wanted to defend Tia from Jeff's judgmental opinions of her. Lately a lot of people weren't happy with Tia and her husband appeared to be one of them.

But that didn't mean she was happy with Tia's decision either. Ron was such a stable guy. She felt real relief that after a long time there was somebody as steady and nice as Ron to take care of her sister. What had come over Tia, she pondered restlessly. If only she could get into her sister's head and dissect whatever was going through that overactive mind. For god's sake, which girl in her right mind would let go of a man as gorgeous and successful as Ron! Heads turned whenever he would walk across a room. And the kind of success he was having for a person as young as him was truly laudable.

Her mind was still full of thoughts about Tia when Krystal opened the door.

"Hey Nysa, nice to see you!"

"Hey Krystal!" Nysa smiled as she handed her the pizza box with a huge bottle of coke.

"Smells nice," said Krystal appreciatively.

"Where's Tia?"

"We were just catching up with an old box office hit on television," she said as she followed Nysa to the living room.

"Hello, Podgy!" said Nysa as she ruffled her sister's hair. "How are you feeling?"

Tia rolled her eyes and looked almost embarrassed. "Someone would think I am dying of cancer."

"Don't say such things, Tia," said Nysa in disapproval, "even in jest."

"Alright!" said Tia apologetically and sighed. "But people don't die from breakups you know..."

Nysa could have bitten her tongue but the words were already out before she could stop herself. "Why did you let Ron go, Tia? He was so good for you..."

It was almost a plea but Tia already clammed up as she turned her back on her and walked towards the window.

"I don't want to talk about Ron," she said quietly while looking out of the window.

The silence was broken after a while with Krystal announcing happily, "Let's just all chill for a while and enjoy this pizza. Hmm, smells nice...I can't wait to dig my fangs on them!"

Nysa immediately took the cue and got up. "I'll bake a few chocolate tarts later..."

The conversation was kept light as all three of them enjoyed pizza with coke and chips.

Tia was quieter than usual but the other two didn't seem to mind and understood her need to be left alone.

"I need to do this more often with you girls," said Nysa as she happily munched on her pizza. "A change from being a mother and a wife."

"True!" said Krystal. "You guys are damn lucky. I wish my sister was close by too. We definitely would have had a ball."

Tia sneaked a look at her sister. Lately her sister was getting a little bit too motherly for her liking. She sighed as she knew that it was all because she worried about her. Tia could understand that very well but she really didn't know what to tell Nysa or how to explain. Her sister would think she was insane if she really knew what was the reason behind her breakup with Ron. In fact, she would insist upon a check-up with a psychiatrist too, she was sure. She wouldn't have understood it as easily as Krystal had and it would have all been too much for her to handle. So she didn't attempt to explain and complicate matters even further.

Personality-wise they were like two alien beings from two different planets, mused Tia. Nysa never got her as to why someone cared so much about the past or people who were no more. She missed their parents and Rianna too but not up to Tia's wavelength. Life was for the living. So why not as well live and enjoy it was Nysa's motto. Nor did Nysa get too attached in any relationship besides her immediate family of course and was very self sufficient emotionally. The woods and the forests were never to Nysa's liking who enjoyed the social circuit that came with her busy life. She loved to dress up and go for parties. And now with her husband, her daughter and her work, she felt even more fulfilled. But Tia understood that that was the reason why Nysa wanted her and Ron's relationship to work out. So that Tia too could have a life as lovely and happy as hers.

Tia felt sad that she was like a thorn – almost – in her sister's otherwise perfect world. It wasn't easy for Nysa too, thought Tia. She had really worked very hard to have the life she had today. Tia knew that most people envied her sister and her life. But she knew how hard working, patient and compromising her sister was. She really admired and appreciated Nysa's tenacity and the way she built her life in spite of all that they had been through as a family. She deserved what she got and more.

Tia ran her fingers through her hair tiredly. But her sister had to understand that *life* was not always like that for everyone. Tia had finally made peace with what life had offered her. And she wished that Nysa too accepted it and made peace with how her life was even though it was vastly different from hers. Intense love flowed in her heart for her sister as she understood how much Nysa cared for her and loved her. Nysa, who was laughing at a comic scene, suddenly turned and their eyes met. She questioned her silently as to what was going on in her mind. Tia simply smiled and got up to clear the coffee cups from the table and then headed off to the kitchen.

"No way!" protested Tia. She was almost outraged. "I don't believe you did this. Cancel it, will you? Gosh! What would have Jeff thought? I won't have it – please!"

"Yes, Nysa not only have you got this fat ticket for Tia, but you got one for me too? It must have cost the earth!" exclaimed Krystal.

"Well, why not? It would be no fun for Tia cruising on her own. Together with you it will be a lot more fun!"

"NO way, Nysa! Get it refunded immediately. I am not hearing of it anymore!" said Tia with a determination in her voice that brooked no argument.

Nysa sighed as she looked at her sister warily.

"How can you think of wasting all this money on some fancy trip for me? I am not so helpless, you know. And Jeff? He must be thinking what a gold digger he has for a sister-in-law!"

"My dear sister, Jeff or anybody else has no right to think of anything like that. We girls have every right to care or spend on our families in any way we can! And why am I working so hard for if I cannot spend it on my family or my little sister whom I care for the most in the world!"

"You are right!" Krystal backed her up with a quick smile. "And I really appreciate it but Nysa, Tia can very well do it on her own. I'd not be happy spending your money like this. I'd be very guilty in fact."

"No way am I going!" cried out Tia. "Spend it on me if there is some crisis befalling me, I don't mind. Not on fancy cruises like this, alright?"

"Alright, alright...calm down. Don't lose all your hair over this now. Think it over once. Anyway I've got to leave for the night. Lola will be back soon and asking for me. I missed her the whole day."

"There is nothing to think, Nysa...you *have* to get it refunded," said Tia.

Nysa raised her eyebrows and her palms as if to say alright. "Crazy girl!" She punched her sister's arm playfully and then left for home after some time.

Chapter 21

Tia woke up to the sound of the cuckoo and a sense of desolation in her heart. She didn't know what caused this sinking feeling right at the crack of dawn. Then it all came flooding back. It was four weeks since her break up with Ron. She had cried herself to sleep last night.

The pain didn't seem to get any less with each passing day. Her heart felt heavier than lead. She felt chains tied around her feet making it impossible to drag herself to the kitchen. She forced herself to move from her bed and make it to the bathroom. As she started to brush her teeth in a slow languid way, she looked at the mirror and saw herself looking haggard. She had huge dark circles and her skin looked parched. She looked years older and her hair was a mess. In fact she looked like some *sanyasini** in an ashram with her tangled hair and her pinched looks, she thought humorlessly. She wiped her face and thought of making some breakfast as she had slept off last night without having anything. In fact, the last meal was at lunch break the previous day when Yuvi had literally forced her to have a piece of sandwich.

Dhruv too had been making the rounds in the past few days asking her if she had eaten something or trying to take her to the office canteen for a light coffee or snack. It was quite unlike Dhruv to be so solicitous and concerned. In fact most people in the office found him weird and anti-social at times. So she was quite surprised at his generous gestures. Not that it was not awkward. Over and above she felt so guilty that he was one of her suspects in her sister's death. Why was he so concerned about her suddenly was the nagging thought running in her mind all the time. Was he trying to appease her? Or was it genuine?

Her heart sank at the thought of the number of people she was distancing herself away from with her suspicions and doubts. What was all this leading to? Everyone had asked her to drop the whole Rianna episode off and move on in life. But she simply couldn't. Was she suffering from some kind of mental disorder or something? What was that sickness that some people were afflicted with – yes...*schizophrenia*. Her heart jerked in fear at the thought and she shook herself to clear her mind. Her thoughts were leading her towards a dark and murky path. She mustn't let this happen. She didn't want to get sick and be a burden on anyone. Especially Nysa. She realized in the past few days how much her sister worried about her. In the midst of all this intense pain it was comforting to know that her sister loved and cared for her so much. She couldn't let her down or be a burden on her by getting sick and lost.

Maybe a cup of coffee would do her good. She looked outside as she brewed herself a cup of coffee. The sun was making its way up. Early risers were busy enjoying a walk or catching up with an early morning run. Everyone looked so fresh and happy, waiting for their day to begin expectantly. She sipped her coffee as she walked to her living room and instantly twitched her nose at the taste. She had made the coffee black, the way Ron liked it. She walked back to the kitchen and poured some milk and sugar to her coffee. Ron always teased her about the amount of sugar she put in her coffee. It tasted more of a coffee candy than actual coffee he would say as his eyes crinkled with amusement. He loved to tease her and never seemed to have enough. He liked to watch every detail of her face, her eyes, and her emotions as she went about their dinner or daily chores. Tia teased him of voyeurism at times and he delightfully accepted it saying he didn't mind as she was the one to blame. Tia realized that she was lost in her thoughts of Ron again. She must stop doing it if she had to get over this terrible heartache. It was so painful every day and she didn't know if she would ever make it through. As she sat heavily on her sofa she was overcome by thoughts of hopelessness as if she would die with this constant suffocating pain in her heart that never seemed to abate.

She noticed a paperback on the centre table with the title "How to Deal with a Broken Heart in 30 Days." How in the world did it get here, she mused. Nina had got it for her a week back. But she had simply dumped it in the library rack of her study room. Who had got it here, she wondered as she took the book in her hand. No one had been here in her house in the past two days. Last evening she had dusted and cleaned up the living room and then thought of watching television. But she simply changed her mind and slept off very early. She took her phone to check for any messages. There were more than a dozen calls and messages on her phone. Her sister, Krystal, Nina, Yuvi...all asking for her whereabouts or if she'd like to go out and so on. She had slept very early at seven. Guess everyone was concerned about her, thought Tia with a mirthless smile.

She had to make an effort to shift this sense of gloom she felt all the time. She was really more blessed than most people in this world. And it would truly be a sacrilege on her part not to make anything of it. Today being Saturday, there was a long day ahead of her. What could she do, she thought, as she felt the sense of desolation at the empty hours stretching ahead of her?

Yuvi had asked her to join him for an hour in the office to work on the upcoming presentation with an Italian client. But she didn't feel like seeing the office for another two days. She had lost the passion for her work lately. Her work or the office didn't seem to excite her any more. Uncle Neal had anyway been asking her to take a break from all the hard work she had been putting into the office lately. Maybe she would take his advice for a change, she thought.

Maybe she would go to the ashram and help the children with their computer studies and spend some time with them. It always made her feel better when she spent some time with the kids. They made one see what life was from an entirely different perspective altogether and yet still be happy about it.

Then maybe she would meet her Yoga guru, Natasha Abraham, whom she really looked up to ever since she had joined her yoga classes a year back. Natasha in turn was very fond of Tia who had quite often helped her with all the events and workshops she held across the city. Krystal also had developed a strong bonding with Natasha from the time she had invited Natasha to do a workshop at her fitness centre. Both Tia and Krystal sometimes visited Natasha at her home as she was always inviting them for coffee or lunch. Her house had a warm ambience with people walking in and out all the time. At sixty, she was years older than them, what with her grandchildren in college, but for Tia and Krystal she was like their best buddy. They regarded her wisdom about life and anything in general with great reverence.

Ron had visited Natasha once too and looked very interested in all their discussion about philosophy and life. Krystal teased him later that he was very good at pretending and she could make it all out. But he swore with all his heart that he had absorbed it like sponge did water, albeit with a teasing glint in his eyes.

"Ron!" Tia sighed as she looked at the ceiling and leaned her head on the sofa tiredly. She dialed Krystal's number and asked, "I am visiting Tasha today. Would you like to come?"

"Yes, that's the reason I was trying to call you yesterday. Tasha wanted us to come to her studio somewhere around twelve and spend some time there. I said I am free and would ask you too."

"Okay, done. Tell her we will come and meet her then."

"I called you like a million times yesterday. What were you up to?" she asked curiously.

"Nothing. Just slept off early."

"Nysa called me up to enquire too. Give her a call, will you?"

"Okay, I will. I did see a couple of missed calls from her."

"Hmm."

"Krystal, did you leave this book – 'How to Deal with a Broken Heart in 30 Days' on the living room table by any chance?"

"No...never heard of that book. Why?"

"Nina gave me this book a week back and I dumped it in the study room. I don't know how it came here."

"Maybe Nysa?"

"It's been days since Nysa's been here. I have dusted up this room and the centre table like a million times after that."

"Oh...hmm. Maybe you sleepwalked last night...," said Krystal, tongue in cheek.

"Anyway, leave it. Now that it's here maybe I will skim through it once." She sighed.

"Yeah, do that. You love reading anyway so why not give this a try too. Maybe you'd find some hidden pearls...."

Tia smiled at Krystal's dramatic voice as she kept down the phone and leisurely dressed up in a mint polka-dot summer dress.

She felt much better at the ashram as she spent time teaching the young kids and clearing their doubts in whatever areas they were facing problems. They loved Tia a lot and hung on to every word she spoke. They went to lengths to please her, carrying her bag, getting her a pencil or a paper, jumping at her slightest query to be the first to do it.

But as soon as she got into the car to leave, someone called her from behind. It was the flower vendor at the gate where Ron would often buy her flowers every time they came to the ashram. The flower vendor, a little girl of fourteen looked at her expectantly today and asked her, "Gerberas or roses, Madam? And lots of tuberoses today too, Madam – your favorite!" She smiled expectantly.

Tia gave her two hundred bucks while refusing the flowers.

"Why Madam?" The flower girl look puzzled. "Are you not feeling well?"

The flower girl looked sad at seeing one of her favorite clients looking upset.

"Now I understand, Madam," she said when Tia didn't answer. "I am sure all will be fine. Your boyfriend isn't here, that's why na? I am sure he will be back soon. Just like the movies...girl-boy fight na...and then back happy again?"

Tia touched her cheek affectionately and silently waved at her from her car window. Tears ran down her cheeks as she drove through the busy road to pick up Krystal. Krystal quickly bustled into the car looking very excited about something. But as soon as she saw Tia's red eyes and tear-drenched face, she looked concerned.

She gave Tia a hug. Tia immediately burst into tears. Krystal kept holding her, saying soothing words till Tia cooled down after a while.

"I am sorry, Krystal. I don't want to spoil your day..."

"It's all part of the grieving process, Tia. I am glad it is all coming out. And don't say sorry, will you? That's what friends are for, isn't it? You would have done the same for me, too?"

"You know what Krystal...it's like some deep knife that has an old score to settle. It goes on cutting deeper and deeper and simply refuses to give up..."

"I understand, Tia. But I am sure time will bring its death eventually. It has to. Just hold on for some more time...."

Tia shook her head as she maneuvered the car out of Krystal's lane.

"Do people die of heartbreak, Krystal?"

"I am sure they don't, Kitkat..."

They picked up Natasha at her home and drove to her health centre.

"How are my sweethearts doing today?" she asked.

"Great now that you are here, Tasha!" said Krystal with a wink.

"You charming little girl – enjoying your freedom too much, aren't you!? Wait till that one guy brings an end to all of this!" She winked.

"Where is he, Tasha? Please take all my freedom, will you, universe!" she spoke to her open window while looking upwards. "It is getting a little bit too suffocating here, on my own!"

They all laughed at Krystal's dramatic dying act. Sometimes Krystal was just too much, thought Tia with a broad grin. What would she have done without her, she thought.

"Gosh! I am really looking forward to this day with you girls. Just a little bit of work at my studio and then we can go to Taj Oberoi for a fabulous lunch. The treat is on me!"

"Ooooh Taj!" Krystal rolled her eyes with pure pleasure.

"Oh, come on Poppins, stop it," said Tia with irrepressible laughter. "Tasha, isn't that a wee bit expensive...we can try a smaller place..."

"Not every day do I get some time with my girls now, do I? Better do it with some style." Tasha was equally dramatic and that was how the rest of the car ride was – filled with jokes and good conversation. Tia looked forward to the day ahead and tried to stop thinking of Ron for a while. She was lucky to have friends like Tasha and Krystal who cared so much for her. She knew Tasha was a very busy woman too what with her very successful Yoga studio, her health centre, her motivational workshops, her social life and her huge family. Yet she was doing all this just to make her happy. She wouldn't be surprised if Tasha and Krystal had both engineered this in fact.

As soon as she got down after parking her car, Krystal grabbed her hand urgently. She was beckoning her towards the lobby of the hotel. It was Jeff and before Tia could walk across the pavement to greet him, she was surprised to see another lady next to him. She was dressed to the nines and talking to Jeff animatedly as they got down the stairs.

"That is Simi, isn't it?" whispered Krystal

"Yes, Krystal...," answered Tia, looking baffled.

Tasha was no less than puzzled to see the bewildered expressions on Tia and Krystal's face. But she refrained from asking anything as she eyed the couple who was the target of their intense scrutiny.

"Why don't you find out where Nysa is?" said Krystal, still eyeing Simi who seemed to be all over Jeff. She hated the lady on sight, for some reason.

"But don't you think it might create trouble..."

"Tch...no, no, no...don't tell her you saw Jeff and Simi together. It might be all innocent for what we know. Just ask her what is she doing and kind of if Jeff is around...just generally enquire, will you?"

Once Tia hung up her phone, she turned to Krystal and slowly said, "She is with her mother-in-law and Lola for a day at the club. And Jeff's gone for a game of golf with his friend it seems..."

"Jeff sure hasn't," Krystal remarked in a dry tone as they saw Jeff and Simi getting into a car together.

At Tia's pinched look, Krystal lightly said, "We might be reading too much into it, Tia. It might simply be an ordinary business meeting after all. Let's have some fun for a change and forget all these hiccups for the time being..."

"Yes, come, come..." said Tasha softly who was consciously quiet all throughout the entire encounter.

*Sanyasini – A female ascetic or hermit

Chapter 22

"Hmm...this tastes good," said Krystal as she closed her eyes to relish the taste of butter chicken.

"What about the palak paneer?" asked Tasha as she scooped up a spoon of the lush, creamy, green, spinach curry with soft cottage cheese.

"Spicy but I like it! The parathas are nice and soft too," said Tia appreciatively as she tore a bit of a paratha and pinched up a piece of paneer with it.

"I am glad you're enjoying the food," said Tasha. She observed Tia from under her lashes. She had grown so thin in the past four weeks. Krystal had told her that Tia hadn't been eating or sleeping well and was having a hard time coping with her breakup. Her heart went out to her. What a beautiful person she was! Not a mean bone in her body. So humble and down to earth in spite of all that she had achieved. Always ready to help her out, doing something for her studio and health centre despite having a busy schedule herself. Most people in the centre admired her for her approachable and friendly nature. Her boyfriend, Ron, whom Tasha had met a couple of times was equally solid and a marvelous human being. They were perfectly made for each other. What could have caused the rift between them, she wondered.

Tia caught her eyes and silently questioned her contemplative look.

Tasha raised one of her shoulders and sighed. "Just thinking about life, relationships..."

She dug into a bowl of glistening, orange, carrot halwa and tasted a spoonful with a sigh. "Remembering my husband Sahil, who is no more. What a special person he was...a gift to humanity. Touched lives wherever he went. He told me that in this universe there is always something or somebody to fill in the empty place. Look...even if I miss him today, I am not unhappy at all. And what a beautiful day for me to share with wonderful friends around. He may no longer be alive and I still miss him at times. But then my life still has so many other gifts that I relish every day. Good friends, good company, my work, great assignments, beautiful moments..."

She looked around her and then at Tia and Krystal who was listening to her with rapt attention. "When good times come our way, we don't even give a thought to it and just go with the flow. But when bad things happen we feel we will never get over it – ever. We form opinions and think this is how life is. React to it as if it is our death warrant and nothing else can go right. But then again that too is just a moment in this vast cosmos of life. A moment in the vast dimension of time not meant to last forever. So we need to learn from it as much as we can and try to develop a strength within us that keeps us stable irrespective of situations – good or bad. These are just situations that might change at any point of time and not to be taken too seriously. Instead we should try to be patient and stay strong till the storm passes over. Our life outside is a projection of our thoughts inside. In other words, a reflection of our inner state of mind.

Have trust and expect the good and that's what your life will be. Live in mistrust and doubt about the higher power's design of your life and again that's what you will get – a life of unfulfilled dreams and dejection. Always believe in the higher power's plan for you, no matter what. Know and understand that even if bad happens, that is only for your own good. Because only if we go through the bad we realize the value of good. It is at times like this when we acquire the tools to live life. Tools such as resilience, patience and strength of mind. Contentment, which is so elusive to us, comes only after we have faced lack and then achieved it. A rich person never values water, electricity or the cooking gas. But a poor person will be thrilled if for a month all his basic needs are served and he doesn't have to worry his head over it. He would never understand what is it that keeps the rich so unhappy when one has so much to be thankful for in life. Because for him every moment is spent in fulfilling the basic needs of life. There is no time to be sad or depressed. He is a happier person because he lives in the present and concentrates at the task in his hand instead of a rich person who needs depression pills, pressure pills and what not. For a rich person it is his worries that become a cause for his setback. Worry for what? For things that might never happen?"

"You are right, Tasha. We are busy scripting things that never happen in the first place," said Krystal.

"Exactly. We can put a script writer to shame at the stuff we imagine but which might never come to pass. So the best thing to do is to stay focused at the moment and not give too much thought to the situations around us because this too will pass."

"But Tasha what if..." said Tia eyeing her ice cream thoughtfully, "what if we lose interest in everything around us...our work...our passions or the people around us? What if on some days there is this massive weight on our hands and legs and we don't even feel like moving...or doing anything whatsoever..."

"Yes, the best thing to do then is to connect. Connect with that higher source which you call God or Jesus, Krishna or the universe – whatever name you'd like to give it. Sit for a while in the quiet and let your inner guidance flow through. Let it guide you, give you the strength and the resilience to support you through that moment. And this you can achieve only with meditation. Make it a habit to meditate every day. Because when you meditate you connect with that higher energy. That higher energy will nurture you, send you thoughts that will guide you to do the right things. It will send you love and strength to lift your spirits. It will help quieten the inner turmoil, howsoever difficult or disturbed your world might be outside. It gives you the stability to handle your emotions in spite of the chaos around you. It brings you the focus that you need for your work."

"I don't know what to do, Tasha. Some days it feels fine but on other days it is like this empty feeling inside that turns my legs into stone. Even ordinary things like brushing my teeth seem like a mammoth task then..."

"It's simply practice, Tia. We have to train our minds every day to stop the negative thoughts from overwhelming us. Take baby steps. Obliterate each negative thought as and when it comes. Live in the present second and do our best at that very second. Every second becomes a minute. Every minute flows into hours and then hours become days till it becomes a part of our nature whatever the circumstances in our life maybe. Only then can we be a master of our circumstances. Come hell or high water, nothing can destabilize us because we make our minds work according to our will. We strive to remain consistent till the bad times shift, making way for the good. And meditation is the key to achieve this stability."

"I don't understand, Tasha...if there is a God then why do bad things happen especially to the nicest people?" asked Krystal.

"That is where 'karma' comes in, Krystal. Karma is the effect of our actions not only in this birth but our previous births too. Sometimes we do our best yet we feel we didn't get the best results or still face bad fortune. It is nothing but the debt of karma from our previous lives or maybe the present. Maybe in a certain situation, we cheated somebody. And although we had a realization of our wrong doing and tried to reform but it wasn't whole hearted then we still have to pay it in the present life till it is fully paid off."

"So, I did some mistakes in my previous birth due to circumstances such as being very poor, then in the present birth even if I don't lie or steal or have any of those vices, I still have to pay?"

"Yes, Krystal. But you can change it. You can change it by raising your thoughts and actions to a higher level. Do good work or raise your vibrations to change the situation. Whatever negative comes, don't get bogged down by it. But keep doing your work and try to change your thoughts to a higher level till the energy shifts in the positive direction. When the energy you emanate changes to a higher level so will your circumstances. Hence you must change your thoughts and actions in the positive direction. And circumstances and life situations are bound to change too."

"It sure feels great talking to you, Tasha," said Tia as she breathed in deeply and finished the last of her ice cream. Tasha lovingly petted her hand, her eyes full of understanding.

"You know what Tasha? I feel my meditation routine has changed me more in a positive direc..." Krystal stopped talking as her eyes shifted towards something at a distance and they widened in surprise.

She looked stricken when her glance immediately darted back at Tia.

"What?" asked Tia curiously as she tried to focus her attention to where Krystal's eyes were at that moment.

Tia's heart gave a sudden dive at the sight of Ron. It was four weeks since she had seen him. He felt larger than life as he almost took over her senses. She could hear a great pounding in her ears. Everything else seemed to dim as the sight of him completely encompassed her mind and heart. But somebody else came in the way. Her heart gave a painful lurch when she saw a tall brunette holding Ron's hand and leaning closely towards him. She was speaking animatedly and Ron seemed to be enjoying the little joke they were sharing. There were other people around them – mostly couples and it looked like they were all together heading to a party.

Tia wasn't prepared to see Ron with anybody else since their breakup and her heart seemed to twist a million times as if fresh blood was flowing through it all over again. Jealousy like she had never known before gripped her as she clenched her fists and tried to look away. Both Ron and the girl looked lost in their own little world and Tia, for the life of her, couldn't look away.

"Are you alright, Tia?" She heard a voice from somewhere droning above the huge humming noise in her ears. It was Krystal and she was worried seeing Tia totally pale and ill. She sought Tasha's eyes desperately not knowing what to do.

"Have some water, Tia," said Tasha very calmly while holding her hand softly. "Breathe in and look around slowly. Change your focus. It will help you calm down."

Tasha was right. She closed her eyes for a few seconds and she drank some water. Her heart beats slowed down a bit and she tried to swallow the huge pain in her throat with the coolness of the water.

Her eyes again moved towards the sight of Ron trying to absorb the reality of him being with someone else. *Her Ron.*

"No need to look that way, Tia," said Tasha quietly and her calm voice was like a balm on her raging nerves. She didn't know how she would have handled it if she was alone and happened to see Ron with some other woman.

"That's better," said Tasha, as Tia breathed in slowly, trying to absorb the pain and take it in her stride.

Just as Tia felt she could sail through it somehow, Krystal gave a sudden exclamation. "Oh no! He is coming this way, Tia!"

Krystal looked frantic with shock. Someone would think that it was she who was handling a heartbreak instead, thought Tia humorlessly.

Tia felt herself go red and warm all over as Ron drew near. He looked even taller and magnetic than he did before. Oh God! She didn't want to face him like this. Why didn't the ground just open up and swallow her right away. She didn't want him to see how devastated she was when he was handling their break-up so well. She wanted to appear cool and least bothered just like he did. And find a replacement – as if it was the easiest thing to do. He had already found *her replacement!* It was so easy for him, she thought with a choke and a gasp.

Tasha held her hand silently below the table as she greeted Ron with a broad smile. "Why Ron! So nice to see you here...small world isn't it?"

"Sure is, Tasha!" he said warmly with a hug. He playfully boxed Krystal on her arm as he teased, "Getting beautiful every day, aren't you? Some good news that I should know..."

In spite of everything Krystal blushed, thought Tia with a slight irritation. He turned to nod at her, rather emotionlessly though.

"Oh come on, Ron! I haven't seen you in ages and look there you are in the midst of a pretty busy social life. What's cooking? Looks like you are having a great time..."

Ron's face looked enigmatic and even if he understood Krystal's direct innuendo, he managed to hide it well. "Oh come on Krystal – destined to be a bachelor for life, aren't I? When good girls such as you think there are better options around the corner..."

It was a direct pun if ever there was one. Krystal ended up giggling while Tasha had an adoring look in her eyes as she threw her head back and gave into laughter too. It was as if they were enjoying all this, thought Tia, petulantly.

Tasha and Krystal suddenly seemed to realize Tia's dismal mood and sobered immediately. Ron seemed to understand what was going through their minds as he pushed his hands in his pockets and looked at the two while hiding his amusement. But his lips thinned when his eyes shifted to Tia and saw the seriousness on her face. The air was fraught with silence and Tia didn't know in which direction it would have gone if not broken by a soft feminine voice.

"Ron," said the voice. "What's keeping you so long...we are getting late."

She held his arm possessively, gave a quick glance at them and then at him with a questioning pout.

"Just met some old friends," said Ron as he looked down at her from his tall height.

She then turned towards them but looked displeased when her eyes moved to Krystal. "Hello, Krystal," she said quietly.

Only then did Krystal realize that she was a familiar face, in fact she was Nina's cousin.

"Oh, hi!" was all Krystal could say.

"You two know each other?" said Ron with a slight smile.

"It's a small world, Ron...of course we do...now let's get back, shall we? Everyone is waiting for us to cut the cake..."

She almost seemed to lead Ron away against his will power.

"See ya'll later," he said as he waved at them and left.

"You know her," asked Tasha in surprise.

"Yes, I do! Tia, isn't that Nina's cousin...wait what was her name...Trina, no, no Trisha!"

"Hmm...I recollect a little...," said Tia slowly.

"How come she never told us!" said Krystal aghast. She quickly dialed her number.

"Nina! Where are you?" Krystal's eyes were agog with surprise as she looked at Tia. "You did? Okay. Actually she is in Taj with me right now...you are what! Oh! Alright...see you in five minutes..."

"What?" asked Tasha slowly sipping her coffee. "You look like a cat who's got the cream..."

"It seems Nina is coming down here. She has been trying to reach you since yesterday and she has loads to tell us," Krystal added meaningfully.

"Where are they?" asked Tia, her voice impassive.

"Who?" asked Krystal, confused.

"Do I have to spell it out...Ron and that girl?" Even his name sounded so difficult to spell out, now that they were apart.

"A few tables away. The waiter arranged the tables in a circle so that their party has some privacy from the rest of the guests," said Tasha calmly. Krystal craned her neck to look behind her. Her position at the table was an added advantage for Tia who was sitting opposite her and it seemed like a good hiding place to peer from.

The girl, Trisha, seemed to gaze at Ron with total adoration as he kept the whole party engaged with something he was telling them. It was like knives piercing all over her skin when she saw the proximity and closeness that they shared.

"She looks totally devoted leaving Ron no room for doubt of her feelings," said Krystal with sarcasm dripping in her voice. She turned her back on them as if she couldn't take it anymore.

They all look startled when Nina made a sudden appearance on them. She gave Tia a tight hug and said a quick hi to Tasha whom she had met a couple of times while accompanying Tia.

"Now shoot!" said Krystal impatiently. "Why have you been hiding this scoop of news from us?"

Nina turned her gaze to where Krystal beckoned with her eyes.

She slowly turned around and shook her head as she said, "Believe me I was in a state of shock myself when I heard about it yesterday. I called up Tia immediately. But I simply couldn't get through! I knew Trisha had a thing for Ron the day she first saw him with Tia at my place before the wedding. She had been eyeing Ron for a long time now. Couldn't believe her luck when she heard of Ron's broken engagement is what she told me yesterday. She tried everything to get Ron's attention. And finally she got it. They have been seeing each other for the past two weeks I heard."

Just two weeks after they broke off, thought Tia sullenly. All of their eyes were on her, sympathetic and weary.

"Maybe Ron is on the rebound, Tia, and it's not serious as it looks," said Nina.

Tia simply shrugged her shoulders while smoothening her hair with trembling fingers.

"What's the party for, Eclairs?" asked Krystal curiously.

"It is Trisha's birthday. Ryan could not make it, so I had to come alone."

"That's quite a party she has thrown in a place like this!" said Krystal with a speculative look in her eyes.

"Apparently she is quite thrilled that Ron is seeing her. Quite the show-off amongst our cousins, that Trisha. Couldn't wait to show the world," said Nina dryly.

"Poised and sophisticated, isn't she?" said Krystal as they all peered at her from afar to Tia's consternation. "But can't hold a candle to Tia by a mile. Ron knows what he is missing..." A sly smile played on Krystal's lips.

"Oh, come on Krystal...stop that. Let's move from here shall we..."

Tia's face looked blanched and they immediately got ready to leave.

"What a day! First there was Jeff and Simi...and now..." Krystal immediately stopped midway, feeling alarmed at what she said. She quickly looked at Nina and asked instead, "When does the party get over?"

Nina instinctively sensed the delicate situation and took the queue. "Well, they just started with coffee and after that they plan to move to the banquet hall where some local band will be playing. And then dinner of course..."

"Hmm...quite a heavy affair looks like." Krystal raised an eyebrow as she glanced at the party again.

"Yes. I told you. Trisha loves to do everything the grand way," said Nina with a derisive smile.

They all bid Nina goodbye and were on their way out but Tia couldn't resist a last look at Ron. Ron too had turned at that exact moment and their gazes locked. Tia managed to tear her eyes away with great willpower. She turned to walk away as fast as her legs could take her, all the while trying to maintain her poise and avoid looking agitated.

Chapter 23

"That's why Buddha said attachment is the root cause of all suffering. Instead of being attached to the external world and its outcome, let us get our inner world right, first. And that we can do is by living our life in an honest way without any expectations. Buddha has laid the eight-fold path to live our life in the most authentic way possible, which in turn can help us achieve stability and peace of mind. The first of which is to have a realistic view of any situation and understand another's point of view without being judgmental. Second, we have to choose the right thoughts because we become what we think. We should not allow those thoughts to harvest that can make our mindset weak or negative. Third, use the right words that don't hurt others or bring about another's downfall, meaning we should not gossip. Fourth, exercise the right action which enables us to live harmoniously with our fellow human beings. We should strive to work sincerely and not indulge in harmful activities like lying, stealing or cheating others.

Fifth, we should choose the right form of livelihood that doesn't exploit others or put others in danger. Sixth, keep trying to do your best compared to whatever we have done in the past. And with sincere efforts keep training our mind to propel it in the right direction. Then seventh, to practise mindfulness every day – meaning living in the present. Living in the past will only bring us pain and regret. On the other hand, imagining things in the future will make us live in a state of expectations, which when not met will ultimately break our hearts. In the process we lose being happy in the present and all the gifts it brings. And last, to spend some time focusing and concentrating at one single point, meaning meditating, as that helps in communicating with our creator who in turn guides us to live a better life. Meditation keeps us calm and steady – grants us serenity through whatever chaos may be happening in our life. So make it a habit to practise it with regularity and consistency."

Mira Dorjee paused for a while as she looked around her with a serene smile. Tia thought she possessed an amazing luminosity around her.

Listening to her had a calming effect on everyone in the room. Tasha had done a good thing by arranging these sessions the past month. Mira was a well-known Yoga specialist as well as a motivational speaker who had made quite a name for herself recently in India and abroad. Being Tasha's good friend, she was generous to lend some time for her health centre.

"Even Bhagawad Gita says, 'Desire is the root cause of all evil'," continued Mira, "so we must strive to focus on our work instead of the outcome; and practise mindfulness every day."

"But Mira Ma'am, I think that seems only possible if we live secluded in an ashram or when we live the life of an ascetic. Not practical for people like us – at least in this materialistic world," said one of the girls in the audience. "And what is the excitement of living life if we have no desire or attachment towards anything. What is the purpose of living life, then?"

"Yes, those are the same questions running in my mind too. Even Buddha desired for peace isn't it, so he went to the forest leaving his life of riches and luxury behind," said another young guy.

"You are right, my dear. That's a good question you have there – a question I have been expecting from you all," said Mira with a smile. "But this is where everyone gets it wrong. Detachment doesn't mean we have to leave our family or job and live the life of an ascetic. It doesn't mean we have to stop going to parties, stop watching movies, or going on cruises, etc. But what it means is that we must focus on our work and goals without being attached to the outcome. Whether it is a good outcome or bad outcome, it doesn't matter except for the kind of efforts we put into our work. We must simply live in the present and focus on the work at hand – give it our best shot. If the results work out in our favour, then good. But even if the outcome doesn't manifest as per our efforts then we must understand that that too is good for us. Because there is the hand of God here and His plan for us can never be any less than our own plan – maybe even far better beyond our imagination. Hence we must not give up and try to get better and better at our goals every day. Every time we keep trying we reach closer to our goal. Same goes for relationships. If we love someone, then we must love them unconditionally. We must not expect that they too should love us back in the same manner. Does God stop loving us whether we are good or bad? Do the natural elements of God such as water behave any differently to us whether we are rich or poor? Water helps quench our thirst no matter what we are or who we are. So also our love for another must have zero expectations. Once we have that attitude, we can make any relationship work in our life. So don't be attached to the outcome or desire for things to happen in a certain way. God or that supreme energy knows each of us like no other. We must have faith that the hand of God is behind everything and even if things look bad today, yet there is some hidden gift or a lesson behind it or maybe a purpose in our favor. Once you live life with that attitude, you will achieve total liberation and empowerment all throughout your life!"

"What if the person we love is evil and we can't control our feelings towards him or her. Or, what again if we are not sure that the person is evil as all the while the person behaves very sincerely towards us. How to overcome this dilemma or which step should we take in that case?" Tia felt the words leave her mouth on its own accord as all eyes were on her, especially her friend Krystal.

"What is evil anyway? Falling in love, remarrying was considered evil in some countries and people were stoned to death for it. Practising a different religion was considered evil. But perceptions have changed with time..."

"No...I mean if the person causes harm to others – that kind of evil. But then again we are not sure if our suspicions against that person have any basis of truth," said Tia.

"Time is the best healer in any situation, my friend. Leave it to time and that supreme energy. While what is left for us to do is to work on ourselves and stay strong. Not to have any expectations but simply love our best and do our best. Time will reveal the answer whether someone is good for you or bad for you. God knows everything. So wait for him to show you the way and reveal the truth."

There were a few more questions and the session came to an end. Tia and Krystal went towards the dais where Tasha was speaking with Mira and a few other people.

"Hey Tia, Krystal, I'm so glad you both could turn up. Mira, meet these two very young friends of mine – Tiala Arya, or Tia in short, and Krystal Wallace. They have done a lot for the centre from the time they joined here."

"Hello," said Tia softly while Krystal protested, "Oh! Come on Tasha, I really haven't done anything – not like Tia at least..."

"You are wrong, Krystal. I really owe both of you so much. Hope you have met Sunita Chopra, my precious accountant without whom my finances would have been a total mess."

Sunita was a vivacious woman in her late twenties that Tia had seen before but from afar.

"We are going for a cup of coffee before we start our next session. Tia, Krystal, it would be great if you could join us?" said Tasha.

"Well, we..." Tia looked uncertainly at Krystal who shrugged her shoulders and said, "I will be going to dinner at Mom's place later. So I'm free for the evening."

They all went to the cafe nearby where Tia got to know more about Mira and her work. Tasha and she had met ten years back at a conference and from then on their friendship grew by leaps and bounds. Mira spoke of her childhood and the hard times they faced as Tibetans under the Chinese invasion. She at ten years walked all the way from Tibet to India along with her parents for thirty days and narrowly managed to escape the Chinese army. They travelled mostly at night and hid in caves and rocks in order to evade being captured by the Chinese. It was interesting to hear about her tales of survival while growing up and ultimately finding success as a yoga teacher and spiritual healer.

Tia heard a familiar voice as she sipped in her coffee. She quickly looked behind and couldn't believe her eyes as she saw Jeff taking a seat with none other than Simi. Jeff gave the orders and as soon as the waiter left they looked quite busy and lost in conversation. Simi was her animated self as she moved her hands and fingers gracefully while holding all of Jeff's attention at the same time. Her long summer dress flattered her figure, accentuating the curvy lines even further.

"Isn't that Jeff Bailey, one of the upcoming entrepreneurs in Bengaluru?" said Sunita, her voice loaded with curiosity. "I heard he is really going places."

"Is it?" said Tia as she looked around the table checking if Krystal had noticed. But Krystal was intently talking with Mira and Tasha, planning up a workshop for Mira at her fitness centre.

"Whiz kid in the animation business, I believe." Sunita's eyes sparkled with interest as she darted glances at Jeff and Simi, her voice lowered in a conspiratorial tone. "Not without a stroke of luck, though. Rumour has it that his partner who was also his girlfriend struck a lucrative deal overseas. She was the brains behind their growing business meaning the technical end while he pulled the marketing ropes. But the poor girl had an untimely death and the whole deal was accounted in his name. It was a partnership that gained him all the moolah in the end. That is how he amassed a lot of money to invest in all his new projects and everything has been a rolling success since then and how – lucky guy!"

Tia rolled the noodles round her fork as she looked at Jeff and Simi busy talking to each other and unaware of them a few tables away.

"Who have we got here now?" whispered Krystal under her breath.

Tia merely shrugged her shoulders as she tore her gaze away and tried to concentrate on something else. She felt Mira's gaze on her and when she looked up she found both Mira and Tasha smiling in amusement.

"We lost you some million of miles away," said Tasha.

"Sorry." Tia smiled apologetically.

"That's okay," said Tasha as she gestured her hand at Mira. "Mira was asking you something. Mira?"

"Tia, I wanted to know if you have lost someone in your life...an older woman...a motherly figure perhaps..."

Tia looked at Krystal in surprise as she nodded hesitantly and said, "Well...I did...my mother actually..."

Mira nodded reflectively as she said, "I am sorry. Does your Mom's name go by something related to a prayer?"

"Yes, her name's Pooja," said Tia with a slight smile. She looked at Tasha thinking she must have told Mira but Tasha merely shrugged her shoulders.

"Sorry, Tia," said Mira, her face keen with interest, "just bear with me. Do you wear a pendant with her initials inscribed in amethyst stones?"

"Yes I do," said Tia in surprise. "At times when I go out..."

"Tia, I am also a medium. Meaning I can connect with people who have passed away and sometimes they want me to convey messages to their dear ones who live on this earth..."

"Okay," said Tia slowly.

"Your Mom, Tia, loves you very much and she is always with you in spirit. She is always watching over you, do you know that?"

"Really?" said Tia, feeling her heart turning over.

"Do you dream about her often?"

Krystal and Tia exchanged surprised glances.

"Yes, I do..."

"Right. Please try to understand what she tells you in your dreams as she reaches out to you through your dreams."

"Okay."

"Did you lose a puppy when you were six years old, one you were attached to, quite a lot?"

"YES!" whispered Tia.

"Yes, even that puppy too is present in spirit with your mom. Do you have a special quilt made of teddies and bunnies that you still use? It's the one your mother made for you when you were in school."

"Yes, I do!"

"Tia, you were away from your home for some time and you felt guilty about leaving your mother, didn't you?"

"Yes, Mira. I studied in Kurukshetra and I was unhappy to leave my Mom. She was very sick."

"She said she was so proud of you then...do you know that? She was so proud that her little girl got through in one of the most prestigious colleges in the country and she doesn't want you to feel guilty about it, anymore."

"Okay..."

"There is some confusion in your life Tia right now and your Mom wants you to stay strong. Things will reveal itself in the right time and she asks you to stay strong – she says that repeatedly in a strong voice."

"Okay..."

"There is also someone you seem to miss a lot, she says...a young female...maybe she passed away too – early for her age...someone you looked up to..."

"Yes, my sister," said Tia amidst her tears.

"Your mom advises you to let go. It doesn't help to be stuck in your past and people who have left you. You must release them, be detached from it. She is fading away, Tia, and she signs off saying she has your back and she will help you through this ordeal..."

"That's awesome, Mira," said Krystal. "You were right on so many counts! How did you know!?"

"A gift from the higher source, you can say. Not many people know about it and I like it that way. But if somebody needs help with connecting to their deceased loved ones and it's really needed, then I do it."

"Mira has helped me cope with the death of my younger son too by connecting me with his spirit. She has brought me closure and I am so grateful to her about it," said Tasha, her voice full of appreciation.

"Aren't you scared connecting with ghosts? I would be spooked out, frankly. What if it's a very evil spirit or a demon?" asked Sunita in awe.

"That's what I don't do, Sunita. I don't connect to ghosts or spirits who are haunted or lost in the earthly realm unless I open myself to it. It's only people who have crossed over peacefully or reached the light, meaning God, that I connect to. Often the spirits who are in heaven come to me, mostly to pass on messages to their loved ones. Although they might have unresolved issues or past regrets yet for the most part they are at peace. And they try to relay messages to their loved ones who are suffering or bereaved at their loss so that their loved ones can free themselves of grief and pain, move on in life and live life as it is meant to be lived."

"That's truly an amazing gift," said Tia with a sense of wonder. "I definitely feel happy and there's a sense of complete fulfillment today that I can't even explain to you. Thank you so much, Mira!"

"It's okay, honey. It was meant to happen. You were searching for something and hence the universe has conspired for us to meet."

"What do you exactly see, Mira?" asked Sunita, fascinated. "Is it like a real person visible to you whom we don't see?"

"Let's say, I see them clairvoyantly. Meaning, images come in my mind's eye – those which the spirit wants me to see. Or, it may be like images in a filmstrip or a flipbook that we had as kids. Then again images can be like those we see in a dream or something we imagined in our mind's eye. But these images don't disappear quickly. In fact they give me some strong feelings and thoughts related to these images. So that's how I decipher them. There are instances again when the spirit appears more physical at times, but more in the lines of ghostly and ethereal figures. Some appear as auras standing next to the loved one I am speaking to. Some psychic mediums have stronger clairaudient skills where they will only hear voices when they communicate with the spirit. Maybe thoughts in their minds or actual voices of the spirit depending on how strong the communication is. I use my clairaudient skills at times if that's the only channel with which the spirit wants to communicate with me. Sometimes I neither see images nor hear voices but simply get messages telepathically. These messages might be a kind of an inner knowing or inner sensing. At times I get physical feelings too. For example, the spirit may have passed by a heart attack. So I'd feel a certain twinge in my heart and know that this was how that spirit had passed away. Sometimes I see symbols, or a contrary image like the spirit is running around happily in case the spirit was paralyzed when he or she was living on earth. So it all depends on how correctly I interpret these symbols. And it sure needs a lot of practice and dedication through the years."

"Can you foretell the future too?" asked Krystal.

"No, I am just a go between. I channel with spirits who have deceased. I don't have psychic or clairvoyant abilities," said Mira with an understanding smile. She got that question all the time. "Actually, it is the clairvoyants who have the ability to clearly see persons and events that are distant in time or space. They can help you see the truth about your past and present as well as predict the future."

By the time they left, Tia looked out for Jeff and Simi but they must have already left. She had forgotten about them completely in the last couple of minutes when Mira was telling her about her Mom.

Chapter 24

"Come on, Tia! I'm not having it. It's a beautiful resort. There's a nice lake for boating and then horse and elephant rides..."

"I'm not a kid, Nina..."

"Ha, ha, ha...I just got carried away. I asked Nysa and Jeff to join us too. Come to think of it, Lola would enjoy it even more."

"Nysa and Jeff too? It's a huge party, is it?"

"Perhaps but very informal...my cousins...then Krystal, you, Nysa and few of Ryan's friends and cousins. The evening snacks and dinner are on us, of course. Most of us are staying back as it would be too late to come back, what with the resort being located at the outskirts of the city. Lodges are not too expensive anyway, so let's make the most of it and stay back. Say yes, babe...long time since we have been together. At least you and Krystal get to be together all the time and I am the only one who's left out..."

"Your fault, Eclairs. Who asked you to get married this early, ha?" said Tia with laughter in her voice.

"So you'll come, right?" asked Nina with hope in her voice.

"I am not sure...Look Nina, don't take it personally. But I am not up to meeting anybody these days except for you or Krystal. I just want to be left alone for some time."

"You think being alone and moping will make this any better?" asked Nina in a quiet voice. "Tia, it's my first birthday celebration after marriage. And the last time it was in school when we three got together on my birthday. It's been almost eight years! I really want to celebrate it this time with my besties and all the people I love. As it is, all of us hardly get to meet these days what with our work and family commitments. This is how relationships drift apart, do you realize that?

200

I don't want that to happen to us..."

"Oh, Nina...that won't happen to us!"

"Then say yes, Kitkat!"

"Alright, I will come."

"Yay! See you darling...love ya!"

Tia sighed. She was really not in a mood for socializing. But, luckily, with Krystal and Nysa around she wouldn't have to socialize with any new people and could quickly recede into the background. The doorbell rang and when she opened, she found Yuvi at the door.

"Hi Tia...what's up? Hope I am not here at a bad time, am I?"

"No, of course not. I was just reading some stuff..."

"I tried to call you but your phone was busy."

"Yes, that was Nina," she said as they walked to the sofa and Yuvi sat next to her. "She is celebrating her birthday in Golden Springs resort for the weekend. Invited me along."

"Are you going?" asked Yuvi lightly as he turned to face her.

"I said yes. She wasn't letting me off otherwise. Almost on the brink of an emotional blackmail!" she said with a light snort.

He brushed a stray hair away from her face as he said softly, "You should go out more. I don't know what caused your breakup with Ron nor do I want to pry. But staying alone cooped up like this doesn't help, you know. Get out, change the scene, spend time with your friends and this will quicken the healing..."

"Healing from what?" Tia laughed with a sneer.

He pouted like a child as if to humour her and then picked up the newspaper and browsed through the pages. They sat like that for some time. It was a comfortable silence. She didn't have to make idle conversation with Yuvi around or the need to fill in the awkward gaps.

"Should I make you some coffee?" she asked after a while.

"No, that's okay. You sit down. I will make some for both of us," he said as he touched her nose affectionately with his finger.

"You will find everything?" she asked as he walked to the kitchen.

"I should," he said with a wink. She sat back comfortably and turned her attention to the book she was reading before Yuvi had come.

"Where is the TV remote?" asked Yuvi.

Yuvi switched to a channel which was showing a hit comedy movie. She laughed her heart out with Yuvi as the scenes were hilariously funny.

"I have got to go, Tia. Have a conference call at ten," he said after an hour. He washed the coffee cups and ruffled her hair lightly as he whispered, "Stay strong!"

Tia stood awhile on the doorway as she looked at his receding figure. Her relationship with him had improved by leaps and bounds, as there were never any demands or expectations from his side. Maybe that was the reason she felt naturally relaxed with him around these days.

Lately they were spending a lot of time together. It wasn't a passionate relationship but she realized that she was getting more and more attached to this feeling of ease with him around. Today too she felt much better and lighter after spending some time with him.

The next day dawned out bright and beautiful as Tia walked towards the car where Ness and Krystal were waiting for her.

"I am glad you are coming back with us tomorrow instead of today," said Krystal happily. "Nysa and Jeff could have stayed back too. What was the hurry to come back? Tomorrow is a Sunday anyway."

"No, they decided they'll stay back too as Jeff's not willing to drive back. Too much work this entire month...so he's quite exhausted. Fresh air, exercise and some quality time for them too. Hence I too made up my mind to spend the whole weekend at the resort. No sense driving back alone..."

"Great then," said Ness. "Although I don't know if the resort will hold all of us as Nina's cousins are coming along too."

"Let me call and find out," said Krystal.

Tia looked outside her window and relished the cool air that blew across her face. The sight of the green of hills and mustard fields calmed her nerves as she leaned comfortably in her car seat. It was really relaxing to leave the busyness of the city life behind them.

"I asked. Rooms are already booked. So no issues, Nina confirmed," said Krystal with a satisfactory grin on her face. "Not many people, just three – four unmarried cousins from her side it seems and two friends on Ryan's side with their spouses. All will be sharing rooms. Mine and Tia's are separate though," she said with a sneaky wink.

"Don't spend too much time with makeup and useless girly gossip, will you? I don't want to spend more time with nature than with you," said Ness with a glint of mischief in his eyes.

Krystal slapped him lightly on his arm. "Girly gossip! What about the boring men talk that you drag us into? It's endless and boring as hell."

They reached the resort in two hours. Tia felt amazingly serene as she took in the beauty of the resort with its undulating green meadows. It was filled with flower bushes and trees neatly lined up around the resort for stretches on end. Once they unpacked in their rooms and freshened up, they headed to the restaurant for a light snack. Nina and Ryan joined them too along with another couple.

"Hey Krystal, Tia! Good all of you could make it," said Nysa as she lightly touched her sister's cheek and sat beside her.

"Where's Jeff and Lola?" asked Krystal.

"Jeff will freshen up and come down in five minutes," replied Nysa.

"My mother-in-law didn't want us to bring Lola as she was sneezing and was afraid she might catch a cold. So we decided not to bring her along."

In no time the girls were busy chatting nine to dozen about their plans for the day while the menfolk were busy discussing the upcoming T20 finals. The manager had switched on the television to check on the scores.

"Hey cous!"

They turned around to see Trisha standing with two other girls.

"Hi...where's Mandi?" asked Nina as she got up to greet her cousins.

"She has a concert to attend. Sanjay came instead, Nisha's friend," said Trisha.

"Hope that's okay, Nina *Di**?" asked Nisha, her cousin, tentatively. "Last minute bookings cannot be cancelled here as far as I know."

"Yeah, no problem. I have met Sanjay before, haven't I?" asked Nina with a naughty glint in her eyes to which Nisha blushed. "He drove you here?"

"No, Ron drove us here," said Nisha. Tia was not the only one reeling with shock at these words but Krystal and Nysa looked equally astounded too. They shifted restlessly in their seats, their glances harried and tactless as they quickly searched across the room.

"Ron?" said Nina, wetting her lips, as her mind seemed to be reacting slower than usual. "I didn't know Ron was coming!?" She looked around to find him taking a seat among the men. Ryan seemed to catch her eye from afar and there was a quiet communication between husband and wife, across the room.

"Is it a problem, Nina?" asked Trisha innocently. "Yesterday you were out when Ryan was calling up the resort and making the bookings. Ron was with us too. So I suggested Ron could come along. Ryan was quite delighted and readily invited him. Hence we made plans to spend the weekend here. As it is, you know how hectic it gets every day, what with our work schedules...a little time away in the peace and quiet of the countryside would be great for both of us, don't you think? We get to be a part of your birthday celebrations too. Two birds with one stone, eh?"

Her wink was conspiratorial. She sounded very excited although the silence that dragged on was charged with a tension one could cut with a knife.

It took a few seconds for Nina to realize that a response was expected from her. So she answered almost brightly, "Yes, yes, why not! Ron is almost like a family friend for me and Ryan...more the merrier."

She passed a quick guilty look at Tia and the others. Tia quickly looked away and tried to look casual. She didn't want Nina to feel guilty about something that was no fault of hers. Her glance accidently fell on Trisha who was looking at her with almost a sly smile on her face. But Trisha quickly shifted her gaze away when she found Tia's eyes on her.

As soon as her cousins left to join the men, Nina looked at them apologetically. Her voice was rushed as she said, "I didn't know about this, Tia. Ryan's going to have it properly from me. How could he be so careless...?"

"It's okay, Nina." Tia couldn't stop herself from looking at Trisha across the room, curling up next to Ron and giving him adoring looks. She almost locked eyes with Tia and her eyes didn't bother to hide her ill-concealed delight.

"It's been almost two months now. It's time I coped with it better. We have common friends and I can't avoid him forever. We both need to move on with our lives. He has done it easily, hasn't he? So why can't I? Anyway, you guys can't go on sheltering me forever. This is what life is! Now quit giving me those insanely tragic looks, all of you. Someone would think death herself has befriended me, judging by your hopeless expressions."

Tia laughed as if to dispel the morose atmosphere around her what with

Krystal, Nysa and Nina looking at her with perplexed eyes. Their jaws were almost hanging down in a defeated reverie.

"Yes!" Krystal attempted to join her in a forced cheerfulness as she raised her coffee cup and said, "Here's to Nina's birthday and wishing her many more celebrations like this!"

"Cheers!" They all chorused.

The day went off in a daze as they all trekked round the area enjoying the sights and sounds of the lush green hills. Nysa and Jeff were way ahead of the rest. Both husband and wife were holding hands and looking all lovey-dovey, thought Tia.

"Seen anything of Simi lately? Everything okay on that front?" asked Krystal curiously.

"I don't know, Krystal. I haven't ever broached the topic with Nysa about seeing Jeff and Simi together, if that's what you mean. Maybe we are reading too much into it and looking for trouble where it doesn't exist?"

"Hope you are right, Tia. I wouldn't want anything less than that for Nysa. She is an amazing person and deserves all the happiness she gets..."

Tia bumped into Ron once but besides a customary hello they tried to avoid paths. His eyes looked very cold for that fraction of a second it held her.

After lunch they all sailed on the boats while enjoying the calmness of the beautiful Hosadoddi Lake. There were loud shrieks as Sanjay splashed water at Nisha and Trisha playfully. Trisha almost fell on Ron's lap while trying to avoid the splashes.

Tia could not stop the torturous wave of jealousy that followed seeing the sight of Ron holding Trisha and steadying her. He whispered something in her ear which made her squeal with laughter.

"They look so cute together!" Ritu gushed. She was Nina's other cousin, who accompanied her on the boat.

The person in charge had seated everybody as couples except for Ritu and Tia who were both singles. Krystal was with Ness, Nina was with Ryan, Jeff was with Nysa and two other couples who were friends of Ryan also had a boat to themselves. Meanwhile Ron, Trisha, Nisha and Sanjay were sharing one boat among themselves due to the unavailability of boats. But they seemed to be having their own share of fun as they made an awful lot of noise and pulled each other's legs. Everyone seemed to be so happy and present in the moment, thought Tia emotionlessly. It was evening and the sun was about to go out.

Ritu was quite a talkative person and she spoke a lot about herself and her life in Pune. She didn't live in Bengaluru but was visiting Nina and her family. She was younger than Tia by about four years and was a highly energetic girl. But after a while her voice seemed to drown in the background as Tia found herself gazing listlessly at the water, her mind elsewhere.

It was quite a lovely evening at a beautiful resort and anyone would have died to spend a day here, she thought. But she couldn't get over the gaping hole in her heart. As much as she tried to get over Ron, it was getting difficult every day. She tried to religiously follow all the advice that Tasha had given her in order to get over her heartbreak. Yoga and meditation she practised every day. She went for Zumba classes at Krystal's fitness centre. She painted and read a lot in her free time. She listened to a lot of spiritual lectures on television or online. But she couldn't seem to get over this gnawing pain eating her heart. Somehow she managed to go through her day by keeping herself busy with work at the office.

Maybe happiness was something very elusive for a person like her, she mused. Tasha had told her that with time everything would feel okay. It was just about training the mind to focus in the present and stop trying very hard. But destiny had other plans it looked like. It repeatedly tested her and sent her new challenges every time she overcame one.

"Tia looks so lost and unhappy. It breaks my heart to see her like this," remarked Nysa as she walked back to the resort with Krystal.

"I know! Did you see how Ritu was talking nine to dozen while Tia was totally spaced out?" said Krystal in exasperation. "Some girls can be really dense!"

"I saw that." Nysa laughed in amusement. "How could Ryan invite Ron to come along at a sensitive time like this?"

"I swear!" Krystal exclaimed in disbelief. "He could have consulted Nina at least once. I am glad he got an earful from Nina."

"Men!" Nysa shook her head tiredly.

"Trisha's all over Ron. It irks me to see any girl behave so foolishly in the presence of the opposite sex."

"She feels Ron is the best thing since sliced bread and who can blame her. Tia just hasn't realized what she has lost," said Nysa regretfully. "Any girl in her right mind would not let go off a catch like that so easily. They would fight tooth and nail for it! But my sister..."

"Did you see how Trisha's flaunting her relationship with Ron?! It's not like it's official or something!" said Krystal disgustedly. "I am sure Ron is nowhere near serious with her and is just enjoying a fling. But look at how she is flashing signals at Tia as if to say he is all mine – don't even dream of looking his side! I think she is a real bitch and not at all like our Nina...cousin or not!"

"You are right, Krystal. I can see the looks Trisha keeps shooting at Tia. What is it that she's so insecure about? She's got the man at her side, hasn't she?"

"But she can't hold a candle to Tia, can she? Tia is all classy, intelligent, loving and a man's dream. That's what she's insecure about. Nysa, I'll go and check on Tia, see if she's okay..."

"Yes, do that. Jeff's been trying to get my attention from a long time. I'll go see what he wants."

"Hey, you okay?" asked Krystal once they had got into their rooms to freshen up.

"Of course!"

Krystal was amazed to see Tia all dressed and ready. She was humming a tune and was putting on the last touches of her makeup. There was something different about her, thought Krystal, as Tia turned to look at her.

"Is my makeup okay?" she asked. Her eyes had an excited glaze about them. Maybe it was her makeup and the way she did her hair. She usually was very light with her makeup but today she took extra pains and she looked more sophisticated.

Yes..." Krystal said almost in a daze.

"Then get ready quick! The resort has arranged a number of activities for us it seems – camp fire, games and then dancing...come on! I am pretty excited. Will wait for you downstairs."

Krystal shook her head as soon as Tia left. She didn't know what to make of it. The next few minutes she quickly took her bath and dressed up. Downstairs Tia seemed to be laughing and talking animatedly with Ritu and two other guys who were also guests at the resort.

Then there were games arranged by the resort's staff which were real fun starting with Antakshari, Dumb Charades, Two Truths and a Lie and last of all the Blindman's Bluff.

Tia tried not to look at Ron and enjoy herself in the moment with Ritu, Sunil and Rishi. They were young people, uncomplicated and full of energy. Luckily they didn't know anything about her. So it was a refreshing change to be with them, instead of being pitied by the other people especially Ryan, Jeff and their friends who had their eyes on her. Nor did she want to be under the prying, overprotective eyes of Krystal, Nina and Nysa.

Ritu seemed to enjoy hanging around with her and so Tia started to loosen up a bit. The guys, who were techies from Bengaluru, were of her age – or maybe a year or two younger than her. Ritu flirted with the one called Sunil outrageously. While Rishi seemed to be paying more than a little interest at her. At least this would take her mind off Ron, she thought – and Trisha, who was displaying a lot of public overtures with Ron. She was simply getting on her nerves.

There was an awkward moment once while playing Blindman's swag, as she almost tripped and toppled over Rishi. Her head was dizzy as Rishi lifted her and held her in his arms. Everyone came running and fussed over her as she held on to Rishi to stop her dizziness.

"She needs to sit for a while and not be crowded around. It cuts off the oxygen. Bring her here." Ron's voice was curt as he seemed to almost bark at Rishi, thought Tia. She felt four hands leading her gently to a chair.

Everyone moved off to let her breathe as she slowly opened her eyes. Ron was on his knees next to her while Nysa and Rishi looked on worriedly.

"Get her a glass of water, will you?" said Ron while he kept his hand protectively around her back.

Rishi went off to get some water for her although he looked reluctant to leave her. What a nice guy he was, she thought, so solicitous and concerned. But here was Ron acting very autocratic and giving orders.

"You don't have to be so rude. Who do you think you are?" said Tia in utter annoyance. She felt an anger boiling inside her as the stress of the whole day was getting a bit too much for her.

Nysa looked a little uncomfortable and was about to say something but Ron cut in, "Relax, sweetheart. I am just a little concerned about your health. Your young boyfriend is too fascinated by you to think straight. He seems to be behaving like a schoolboy who has just found his new crush."

"Oh! Don't be so patronizing! You..."

Tia left off whatever she was saying as Rishi hurriedly appeared with a glass of water.

"I told the staff to prepare some orange juice. It will make you feel better."

"Thanks, Rishi."

"Would you like to go inside?" he asked her.

"I think she needs some fresh air," said Ron, in a voice that brooked no argument.

"Yes, Tia. It's better you sit outside for a while. I feel parched...will be back in five minutes," said Nysa hastily and walked off to the lounge.

"Ron...is she okay?" It was Trisha and she looked awkward as she came to stand beside them.

"Yes, I feel better," said Tia. She looked at Trisha and could almost feel her discomfort at finding her man being occupied with his ex.

"Oh! Glad you are over it," she said with a smile which was very indifferent and empty, thought Tia.

Trisha quickly turned to Ron as she said, "Ron, can we take a walk by the lake. I am really exhausted with all these games and activities. Feel like unwinding a bit..." Her hand held on to Ron's as she closed the distance between them and looked at him from under her lashes with undisguised flirtation.

"Yes, you'd better go, Ron. Rishi and I will go inside for a while, anyway. I feel like lazing a bit in the lounge too."

Ron flipped a cold look at Rishi and then at her. He abruptly turned away and let himself be led away.

"I am at your command, princess...show me the way," he spoke lazily as he took Trisha's hand.

Tia could feel the hot pang of jealousy as she saw them both shamelessly flirting with one another as they walked away.

"What a cold fish that guy is!" said Rishi and exhaled in relief. "The girl's a total show-off. Butter won't melt in her mouth, looks like. The pair's so made for each other if ever there was one."

The dances had started and everyone seemed to enjoy themselves as they gave into the light mood of the evening. Trisha was latched on to Ron almost like a twine round a tree, thought Tia morosely. But Rishi in turn gave her more than a little attention. She flung herself into the moment, enjoying every dance with him. Ritu and Rishi persuaded her to have more than a glass of wine. She was not used to it and felt much lighter than usual. She found herself laughing more and almost playing the fool with Ritu, Rishi and Sunil.

She caught Ron stare at her a couple of times but his eyes appeared to be full of contempt. He was very gentle and attentive to Trisha, however, and that really gnawed at her heart. Krystal came and asked her to come and sit with her for a while. But Tia shooed her away saying she need not bother about her and to go have some fun with Ness instead.

"I don't think you should drink anymore, Tia," said Nysa as she came next to her side, worry creasing her brow. "Ritu, she is not used to this. So please refrain from handing her any more glasses, will you?"

Tia couldn't help giggling at Nysa's worried face. "You are sounding like a school headmistress now. Look there, Jeff's looking cross now at being left alone by the mistress..." Ritu seemed to find that funny too and started giggling with her. Nysa shook her head warily and left them giggling away helplessly again.

Rishi was like a faithful puppy following her around everywhere and after a while she found him getting physically closer than usual. He was almost squeezing in the space between them when they sat at the lounge, holding her hand even when not required and laying his hands on her at every opportunity during their dances. She was tired after a while and wanted to go to bed.

Ron came to her just as she was leaving and held her hand. Ripples of shock ran through her at the feel of his skin after a long time. He looked into her eyes with an intensity that made her heartbeats race. She didn't want him to know the trembling she felt inside at his close proximity.

"Want to have a dance with you," he said. He slowly led her to the dance floor and held her close.

She could feel Trisha's eyes from afar, burning holes into her skin. She took his hand and led him to the far corner of the dance floor.

"Why not?" she whispered as she pulled a hand from behind her and put it in his hand. It was Trisha's hand and she looked quite startled but nonetheless happy. Tia's lips curved into an ironic smile as her eyes flashed defiantly at Ron. With that she left him with Trisha, though the look he gave her was far from pleased.

Di - A term used for an elder sister/female cousin in India. Short form of Didi.

Chapter 25

"Good morning..." Tia's voice was a croak as she answered her mobile which was ringing incessantly amidst her semi-awakened state.

"Hey, time you woke up! I am coming over to take you with me. Need some help shopping for Nina's parents' anniversary party."

"Oh I forgot...another party." She groaned as she dug her face into the pillows. "Nina is living it up a bit too much, isn't she? Only last weekend we had celebrated her birthday at the resort, didn't we?"

"Ya, you had too many drinks and quite a large dosage of young Mr. Rishi. And then you had come down with a splitting headache. Anyway, the party is for Nina's parents and it will be their 30th wedding anniversary. Uncle and Aunty have been very sweet to us all our lives. So we'd better make it special for them and help Nina arrange the party."

"Yes, you are right," said Tia as she sighed and got up. "I have been such a whiner lately and so ungrateful. Sorry about that, Krystal."

"It's okay, Kitkat," said Krystal with a smile. "We are all used to you by now."

"Shut up, you meanie!" She laughed.

"It's already 8 am. You slept late. Coming in another 30 minutes. Breakfast at Udupi. Get ready."

"No way! I am sleeping for another hour. Don't ring me for another hour as I am keeping my mobile in silent mode. Come at nine thirty. I will be ready then!"

Tia slept for another hour and then quickly got up to have her bath. By the time Krystal came she was already famished. The breakfast at Udupi was ravishing and Tia felt ready to shop for the day. They got some decorative items for the party that Nina had asked them to get. Then they started looking for decorative candles. Nina had planned to light up the whole house with them. There were some with awesome sandalwood fragrances that smelt really good but weren't strong enough. Maybe the ones with rose fragrances would be right, thought Tia. Their essence was stronger.

"Looking for something?"

"Oh Yuvi, you almost gave me a fright!" said a startled Tia.

His eyes crinkled as he hugged her with ease.

"Sunday shopping?" he asked.

"Yep! For Nina's parents' anniversary party. Are you coming for the party?"

"Oh, yes...it almost slipped my mind. It would be great to see the old couple after a long time. Always been a very sweet couple."

"Yes, we are planning to go early, as soon as we finish shopping to help decorate the house."

"Is it? Then why don't I accompany you too. You could do with another helping hand for sure. Long time since I have been involved in a family celebration," he said.

His face looked quite vulnerable as he said that. Tia could feel the familiar tug in her heart for Yuvi, as she remembered how hard it had always been for him. With no family or siblings around, it must have been quite tough for him emotionally on his own.

"Well, of course you can! Do join us if you are free. The more the better," said Krystal from behind.

"Hey Krystal! How are you?"

"I am good, Yuvi. Good to see you," said Krystal with a heartwarming smile. Lately she felt happy that Yuvi was always around with Tia. She hadn't been too happy about Tia and Yuvi's growing closeness at the time when Tia was engaged with Ron, yet now she welcomed it.

Tia looked quite relaxed with Yuvi around and now that Ron seemed to be already too eager to move on with Trisha, it is best that Tia had someone to fall back upon, emotionally at least. Besides it looked like everyone had someone in their lives and also was pretty busy with them. Except for Tia of course, and that made Krystal's heart ache for her friend. Her relationship with Ness was also growing deeper, lately. She didn't want to see Tia moping on her own.

Yuvi was quite smitten with Tia if one observed closely, thought Krystal. They looked quite good together actually, she mused. He always seemed to keep her happy and amused, his look full of adoration. Though not up to Ron's standards, yet there was something very boyishly attractive about his face as well as his very tall and muscular physique. Actually, there was more than one female at the mall stealing glances at him.

Once they finished with all the shopping and a nice lunch which Yuvi treated them to, they headed towards Nina's house. Nina's house was a bustle of activity with helpers and vendors decorating the house. Her parents were happy to see the trio as they were all children of their friends from a long time. Her mother treated them to a delicious pudding and she made sure they were more than full.

Yuvi helped Tia decorate the living room wall with crepe paper, paper chains, balloons and honeycombs. Yuvi kept teasing her that her crepe paper chains were more that of a kid's handiwork. She retaliated by throwing crepe petals at him which he made a great show of evading.

Her eyes were suddenly caught by Ron's who was leaning in the doorway casually with his hands inside his pockets. His gaze looked like it could almost freeze hot molten lava as he stared at both of them coldly. He was soon joined by Trisha who looked quite taken aback at the strained silence that stretched between them.

"Hey Ron? Long time..." Yuvi spoke lightly as he tried to dispense the tension in the air. "What's up?"

"All good, so far. What about you...work and fun, is it?" Ron smiled crookedly yet his eyes were loaded with meaning.

"Yeah...you're right on that score, buddy." Yuvi's smile was equally loaded.

"Looks like..." Before Ron could complete what he was saying, Trisha intervened in a petulant voice. "Ron, Nina's waiting for us to help her with the caterers. Can we get going please...?"

"Hmm, looks like someone isn't too happy," said Yuvi with a lift of his brow, after they left.

Tia merely shrugged her shoulders and got back to decorating the wall. She didn't feel like talking for a while and Yuvi left her on her own. One of the helpers got them glasses of orange juice which helped to cool her parched throat. Just as she finished it halfway, her shirt was spilled with the remaining juice as one of the kids dashed into her.

The kids, two girls and a boy, apologized profusely but she ruffled their hair, saying it was okay. She told Yuvi she'd be back quickly and rushed to Nina's guestroom. Luckily it was unlocked and she used the restroom there. Just as she was about to come out, she heard someone giggling excitedly.

"Ron, will you please stop making jokes and help me with my pearls," said a laughing Trisha as she looked at herself in the mirror.

Tia could feel herself blushing behind the curtains that hid her as she saw Ron helping Trisha hook the necklace behind her neck.

"Is that okay?" asked Ron in a smooth voice.

Trisha's voice was almost husky as she said, "Perfectly okay."

"I think we should go now. Nina will be waiting."

"Let them wait," said Trisha. She drawled seductively as her hands locked behind his neck. "We hardly got any time for ourselves today?"

"Didn't we?"

Tia's phone buzzed at that time and she almost panicked at being found out. But luckily she had kept her phone in silent mode early morning itself and forgot to turn on the ringtone. It was Nysa calling her. She tapped on the ignore button and cut her off.

"Hmm, let's go far away for sometime...away from the crowd." Trisha purred and Tia could hear the sound of moving bodies.

"Why?" asked Ron softly.

Trisha laughed again in a seductive way and said, "This is why..."

Tia's nails dug into her palms none too gently as she could hear the sound of a passionate kiss. She could feel the hot rush of blood across her face and sound of a loud crash booming in her ears. Her heart hammered as if it would burst. She could feel her heart break into a million pieces – as if a massive boulder had struck it inside out. Meanwhile her phone was buzzing insistently with Nysa refusing to stop calling.

She knew she'd be seen but she didn't pause to look at the startled glances of Ron and Trisha as she quickly rushed out. She muttered a muffled sorry while looking nowhere and ran as far as her legs could carry her.

She paused at the corridor to take Nysa's call that continued ringing.

"Hello, Nysa..." Her voice was breathless.

"Podgy, where are you?"

"I am at Nina's...tell me..." she was choking with emotion but she controlled her voice with great effort.

"You know what? I am out of ideas on which flavor of frosting to use on Uncle Sareen's cake. I..."

"Nysa...I...I'll call you later..." She quickly hung up lest Nysa makes out that something was wrong. She ran out into the garden before anyone could see the hot rush of tears scalding her cheeks.

It was late evening and Tia finally found a bench into which she almost crashed and gave into her tears. She cried her heart for some time when she felt the phone ringing again. It was Krystal this time who was dialing incessantly. It stopped after a while but her tears simply refused to stop as she kept wiping them off. The phone rang and it was Nysa again this time. Suddenly, someone grabbed the phone from her hand and she was shocked to see Ron at her side.

"Yes, Nysa, right time you called! Because your sister here is living a lie and it's breaking her apart! She is hiding what she really feels from the world and from me! But you know what happens when we go on killing our feelings, no matter what? When we try to force ourselves into behaving different? It breaks us in time till there is nothing left except unhappiness and heart break. We are fooling ourselves if we think we can lie to ourselves forever..."

Ron handed back her phone. "Talk to your sister, Tia!"

Tia clutched the phone and fell into Ron's arms.

"Tia!" He hugged her tightly as she cried her heart out. She shook profusely in his arms. It was as if she was letting go months of pain and agony with her tears.

Ron felt her warm body in his arms and caressed her back gently as if to rub the pain away. He pulled her even closer. She had become painfully thin and he felt as if her bones would almost crack. If only she would come to her senses and stop denying these feelings between them, he thought frustratingly. If only she would let go of all her fears and trust him for once. He could walk the earth for her. He hadn't felt so much love for anyone else in his life. It was absolute torture to be away from her. Trisha had been a distraction. He felt bad that he was using her to fill the emptiness inside and also to make Tia jealous. He had seen Tia going inside Nina's bedroom and let Trisha pull him into a passionate clinch just to make her jealous.

"Tia, will you stop fighting your feelings for once? Sweetheart, you know you are building up this barrier between us simply for something that you believe, which is not true at all." His voice was gentle and very soothing. "We love each other and that is the only truth we must face. Why don't you just forget whatever's happened as a bad dream and make our relationship work? You love me a lot and you can't deny it any more. I can feel it in every pore of your body...maybe with a little bit of professional counseling everything will be alright between us?"

"A friend of mine is a reputed psychologist who deals mostly with people trying to cope with the loss of their loved ones. In fact I had spoken to him once on the pretext of asking after a friend...he suggested that with a little bit of therapy and counseling, many easily come to terms with grief like this and live happy lives. We can have the same sweetheart. Why don't you just admit that you love me and give me a piece of your trust? I'll take care of everything – just trust me!"

It took some time for Tia's sobs to quieten down as she broke away and wiped her face with her shirt.

She tearfully looked at him as she said, "I do love you Ron...I do..." Her voice almost broke as she tried to get a hold of herself.

Her body shook as she tried to speak again through the sobs that kept breaking her sentences. She swallowed them painfully as she said, "I loved you when I first saw you in school, Ron...when you walked through the school corridors...when you helped me with my homework...I loved you then...and I...and I love you now...and I will always love you...one cannot forget their first love, can they?"

The pain and the hopelessness in her voice cut like a knife. Ron could feel his heart dive to his knees as he feared what was to come next.

"I will always love you, Ron..." she let her palm touch his cheek tenderly as she gulped another sob that threatened to spill out, "...but only *as a friend – a very good friend*. A friend who really cares for you...now and forever..."

She rubbed her nose and face again as Ron looked at her helplessly. He wanted to shake the life out of her but he restrained himself somehow.

"I just don't know what came over me, Ron..."

She tried to smile through her tears although it looked totally forced. "Krystal always teases me about being a tragedy queen and so did my sisters...called me a cry baby. I just can't help myself sometimes...feel so overwhelmed for the stupidest reasons and end up crying! So stupid of me really...I am really sorry...please don't mind, ok?" she said as she backed away slowly.

"Tia..."

"I think you should be going," she said. "See you later, huh?"

She turned away and ran her fingers dejectedly through her hair as she started to run. She turned once more before she hurried away and looked at him through her tears. "I'm sorry, huh?"

As she ran across the lawn, Ron could see her weary shoulders shaking with tears that still kept flowing down her cheeks. Ron didn't know who was more heartbroken between the two as he kept looking at her dejected figure slowly disappearing in the dark.

Chapter 26

"Wake up, Aunt Tia. Lola go school."

Tia felt soft chubby hands caressing her cheeks.

"Oh sweetheart, all ready to go to school? What's the time?"

Tia felt the sunlight making deep forays on her eyes and she rubbed them to bring herself fully awake.

Lola in all her cuteness was sitting beside her bed with her hands holding her chin and knees drawn up.

"Now Aunt Tia wants a cute kissy from her little princess..."

Lola raised her face to give a baby kiss on her cheeks and Tia hugged her lovely niece with all her heart. What purity these little ones had, she mused. One could feel so much tenderness simply by the feel of their soft skin, smell of their baby hair and every little expression on their face.

"Lola late to school, Tiala...Jaya waiting downstairs...you have breakfast and I go...okay?" she said in a motherly tone and Tia couldn't help smiling.

"Okay, honey. Have a great day!"

Lola ran as quickly as her little chubby legs could carry her not, stopping midway to give a backward glance and wave at her aunt from the doorway.

Tia quickly got up to shower and have a bath. After the party at Nina's on Saturday, Nysa had insisted on her coming to stay at their place for the weekend. Tia couldn't say no to Nysa's heavy persuasion, so she agreed. She planned to go home today as it was a Sunday and she had to do the laundry and some household chores before facing another hectic week ahead.

At least Jeff would be relieved that she left, thought Tia. Lately she sensed some kind of distance from his side. As if he didn't want her around the house too much...or even in their lives. Maybe he resented Nysa devoting too much time on her, especially with her being a drag lately. Or it might be because he was not happy that people were talking about her a lot. With her and Ron's relationship breaking off, many of their colleagues and acquaintances had noticed her wary aloofness. News spread fast and people were saying things like she was depressed and getting weird by the day. Maybe Jeff didn't like to hear any kind of stories related to his family. It embarrassed him socially and was bad for his image to hear that his sister-in-law had gone cuckoo. It felt really uncomfortable being at Nysa's house lately although Mrs Bailey, Jeff's mother, was always very sweet and affectionate towards her.

She went to check on Nysa and find out if she had breakfast before going downstairs. As soon as she neared Nysa's bedroom, however, she could hear angry voices filling the corridor.

"This is all getting too much, Jeff! She is getting on my nerves now..." said Nysa.

"Now be reasonable Nysa, you know it's all business..."

"Business! Don't give me that shit...my friends have seen you in some happening places doing romantic lunches, dinners and what not..."

"Your friends are crazy gossip mongers. They are only business luncheons or dinners and not romantic at all..."

"Business can be conducted in the office with people around and not in secret places. And my friends aren't gossip mongers. They are my childhood friends who have only my best interests at heart..."

"Yes, but they don't have any clue about how business is run and are pretty ignorant. You know this is all networking and additional props to make a business deal work. You are a business woman yourself, Nysa, you should know better than to listen to all this shit!"

"I don't trust Simi, Jeff."

"Nysa, this deal that Simi is working on can do wonders for our company...if we win it, of course. She knows a few of the influential politicians who have a great reach in some of the government projects proposed. The tenders are all at competitive prices and if she talks in our favour, we might win the tenders of some of the most lucrative projects here."

"She makes me insecure...just like I was insecure with Priya - and I was right! Wasn't I?"

"You were right!? You found out there was nothing between Priya and me, right Nysa?"

"Only because I didn't allow it and you know it..."

"It is only because I love you...and only you...you know that very well!"

"Yes? You have a great way of showing it don't you..." Nysa left the remaining unsaid as her voice broke into sobs which tugged at Tia's heart.

"Nysa...honey...how wrong you are...there is no one for me...just you and only you..." said Jeff in a cajoling voice. Their voices muffled and receded after some time.

Tia walked unhappily to the dining table.

"Dosa and chutney, Tia Ma'am," said Jaya. "Hope that's okay?"

"Thank you, Jaya. That would be absolutely lovely."

Tia bit into her breakfast but she felt nausea overwhelming her. She left it uneaten and had her tea instead.

"Ma'am why haven't you eaten anything...is the dosa not good?"

"No, Jaya. I am so not hungry. Dinner was a heavy affair last night and I am not hungry at all..." Tia apologized profusely.

"Please try to have a little, Ma'am. You have lost so much weight. Such a beautiful girl, I always say to my mother and sisters. All my sisters who have seen you agree too. Madam Nysa's sister is one of the prettiest girls they have seen they say..."

"Oh, Jaya! You know I am not. There are far prettier girls than me...but thank you for being so nice."

"Oh Ma'am, what a modest girl, you are! Even Mrs Bailey says that you are one of the prettiest and most charming girls she's ever met. And do you know what's the next best thing my family says about you? They say that you are very well-mannered and kind to everybody. Not many people are kind to helpers like us or bother to talk to us. But everyone working for Nysa ma'am agrees with me - Raju, Birju...they all say that very few people are friendly like Tia Ma'am."

"Aww...that's too many compliments for me to handle in one day..."

"Ron Sir is a truly lucky guy to have someone like you. There are so many beautiful girls in this city but only a few very nice ones. Ron Sir knows that for sure and that's why he did his best to win you. A diamond sparkles even in the dark..."

"Is it?" Tia smiled. Jaya didn't know that she and Ron had broken off and she didn't bother telling it to her. She will know in time, thought Tia dully.

"Thank you, Jaya. Even you have taken so much care of us from the time I knew you. And we are lucky to have you too."

Jaya blushed saying, "Oh Tia Ma'am, what are you saying..."

Jaya went happily back to her cooking and Tia left her to find her sister. But then she had second thoughts and went to pack her stuff instead. After leaving a message with Jaya, she drove home, her mind occupied with thoughts of Jeff and Nysa.

The words of Sunita, Tasha's accountant, rang in her ears. Jeff was very ambitious and he was very good at making money. In fact he had an amazing knack for it. But she wished it never compromised with

225

their family happiness.

Krystal rang up asking if she would drop in the evening and Tia readily agreed. At least she could talk it out with Krystal and find some relief.

After being busy the whole day dusting her rooms, mopping, and doing the laundry, she baked a cake for Krystal and herself. It was 4 o'clock by the time she made some *pakoras** and the doorbell rang.

"Exhausting weekend if ever there was one," said Krystal as she sank tiredly on the sofa.

"Why? What's been happening?"

"I hardly slept after Nina's birthday party. My niece Britney had a fall, so had to take her a couple of times to the hospital. Then Mom wanted me to help her shop for the upcoming housewarming party at her sister's place. And today I had to call the plumber to repair some of the damages caused by rains. Gosh I don't think I can make it through the week." Krystal groaned as she sipped her tea.

"Krystal, I am again having these bad thoughts about someone close to me and I feel so guilty about it..."

"Bad thoughts...what do you mean?"

"Actually I heard Jeff and Nysa quarrelling this morning. It wasn't nice..."

"What were they quarrelling about?"

"Simi."

"Simi? Simi Panag, you mean.

"Yes!"

"Really! What were they fighting about?"

"It seems Jeff's been seeing a lot of Simi at...say special places and Nysa isn't too happy about it."

"I see," said Krystal as she nodded her head slowly. "So they have been seen by few others too besides us. Sounds suspicious. What did Jeff say to that?"

"Jeff kind of pledges his love for Nysa, if that's what you are asking..."

"What do you feel about this, Tia?"

"I don't know what to think, Krystal." Tia rubbed her fingers on her forehead thoughtfully. "You know I haven't told you before but even Dhruv kind of points at Jeff regarding Rianna's death..."

"Really? What did he say?"

"It seems there was a lot of cash flowing for Jeff after her death – the cars, the houses and so on..."

"Hmm..."

"I kind of blocked it off for some time what with harbouring suspicions against Ron and Dhruv, I really wanted to take my mind off this and didn't want to suspect somebody anew. Maybe I was going crazy or something, and then..."

"What then?" Krystal asked as she lost Tia in the silence.

"Remember that day when we went for coffee with Mira Dorjee, Tasha and her accountant, Sunita?

"Yes, very well. You had connected with your mom."

"Yes, connection with my mom again kind of helped me block whatever I was thinking about Jeff."

"Ok..."

"Actually that day at the restaurant while we were having coffee I noticed Jeff and Simi too sitting a few tables away from us."

"Oh yes, I remember! Though I noticed them only later."

"Sunita noticed them too."

"Sunita? Tasha's accountant? She knows Jeff?"

"Yes! It seems she has heard a lot about Jeff from the grapevine."

"Heard what?"

"Just that he is doing very well for himself – upcoming entrepreneur and all that..."

"I see..."

"But she mentions the same thing as Dhruv."

"What?"

"She kind of suggests that Jeff was lucky because his partner who was his girlfriend died an untimely death and there was one deal which they won. And then all the funds were accounted in his name. It seems his girlfriend, although she didn't suggest any name, was the brain behind their business and all their deals."

"She said that, did she?" said Krystal slowly, her eyes and mouth stupefied in wonder. She sighed as she folded her legs under her knees and said, "All this is getting so mysterious. I mean it's been like five years since Rianna died but somehow the mystery is unfolding again and gets more baffling by the day."

"I feel that too, Krystal! I mean as if Rianna wants her death to be resolved and she will not be at peace till it is done so. So she keeps showing me these dreams and nudging me to get it solved. Am I wrong, Krystal?"

"No, Kitkat. I'd feel the same way too, I guess. But I don't know how to help you..." said Krystal helplessly.

"You don't think I am going mad or something..."

"Of course not! But what can we do, tell me?...I mean the police never found out anything. They indicated a suicide, didn't they?"

"Rianna can never commit suicide, Krystal!" said Tia, her voice agonized.

"Well, yes...then if it's...I mean..."

"You mean to say murder, right?"

"Yes...."

"I really don't know...and I won't rest till I get to the bottom of this!"

"Do that if you must, Tia, till you get all the answers. But the question is what do we do and how to go about it? And these dreams about Ron..."

"I know, Poppins! What if Ron is not responsible? And what if he is? At least till my mind finds an answer, it will not let me rest Krystal..."

"So, why don't we talk to Mira about this, Tia. Being a psychic who connects to spirits she might be able to shed some light on this?"

"Yes, I thought about this the other day. How uncanny that you think so too!"

"And Jeff? He is your brother-in-law, isn't he? If Nysa gets some scent about this, then God save you!"

Krystal shuddered as she left the remaining unsaid.

"I already feel so guilty even thinking about Jeff like this. I don't know how to go about it Krys. And what if...if...it's true?" Her voice was a whisper and her look panic stricken. Krystal looked equally astounded.

"I don't want it to be Ron or Jeff...I'd die in fact..."

Tia rested her head on her drawn-up knees. She closed her eyes as if to block the scenes that agonized her mind. "And Dhruv, he has always been so nice to me. Poor guy. I have always felt this strange empathy for him. Hasn't he been so unlucky in his life? Losing Rianna right in front of his eyes to Jeff when she was alive and later to death. He looks so alone at times..."

"Let's not even go there, Tia. We don't even know if it's murder whatsoever. Let's take things one at a time..."

"Yes, you are right Krystal," she said slowly. They both sat in silence as the sunrays receded far into the corners. None of them thought of switching on the lights as they both got lost in their own mental plane.

"These love affairs gone awry with the added daggers of financial and legal issues are becoming so common these days," said Krystal, after a while. "Why, the other day I was reading in the papers about an actress who, after having a tempestuous relationship with a business tycoon, was charging the tycoon for harassment. It seemed the actress charged the tycoon for online harassment because he sent her innumerable mails every day. But then again, the tycoon says it wasn't his email id but some impersonator's. On the other hand, he now says that it was the actress who was bombarding him with around 50 mails per day. So there are legal notices issued on both sides..."

Krystal stopped midway when she saw Tia looking jolted about something, her brows flying almost to her hairline. "Hey Krystal, why don't I check the emails between Rianna and Jeff during her last couple of days. I am sure we can find something there?"

Krystal looked at her thoughtfully. "Hmmm...that's not a bad idea, Tia. Maybe, some light will be shed on the matter..."

Pakoras - Pakoras are fried, crisp snacks made from different veggies. They are basically Indian fritters made with gram flour.

Chapter 27

"Let me talk to Regan first," said Tia and dialed his number.

"Tia, what's up?" asked Regan.

"Regan, after Rianna died, did the police team check her emails and online stuff in case it shed some light on her death?" asked Tia.

"Yes, the police usually do it if the need arises and in Rianna's case too we followed every possible lead we could find."

"Regan, I don't know how to put this...but...but there is a nagging suspicion in my mind that's been troubling me for..."

"What is it, Tia? Cut to the chase, dear...you know you can tell me everything. Go ahead." His voice sounded encouraging.

"I wanted to know if...if Jeff amassed a very large amount of fortune after Rianna's death?"

Regan was silent for some time. "Yes, he did..."

Tia gulped as she forced herself to ask the next question, "So did the police harbour any suspicions about his motives to be the cause of Rianna's death."

"I don't believe this Tia..." Regan said in a quiet voice. "You want to get your sister and brother-in-law in trouble now!?"

"I..." Tia's voice shook as she didn't know how to answer Regan. "I need to know, Regan..."

"You know what all this will lead to, don't you!?" said Regan, his voice aghast. "Nothing but a lot of pain and misery! It will cause severe heartbreak in your family and break a lot of relationships – and for what? All because of some psychic intuition which might be a piece of red herring for all we know." Regan sighed painfully. "Once broken, nothing can be easily repaired, do you realize that? So please let sleeping dogs lie, Tia...I beg you as one of your true well wishers. Rianna is no more but let the others move on. Don't do this Tia...just don't do this..."

There was silence as tears flowed unbidden down Tia's cheeks.

"I am doing my best, Tia, amidst all my work. This will take time...it's already a dead case but I am trying my best. And I don't want you to go behind something that is just a figment of your imagination. Accept things as they are till I find some evidence that can convince you finally and put your mind to rest. But for that I need some time..."

Krystal took the phone from Tia and spoke to her cousin, her voice firm. "Regan, she just wants some answers so that she can find some closure to Rianna's death. Admit it – there has been some missing gaps in the case. You know that very well. The police as a whole failed to solve this case and it was hushed up as a suicide when we all know that Rianna is not the kind to commit suicide. Cold cases are opened all the time. So why are you being so hard on her?"

"I just don't want their family to get hurt, Krystal. Last time we found nothing. What if this again leads to nothing but on the other hand cause undue anguish for everyone."

"But we need to find the truth and put the matter at rest once and for all, don't we? We need to remove the 'if'."

Regan sighed. "Ok, I am there to help but don't say I didn't warn you."

"Ok, Regan, we will be as discrete as possible...no one needs to know," said Krystal earnestly. She was glad her cousin had relented a little. All through their lives Regan had always been an awesome brother, more of a friend, in fact.

"Ok, give it to Tia now..."

"Tia?"

"Yes, Regan?" said Tia in a quiet voice. Her emotions were all shattered after the way Regan had reprimanded her.

"We checked her emails, her social media accounts and didn't find anything out of the ordinary. The official mails between her and Jeff smelt of no fraud whatsoever. The bank accounts on both sides were in perfect order – all credible and legally operated. Their's was a partnership firm and by that rule Jeff inherits everything in case the partner deceased. Especially since there was no will whatsoever. So no fraud or foul play there."

"Ok."

"We returned her computer and personal belongings to Dev. You can check with him if you want to go through her mails. I can't give you any information, though, regarding her mail accounts as that will be a breach of ethics," he said gravely. There was an underlying suggestion in Regan's voice as he said, "Most of the internet browsers store email id information, as you may very well know – being an advanced programmer yourself."

"Thanks, Regan," said Tia in a solemn voice.

"Be careful. These cold cases once brought up can cause severe damage and discord between families and friends."

"Alright, Regan."

Once Tia kept the phone, she hugged Krystal for a while. Krystal petted her back in understanding.

"Thanks, Krystal. Don't know what I'd do without you."

"Don't say that. Rianna was more my sister than friend. We owe her bereft soul some sense of justice if that's what she's looking for...so what do you plan to do now?"

"I think I will go upstairs to Dev's apartment first thing in the morning and check up Rianna's stuff."

Dev was on a business trip but both Maya and Alisha were at home when Tia visited the next morning. If Maya was surprised to hear Tia's request to check on Rianna's computer, she managed to hide it well.

"We have kept most of Rianna's stuff in the old study," said Maya as Tia followed her to the study. "Alisha, can you help out your aunt? I have lots of cooking to do today. Some guests are coming for dinner tonight."

"Yes, Mummy," said Alisha, as she flopped on the sofa with her tablet.

Before Maya left, however, she stopped at the doorway and asked curiously, "Have you told Dev about this?"

"About what?"

"Checking on Rianna's stuff? He somehow doesn't like anyone tampering with her things."

"Maya, I am not tampering with anything, you know. I just want to check if there are any old pictures of my sister who has passed away. Anything of her that I can preserve – to keep her memory alive. Is that too much of a hassle?"

Maya's lips tightened and it was an awkward moment. "I didn't mean that Tia...anyway, never mind...I've got to go. Alisha, you have to go for your piano practice after lunch. So come out in an hour, ok?"

"Mom and Dad gets really tense when people come around snooping for Aunt Rianna's stuff," said Alisha almost apologetically to her aunt.

Tia smiled at her niece in understanding. Hadn't she just turned thirteen a week ago? But she already sounded so mature, Tia thought. How fast they grew!

"Hmm? Meaning? Who else came snooping around?" she asked.

"Mainly the police and the detectives, of course. Rounds and rounds of endless questioning, I remember. And some from the press too!"

"You do? You were quite young, na, honey?"

"Yes, some of it. It did go on for some time – the investigation, didn't it? Mom and Dad were really tired of it all. What are you going to check now?" Alisha asked curiously.

"Just a few things like her pictures or maybe anything special she wanted during her last days. Something like that maybe..." Tia smiled.

"Alright," she said.

"How come school's closed today?" asked Tia.

"The seniors are having a seminar and students from many schools all over the city are coming over to participate. So all the classes from primary to middle grade have been called off."

Alisha went back to reading a book on her kindle while Tia checked the hard disk to see if she could find anything involving Rianna's firm. There were mostly projects specs, reports and invoices in most of them as well as some design proposals. She opened the browser to check her Jino mail. The email id flashed as soon as she clicked on the text box but it didn't have a password stored. She tried opening Rianna's Facebook account and here too just the email id suggestion appeared; the password wasn't stored.

Regan had given her a hint on how to find Rianna's email information and left the rest of the work to her, knowing that she had a background in programming. As the passwords were not saved, she had to hack her way in through Rianna's mailbox. Immediately a name flashed in her mind – Karthigeyan!

He was one of her best buddies in college and a whizkid in programming. He was crazy about hacking and in fact done a project on it in their final year. She searched her Facebook friend list to contact him and sent him a message. It had been four years since she had gotten in touch with him. She hoped he would not be pissed off with her and answer her mail. How selfish we humans are, she thought in retrospect. Her heart skipped a beat when she saw he had answered immediately. Once he sent his number she immediately went to the other part of the house to talk to him. She didn't want Alisha to find out that she was getting into hacking and all.

"Hey Tia, how are you friend...long time!"

"I know Karthik...it's been a long time!" she answered in an eager voice. They easily got into talking about old times. Tia was excited when she learnt that he worked as a white hat hacker in a law enforcement agency.

"Karthik, I need your help regarding a private investigation that I am doing. In fact, that was the main reason I got in touch with you today," she said urgently.

Karthigeyan went silent for a moment and quietly asked, "What is it, Tia? Tell me."

"Karthik, you remember, I had an older sister who died under mysterious circumstances. The police had closed down her case as suicide..."

"Yes, I remember that time in your life. Most of us didn't know how to help you, although we really felt a lot for you."

"Karthik, I strongly feel that it's not suicide but there is something more than that. Although it's a closed case now, I want to get into my sister's email account to check her mails during her last days...," she said in a painful voice.

Karthigeyan sighed at that.

"I know, Karthik, it's wrong of me to contact you for this. Downright selfish of me in fact and I know it's against your ethics to hack into a personal account. But I am so desperate now...I don't know how else to go about..."

"Okay, Tia," said Karthik slowly. "I understand what you are going through. And of course that's not selfish. I remember that time in my life when you were the only one who stood for me..."

Tia's mind went back to the time when Karthik and another guy were accused by one of his rivals of hacking into one of the university computers to access the test paper database. It was a very difficult time for him, she remembered. It was only Tia who had stood by him and provided alibi. All the others had retracted as they feared getting into any kind of mess with the police and thereby inviting a black spot in their academic careers.

"Though this is against my professional ethics, I am giving it to you not only because I know you very well but also because the account is that of a deceased person. That too she is your sister. So not much harm in this as it is already a cold case. We do help people sometimes once they have submitted a death certificate and power of attorney documents."

"I am sorry for putting you through this, Karthik..."

"No, Tia. Actually it's me who can't thank you enough for the support and faith you showed me during a difficult time. Give me all her email ids as well as the account ids of the websites she used. It will only take me a couple of minutes."

Once Karthik told her the passwords, she opened Rianna's Jino mail box and browsed through her mails especially the ones with Jeff. There was nothing much in the mails except for discussions about their office projects. There wasn't much discussion about their financial dealings either. She checked Rianna's Facebook account, but here too there wasn't much except for pictures with Jeff or her friends. There were some with Dhruv too. He looked very young and happy in his pictures with Rianna unlike the morose and haggard looks he carried now.

It was five o'clock in the evening and she was still going through the mails. Alisha had returned from her piano classes and made some tea for her. She then sat down cozily on the sofa with a book in hand.

"Aunt Tia, have you finished?"

"No, dear. Still going through..."

"Why don't you stay over for the night? Long time since we had a sleepover..."

"You are always busy with your school, piano classes, projects and tennis. Where is the time for your old aunt here?"

"Of course you are not old..." She giggled. "You are one of my prettiest aunts with the most handsome boyfriend ever on planet earth. I can't believe you let Uncle Ron go!"

Tia blinked at her niece's outburst.

"I mean he is the dishiest guy I have ever laid my eyes on! I couldn't believe when mom said you had broken up..."

"This kind of things happen, Alisha. Breakups are a part of adult life. You will understand once you grow up...." Tia smiled at her niece sadly.

"Oh, Aunt Tia! If only you had consulted with me once before taking such a drastic step..."

"I know...," said Tia, amused and laughing.

"Please say you will stay tonight! We will talk till we drop and have some midnight snack and coffee too?"

"Oh, alright!" said Tia with adoration shining in her eyes for her niece.

Maya came in once and Alisha excitedly said, "Mom, Aunt Tia is staying with me tonight for a sleepover..."

"Oh, good for you. Stay over then, Tia. I am cooking a chicken dish today. It's one of Alisha's special dishes. Are you done with your work by the way?"

"Yes, almost," said Tia.

Once Maya left, Alisha said in a wistful voice, "I miss Aunt Rianna a lot. I had sleepovers with her all the time when Mom and Dad went out. She told me such awesome bedtime stories and we often used to hang out in the malls and parks. How I miss her...."

"We all do, honey," said Tia softly.

"You know sometimes I still dream about her, especially about our times together..."

"You do?" asked Tia.

"Yes. But in the dream when she leaves me she always looks sad...and it's as if she wants to tell me something."

"Really?"

"Yes, but she changes her mind and says, 'Never mind honey, you're too young...'"

"Oh!" Tia could feel shivers down her spine but she schooled her face to look calm.

"Yes, Aunt Tia."

"Maybe you miss her...so in the dream she looks as if she is sad too. Your feelings for her reflect in the dreams that way I guess..."

"Yes, but whenever I dream about her, this is how it ends. Usually dreams change and you see a different one every day. But with Aunt Rianna, the dream somehow ends this way – only."

"You mean she wants to tell you something but she changes her mind and goes away..."

Alisha nodded her head vigorously to that.

"But anyway her dreams come less and less to me now. It is no longer frequent as it used to be. Do you believe in ghost, Aunt Tia?"

"No, not so much." Tia lied as she didn't want to freak her little niece out.

"You know, when you were not around, Mom used to open the windows and doors of your apartment once a week – meaning downstairs. She used to do the dusting too so that it remained fresh and useable any time."

"Okay..."

"So, I used to go downstairs and play often. Especially when my friends came, Mom used to send us downstairs so that we didn't get in her way. And I often felt Aunt Rianna standing there and watching us."

"Really?"

"Yes. Not like she was really standing there but just a sudden image of her quickly passing by or her shadow – if you get what I mean. Even the familiar perfume of her which I remember so well would come in a sudden whiff..."

"I see...," said Tia casually, trying to hide her surprise.

"And sometimes the bathroom tap would open for no reason. And if for some reason I left my dolls or a toy or any other storybook of mine in the living room downstairs, then next day I would have to search for it for ages. And then I'd find it in some other room. For example, the bedroom that you use now."

"Oh!"

"It freaked out my friends and they didn't want to go downstairs anymore."

"Did any of this happen upstairs?"

"Not at all. Except for her dreams, I never experienced any of this upstairs."

"Did you tell any of this to your Mom and Dad?"

"I did several times but they felt that it was my imagination since I was attached to Aunt Rianna so much."

"Why didn't you tell me any of this before?"

"Mom asked me not to talk about this anymore. And after I stopped coming downstairs I sort of forgot about it. Did you ever feel her presence down there? I mean now that you have lived there for the past four years?" Alisha asked, her voice filled with curiosity.

"Nothing like that...you know I miss her too. So I feel her very strongly at times. Nothing like a ghost or something," said Tia, feeling bad for lying to her niece. But she didn't want to upset her by telling her the truth and unnecessarily scare her about ghosts and similar paranormal stuff.

"I heard Mom and Dad once talking about the terrible nightmares you were having. I think Mom kind of fears that the ground floor is haunted by Aunt Rianna..."

"What?!"

"Yes, Mom wanted to do some ghost cleansing by calling paranormal investigators or what they call...yes, the ghost hunters. You know the kind who are called for chasing off ghosts or deceased spirits who haunt a house."

"Oh!"

"Yes. But Dad brushed it off as superstition. I overheard them once when they didn't realize I was around."

"Maybe he's right and it wasn't true after all since you never felt anything here except for the times you played downstairs. If you actually come to think of it, that's only natural that you'd feel her downstairs as she lived there and her memories feel almost real there."

"Maybe...," said Alisha as she turned a page of her book.

Tia's mind was reeling with whatever Alisha was saying. She was not far from the truth as she felt the same sometimes. Lately her presence had got stronger especially after Ron had come into her life.

"There is nothing here," murmured Tia. She felt really tired and abruptly shut the computer down.

"Oh, were you looking for something specific?" asked Alisha.

"No...nothing like that. I just wanted to check some specific mails of hers...oh never mind!" said Tia with a sigh.

"Aunt Tia, there is one more place you might like to check if mails are what you are looking for specifically."

"Where is that?"

"Aunt Rianna also had a laptop. She often brought it here and let me use it sometimes. She had left it in my room. Dad totally forgot to hand it over to the police. Once after the police left, I remembered and told dad about it. Dad wanted to hand it over but Uncle Jeff who was also here at that time, said he would hand it over instead. He had some software packages and data he wanted to retrieve before handing it over to the police."

"Where's that laptop, can I check it?"

"Oh, it's with Uncle Jeff. From what I know, Uncle Jeff told Dad that it stopped working because of some faulty hardware...and so he didn't bother to hand it over to the police later. I lost some of my poems too that I had saved there."

"Oh...so it's with Uncle Jeff now?"

"Yes. I saw it in Aunt Nysa's study the other day. I remembered it because it's a beautiful red one, on which I learnt a lot of stuff about computers. It was almost like my first computer!"

"Okay," said Tia, her eyes watchful as she nodded slowly.

That night Tia felt restless with all the things that her niece had told her. She looked at her niece's figure shifting slightly in her sleep. She was thrilled that Tia had decided to spend the night with her and spoke excitedly all about her life in school and her friends. Tia would get distracted sometimes to which her niece would pout. So Tia tried her best to keep her mind on what Alisha had to say. She was relieved when Alisha finally went to sleep and she covered her thin body with a quilt.

She went to the kitchen for a cup of coffee. Alisha was right about feeling Rianna downstairs a couple of times. It wasn't so strong before but lately after her recent accident, she felt her presence more and more strongly. It was as if Rianna was trying to get in touch with her desperately — in fact tell her something. She didn't know if anyone would believe her if she said that.

Krystal was fascinated to hear all about the stuff that Alisha had told her. Fortunately, there was one person with whom she could discuss freely without being judged, thought Tia. And that was Krystal. Everyone else thought she was crazy or was in need of some help. Tomorrow she had to go to Nysa's place, and find Rianna's laptop. She might have to skip office too if required, she decided.

Chapter 28

"Hey Nysa, can I come over to your place today. I am just not in the mood to attend office. Thought would spend the day at your place?"

"Are you okay?" asked her sister in concern.

"Yes, I am. Just not in the mood and want some company. Maybe spend some time with Lola."

"Yes, come over. Need you ask! Lola will be excited. She won't let you leave easily though, be warned." Nysa laughed in amusement.

"I don't mind." Tia smiled at the thought of her little niece.

"I will be out for the day. But will meet you in the evening. No need to leave tonight. In fact why don't you stay for two more days? Today there is a small dinner party and I will be slightly busy. So we can catch up on all the gossip and news tomorrow night?" Nysa suggested. "I hardly get to meet you these days..."

"Okay, maybe I will."

"Oh by the way, Jeff called on Ryan and Ron for dinner tomorrow night. He wants to have some discussion regarding an upcoming project. Ryan will be involved in this project and Jeff wanted some financial advice from Ron too. Is that okay with you?"

"Yes, no problem," said Tia in a small voice although her heart beat very hard.

"I will ask Nina to come along so that you can have some company."

By the time Tia reached Nysa's house, Lola was all set and ready to go with Jaya to her playschool. She was excited to know her aunt would be spending the night at her place.

Tia met Jeff at the dining table buttering his toast.

"Good morning, Jeff," she said. Maybe it was her guilty conscience that made her voice sound very awkward and uneasy.

Jeff who looked preoccupied gave her a clipped hello and went back to reading his newspaper.

"Hello Podgy," said Nysa as she breezily came into the dining room and waved her to sit down.

"Have some breakfast," she said as she quickly gulped her coffee.

"No, that's okay. I already had some at home. Let me keep my overnight bag in the guest room. I'll be back."

"Alright," said Nysa in a peppy voice. Jeff was still with his paper and didn't look up.

Tia kept her stuff in Nysa's guestroom and changed herself into tracks and tee.

"Podgy, I have to get going. Make yourself comfortable and ask Jaya to make some snacks for you – whatever you feel like having..."

"Alright, I'll do that," assured Tia as she smiled at her sister.

"Hope you're feeling okay? I have never seen you take leave like this in the middle of a working week..." Her sister's eyes were full of concern.

"I am fine, Nysa...stop worrying so much."

"I can't help worrying, Podgy. After losing Mom, Dad and Rianna, I couldn't take it if anything happened to you. You are the only one I am closest to and the only one with whom I can be myself. As I get older, I realize how much I need you with every passing day."

Tia felt a gulp in her throat and a great prick in her conscience at what she was planning to do. She smiled forcefully as she said, "Now that surely will make your very possessive and loving husband jealous..."

"Oh, Jeff!" Nysa laughed and winked. "Husbands can never take the place of sisters – however hard they may try..." She walked away looking lighter and happier, the shine back in her eyes.

Tia sat heavily on the armchair once Nysa had left. What was she doing to her sister and her life with all this searching and investigating, she thought. It was as if she had to choose between her two sisters. Was redemption for Rianna more important or Nysa's happiness that really mattered? Rianna was no more in this world anyway. It was Nysa who had to live through this whole life with whatever outcome that came of her search. And who knew what really went on in the afterlife. It might not exist for all she knew.

But what if Jeff was *really* guilty of Rianna's death. Then was it okay for Nysa to live with a man like that? Wasn't she living a lie, a voice rang in her ears. What if Jeff caused her sister harm too some day if he had a ruthless streak like this? Wasn't it her duty to protect her sister? And what if Jeff was not guilty at all? Then one more suspect would be eliminated and she would reach closer to the truth, wouldn't she?

She had to do this not only for herself but also for her sister's happiness as well as her niece Lola's too whom she loved with all her heart. Her resolve got stronger as the future loomed ahead like a dark hole in front of her. She had to go through that dark hole in order to find the light of redemption for all of them. She then remembered about the study room and dialed her sister's number.

"Nysa?"

"Yes, Podgy."

"I am sorry to disturb you at your office, but I needed the keys to your study. I want to check on some programming books as well as work on your computer. My laptop is really giving me huge problems."

"Alright, no problems. Use it. The keys are with Mummy, though. Can you take it from her?"

"Alright. Thanks!"

Tia got the keys from Mrs Bailey and went to Nysa's study. It was beautifully decorated in classic style with natural colours, elegant fabrics, floral and vegetable prints. There were lovely paintings everywhere and a view overlooking the garden.

Tia looked for Rianna's laptop in the shelves, cabinet drawers and cupboards. She finally found it in one of the lower shelves.

Her happiness was short lived when she found that the battery was dead. Luckily, she found the power chord in an adjacent drawer and it powered on smoothly with a light humming noise. Rianna's face flashed up on the screen and she felt almost taken aback at how real it felt. Her smile lighted her eyes and it looked almost encouraging as if to say, "You're on the right track, Podgy."

She browsed around the files and folders of the hard disk to see if she could find anything out of ordinary. There was an official folder which mostly contained their project specs, invoices and other payments. She opened up the internet browser, Google Chrome, which straight away went to Jino mail asking for a user id and password. She clicked on the text box to see if Rianna used any other email ids besides the one she had used on her desktop.

But apart from the accounts *rianna_arya23@jino.com* and *jeffbailey01@jino.com,* there were no other suggestions. She searched for other mail programs in the laptop and found that Rianna also used Infosoft Mailchat, an instant messaging app.

When she opened the program, it promptly asked the password for *rianna_arya23@infosoft.com.* She tried Rianna's Jino password in the password box but it didn't go through.

"Shucks!" she exclaimed. She didn't want to trouble Karthigeyan again. She tried keying in Rianna's Facebook password in the text box this time and luckily it went through!

She checked through the app's chat history and found it to be mostly about official discussions regarding projects. On the left, she saw that Rianna had neatly organized her contacts in different categories. There was a contact list which comprised her clients, while the 'Favourites' section listed the contact ids of Dhruv and Jeff. Dhruv's chat history were mostly about instructions for the design of websites and other similar works. Rianna's chat history with Jeff were mostly about their plans for future as well as their work. Some of them were intimate and romantic too. Tia couldn't help feeling awkward knowing that Jeff was Nysa's husband now. Jaya came to call her a couple of times and in the end she brought her lunch tray to the study. It was evening and she was not even half-way through the chat history. Till now, nothing felt suspicious or out of the ordinary.

"Hey, what's up? Jaya tells me you have been busy all day," asked Nysa curiously, when Tia went down to meet her.

"Yes...thought of working from home." She waved her hand vaguely.

"Okay, I will be going for the dinner party tonight. See you tomorrow at breakfast," Nysa said.

Tia stayed up late but could only finish checking half of the Infosoft chat history. The next morning she woke up early and went out for a jog. She saw Ashok Goyal, the owner of a small nearby tea and snacks outlet, standing at the park gate. It was a long time since she had seen him and she went up to greet him. She had known him from childhood when she used to come with her father or sisters.

"Hello, Uncle Ashok!" she said to the bearded man almost in his sixties.

Ashok looked shocked when he saw Tia, but soon recovered.

"It is little Tia, isn't it?"

"Yes, Uncle Ashok, how are you?"

"I am good, dear, I'm good. You look so grown up and almost like...like Rianna. I was shocked for a moment as I thought it was her in front of me!"

"Oh, is it?" she said with a quiet smile.

"You look more like her every day you know," he said, amazed. "Her smile, her eyes..."

They started talking about old times and Ashok asked after her family.

"Your dad, I miss him so much. What a great man, yet so humble! He never made any distinction although I came from a humble background. We had some long conversations."

"Yes, I know. Dad was always so down-to-earth and easy going... hardly any people like him these days..."

"Very true," he agreed in an effusive tone, "and Rianna... what a gentle soul she was! What a tragedy it is that she died so young..."

"Yes, we all miss her a lot."

"I remember the last time she came here..." he said, "it was with Jeff actually..."

He looked almost embarrassed to say that.

"It's okay, Uncle Ashok," she said dryly. "They were engaged at one time...so it's okay to mention that..."

"But I felt bad that the last time I saw her, she was in a depressed mood. That was the only time I saw her so dispirited. She had always been so full of life and cheerful, wherever she went. And that's how I would always like to remember her as. Maybe that particular day was not her day...some trouble most probably between her and Jeff – they were almost...almost in a fight..."

"Is it?" she asked curiously. She felt she should know more, somehow. "What kind of fight?"

"I don't know if I should say this...it was a long time ago..."

"No, tell me Uncle Ashok. It's okay. Every memory of Rianna is very important to me because that is all I have of her now."

"Ok. It was the day of *Janmasthami** festival and everyone was in a

249

celebratory mood. My small shop was busy with people coming and going all the time and so I was happy too. But Rianna was the only one in a morose mood. She and Jeff were fighting about something, I noticed. Everyone in the shop started staring at them. I didn't want Rianna to do something embarrassing in front of everyone because she was like my daughter and I had known her since she was a toddler. Before I could get to her side and stop her, she spilled all her coffee over Jeff's face. Poor Jeff was humiliated of course and I remember he shouted at Rianna, 'You will regret this!'"

Ashok was silent for a moment. "They both walked off angrily, but I felt sad that the last time I saw Rianna it had ended this way. Of course, Jeff must have been unusually upset because I have always known him to be a quite cool and level-headed guy."

Uncle Ashok's words rang in her ears as she resumed her search through Rianna's laptop. Finally it was evening and she was about to give up when she found a chat conversation regarding a huge financial profit that had just come their way. Rianna and Jeff seemed to disagree on the sharing of profits of the project. There were a series of conversations regarding this but then Tia suddenly noticed the time on the right hand corner of the laptop. She realized that it was time for Nysa to walk in any minute. She hastily unhooked the laptop and took it to her bedroom. And as soon as she placed the laptop on the bedside desk there was a knock on her door. She quickly hid it and went to answer the door.

"Get dressed, Tia," said Nysa, hooking a diamond stud in her ear. "We are expecting our guests any moment. And Nina can't make it. So it's only Ron and Ryan."

"Then why do I need to be there," said Tia in a bored voice. "It will be mostly business talk, after all."

"Gosh! Say hi to Ron and Ryan if not anything else. I need some help in the kitchen too as Jaya needs to leave now for some puja function at her mom's place."

"Alright..." Tia forced a smile at her sister. She didn't even want to see

Ron tonight and couldn't wait to delve into the remaining chat history. She was restless to find out more.

Once she showered and dressed up, she walked into the living room. She caught Ryan's eyes first as Ron and Jeff were sitting with their backs towards her. Ryan quickly got up to greet her effusively and gave her a high five. After muttering a quick hello at Ron and Jeff, she scurried to the kitchen. She could hardly meet Ron's eyes but felt his cold stare boring her back.

"Tia, I am almost done here. Just frying some cheese balls for starters. Can you serve the cocktails, please?"

"Nysa, let me cook the starters, please. You can go and serve the drinks. I am really not in the mood to face Ron's prying eyes...," she said in a sullen voice.

Nysa looked surprised. Tia usually never said no to anything she requested and did her best to please everybody no matter how bad she felt inside. By nature it was always difficult for her to say no to anybody. She immediately understood how difficult it must have been for her to face Ron in spite of the long gap after their break up. However she couldn't resist herself from teasing, "Still flirts with you, does he?"

Tia didn't say anything to that and Nysa left the kitchen quietly.

When Tia entered the living room with snacks, they were busy conversing on some projects that they wanted to soon undertake.

"Nysa, I will join you guys for dinner later," she spoke softly in Nysa's ears. "I am really bored."

"Alright." Nysa nodded distractedly as she too was heavily involved in the discussion. Tia couldn't resist a sideways glance at Ron who seemed to be looking equally bored too. But before she could look away, her eyes locked with him. He raised his left eyebrow slightly and Tia looked away, flushed at being caught.

She went back to her bedroom and opened the laptop to check the chat history. She tried to find out more about the project which had brought a huge profit to both Rianna and Jeff. It was an overseas project and Jeff was excited that they would be minting millions out of it. Rianna, however, wanted to allot twenty per cent of their profits from both their shares to Dhruv who had worked his butt off on this project.

But Jeff wasn't too happy about it. He didn't trust Dhruv and he warned Rianna that he was trying to play with her affections to further his own career ends. He was just an employee and hadn't done anything to win their trust as an employee after all. There were other members who had worked equally hard on this project as well, so why play favouritism, Jeff reasoned.

But the consequent correspondence looked like Rianna wasn't happy with Jeff's attitude regarding this. There was a final chat conversation from Rianna in which she laid her foot down stating that she would be allotting forty per cent of profits to Dhruv whether he liked it or not. Jeff seemed to be livid with rage as his final reply accused her of utter foolishness saying she had no clue as to how a business was run.

Tia's heart was heavy by the time she finished reading the whole chat history. It was late, almost eleven pm. She wondered if the guests had left. But she was too tense to think about them as she paced around the room restlessly. Finally, she made a quick call to Krystal, instead.

"Hello."

"Krys..." Tia pulled in her breath, her heart beating fast, yet not knowing how to bring the words on her lips.

"What's up, Tia?" asked Krystal slowly, sensing her hesitation.

"I...I found one of Rianna's laptop in Nysa's study..." She gulped and paused to get some fresh air. "Actually it was our Alisha who led me on this trail."

"What did she say?"

"It seemed Rianna had a personal laptop which she had left at Alisha's when she had spent the night at their place. Dev wanted to hand it over to the police later but Jeff volunteered instead."

"Okay..."

"Jeff said that he had some software packages and data to retrieve before handing it over to the police. But later, since it had some faulty hardware problem, Jeff never bothered to hand it over is what Alisha told me. So it never reached the police somehow..."

"Oh...and you found it there..."

"Yes, Alisha remembered seeing it again in Nysa's study. So I looked for it and found it easily. I was looking through the chat history of the messaging app Rianna used and found a lot of their private stuff, of course. Then there was this one big project that Rianna had worked for a client. I looked for the client information on the net. It is a very rich player in the animation business, even today. Apparently, Rianna and Jeff created a software to make animations look more real and human-like with the help of their team which also included Dhruv. They got a huge, huge, amount of profit out of this."

"Okay..."

"It seems Rianna wanted to allot twenty per cent of each of their shares to Dhruv but Jeff was totally against it. He asked Rianna to treat him as an employee who merely worked his part of the assignment, that's all. In fact, he repeatedly tried to convince Rianna not to trust Dhruv at all. Rianna disagreed and gave him an ultimatum that she was sharing forty per cent of profits with Dhruv, whether he liked it or not."

"Uh...were they engaged then?"

"I think after this Rianna broke off their engagement. It seems Jeff was having a fling too with one of the co-workers..."

"You're sure about this?"

"Yes, that's how the sequence of chat conversations go."

"So you feel that...umm...ahem...that Jeff has a motive to..."

"Yes, Krys. It breaks my heart to say this but Jeff has a motive for Rianna's murder. Dhruv kind of kept sending me feelers about this. A huge amount of money did divert to Jeff's account after Rianna's death...The fling hardened Rianna even more and helped her get over Jeff although it was not to Jeff's liking. Jeff wanted to get back with Rianna but she refused."

"So it was not Jeff who broke off with Rianna but the other way round."

"Yes, they broke off a month before her murder..."

"It's so hard to believe this about Jeff...I mean Jeff!?" said Krystal in a puzzled voice.

"Yes, Krystal!" cried out Tia in sheer frustration as she ran her fingers through her hair. "I don't want it to be Jeff...but if it is, then Nysa is living a lie. Sooner or later the truth will come out and it will totally shatter her..."

"What are you going to do now, Tia?"

"I am going to talk to Regan about this. If the laptop was handed over earlier, at least the police could have brought some semblance to this. But Jeff kept it with him. He withheld evidence which is a crime. How could he?" said Tia, as tears streamed down her cheeks.

"Yes, why did he not hand over the laptop to the police? That really throws me!" cried out Krystal.

"I don't want to do this Krystal...but I just don't know what else to do!"

"It's heart breaking Tia...I would have got cold feet and...I don't know..."

"I just feel like I would die! How I wish all this never happened...why does this only happen to me and my family?!" Tia was crying profusely as she felt her heart ripping apart.

"Tia, please calm down for a while. Talk to Regan first...he will know better."

"Talking to Regan means reporting about Jeff as a murde...murderer...and I just can't do it. And here I am in Nysa's house..." Tia cried in despair as she felt nausea overwhelming her. She was about to move to the bathroom when the sight of Nysa's white face shocked her into a stand still.

"How dare you!!!" screamed Nysa as she threw something out of her hand and it crashed into minute pieces on the floor. It was Nysa's mobile and Tia could see rage pouring out of sister's eyes as she advanced towards her, her posture threatening.

"Nysa, I..."

"Keep quiet!!! How could you!?"

There was a scuffling of noises as Jeff, Ron and Ryan burst into the room.

"What's the matter Nysa...we heard some noise...and...," Jeff was saying but he stopped midway when he saw Tia and Nysa looking out of their element. Nysa was livid with anger while Tia was crying profusely.

"Ask her, Jeff! Ask her what she's up to!"

There was silence as Ryan, Ron and Jeff looked at each other in bewilderment.

"She wants to destroy all of us. Only then she will breathe in peace!" screamed Nysa.

Tia's fingers dug into her palms and her sight was blinded with tears.

"Nysa...this isn't easy for me at all," her voice shook as she tried to speak steadily. "There are a lot of things that has gone unanswered. I just want to bring a semblance to Rianna's..."

"Is that why you make us all to be murderers!!!" Nysa's voice was a shriek across the room.

"Nysa...what is going on?" said Jeff in a composed voice. "Will you both calm down?"

"Jeff, you won't believe what this sister of mine has been up to. You were right about her! I should have kept away from her...she is destruction itself!" Nysa's voice was hoarse with fury and her eyes glazed crazily as she looked at everyone around her. Mrs Bailey too had come in and was standing in the doorway in a state of shock.

"You don't know what you have done to us, Tia!" Nysa pointed her finger at her as she closed the distance between them. "I always put you first besides anyone in my life. Even with my husband, it was you before him! And you call him a murderer?? Does he look like a murderer from any angle? He is your brother-in-law – my husband and the father of your niece who you profess to love so much. How dare you!" Nysa's voice rose hysterically as she ranted at Tia.

"But Nysa, even I don't want any of thi..."

Nysa swung her hand at Tia's cheek with a force that almost threw Tia off balance had Ron not caught hold of her.

"Nysa!!" said Ron in a shocked voice. He protectively blocked Tia from Nysa's view while holding her at the same time.

"She broke your heart, Ron, and now she broke mine too like no one ever did!"

Jeff held Nysa as she too was choked with tears now.

"You better get her out of the house, Ron," said Jeff in the coldest voice possible while holding on to a trembling Nysa in his arms.

"Yes, get her way from me!" shrieked Nysa. "I don't want to see her ever in my life again!"

Ron looked around helpless as he held a broken Tia in his arms, wrought with tears.

Ryan nudged him silently. "Let's go," he murmured.

Tia let herself be led by Ron, as she felt like a zombie, her body numb and her eyes awash with tears.

"Where are your house keys, Tia?" asked Ron for the third time.

She didn't know what she mumbled but heard him asking Ryan to get her handbag.

The car started after a while and Tia looked out silently not seeing anything.

"Yes, Krystal," spoke Ron quietly on his mobile. "Sorry, I didn't hear. I was in Nysa's house and there...umm...okay you know. Alright, come over then. She really needs you today."

When they reached her house, Krystal was already waiting for them. She took Tia's handbag and opened the door lock. Ron made her sit on the sofa as Krystal went to get her a glass of water.

"Tia?" Krystal looked at her questioningly.

Tia broke into tears as she clutched on to Krystal. "What have I done, Krystal!? Maybe I should have listened to Regan..."

"Shhh...it will be all okay...have faith in God...he doesn't give us a burden too heavy for us to carry," she consoled as she petted her back. "This too will pass...have faith in Him."

Ron took leave after a while and Krystal put Tia to bed.

It wasn't difficult for her to fall into a deep sleep. She dreamed of a huge sea in front of her and she was sitting on the beach, building sand castles with Nysa. Rianna and her Mom were lazing on the mat, a little further away. They were engrossed with their books.

Nysa was irritated with her because the castle was too broad when it should have been a little taller. But Tia felt this design looked better as she looked proudly at her sand castle.

Nysa was being too smug about her opinions as usual, she thought. She always got away with what she wanted. But at seven, Tia knew better about castle designs, she decided. She wouldn't give in, come what may.

"Tia, would you stop messing everything up! Sometimes you should sit and try to learn things instead of being a know-it-all!"

"You are being a know-it-all, Nysa! Not me!"

"Oh! Do it yourself then," said Nysa, irked and walking away.

Tia looked for a while at Nysa's receding figure and then ran to her Mom. She leaned her head on her back as she sat beside her Mom.

"That Nysa can be so difficult at times, Mummy. She never listens to me. Thinks she is always right." Her baby voice sounded petulant in her mother's ears.

"It isn't like that, Tia. She is older and thinks she can teach you better." Her mother gave her a warm hug and a kiss.

"Now she will not even talk to me." Tia grumbled as she wrapped her hands around her mom's neck with a pout on her lips.

"Don't worry darling, it will all be okay," said her mother in a soothing voice. "She will come and play with you after a while – when she has cooled down, of course."

Janmasthami* - Janmasthami is an annual Hindu festival that celebrates the birth of Lord Krishna.

Chapter 29

The next week Ron kept visiting her more than often. Sometimes he'd take her to her office or sometimes drop her home. She didn't mind as she felt so listless and drained of energy with every passing day. They didn't speak much but Tia felt better to have his company instead of facing the empty silence.

"Won't your girlfriend mind? Your coming here like this?" she asked.

"Which girlfriend?" He mocked.

"Trisha? Trisha Sareen?" she asked lightly.

"Who told you she is my girlfriend?" was all Ron said and she didn't press further.

She felt more of Rianna in the house these days, as if she was watching her. Sometimes it was her perfume or she would find her stuff frequently misplaced when she was very sure of where she had kept them. She started reading more about the afterlife and spirits on the Internet. She realized that Rianna's presence wasn't her mind playing tricks and she acknowledged her presence more than ever. Somehow the more that she accepted her, the more confident she felt and not frightened at all.

Sometimes she would ask, "Rianna, are you around?" She would notice the lights flicker or a tap opening in her bathroom or kitchen.

"What are you trying to tell me, Rianna?" she would ask in the empty silence. But she never got any answers to that. And the worst part was as Ron frequented his visits to her place, she dreamt more unhappy dreams about Rianna. In her dreams she would be walking in the beach with Ron or sharing any happy moment with him outdoors and Rianna would show her displeasure, shake her head from afar as if to tell her not to be with Ron.

She woke up one morning from her dream and felt so depressed that she didn't feel like going to her office at all. Ron called her but she told him she didn't want to go out and be left alone.

"Ron, you don't need to worry so much about me, you know. It's not like we are going around or something? You really don't need to feel obligated to me any way – please understand that." Her voice was almost pleading.

"It's not in my hands, sweetheart," he said in a self-mocking voice.

"Ron, please be serious. Anyway my emotions are all messed up now. I really need some space from you, believe me!" She ran her fingers wildly through her hair in utter frustration.

Ron sighed at that and after a few seconds of silence, he said slowly, "I tried. But I can't. I am sorry I can't." Her heart ran a quiver when he continued gently, "Staying away from you is something beyond my control. You don't have an option. Stay safe, sweetheart."

Krystal rang up late one afternoon.

"Hi, Tia. How are you feeling now?"

"How else..." she vented, then sighed. "Sorry about that. I feel so heavy and don't feel like moving or walking anywhere. Simply feel like sinking myself into a big dark hole..."

"You can't break down like this, Tia. Be strong..."

"I am trying, Krys. I wonder how is Nysa? Maybe I should call her...I feel..."

"Don't do that, Tia. Just cool off for a while will you and keep some distance from Nysa."

"What do you mean?"

"I don't know how to tell you this but Nysa strongly feels you need psychiatric help. She discussed with Dev regarding this. She called me to convince you somehow although she doesn't want to get in touch with you. In fact, she called up Ron too..."

"What! I don't believe this!"

"Don't take it otherwise. She is very worried about your mental condition. Although she is concerned about you, she says, she is finding it very difficult to forget what happened." Krystal sighed. "She said she felt betrayed by the person she loves most. So it's better you'll give each other some space to heal..."

Tia almost laughed wildly at that. Psychiatric help!

"You can't blame her, Tia. It's not easy to believe into this paranormal stuff or whatever name you'd like to give it. It sounds bullshit in fact if you kind of talk about it with a normal person. If I myself didn't feel that odd vibe in your house or a weird kind of presence, I wouldn't have believed you either..."

Tia sat lost in her thoughts curled in the living room sofa for maybe two hours when the bell rang. She thought it was Ron and as soon as she opened the door she said in a weary voice, "I don't want to go out, Ro..."

"Hey!" Yuvi smiled at her frustrated expression. "I was not asking you..."

"Oh Yuvi...I thought it was..."

"It was?"

"Never mind. Come on in. I am shabby and badly dressed...hope you don't mind."

"Oh Tia...I do mind from the time I saw you in your pigtails," said Yuvi, his eyes crinkling. "What's wrong with you by the way? Blinds down...still in your pajamas...and bunking office a lot these days. Just because you are one of the bosses, doesn't mean you get away so easily, you know."

"Oh Yuvi...I'm sorry. Uncle Neal is the boss – not me...." She laughed.

"He must be thinking Tia's taking him for a ride..."

"Of course not, Tia. He knows you have poured your blood and sweat into the company. You have been his right hand all along. You are entitled for a break too. By the way, is there anything I should know? I haven't ever known you to stay away from office this often."

Tia sat on the sofa tiredly as a sense of desolation came over her.

"Anything wrong, Tia?" asked Yuvi in concern.

"I can tell you but you won't understand, Yuvi," said Tia in a self-mocking voice. "In fact no one understands! Except a very few like Krystal or my niece, Alisha..."

"Try me, Tia," said Yuvi softly.

"Oh! What's the use..."

"Come on, Tia!"

"It's something hard to explain. If I tell you, you'd think I am crazy mad or something. Some people are starting to think that, in fact even my own sister!"

Tia broke down into tears.

"Tia..." Yuvi sat beside her and held her shoulders, trying to comfort her while she sobbed out.

After a while the sobs died.

"You can tell me, Tia. You will feel much better...let it off your chest..."

"Yuvi, I have a strong feeling that Rianna's death wasn't suicide. She was murdered!"

"What! What are you saying, Tia?" Yuvi said slowly. "Rianna's death was investigated thoroughly. The police checked every angle and found out that it was suicide."

"Yuvi, you've known Rianna for so long. Can you believe she could do that! Can you, can you!?"

"At that time I was shocked of course...but later I accepted whatever was laid down in front of me by the police – like everyone else, of course. Then it all became a memory after a while. She was a beautiful person inside out. But things happen in life and we have to move on and not be stuck in the past. Why...it's been five years since her death. I didn't know you still felt so strongly..."

"I do...Yuvi." She pulled up her folded knees and rested her chin on them desolately. "I miss her a lot. And I still feel her presence. I have a feeling that something was not right about Rianna's death. I dream about her a lot. It's as if she says she wants justice...!"

Yuvi went into a thoughtful silence as she looked at him intensely, waiting for a response.

His eyes were watchful, as if he was trying very hard to understand her pain.

"I am sorry you still have to go through this, Tia. Why didn't you tell me any of this before? If not anything I could have at least lent a sympathetic ear and you would have felt much better..."

"Thank you, Yuvi, for understanding. That makes everything so much better..."

"But what made you feel Rianna was murdered by the way? Anything you saw or heard?"

"First it was these dreams..."

"Dreams!?"

"Yes, Yuvi – dreams! Something which is so difficult for everyone to believe. Dreams and my intuition! And it got stronger with time...I have been investigating for a while in whichever way my gut feelings have led me and I am convinced that she is murdered."

"You have been investigating? How?"

"I have been talking with Regan, the police officer who was in charge of her case. Checking her mails and who she corresponded with on her last few days. Checking on people who were closest to her before she died..."

"Gosh! You have been really busy..." he said slowly, his eyebrows almost touched his hairline in bafflement.

Tia shrugged helplessly.

"I checked out the motives first, Yuvi. And a few accidental clues were flashed right in front of my eyes lately, in the form of people or things..."

Yuvi's face squinted, trying to follow her train of thoughts, "What do you mean?"

Tia sighed, her eyes revealing her pain and anguish. "I mean, at first I suspected it was Ron because of certain dreams that kept coming to me about him. It sounds crazy but they were so powerful that it didn't let me free till I kept asking Ron about them."

"What did Ron say?" He rubbed his forefinger over his chin to and fro in a distracted motion.

"He recalled dates and meetings and by putting two and two together we both realized that he had met Rianna just before the day she died. Though his version was that he had to rush off on account of his mother's illness, and received the news much later. He told me he hadn't known anything about her death prior to that. But that made me even more suspicious and distanced me from him. This constant suspicion made me break my engagement with Ron. I couldn't live with a person who was my sister's killer could I – although I hadn't found any concrete evidence against him except for my dreams. And again if he wasn't responsible then I was killing him with my doubts about him, wasn't I? But I couldn't help myself. So I broke up with him so that he could be happier away from me. We were only causing each other undue grief, weren't we?"

Yuvi pursed his lips, nodding slowly, his eyes empathic, "I am sorry, Tia. This hasn't been easy for you...."

He patted her back reassuringly as she went on, "Then for a while I suspected Dhruv..."

"Dhruv!?"

"Yes, because he had a motive too. He loved Rianna but couldn't get her because of Jeff. Regan also found a love letter carrying some symbols of Wicca in Rianna's purse which he handed over to me. Dhruv had a lot of decorative designs on the wall hangers, paintings and show pieces of his room with similar Wicca symbols as on that letter. But he told me that those were simply stuff he bought for his office and home decor from a client – Tara Mehta."

"Tara Mehta?"

"Hmm...she is a Wicca practitioner, tarot reader and an astrologer. My sister and Dhruv designed her online shop and brochures where she sells a lot of her Wiccan stuff..."

"Then...?"

"Then there was also a chain he wears. It has a locket that carries the design of a pentacle, another important symbol of the Wiccans. I saw the twin of that chain in my dreams and that it was lying buried in Pearl Valley. Krystal and I went to that place and dug it out from the very place I saw in my dream. I felt that it was meant to signify that Dhruv was related to this somehow. But once I started investigating, Dhruv kind of pointed to me that it was Jeff who I should be investigating about. And he was the one having a motive..."

"So you've become a real detective, haven't you?" Yuvi lightly teased.

"Ha ha ha..." She snorted humourlessly. "It would have been funny if my family was not involved – and Ron specially," she said quietly.

"Yes, I remember what a crime buff you were in school...Agatha Christie was one of your favs, wasn't it?" Yuvi said lightly as if to bring her out of her gloom.

"You are not far from wrong, Yuvi. I did have a passion for detective novels and television series at that time. Mom and Dad were worried that it would drive me crazy...but I wish this too was a book I was only reading and it never really happened..."

"So, you believed Dhruv then?"

"I don't know...I mean I couldn't find any concrete evidence against him. Regan also told me that Dhruv had a strong alibi to prove that he wasn't anywhere near Rianna the day she was murdered."

"Okay. So you ruled out Dhruv from your list of suspects."

"Not ruled out...but...umm...things happened in such a way that it distracted me from him for some time. And then, I found my focus shifted towards Jeff who looked as if he had a strong motive for murder. I couldn't help myself, Yuvi," she cried. "It was as if something was propelling me to find the truth..."

"Okay, go on..."

"Jeff had a real motive to murder Rianna as there was a huge amount of money that he would own after she died. In fact he and Rianna had an argument regarding their finances a month before her death. As it is, there were already pressures mounting on their relationship. Then there came a point where she wanted to hand over a certain percentage of their project's profits to Dhruv. It was from a very lucrative overseas project that they were dealing with and it had brought them huge returns. Jeff didn't agree to this and he wasn't willing to part with any share of their profits, especially with Dhruv whom he didn't trust at all."

"So you feel that Jeff feared that with his breakup with Rianna, her profits would be diverted towards Dhruv. He wanted to amass all those profits only for himself..."

"Yes, Yuvi," said Tia in a confused voice. "I was working on that but Nysa found out and hell broke loose..."

They were silent for a while, lost in their thoughts.

"That's quite a theory you have come up with, buddy." Yuvi's lips curved into a crooked smile. But Tia looked back at him listlessly.

He sighed, his eyes serious and introspective. "I don't know what to say, Tia. They are all your family – Nysa, Jeff...and Ron too as he is the man you loved and maybe still love. I think the best option would be to not do anything for a while and sleep on it. Take some rest, do something else. Sometimes the answers come just when we give up or are not looking..."

"You are right, Yuvi." Tia shrugged wearily. "Thanks for listening, though"

"I gotta go," said Yuvi as he ruffled her hair. "Just hold on. You will be fine. Believe me."

Tia saw him to the gate and waited till his car left. As she was about to come back, she heard a loud crash in the bushes. She ran to check what had fallen and was surprised to see a figure looming from the bushes.

"Who is it?" she asked sharply.

The voice didn't answer as it was a man getting on his feet and rubbing away the leaves and grass from his body.

"Dhruv!"

"Hello," Dhruv said simply.

"What are you doing here, Dhruv?"

"Taking a walk round the neighbourhood. Something that you like to do...investigating maybe?"

"Investigating for what?"

"You are not the only one who likes to play the detective here, Ma'am." He mocked.

"Don't joke, Dhruv! I could call the police on you!"

"Oh, really? And say what? I was just taking a walk to my boss's house after all. Is that a crime? I am sure the police would have a laugh! Or maybe the tables may turn on you for unnecessary hue and cry," he said smoothly.

She looked shocked at his gall to get away with anything.

"By the way, looks like you are on the rebound, aren't you? You think Yuvi suits you better? Maybe some time alone with oneself helps better than any cheap substitute that is available around the corner, don't you think? I learnt it the hard way and I hope you don't make the same mistake, kid. See ya!"

He turned and she kept watching him walk coolly away while reflecting on his words. What did he mean, she thought, and what was he doing here? This was the first time she had seen him in her part of the neighbourhood.

Chapter 30

"Damn! I'd never find this," said Tia as she walked down the corridor to the store room. She couldn't find the backup tape cartridges anywhere. The office was totally deserted. Pradeep, their security guard promised to come after an hour and lock up the office once she'd finished. He had requested leave for an hour for some last minute shopping for the Ganesha festival round the corner and Tia had relented.

But, unluckily, the store room was locked and the keys were with Pradeep.

"Damn! I should have kept the keys...how careless can I get!" She ranted at herself. She had to upload the final images before making the website live. The client was already annoyed that her team had not made the design changes as discussed the previous day. As it is they were constantly demanding new changes every day as per their whims and fancies, she sighed. That was the reason she had come to the office on a Saturday to work on the desktop that contained all the files. But now that the images were corrupted by a virus, she needed to retrieve them from the backup tapes of the project.

She decided to check for it in Yuvi's storage cabinet as her backup team had also kept an extra set there in case of emergencies and disaster recovery. But before she could take a step further, she felt the wind knocking out of her chest as someone grabbed her neck from behind and then hurled her towards the wall. Tia fell heavily on the floor and her head was swimming. Large hands grabbed her legs and she was dragged roughly across the tiled floor.

As she looked through the haziness in front of her, she saw a masked man drag her through the cubicles of her office. He released her for a second and came close to check on her, maybe to see if she was breathing, thought Tia. She closed her eyes and felt the loud thuds of her heart hammering against her ears. She tried not to blink her eyes and remained steady as the man bent closer to her face. After a while she sneaked through her eyelashes to see the man getting a thin blanket and laying it next to her. He sat down next to her feet and pulled out a huge rope. She felt heavy and her body ached all over but she knew that this was the only chance to get away. The masked man was busy now trying to tie her legs. With great effort she pulled in her right leg and thrust it right into the man's masked face. The man cried out as he grasped his face in pain.

"Why you...!"

She struggled to get up on her feet with the help of the table leg that was right next to her. By the time she could get on her feet the man managed to recover somewhat. He was about to grab her when Tia flung the nearest object she could find and that was an inkjet printer on the table next to her. The printer hit the man's head and he temporarily swayed on his feet and crashed on the ground.

Tia forced herself to turn around. She was limping as she tried to get away. She looked back quickly and saw that the man was massaging his head while trying to get on to his feet. She felt better with each step she took and dashed down the nearest staircase she could find. She could hear footsteps behind her and the best possible action was to plunge into the restroom ahead of her. She nearly hooked the latch when the man banged into the restroom door. Tia slammed the door back with as much strength as she could muster and somehow managed to latch the door.

The man kept on banging the door and it looked like it would be forced open any minute. She leaned on the wall behind her for a second to catch her breath and looked around the rest room frantically to find a way to get out. The banging stopped for a while as Tia got into one of the toilet stalls, climbed on a toilet seat to open the ventilation window above it. Although she could open the window, she couldn't climb up to it as it was way higher for her to reach.

The banging increased again. Tia got down to check on the door of the rest room and she could feel the door breaking down any second. She felt paralyzed as she looked desperately around her. She couldn't get out of the restroom anyway and only way she could save herself was to attack her assaulter. She checked for any sharp object she could find but was a second too late. The masked man lunged into the rest room as the door fell down with a heavy bang. Tia felt cornered and helpless as the assaulter closed the distance between them.

When her assailant swung his hands to grab her, Tia used her knee to hit at his crotch. The attacker squirmed in pain and his grip loosened on her. At that very moment Tia's eyes fell on a towel ladder. She immediately pulled it up and swung it over her assailant. She held him captive with the ladder and pushed the ladder away with all her strength. She rushed out of the rest room and ran between the cubicles to reach the exit door of the second floor. As soon as she reached the door, she found hard hands again grabbing her waist.

She elbowed him hard into his stomach and stamped his feet while swinging away perpendicular to him as he swore in pain. Holding his forearm very hard, she dropped to her knees while keeping a strong grip on him. This propelled him to loosen his grip and fall heavily on the ground. Luckily she found another restroom close by and immediately got in. She locked it quickly from inside. But her minute of respite was short-lived as the assailant came banging on to the door.

Tia ran to the countertop wash basins which had ventilation glass windows above the mirrors. She climbed up the basin to push open the ventilation window and swung her legs to climb out through it. Before she could reach the ledge outside, she felt herself chunked back down by a brute force. She crashed on the ground along with her assailant. Her fall was buffered by the assailant's body below her. She pushed herself off the floor but her assailant grabbed her by the neck and slammed her outside the restroom. She banged heavily against the cubicles, hurting her face badly. Tia was fully under his mercy as she looked around hastily for some means of escape.

With all the strength that she could muster, she swung her leg into a roundhouse kick at his face, coupled with a quick back kick. The assailant didn't expect that and hurtled against the wall behind him. Though temporarily weakened, he was in a mad rage and made a quick comeback. He squeezed her neck very hard and swung a knife over her.

She screamed in horror and everything in front of her blacked out as she crashed to the floor. She could see Ron's face swimming in front of her as she opened her eyes and her head felt torturous with pain. She must tell him goodbye now as this was the end of her life, she thought, amidst the haze. Would anyone tell him that she thought about him during the last moments of her life? She lost a million chances to tell him how much she loved him and now it was too late to say goodbye. His face faded into oblivion as she saw someone running away from her with heavy footsteps. Who was that? Maybe it was Ron being separated from her at the inevitability of her death.

But no, he was coming back to her. She could see him clearly now as he sat down beside her, his eyes inundated with pain. She could hear sirens in the background as she heard him talking to her but she couldn't hear his voice.

Then after a little while his voice seemed somewhat audible as she heard him ask her, "Are you okay, Tia?"

He was sweating and his eyes were huge in distress.

"Where is that man?"

"Your attacker? He released you as soon as he saw me. I was about to go after him but I was too worried to leave you behind. Anyway, the police too are on the way..."

She tried to get up but Ron held her down.

"I think I can get up now. How did you reach here? I was all alone and today is a Saturday."

"I tried your number and couldn't get through. So I called Krystal. She told me that you would be working at your office today. I saw your car and tried your number again, but you didn't take the call. I decided to get into your office building and give you a surprise when I realized it was locked."

"Yes. Pradeep, the security guard said he would leave the back door of the building open if I wanted to go out."

"Yes, I decided to wait for you downstairs when I heard this loud banging and some noises. I didn't know how to get in and called the police. Meanwhile I explored and found the back door. I quickly got in and searched for the source of noise. As soon as I entered, I saw you kicking him and him making a grab at you. Luckily he heard my footsteps before he could stab you with his knife. He immediately released you and ran. That's why you crashed on the floor. He was about to swing his knife at me when I reached his side but then he heard the police sirens and decided to run instead. I went after him but realized you needed me more..."

"Yes, I need you so much..." Tia sighed as she leaned into him. "Can you help me up?"

Ron held Tia as they walked downstairs, slowly. The police halted where they stood and Ron quickly explained. The police started their search for the attacker while Tia kept moving downstairs with Ron's support.

As soon as they reached the ground floor, the door to one of the main halls flung open and a man dashed out.

"Dhruv!?" cried out Tia.

Dhruv looked out of sorts and there were grazes all over his face. A huge streak of blood rolled down his forehead. Dhruv halted as soon as he saw Tia and Ron while breathing a sigh of relief at the same time.

"Tia, are you alright?" his eyes were full of concern.

"Yes...but what are you doing here?"

"I was walking by and saw your car, Tia. I knew that you were working alone in the office today. Neal had told me that you were working on client demand. I thought I heard some banging noises and wanted to check on you..."

"Really!" Tia's voice was almost disbelieving.

Dhruv's face changed expression and he closed his eyes for a second.

He looked wary and hugely frustrated as he scowled back at her.

"You don't believe me, don't you? Why is that so surprising?" His mouth curled into a sneer although he was still breathing a little heavily.

"What are those grazes, man?" asked Ron curiously.

"Ron, would you believe it if I said I heard noises! And as soon as I got inside, I saw this masked man scurrying down the staircase. He ran as soon as he saw me and I chased him all the way. We had a scuffle but that bloody guy managed to escape..."

Before he could say anything else the police inspector interrupted him. He wanted to speak to Dhruv in detail about the assailant, so he took him aside. Ron helped Tia to the car and drove her home.

"I couldn't see the man's face...he was masked as Dhruv was saying. I hit him a number of times..."

"Hey, I saw those kicks you swung! From where on earth did you learn such moves, Tia?!"asked Ron, surprised.

"I hold a blue belt in taekwondo, Ron. Both Nysa and I learnt it when we were in school. Nysa holds a black belt actually. In fact she was the one who dragged me to all the taekwondo classes at our neighbourhood academy. I owe her that..."

Ron whistled appreciatively at that.

"Ha ha ha...stop being dramatic will you," she said, amused.

Her eyes looked grave as she turned his side. "Ron, I am suspicious about Dhruv's story. He had a number of grazes on his face. Could he be the attacker in the mask? I did hit my assailant a number of times on the face and forehead..."

Ron rubbed his face tiredly as he parked the car near her gate. "His sudden appearance did appear suspicious, I admit. And why on earth is this sudden concern for you?"

Chapter 31

Krystal looked worried as she sat beside her friend. Ron had left a few minutes back with the doctor who was kind enough to come on short notice. After prescribing a few pain killers and dressing her bruises, the doctor had assured them that she would be fine.

"Did the police catch the assailant?" Krystal asked.

"No," said Tia.

"Who would want to harm you, Tia?"

Tia simply shook her head as she sipped her coffee. Her eyes looked blank.

"Did the police find out anything?" Krystal asked.

"Not yet," said Tia. "They are still working on the case."

"Did something come out of questioning Dhruv?" asked Krystal.

"Dhruv told the police that he was walking by the office and saw my car. At the same time he heard some banging noises and wanted to check on me. He met a masked man tearing his way downstairs and he chased him for a while. Dhruv wrestled to catch him but he got away," Tia said as she leaned back on the sofa tiredly.

"Do you buy that story?" asked Krystal.

Tia shrugged her shoulders and shook her head in confusion. "I don't know what to believe, Krys. Two days back I found him prowling by my house. Just taking a walk around the neighbourhood was his flippant reply, adding that I was not the only one who could play detective..."

"Gosh! How cheeky!"

"I know!"

"What could be the reason behind the attack?" said Krystal, tapping her forefinger over her lips thoughtfully, when the phone rang.

"Hello, Regan."

"How are you feeling now, Tia?"

"Much better. The doctor was here. No broken bones he said but asked me to take an x-ray test tomorrow...just in case."

"Good. You really gave me a scare, Tia. I am sending two policemen over there for your security. They will keep a strict vigilance near your house."

"Is that necessary, Regan?" said Tia.

"Don't want to take any chances, Tia. You have been doing a lot of asking around lately. Who knows you might have opened up a can of worms and someone somewhere is not too happy about it."

"What do you think about Dhruv appearing out of nowhere on the scene?" asked Tia, her voice curious. "I found him right by my garden two days back too."

"Again, can't say, Tia. It was a Saturday and it does look suspicious to find him there. But again we need a motive and evidence...I am working on it. By the way, it seems you and Nysa had had a major fallout. Is that true?"

Tia sighed as she answered a yes softly.

"Who else might know that you are investigating about Rianna's death? I mean who else was there when you had a major row with Nysa?"

"Only Ryan, Ron, Jeff and Mrs Bailey."

"Okay. I am with you now and working actively on this case. I am sorry that I didn't take you more seriously before. Stay strong and be careful."

"Thanks, Regan!"

"Tia!" said Krystal brightly as soon as she finished her call.

"What?"

"It's high time we contacted Mira Dorjee. She connected with your Mom, didn't she? And everything that she said rang out to be true. Maybe she can find some meaning to all this. The dreams that you have...this feeling of Rianna in this house...this confusion between you and Ron..."

Tia looked at her thoughtfully, her chin in her hands. "Ok, let's try that out," she finally said.

"Right! I will call her tomorrow," Krystal announced.

Ron called her the next morning and Tia couldn't help the surge of excitement at hearing his voice. He asked after her health and told her he would come within an hour to take her for the x-ray check up.

She sighed as she hang up and wished that their love story was a simple one just like any other boy-girl story.

"I spoke to Mira at length about this. She says it's quite interesting and wants us to come and meet her," said Krystal as she sat next to Tia.

"Okay, what about late afternoon after I finish my medical check-up?" Tia suggested.

"Yes, she said she would be free around that time. She also asked you to get some personal items of your sister and mother. That would make her sense their spirits better."

Ron took her for a medical check-up and her x-rays confirmed that everything was alright. They were quiet on their entire trip and Tia felt easy that way. It was almost like old times. Will it always be like this between them, she mused. These up and down swings in their relationship never seemed to abate. The chances of it ever surviving were nil what with this constant suspicion and distrust, especially on her part.

After Ron dropped her, Krystal came along and they drove over to the Taj hotel. Mira always seemed to emanate that Buddha-like serenity and Tia at once felt at home in her company. She gave them both a warm hug. They took their seat at the restaurant, which looked relatively quiet and deprived of guests.

"It's great to have the restaurant all to ourselves, almost." Mira smiled. "Okay, tell me everything from the beginning – leave nothing out."

"Mira, I lost my sister around five years back when I was in the third year of my engineering degree. It really broke me badly and there was this black depression that totally overwhelmed me. According to the police, my sister's death was a case of suicide. This, in addition to losing my mom two years prior to that, made me quite lost and broken. Mom died due to a heart stroke although she was paralyzed and wheelchair-bound for a couple of years before her death. I had awful dreams of Rianna after she died, where she was always crying or was in extreme pain, but then Mom also used to come in my dreams and strangely her dreams were calm and peaceful. In the dreams she asked me to meditate and say prayers from a book. Slowly the bad dreams stopped and I worked over my depression by studying very hard for my semester. Life went on, I got a job and then quit it to come home three years back. I live downstairs in my parent's house where previously Mom, Rianna and I had lived, and after my mom's death, I and Rianna. Once I came home for good, there were times I felt Rianna's presence in the house as if she was watching me or something. But I didn't give it much thought, thinking I missed her since we shared a lot of memories in that house..."

"You just felt her presence...that's all? Nothing paranormal or something similar in those lines?" asked Mira.

"Sometimes I'd get a whiff of her perfume suddenly from nowhere. But such occasions were very far in between and very mild so I didn't think of them much. I thought it was my yearning for her that made me feel her so sharply. Then I had a car accident almost a year ago. After this, the dreams of Rianna started again. I dreamt of her quite often and the dreams were gory. I felt she wanted to get my attention, however bizarre it may sound...and then Ron came in my life. I knew Ron since school. He knew most of my friends – Krystal, Nina and even Rianna. And once Ron came in my life, it was then that I started to feel Rianna more than ever. It was like she didn't want me to have a relationship with Ron at all. She showed me dreams as if...as if Ron was somehow responsible for her death. That drove a wedge between me and Ron...'

"How closely did Ron know Rianna?"

"Not much. He knew Rianna as my older sister who he met on and off at social events or around our locality. They met for the last time at a charity event just the day before she died. Ron was conversationally mentioning that he was looking for a professional photographer to carry out an assignment of his. Being a reputed photographer herself, she pitched in to help. She was to meet him at Pearl Valley and take professional shots of the place for a real estate client of his. But that never happened because he had an emergency call from home and had left that night itself. His mom was seriously ill."

"Ok. Krystal had told me about your broken engagement...is that the reason why..."

"Yes. Somehow I felt that's what Rianna wanted. The day I broke off with him she came in my dream and comforted me. She said that it was meant to happen as I cried over the dog that I had lost when I was six. It was one of my most favourite pets."

"Oh..." Mira looked at her with full empathy.

"As I was saying, after Ron came in my life, I felt she was trying to get my attention more than ever. Water taps would be opening for no reason or I'd feel her perfume for a longer time than before. Her photo frame on the wall would be slightly tilted at times, especially in the evenings after I came back home from office. I would also find my stuff misplaced and so on...In fact my niece Alisha who stays upstairs also used to dream a lot about her when she was younger. Nowadays she doesn't dream as much, though. In every dream Rianna looked sad and wanted to convey something to my niece. But then she would change her mind towards the end of the dream saying she was too young. Alisha sensed Rianna when she used to come downstairs to play. It freaked out her friends too and gradually they stopped coming downstairs anymore."

"Even I have felt her a lot lately," said Krystal. "Just a presence though – as if I am being watched. And then again I thought maybe it was because I was hearing too much of Rianna from Tia, or simply my superstition. So I am not sure."

"Let me see...give me some personal belongings of Rianna...something she might have had during her last days."

Tia put across the chain with the pentacle locket on the table. "I found this at the place where she died. She actually showed me how to find this in my dream..."

Mira held her hands in a prayer position, closed her eyes and chanted, "Dear angels and spirit guides, seal me with your white light from all sides. Keep me protected in your light and connect me to only *those* who are in the light."

Mira then took the chain kept on the table and ran her fingers over the locket for a while. She suddenly pulled in a sharp breath as she closed her eyes. Then her face turned blue as if in pain.

"Gosh!" she dropped the chain on the table and leaned back on her chair while taking deep long breaths.

"What's wrong, Mira!" Tia asked as she got up to hold Mira.

"Are you okay?" Krystal was on her toes, quickly pouring her a fresh glass of water.

"I am okay...sit down, sit down..."

She was quiet for sometime as she said, "I can't connect to Rianna. Maybe because she has not crossed to the other side. But when I held the chain I felt an immense pain in my head, as if somebody had hit me very hard with a huge rod or something. These feelings might be transmitted in the locket while Rianna was wearing it or holding it. Clearly it was not a nice feeling and it carried sheer discomfort. I have not been able to connect beyond that. Again, as I said before, this maybe because Rianna has still not reached the other side...I am not sure."

Okay," said Tia slowly.

"Now give me your Mom's belongings if you have any. But Tia, remember I can connect with her only if she comes through and that is not always in my hands. It all depends on the spirit."

"I understand," said Tia as she handed her a ring of her Mom.

Mira took a notepad and started jotting down stuff as soon as she held the ring. She was nodding and whispering things and it all looked very strange.

"Okay Tia, your mother is on the other side as I told you the other day. And she guides you all the time. She worries a lot about you and senses some danger around you at this time. So she asks you to be very careful. She is aware of the accident you had the other day and ask you not to trust anyone but your instincts. Some friend or...maybe a relative...someone close to you in fact will betray you, so she's asking you again to be very careful..."

Mira looked surprised as she said, "She stresses it again and again, not to trust anyone at this point of time – however secure you might feel with them, Tia..."

"Okay Mira..."

"I am losing her, Tia...she is going away and wants me to say she loves you a lot..."

"But what about Rianna? Can you ask her to tell us something to guide us...?"

"I asked and she says she can't do that. They are not supposed to tell us of the unknown, Tia, as it will interfere with the free will of a person and in turn their karma. It is our journey and we have to make it on our own. Only then we will learn the life lessons for which we have come to this earth. In every life we have a lesson to learn for the growth of the soul – there are no short cuts to it. And if our life is cut short for some reason without learning the lesson we were supposed to, then we have to come back to learn the same lesson all over again. Your mom does mention though that your sister is not in a good place and they are doing their best to help her..."

"Oh, thank you, Mira. Tell her I love her."

"Okay, she is going now, Tia, and she says she is sending kisses to her youngest baby daughter. So that's it, Tia. I can't connect to Rianna maybe because she is an earth-bound spirit..."

"Earth-bound spirit...?"

"Earth-bound spirits meaning those who haven't reached the other side or aren't with the light – or with God if you believe in one. They are the lost souls..."

"So Rianna hasn't reached heaven is what you are trying to say...?" asked Tia.

"Tia, I connect only with people who have passed away peacefully or are in heaven, as some may like to call it. Just like I had connected with your mother the other day. More often these spirits contact me to pass on messages so that their living relatives find some closure and assurance that they are fine. I absolutely do not connect with any other form of ghosts or paranormal activity as that isn't my specialty at all. It's a very delicate boundary with us and those in afterlife. One small mistake and it might cause havoc to both the living and the deceased souls.

"But I do have a friend, Sushma Ahuja, who deals with these cases. She belongs to the group who are popularly known as the ghost hunters or the paranormal investigators. Some of us call them spiritual healers. She herself likes to be called as a spiritual healer as she heals lost spirits and sends them to the light. She works in haunted places and cleanses them of spirits. She has created quite a name for herself working as a spiritual healer or a rescue medium. She is a medium between the living and the dead – particularly the dead who haven't peacefully crossed the other side or is lost here on earth. Usually these earth-bound spirits or ghosts do not cause any harm whatsoever as it is portrayed in our movies. But it does cause disturbance to people in a particular place when they sometimes makes their presence known. And who on earth would like an unknown presence around them, who they cannot see.

"The sounds, impressions and activities that they cause, such as a change in temperature or displacement of personal belongings etc, could be no less disturbing for many. So people who feel that their houses are being haunted call Sushma to check if it really is so. If it is haunted then they do a cleansing and this helps to clear this disturbing energy which we call a ghost. It also helps the earth-bound spirit to cross over to the light and finally be at peace."

"I have read some haunted places can be really evil?" asked Krystal.

"In my entire career I haven't met any such evil ghosts, Krystal. Of course, some energies are very strong that they can make you feel sick. But that is because they themselves feel very sick to relive whatever bad experiences they had gone through while living on this earthly plane..."

"Why don't some souls cross the other side, Mira?"asked Tia.

"Many reasons...such as an unfulfilled wish or an attachment to a particular place. Sometimes they are confused and stuck, not knowing how to cross the other side. That is where the spiritual healers come in and help the soul to cross the other side. I will ask Sushma to visit your house and check if Rianna is haunting your house. She charges her clients usually but being my friend she won't be charging here..."

"That's okay...we will pay her..." said Tia, almost embarrassed at Mira's generosity.

"Ha ha ha...you might just regret what you said!" She laughed.

As they got up to go, Tia's gaze was caught by someone familiar, a little further away in the hotel lobby.

"Hold on, Krystal." She left her quickly to follow the couple across the corridor. She was careful to hide in the shadows so as to avoid being caught by Jeff and Simi. She lost them for a while and then she heard loud voices as if in argument from a conference room nearby. The door was open and she got a feminine perfume lingering in the air. When she crept closer to hide outside the door, she was certain that the voices were of Jeff and Simi.

"But you knew, Jeff, you knew!" Simi seemed to be on the verge of screaming.

"It was only a business partnership, I always made it clear," said Jeff in a cold voice.

"How dare you!" cried out Simi.

"Don't raise your voice at me, Simi. I might just lose my cool."

Suddenly Simi's voice started pleading as she said, "Don't do this to us, Jeff. You know how much I love you...please. I would die without you..."

"Nysa, my wife, is the only woman I love – now and forever."

"Come on, you don't love that bitch, Jeff! She is nothing compared to what I am...I can take you places! You know that as well as I do."

"You're getting delusional, Simi. Time you checked up with a shrink."

"Jeff you don't mean this..." Simi's voice broke into sobs.

"Get off me, Simi! I don't want to see you again in my life..."

"NO!"

"Get away from me. You have caused enough problems as it is between Nysa and me. There is no other woman in my life besides Nysa. Is that understood?!"

There was a loud sob as Simi swept out of the room before Tia could get into hiding.

She was in rage when she caught Tia lurking near the door. "You eavesdropping bitch!"

Jeff was next to her as she tore her gaze from Simi's receding figure.

"So what's the next story you want to carry back to Nysa, Tia?" Jeff jeered at her.

Tia fought hard to stop the sting of tears that threatened to overwhelm her any second. "Jeff, I am sorry…I…"

"Oh! Please spare me your fake apologies!" He spun on his heel and walked off leaving Tia feeling guilty and bereft.

Her thoughts were running round in circles once she reached home. On the one hand, there were Mira's words ringing in her ears and on the other hand it was Jeff's. She threw her shoes off and slumped on the sofa, feeling desolate. So is Rianna still around her right now, she mused. Somehow it never frightened her; it was simply unsettling. What did Rianna want to tell her, she asked herself silently. What did Ron do to her that made her so dead against their relationship?

But there was only the swaying of the curtains and the sound of wind chimes softly as cool breeze fanned her face. She closed her eyes and let her mind go blank, not wanting to stress over it any more. She felt better as tension released from her body and glided her slowly into the land of slumber.

The sharp ringing of the bell jolted her out of her drowsy state.

"Does it have to be now!" she muttered and got up to open the door.

"Hey…"

"How are you feeling now?"

"Much better…" she said as she held the door wide open. "Come in…"

Chapter 32

"Sir, do I file Mr. Sharma's papers for now?"

"No, leave it. I want to go over them once before leaving," said Ron to his assistant.

"Can I get you some coffee before I go?"

"No, thank you, Mili," said Ron with a warm smile. "Go ahead. Have a great weekend."

The office that he had rented at the city centre almost a year ago had gone quiet after his staff had left. Ron stood and watched the slow moving traffic outside his window. He was feeling restless the whole day. Should he call upon Tia once before he left for home, he debated in his mind. He didn't want to scare her by getting too close. He took the photo frame of Tia on his desk and looked at her childlike face.

No other women had this effect on him. It broke his heart that she didn't trust him. But he understood that it hadn't been easy on her, whatever she was going through. Losing both parents at a vulnerable age and then a sister in very tragic circumstances could leave a devastating effect on any sane person, he mused. Whatever she was going through was creating a great havoc in her life, although it was totally beyond his comprehension. What would it take to convince her that he loved her like no other, he thought with a deep-seated ache.

Her sister always seemed to come between them even though she was dead. It was all a mystery that he could give anything to solve. It was not as if she was making it all up. There was something very supernatural about her sister's presence in her life – that he was sure. And he didn't want to block his mind against the possibility, however practical and realistic he was as a person. He knew that while on one hand, there were all kinds of superstitious stuff that people believed when they were in a weak state of mind, on the other there existed matters in this world that science couldn't explain.

He had always laughed at guys who made a fool of themselves for love and women. But this was the first time in his life that he felt this kind of weakness – this kind of crazy helplessness for a woman. He looked at Tia's photograph again. He felt like being harsh at times, ranting out and shouting expletives so that she would stop playing with him like this – stop hurting him!

But when he saw that childlike, vulnerable face of hers, something very deep inside him moved. She touched him at the very core of his heart, made him feel so tender and he couldn't hurt her for the life of him. It was amazing how so much innocence and beauty could be in one single person who could simply take his breath away. He admired her for the way she led her life. She was always thinking about others and trying to do something meaningful instead of gliding through with the same old materialistic values and self-centric goals like many others.

He looked closer into her beautiful eyes – one of her best features. He felt drawn to them and a quick surge of emotion as he looked into them. Strangely, he was overwhelmed by a strange and weird feeling at that very instance, as her eyes stared back at him. It was as if her eyes were speaking to him and saying she wanted him at her side. A slight queasiness built up in the pit of his stomach. He had a sudden urge to speak to Tia at that exact moment. He dialed her number but it went on ringing and there was no answer. He tried two more times and when she still didn't pick up, he dialed Krystal's number immediately.

"Krystal, I can't seem to reach Tia. I've been trying her number a couple of times. Do you know where she is?"

"Maybe she is resting? We got back from an appointment around two hours back. I am sure she is fast asleep, especially with all those painkillers."

"Oh, alright," said Ron and hung up the phone. It was only six in the evening. Maybe he would drop in and check after all. Something didn't feel right and he didn't know what. He locked up his office and headed towards Tia's house, beating Bengaluru traffic as cleverly as he could. He reached in twenty minutes and saw that she had not pulled the blinds down nor switched on her lights. He rang the doorbell a couple of times. No one answered. He knocked at the door, which swung open at the slightest pressure of his knuckles.

"Tia..." he called out. Nobody answered. He went from room to room but there was no sign of her. Nor were there any signs of a break-in or any other suspicious activity, he mused. Nothing to be alarmed about, he calmed himself. Did she go for a walk or a jog leaving the door open, he wondered. He walked back to the living room. His hands were poised on his hips as he carefully looked around.

There was a sudden gust of wind and a loud crash that startled Ron. He looked around to see where the sound came from. There, below the designer wooden shelf, he saw something had fallen to the ground. He bent down to retrieve the glass keepsake which he had seen earlier too when he had come to visit Tia. It carried a beautiful quote that said, "You don't need a reason to help people."

Ron pulled in his breath when he kind of sensed the meaning of the scene that flashed in front of him. Along with the glass keepsake, the photo frame carrying Tia's photo had also fallen and cracked a bit. And just on top of Tia's photo frame there was a smaller broken piece of glass that had chipped away from the keepsake. The broken glass piece carried the word '*help*'. He felt swept by a cold eerie feeling, as if the photo frame of Tia was calling out to him, saying - "help me!"

"Krystal," he spoke urgently into his phone. "I can't find Tia. Please call all places where Tia is likely to be – her sister, Nina, Tasha...everywhere and find out if she is there..."

"Ok, I will do that...where are you by the way?" asked Krystal, her voice frantic.

"I am at her house. I am going to her office once to check. Can you get back to me quickly while I make calls at other likely places she might be? Sooner we notify the police..." Ron left the rest unsaid, as he dreaded to think any further.

Chapter 33

Tia could feel her whole body ache. She tried to move but her head felt heavy and her sight hazy as she tried to adjust her eyes. She found herself facing a dull yellow wall. There was a loud chatter of voices which stopped when she tried to get up on her knees. Her body was weak and her mind fuzzy as she tried to recollect what had happened to her. She remembered Yuvi coming down to visit her and then she felt total darkness as something heavy struck her from behind.

She was inside what looked like a storeroom where boxes were lodged one over another and wires lay scattered around the room. It was an untidy room although it smelt of fresh paint. She could see two men walking towards her as her eyes adjusted to their faces. She didn't know the men although one of them looked familiar. The one with a hugely built body made Tia feel almost threatened and somewhat naked. He had a lewd expression and his lecherous eyes ran all over her body. Where was Yuvi, she thought, feeling totally disoriented while her heart raced crazily. Did these men do something to him too?

At that very moment a door flew open and a tall man walked into the room.

"Hey, there you are, Tia," Yuvi smiled at her gently. "Thought you'd never wake up."

"Yuvi!" She was relieved and was about to get up but realized her hands and feet were tightly bound with duct tapes. The men beside Yuvi chortled in amusement. They seemed to enjoy her surprise.

Yuvi gave a hard look at the other two guys and asked in concern, "Are you alright, Tia?"

"I, I...Yuvi, my hands!" She couldn't fathom why Yuvi was standing away and not helping her untie her hands.

Yuvi flashed one of his most charming smiles as he softly said, "Does that hurt, Tia?"

Like a movie changing scenes, Tia's face reflected a gamut of emotions, right from confusion to shock and then betrayal. Yuvi seemed to be amused by them all.

"Yuvi, what is this?" she whispered, outraged.

"What is what, Tia?" Yuvi slipped his hands into his pockets as he looked at her with eyes half closed, his mouth turning into a slight curve.

He sat leisurely on the edge of a table that lay in the middle of the room. He seemed to almost enjoy her agony as he waited for her to react.

"Surprised, Tia?" he softly taunted.

"Why are you doing this, Yuvi?" Her voice croaked. "What's happened to you!?"

"Don't you know?" said Yuvi, his voice soft.

Tia gulped not trusting herself to put her thoughts into words – thoughts that were crazily racing in her mind. All this felt completely unreal – almost like an unfathomable psychotic movie.

"You let me down, Tia...that's what you have done – first Rianna and now you!!!" He lashed out. His face was twisted with anger and intense hatred.

Tia looked around slowly while trying to calm her frazzled nerves. She was baffled and grappling with the terms that this was Yuvi, her childhood friend who held her captive like this.

"I don't understand, Yuvi?" Her lips trembled as the sinister quality of the surroundings was taking a grip over her senses.

"She doesn't understand, guys...what do we do now?" Yuvi almost mocked as he glanced at the other two men standing beside him.

Tia's head reeled at the impact of the heavy smack right across her face. She could feel her lips split and blood oozing out as she tried to stop the sudden dizziness overwhelming her.

"That's her answer, Yuvi." It was the guy with the familiar face who massaged his hands as if to ease the pain of hitting her.

"Ouch! What are you saying, Jai? It hurts!" said Yuvi, looking pained.

"Does it?" Jai laughed, totally enjoying himself. "She's been asking for it, Yuvi. It's time you stopped being so charitable..."

"You are right, Jai. She took advantage of my kindness, more times than I can remember." His face looked ugly as he snarled at her, "I loved you so much, Tia, and tried to protect you always. And look what you gave me in return..."

Tia was too shocked to show any reaction. What was Yuvi saying? Sensible and understanding Yuvi – her friend. She literally felt someone pierce a knife right into her heart and scrape it into a million pieces.

"I guess it's never too late, Yuvi," said Jai almost with a jeer.

"It is, Jai! It is!" Yuvi restlessly paced back and forth around the room. She flinched when he sat down next to her and softly traced the blood oozing out of her lips "Actually it serves me right, Tia, for not allowing Jai to finish you off when he wanted to..."

He shook his head as if to mock at himself and walked away.

"Jai?" she asked weakly.

"Forgot me, Ma'am?" She cringed as she saw the guy named Jai come at her like a bull charging at a matador. He pulled at her hair painfully and raved, "Look at me, Tia Ma'am!"

In a flash Tia remembered the accountant she had fired less than two years back for the embezzlement of company funds. "Get your memory back because it's payback time now – for the way you destroyed my life and my career!"

"Hey cool down, Jai *Bhai**, will you?" The sturdy guy behind Yuvi jeered. "I am yet to taste every inch of that luscious body."

Jai pushed her head away and came back to sit beside Yuvi.

"Bloody lucky her car skidded into those wild bushes and a few hitchhikers gathered in time," he ranted.

Tia suddenly remembered how the accident had happened last year in May and all the missing pieces fitted in place. While giving way to the car behind her, she was puzzled that it didn't try to take the wide space to the right of her car. In the darkness that followed she almost forgot that the other car had actually jammed very hard sideways into the body of her car not once but repeatedly. It all came flooding to her only now...maybe that part of her memory got temporarily lost due to the trauma of her accident. Doctors had warned her that it sometimes happened in some cases of motor accidents.

"So it was not an accident...you tried to kill me..." Her eyes mirrored confusion as well accusation as she looked at Jai.

"What do you think?" Jai's lips curved into a gloating smile. "Anyway, it doesn't matter now. Time changes and so does luck!"

"Huh! He would have done a lot more if I hadn't stopped him, Tia..." said Yuvi slowly in a tone that boasted of his generosity towards her.

"Serves you right, Yuvi, for falling in love with a woman," said Jai in a mocking tone. "Women are to be used not loved..."

He kept quiet at the cold look flashed by Yuvi.

"I will let you know when I need your advice about the matters of the heart, Jai," he said with sheer contempt. Jai flushed and looked away in annoyance.

Yuvi turned his gaze at Tia.

"And what do I get after all this, Tia? Your undying devotion to that bastard, Ron!" his voice rasped. "When everything to that scumbag was about winning – and winning only! Even friendship to him was only a game!"

Yuvi breathed hard and his face was red with rage.

"After all these years he comes sneaking back into town to take you away from me. Everything was going so good for us, Tia! But no! This was another game to him again – just like in college – just like old times!" He almost whispered the last few words in utter disgust.

He came and grabbed her chin to look at him, "And you, Tia! You don't even try to understand how patient I have been! Patient to give you time in all these years to make you feel my love for you. Patient enough to give you time...give you space to get over your infatuation for Ron."

He laughed without mirth.

"Instead you are restless to start a new adventure altogether. Going around snooping about Rianna's death which had already been a closed chapter five years back." He threw his hands in the empty air with frustration. "Given up even by the police altogether! You forced me, Tia...you forced me to hate you. Just like she did..."

"Who?" asked Tia, her heart beating hard.

"Your sister! Who else? Rianna!" He spitted out her name with downright hatred. "I grew up madly loving her. But she too never had a desire to even look at me. What is it that I lack, huh? A family? Wealth? Or a background?! What!" He kicked a box out of the way. "What is it with you girls, huh? A snobbish lot – aren't you? In spite of loving her all these years, she too goes around snooping about me...and my work in the office...almost making a mockery, a fraud of all the hard work that I had put in all these years!"

"What did she do?" Tia asked, puzzled, her body aching severely at being held bondage in the last couple of hours.

"Oh, now you ask me! Your sister Rianna starts playing the detective too – just like you! No wonder blood is said to be thicker than water! You always did try to follow her footsteps, didn't you?!"

Tia digested all this in shocking silence which was suddenly disturbed by the ringing of the phone.

"We need to get away, Yuvi, and let Chandru take care of the rest," said Jai urgently as Yuvi was about to answer his phone.

Tia could see Yuvi and Jai exchanging tense looks.

"Hey, Ron! What's up," said Yuvi brightly. "Tia...umm I don't know...haven't seen her today...okay...the police! Oh, that's okay..."

"What?" asked Jai in a tense manner once Yuvi hung up.

"Apparently lover boy Ron's worried and has also notified the police...," said Yuvi, looking at Tia speculatively.

"What do we do?" Jai's eyes darted watchfully from her to Yuvi.

"Keep up appearances...what else? Come with me," Yuvi ordered.

After the three left, Tia tried to clear her head and shift her aching body. She tried to close her eyes and rest a while to stop the intense pain in her head caused by being smacked very hard. She breathed deeply as she tried to stop the sense of panic that was threatening her sanity.

She had to hatch a plan to get out, she thought weakly. There didn't seem to be any means of escape as the room looked sealed from all sides except for the metal door that Yuvi had locked from outside. She was in a cold sweat. There was no way to get out of here and her heart started to race like crazy at the thought. All the three, including Yuvi, looked like they would kill her any second.

She looked around frustrated and then decided to get the duct tapes off. She had got some lessons in self-defence many years back and she tried to remember the steps to break the tapes. At that moment there were the sound of footsteps and Tia knew that they were back again.

As she looked at Yuvi who looked smug, she decided that there was only one slim chance for her now. And she must make it work somehow. It was her only chance! Heavens knew if anything of the former Yuvi, her friend, was left anymore. This was a monster she was facing, someone she had never imagined Yuvi to be, even in her dreams.

"I don't know what happened between you and Rianna, Yuvi, but I always knew that she considered you as a friend. Just as I did...a very good friend. Yuvi, you were always family to us," she said in a beseeching tone.

"A friend?" he swore under his breath while his smile was devoid of any humour. He said with a deadly calm, "So is that why she tried to hoodwink me? Cheat me?! Hold me for charges on fraud and get me in prison?"

Tia wet her lips worried that whatever she was going to say or react would aggravate the situation. She felt as if she was walking on egg shells...one wrong word and it would unleash the animal in Yuvi. She already had a terrifying taste of it. Instead she kept quiet and let him rant out the spite and hate that gleamed in his eyes.

"As if she could do that to me!" he sneered. "What did she think of herself, huh?! This was Yuvi Raval she was dealing with!"

He looked at her with an arrogance of a man that knew only success – by whatever means – scrupulous or not!

"Yet for her I humbled myself," his voice lowered to a softer tone. "Like a loyal puppy, I loved her from afar, trying not to scare her off. I always followed her around, would you believe it, just to have a glimpse of her! There was a time I also sent her ridiculous love letters sprinkled with black magic from Tara Aunty's store – just in case it would make her fall in love with me."

"Tara Aunty? Do you mean...Tara...umm…" Her mind was fuzzy as she tried to recollect the Wicca practitioner's name.

"Yes, Tara Mehta," Yuvi chuckled wickedly. "Rianna's client and my aunt. The most sought after woman by teens and young women to make their heart's desire fall in love with them."

"I didn't know she was your aunt...you never mentioned..."

"She is my Dad's cousin. All through her life she struggled to make ends meet, but then her business suddenly picked up and she is quite a success now." His lips crinkled in amusement as if some far away memory caused it. "My witch Aunt Tara! Her love spells are quite a rage I believe. She gave me a chain too and advised me to wear it – the one with a pentacle locket which you professed to have seen in your dreams!" He sneered. "She told me it had the power to make the person of my affections fall in love with me. And like the superstitious fool that I had become, I used to wear it everywhere I went."

He seemed to mock at himself as he shook his head and looked away.

"So you sent those letters with Wicca symbols," said Tia with a sense of disbelief.

"Crazy to believe, isn't it? For a man like me? But that's what love makes you do, Tia. And I could do anything to make her see me as the man for her." His voice sounded almost vulnerable for a second.

Tia tried to look as sympathetic as she could although she was filled with disgust and loathing with every passing second.

"That was the day I wanted to confess my undying love for her." Yuvi laughed emptily. "But little did I know as I shadowed her on the day of Mr. Mittal's charity event that she had gone to Uncle Neal's office to investigate about me. Back in my mind there was a tiny voice though, nagging me and asking what was she doing on a Saturday when the whole office was closed down. Most of the staff was at the event, in fact. But I pushed the thought off like a blind man in love and waited to surprise her outside Uncle Neal's office with roses and a diamond bracelet.

"As I stood pacing the office for some time, I decided to check what was taking her so long. And lo and behold, I found her making calls to our client companies! Asking the companies, who were supposed to deliver us some software packages, why they hadn't? Of course we had bought only three copies and the rest were cancelled."

Yuvi laughed while exchanging glances with Jai.

"And so our very intelligent girl, Ms Rianna Arya," his voice was contemptuous, "finds out that I haven't used any of the new software in the rest of the computers except for the free versions of them. So what does she do next? She makes similar calls to other companies, puts two and two together and calls up Uncle Neal. 'Oh Yuvi hasn't implemented all the software packages as per the project specifications, Uncle Neal! He has used only three copies of the license and the rest of the computers are installed with only the free versions of the software. But payments have been made for around 100 licenses. What happened to the rest of the paid copies?'" his voice mimicked that of a female's.

"Of course, Uncle Neal was out of station and luckily he couldn't get into the heart of the matter immediately. So once he was back I had all the time to convince him that there was a misunderstanding. He never had any clue of the technical side of our work anyway. I could easily manipulate him."

"You always had Mr. Neal Arya at your fingertips, Yuvi!" Jai smiled appreciatively.

"Yes, the old man trusted me like his own son. I was his business partner's son after all. A business partner who was more of a friend and helped him build the company that he got full ownership of, once my father died. He took me for his son and worried that I grew up as an orphan, unlike the rest of the world." His glance ran over her sarcastically. "Things would have remained that way had it not been for the meddling witch who wouldn't let things be..."

His eyes were filled with rage that almost spilt like hot lava.

"Your sister, that witch, calls up some friend – some whiz kid in finance, and starts investigating the anomaly found in the invoices. There is a list of software in the invoices that she had never seen used in our office, she tells the whiz kid. Those that are used are mostly the free versions of the software and she had seen only three copies of the paid version. Of course, the financial whiz kid from the other side informs our honest Rianna how fake invoices are used all the time to embezzle funds in companies."

"Is that why you killed her?" asked Tia, her voice almost choked with pain.

"She left me with no other option, Tia. As soon as I walked into her, which I feigned as coincidence of course, she had the gall to ask me about the purchases. She wasn't sure as to why we didn't have the paid copies installed in all the computers as per the number mentioned in the invoices. I told her that we had installed them all in the client places and some of them were found corrupted. But she thought she knew better, tried to sidetrack the issue and change topics. I knew then that she was going to create trouble for all of us." His voice slowed down as if in a flashback, "Tch...I could it see it in her eyes – big trouble with a capital T."

Bhai* - Brother (Hindi)

Chapter 34

"How did you kill her?" she asked, her heart beating very hard.

"Aha...that wasn't very difficult. In course of the party at Mr. Mittal's, I heard her making a date with Ron to meet him the next day at Pearl valley. Ron wanted to use her photographic skills to take some shots of the valley. Amazingly, luck was on my side that day. While Ron and I were sitting under the pergola of the lawn, discussing about a future project, he got a call from home saying his mother was almost on her deathbed and wanted him back. He was totally flustered, poor fella, making calls to find a flight back to Delhi. He left, asking me to pass a message to Rianna and I was of course too happy to comply. Poor guy left his jacket on the seat too. What a stroke of luck!" Yuvi seemed to revel in that memory.

"Of course, I didn't pass on the message to Rianna and his jacket fitted me well too..."

"Rianna thought you to be Ron..." Tia whispered, aghast. Everything started to make sense now.

"Clever guess!" Yuvi raised his eyebrows in a taunting smile.

"She was waiting for Ron at Pearl Valley. Couldn't help playing a bit of hide and seek at the temple ruins as she kept calling for me. 'Ron! Ron!' Her voice echoed through the emptiness of the Valley." Yuvi smiled at the memory.

"Come to think of it I almost passed for Ron with his jacket and his height. From behind we almost look similar. Yet Tia, in spite of the similarities, you too had to choose him over me!" His voice rasped in agonized anger. "How I hate him and always hated for grabbing everything from me, right under my nose..."

His eyes bulged with hatred.

Tia closed her eyes at the scene of Rianna – so trusting and not knowing what lay ahead of her. Her beautiful sister, she thought, as tears streamed down her cheeks. A life cut away so unfairly and a person who no way deserved such a death.

"Gosh! I couldn't bear to hear his name on her lips." Yuvi's voice was dripped with bitterness as he ranted and raved uncontrollably. "From the time I knew him he always competed with me in every sphere – whether it be in the playground, in college or with the ladies. Especially the women – they were attracted to him like moths to a flame. And some way or the other, he always managed to destroy any bit of happiness that was promised as mine. And here was this woman I loved and hated at the same time calling out for him."

"And what did you do to her!" asked an agonized Tia. She remembered Regan's words about how Rianna's body had lost all traces of a human being. It was badly mutilated.

"Actually at that moment, I couldn't stand to see the sight of your sister – especially after I heard Ron's name on her lips..." He spitted out and his voice turned venomous. "She was with Ron too – my enemy, my nemesis all my life! I didn't want to malign my hands with her. Instead of giving her a piece of my mind, I decided she deserved the likes of Chandru, an inhuman, necrophiliac killer that Jai had brought with him." Yuvi slanted his head to point at the bulky guy next to him who had stared at Tia all the while with the most lewd expression on his face. "After all that she had done to me and my life, that was what she deserved!"

His laugh was ugly as he seemed to gloat at his victory. Tia could feel nausea build inside her as images ran through her mind. Necrophiliac killer!!! For the first time in her life, Tia saw pure sinister evil in human form as Chandru looked almost proud of himself.

"Oh, come on boss...each to his own taste," said Chandru with a sly grin. His gaze at some far memory seemed to be filled with feverish excitement.

"Control yourself, Chandru," Yuvi mocked at him and turned to her with a self-congratulatory smile. "I threw that chain at her – the chain with the pentacle locket that I used to wear for her! I beckoned Chandru who couldn't wait to get his hands on your sister. And he did the honours, of course – on your unsuspecting sister..."

Tia swallowed the uncontrollable whimper that almost threatened to overwhelm her. She closed her eyes to hide the tears from the monsters that gloated at her every reaction.

Yuvi turned to Chandru as he said in fake concern, "Chandru, actually that was hitting below the belt, man...you know – striking her from behind, catching her unawares. If you ask me, you must at least give a little warning to your victim beforehand...kind of give them some time to prepare. Very indecent of you, huh?!"

Yuvi shook his fingers at Chandru as if to a child and they laughed, thrilled at the memory. These bastards were enjoying this, she thought incredulously, seething inside.

"Oh, she was busy looking at the chain that hit her skirt from nowhere," Chandru mocked. "And when I hit her with the wrench from behind, even then she thought I was Ron, Boss!"

"She did? Come on...how could you know?" Yuvi's eyes looked frenzied as he seemed to enjoy Rianna's last painful moments, thought Tia in incredulous disgust.

"Yes, Boss! When she turned around, she was almost swaying trying to maintain her balance. Yet, with her hands holding her bruised head and her eyes half open, she cried out, 'Ron, is that you...why Ron...and blah blah blah'" He imitated cruelly as they all laughed. "Maybe her vision was hazy or something...and I was like – who is this hero? But dizziness seemed to catch up and she crashed off within a second – swish to the ground!" He motioned to show his hand falling quickly at a 90 degree angle. "Madame was quite a strong lady, though. In spite of the heavy concussion she was still semi-conscious!"

"Wow!" Yuvi's lips were curved cruelly as he seemed to enjoy every bit of Chandru's account.

Chandru's eyes lighted up at the memory as he gushed, "Ohh, I'd never had sex with a half-alive woman before. It was an exotic adrenalin rush of blood for me. Didn't go to say she wasn't equally bad after I strangled her. A rape to relish, for sure!"

"You make me sick, man!" said Jai with a disgusted look and he did turn a bit of green in his face.

"It's just a different kind of addiction, Jai, or a vice you could say. Nothing different from yours! Don't give me that holier than thou look, will you? Especially after we know how you tried to kill Tia but failed!" said Chandru with a jeer.

"I am getting out of here. Can we stop wasting time and get out of here, Yuvi?" Jai fumed, his patience wearing thin. "Let Chandru do whatever you called him for..."

"Wait, I was just beginning to enjoy this moment after a long time, Jai," said Yuvi like a man possessed by the taste of revenge.

"You're dragging this shit unnecessarily," Jai lashed out in disgust. "What if the police get a scent of this before we can dispose her off?"

"Scared of the police, aren't we, Jai?" Chandru's chuckle was malicious and patronizing. "But I guess he is right, Boss. I think you should carry on with the rest of the plan and leave her to me...I am kind of getting restless anyway. This usually happens when a hot, sexy lady like her lies wasted in front of me..."

"Leave her, Chandru!" commanded Yuvi as Chandru looked like he was about to touch Tia.

"But you promised me I can have her once I help you..."

"Promises depend on my feelings..." Yuvi's voice was autocratic as he raised a mocking brow at Chandru.

"I hope you will not go back on your word, Boss?"

"Mind your language, Chandru, and don't forget who is the boss!"

"So you mean I can't have her?!" Chandru's voice sounded impatient and almost threatening.

"It depends on what I feel of the situation at the moment. So why don't you just go and cool your heels for a while. I will call you when required," said Yuvi coolly.

Chandru walked away in a huff but not before giving Tia a lascivious look as if to say my eyes are on you.

Jai seemed to pace around restlessly.

"Hope you're not getting emotional now, buddy, and decide to change your plans. She might just bring doom on all of us..."

"Relax, Jai. Tia hasn't heard the full story yet," said Yuvi as he moved closer to Tia, assessing her, almost as if he was reliving a memory.

His voice was soft as he said, "After Rianna died, I was almost a broken man and living like one who was dying every day. Although my work kept me alive, still everything around me seemed lifeless and dull. And then there came the day when I saw you again, Tia, in Uncle Neal's office, all grown up and beautiful! Something tender stirred inside me again, Tia. I wanted to live again not for money this time but for happiness and a family. A family that was lost to me before I could come to terms with life and the world. It was just like finding Rianna all over again."

"If I only knew the pain you were going through, Yuvi. If only you would have trusted me and told me everything!" said Tia in earnest.

"Then what would you have done, Tia? You already let me down when you too began snooping around the company files like a hungry dog trying to help Uncle Neal with his bloody losses. Of course I was on my toes this time and could cover up. Poor Jai got fired instead." He jeered.

But Jai looked really pissed off now. "We don't need to hear the whole story again," he said. He sounded like a man who was somehow managing to hold on to his temper with great effort.

"We do, Jai, we do," Yuvi said with a controlled patience. "At least Tia does. I tried so hard not to get too close as I didn't want to lose her. Kept offering my friendship but she never seemed to get how much I loved her!" He almost shouted the last bit as he threw his hands in the air, acutely frustrated.

"When you tried to kill her on that hilly road, I kept protecting her from you and your brother, Jai. But she still seemed not to see it!" He let out a sigh of bitterness.

"To be frank, you were only digging your own grave, bro," said Jai, shaking his head disgustedly. "She would have found out all about it anyway – at least with all the snooping she was busy with..."

"Ha ha ha...but I found out eventually, didn't I?" He looked at her with spite and triumph. "Nobody plays dirty with me and gets away, Tia, nobody!"

All kind of thoughts were racing in Tia's head as she looked at Yuvi letting out all the things he had concealed in his heart for so long. He was giving full vent to his vindictive feelings against all those he felt had done him wrong and was glorifying at having survived it all. It hadn't been easy for him she always knew that for a fact and sometimes felt sad too. What with having no parents to love him or a sibling to share his pain, the tragedy of losing his parents must have taken quite a toll on him. Uncle Neal had taken care of his accommodation, school and college education besides being a trustee till he completed his studies. But Uncle Neal had his own business and family to concentrate on. Maybe that's why Yuvi always felt deprived of love and trusted no one. He grew up with cynical eyes thinking that the world was out to get him. Why, after she hit her teens she too withdrew from his life and saw less and less of him what with the tragedies in her own life. Ron had told her that Yuvi had been very possessive about their friendship too. Maybe this feeling of competitiveness and distrust grew from years of loneliness and having to fend for himself, she mused.

"You thought yourself to be very clever by trying to get more evidence against me didn't you, Tia? Just like your sister? It was history repeating itself with Ron in the picture again, wasn't it?" he snarled.

"But it all backfired! Your plan to hand me over to the police and marry that son of a bitch Ron..."

"If I loved Ron, would I have confessed everything to you that day, Yuvi? Actually...for a long time I had stopped having any feelings for Ron....Oh Yuvi, if only you trusted me!?"

"What do you mean...?" he asked, a concealed bafflement creeping into his voice.

"I wouldn't have done what Rianna did. That's the difference between me and her. If you only gave me a chance! I would have talked about it and tried to understand why you did the things you did..."

Yuvi was silent for a moment as he looked at her with narrow eyes.

"I can understand what you have been through only now, Yuvi. After all we go back a long way, don't we?"

"You are lying!" He bit out furiously.

"I'm not! Believe me! You have been my childhood friend, Yuvi. The best moments of my life were with you...I remember every time you saved me from Mom and Dad when I got into trouble. You taught me to ride my first bike...nursed my wounds every time I hurt myself...how can I forget that, Yuvi? Ron has been there only for what – a few months in my life? But you were there for a lifetime...no one can take that away!" she said in a soft voice. "Ron was just my outlet to beat the loneliness in my life. If I only knew that you were going through the same loneliness as me, Yuvi, things would have been very different today, I assure you."

There was the sound of a sharp intake of breath and it was Jai, who looked incredulous enough to almost fall off his chair, "Gosh! That's a lying bitch if I ever saw one!"

Yuvi didn't answer as he contemplated his shoes for a moment.

"You think she is lying, Jai?" he asked quietly.

"Need you ask?" He was interrupted by the sudden ringing of the phone again.

"Hello Ron – buddy, what is it?" answered Yuvi in a cool voice. "What for...well I am actually visiting a friend right now...can't it wait till tomorrow? Well, alright!"

"What's up?" asked Jai, every inch of his body looking stiff with tension.

"Ron wants to come visit me with a police officer and ask a few questions. Says it might help shed some light on Tia's disappearance."

"So they suspect us?" asked Jai in agitation.

"Ron says they have asked the same questions to the rest of her family and friends. Just a customary routine check on the part of the police. Relax, Jai. No way Ron or anyone else can be suspicious of me as I have kept quite a distance from Tia in the last few months. If I am not wrong, it should be Ron who could actually be seen as a suspect."

His voice was mocking as he gestured at Tia and said, "Tia has voiced her suspicions to more than one about how Ron could be involved in Rianna's murder."

"I will relax once you have done away with her," Jai muttered in anger. "Aren't you just delaying the inevitable..."

"Let me deal with Tia the way I think best," said Yuvi in a sharp voice while he slapped a duct tape over Tia's mouth to stop her from making any noises. He then beckoned Jai outside and locked the door from behind, leaving her a hostage inside.

Chapter 35

Tia raised her tied hands high over her head and swung her arms down a couple of times but she was unable to get the duct tapes off. She tried to recall every single detail of the lesson she had received from the instructor when she was in her teens. The memory was hazy and she strained her mind to remember it as clearly as possible. She had to bring the elbows close together so that duct tape was tight around her wrists. She remembered the instructor's words that rang out more clearly this time and slammed down her elbows by bringing them towards her ribcage. Her elbows slid sideways over her flanks and her palms splayed onto her stomach at the same time. The swinging pressure of her hands caused the duct tapes to come off successfully.

Now that her hands were free, she quickly pulled off the tape on her mouth and concentrated on freeing her legs from the duct tapes tied round them. She put her palms together between her knees and forced down her joined palms below into a hard fast blow. She got it right at the first try itself as the blow forced her legs apart and that helped tear off the duct tapes.

She tried pulling and pushing the door alternately. But the door didn't even budge a single inch. She looked around and desperately felt the walls around her with her hands to find some clue as to how to get out of the room. But there was nothing she could find that would help her get out of the room. She sat on the floor in defeat when she heard some squeaking noises from around the corner. It was a rat coming out from below the narrow space of the single cupboard in the room. Then there was another rat and then one more. They ran hither thither in confusion as well as excitement at seeing a human approaching them. Tia wondered from where the rats had come as the room looked sealed perfectly with not a single crack anywhere.

She felt an urge to check the wall behind the cupboard. But the cupboard was heavy and refused to move. On trying to open the door of the cupboard, she found it locked. She searched for the keys all across the room though without any luck. She ran her fingers over the top of the cupboard that was as high as six feet. To her pleasant surprise, her hands moved over a bunch of keys! She was thrilled to find that they were the right keys to the cupboard. Opening the door, she discovered that the cupboard had a lot of hardware inside And she quickly threw them on the floor and emptied it. Tia could easily displace the cupboard this time and behind it she found a narrow outlet of about three feet. Quickly opening it, she found a dark tunnel inside. Voices and footsteps were drawing near and without a second's thought, she got down on her feet and scuttled through the hole.

The door opened and she heard Jai's voice saying urgently, "We need to finish her off before Yuvi gets back or..."

There was a second of silence when Chandru saw her feet and muttered, "The bitch's running..."

"Quick! Go get her..." Tia lost the voice as she scrambled blindly through the dark hole. She hoped desperately that the hole led her to something before the men caught up with her.

Her heart did a crazy beat when she felt some movement behind her. With all her strength she raced as fast as she could on bended knees. The tunnel seemed to have no end as she found herself scratched multiple times and layers of cobwebs sticking on her face. She felt tiny insects crawling on her face too and she disgustedly rubbed them off. Suddenly, she saw a ray of light making its way and she climbed out into the open space ahead of her. Looking around, Tia saw that she was inside a computer warehouse with racks and racks of computer hardware. She looked around frantically for the exit door of the warehouse when she was forced to halt in her steps. She found herself facing none other than Chandru – a monster in disguise of a human being and she was terrified.

"Hello, Tia. Looking for me?" His slimy smile bespoke evil – savage evil!

Tia quickly glanced behind her and started to back away.

"Stop it, Tia. Tch...stop making it so hard for us," he drawled lazily.

Her feet felt almost paralyzed as the monster charged at her but somehow she forced herself to backtrack at an equally increasing speed. Her hand unknowingly nudged a tower of cartons on her left and she blindly pushed them at him. She instantly ran to increase the distance between them as he floundered among the boxes that fell on him one by one. She bolted through the rows of racks and crouched silently in the shadows to hide herself. She was panting painfully as she tried to listen very hard for her assailant's footsteps. She didn't hear anything for a while but footsteps coming from afar.

"Tia! Where are you, Tia? You know I am going to find you anyway...so stop delaying it, will you, darling."

Suddenly she found herself staring into the feet of her assailant who was just two rows away from the rack hiding her. She clamped her mouth hard to stop whimpering in fear. She was sweating all over. Her hands and feet felt like jelly as he kept calling out to her almost in a melody. She quietly crept backwards on bent knees as her assailant turned around to reach the adjacent rack. She kept backtracking away quietly to cover as much distance as possible.

Once she felt there was some distance between them, she quickly took off her shoes and ran quietly through the rows of racks ahead of her. She felt tired as she couldn't find any exit but endless rows of racks, one after the other. In one corner, there were a few big cartons thrown carelessly in a heap. She quietly got into one of them and hid herself by pulling another carton on top of hers. Her heart beat wildly as she listened to his footsteps that seemed to be quite a distance away from her.

"Help me please, my dear God! There is no way I can get out of here without your help. Only you can save me from this monster. Get me out of here God, pleaseeee!" Tears and sweat rolled down her cheeks as she joined her hands and prayed earnestly.

Chapter 36

"He's getting quite restless, Dhruv. Do you think I should make the call now?" asked Ron.

Dhruv checked his watch and bit his lip thoughtfully. "Umm...it's twenty minutes since he got here. I think it should be okay now...go ahead and make the call."

Ron nodded as he looked at Yuvi's figure pacing restlessly up and down the patio. "Right! I don't want him to get suspicious and change his plans."

He dialled Yuvi's number and spoke in an offhand manner, "Hey Yuvi, are you back?"

"Yes Ron, where are you? I am waiting," said Yuvi in a quiet, impatient voice.

"Actually, I will not be able to make it and Regan – hope you remember Krystal's cousin...yes that's the one. He got some other leads related to her disappearance and they are headed that way..."

"Oh! Is it? Any idea where that might be?"

"No, they didn't divulge much."

"Alright. Hope they find her soon..."

"Yeah, I know. It's been like twenty-four hours since she's been missing...we are really worried."

"Me too." Yuvi sighed unhappily. "Have they checked if she's gone to the countryside...she does paint a lot in the woods..."

"Yes, the police are on the lookout there too."

"Ok. Keep me informed, Ron. It would break my heart if anything happened to Tia. We have been friends for so long..."

"Sure, Yuvi."

Dhruv and Ron saw Yuvi lock up his door and hurry to the car. They were hiding behind a few trees across the road. They got into their car quickly and started trailing him unobtrusively from behind.

"We better keep four-five cars between us, Dhruv, or he might get suspicious," said Ron, worry creasing his brows.

"Hmm. I am trying...haven't ever trailed a car before. Although it wouldn't be too difficult to hide ourselves, what with this slow moving, busy traffic. But if he takes the highway or some empty street, then it would be another matter altogether."

"I, for the life of me, can't imagine Yuvi as a part of this or writing any of those letters." Ron sounded baffled.

"Are you sure? There is something about him that made my toes curl all the time. Especially his eyes and the quiet way he kept his watchful eyes on you, and I am not a bad judge of character. He always got on my nerves. If not for Neal, I'd have left the company long back."

"I remember we had some good times together in college," Ron sighed. "But he had this need to control, be it in his habits or people. And sometimes he was too petty in his outlook about things and that really got to me. Wanted us to hang on in that small world of his. Trusted no one. Later it got too suffocating for me. He didn't like it when we drifted off, that I knew for sure."

"But you did business too with him later, didn't you...after you left college?" Dhruv asked curiously.

"Yes, we kind of met after maybe two-three years and were nostalgic about our college life. So in that spirit we decided to start one or two projects together. I soon realized his dealings weren't ethical and I stopped doing any business with him from then on."

"I don't understand how Tia got along so well with him...that baffles me too," said Dhruv in a puzzled voice.

"Well, she always did see him as a childhood friend. Dhruv, look out...he's taken a left," said Ron.

"Ya...I got him..."

"I think it's time I alerted Regan too..." Ron mused.

"I realize Regan thinks this could be a red herring...but we can't take chances. It's already six pm now. Twenty-four hours since she was last seen," said Dhruv.

"Hello, Regan!" Ron said. "Yuvi did come to meet us at his house...yes, we are now trailing him through MG Road...Alright."

"What did he say?" asked Dhruv.

"He is coming with two of his officers. He doesn't want to take any chances by not believing us, he says. If we feel there might be some missing piece here, he thinks it better to look it up."

"Good!" agreed Dhruv in relief.

"Wonder what she is doing right now...is she alive or..." Ron couldn't bring himself to complete the words. Never in his life had he felt so powerless, so choked with fear about anything or anyone.

"Keep the faith, buddy, keep the faith..." Dhruv put his hand reassuringly on Ron's arm. "Heavens! Looks like he is in quite a hurry..."

"Yes! You better speed up, Dhruv, or we might just lose him."

Chapter 37

"Great hiding place, Tia!" he chortled triumphantly as he caught her neck in a vice and shoved her out of the box. He then curled his other arm around her neck from behind.

Tia felt an intense spasm of pain flow through her neck and shoulders as he increased the pressure and dragged her with him. She pulled at his arms to prevent him from choking her but felt powerless against the beast's superior strength. Instinctively, she sunk her hips down while thrusting her right elbow forcefully behind into his ribcage. With her left hand stopping his arm from squeezing her neck, she quickly curled her right hand into a fist with the thumb jutting out and swung it up to stab at his face. He grunted as her thumb made contact with his eyes. This move helped loosen his grip for a split second which mutually provided her some leeway to slide her hips and step sideways to the left. She quickly head-butted the side of his face while thrusting her fist into his groin. As he bent in pain, she pulled at the trouser of his right leg which weakened his balance and in a flash she moved to throw him to the ground.

Tia pushed herself to run as fast as she could. Her chest felt as if it would burst from exertion. She hardly crossed a couple of yards when he quickly closed the gap between them and locked his hands around her waist to grip her hard. She cried in anguish while slamming her rear end back into his hips as hard as she could. Quickly sidestepping on his right, she bent slightly to hammer fists repeatedly at his groin.

"You bitch..." he swore as he grimaced in pain while she gripped his locked hands and pushed her hips forwards. At the same time she pushed down her arms to break down his locked hands around her waist and run.

She hurtled between the rows of racks at an outrageous speed, feeling her lungs almost spasm out from overstrain. Tia had no clue as to where she was heading except that she had to get away from the clutches of the monster. She felt her breath almost giving up when she felt him grab her and swing her towards him. He then flung her very hard against the wall behind them.

"How dare you!" Chandru pinned her to the wall and grabbed her neck very hard. He was out to choke her till her last breath. She could feel her head reeling with dizziness and she tried to suck in air to keep herself alive. Through her blurred vision she forced herself to push both her joined palms up through the space inside his arms. As soon they swung up towards his face, she dug, scratched and poked his eyes, which made him squirm and crouch in pain. She massaged her neck while trying to gulp air into her lungs. She pushed herself away from the wall to bring some distance from him although she felt totally deprived of any energy. Her legs were wobbly and she felt too weakened to move away. As she struggled to move her feet she felt the wind knock out of her body when something flung at her from behind. It was a laptop with which Chandru had hit her and she crashed to the floor with a loud thud. As she turned on her back she saw Chandru advancing towards her.

She pushed with her feet and kept sliding away on her back across the floor. But Chandru flung himself over her and pinned her arms on the ground leaving her no room to hit him back.

"What are you going to do now, huh!?" he breathed near her mouth, his eyes glistening with feverish excitement. Tia tried to bring her knees inside and kick him but failed against his superior strength.

"This gets even more exciting, girl! Tia, you are a better lover than your sister ever was...or anyone for that matter," he snickered. "In fact no one has excited me like this before!"

His heavy body seemed to convulse as he breathed into her hair

"Let me go, pleasseee...," she cried, "please leave me...I beg you please..."

"What are you saying, Tia?" he questioned her in mock innocence as he licked his smelly tongue all over her face. "Oh Tia, this will be a night to remember."

Tia could hear a deep ugly animal moaning from afar.

"Oh! What a rush of adrenalin you bring in me, Tia, do you realize that?" He leered at her and then bit very hard into her neck. She screamed as a sharp needle-like pain coursed through her skin.

"Stop screaming, it hurts my ears!" he ordered as he sat on her hips and smacked her right across her face. He hit her so hard that she felt her jaw almost breaking into two. He boxed her again on the other cheek which made her scream with inexorable pain. Her eyesight blurred and her head was so numb that she felt she didn't exist anymore. Last she knew, Chandru was biting her everywhere and alternately pulling at her clothes while she slowly sank into darkness. There was no feeling here, or pain, except for a dark void where she kept sinking lower and lower.

There was a slight humming noise in the darkness which grew a little more audible and then droned like a vacuum cleaner running in the background. It was like white noise and she felt a little comfortable actually as she glided into the empty dark space. Suddenly, there was a tiny beam of light shining amidst the darkness that grew larger and larger. A silhouette of a figure was approaching her. She realized that it was a lady and her face looked familiar. Her heart skipped a bit when she realized that it was none other than her mom. She glowed all over, almost like an angel, as she walked slowly towards her. Her mother's face broke into a smile in absolute reassurance, as if to say, nothing would happen to her and she would be alright. She sat a little distance away and then the whole room lit up again with the glaring bright light. Tia felt herself back in the scene, in that warehouse with that monster plundering her body and mind.

Pain seared through her body as the beast Chandru pulled and tore her shirt away. Her mom was gently pointing at something and through the haze, she slowly moved her head on her right to check what it was. She could see that there were some tools lying on the bottom shelf of the rack that they were lying next to. She looked back at her mom who raised her arm to show something. It was a wrench she was holding.

Her lips didn't move but her eyes seemed to speak the words instead and say, "Use that".

When she turned back, she saw a wrench lying among the many tools left untidily in a mess. The beast had torn her shirt completely off and now he was pulling at her jeans. She tried to reach for the wrench. It was just too far off. Tears streamed down her face as she stretched her hand as much as she could.. Her mother nodded her head as if to say, 'go for it, you can do it, darling.'

Tia stretched her hand even further but still it was difficult to reach it due to the weight of Chandru sitting on top of her. Chandru had a hard time pulling her jeans and was swearing as he struggled to get it off. Finally she could manage to touch the wrench somehow but found it very hard to make a grab for it. Just as she thought she couldn't do this anymore, she felt a strange kind of warm energy flowing through her veins. This surge of energy helped her to catch hold of the wrench above her head. Chandru who managed to pull one leg off her jeans, noticed her trying to lift the wrench.

"Why, you bitch..." He snarled and reached across to grab her hand. By some miracle she found herself swinging the wrench and hurtling it hard on his head. There was the sound of a crack as the wrench hit his skull and bounced off tangentially the opposite way. Blood oozed out of his skull and Chandru fell heavily over her chest. She wiggled from under him and pushed his heavy body away as hard as she could. She felt a wave of dizziness as she sat upright but slowly managed to shake it off. She looked around for her mom but there was no one around. She thanked her silently as she unsteadily got to her feet and pulled her jeans to secure it around her hips. She pulled her torn shirt across her shoulders and tied the end lapels to cover her bosom. She felt almost naked but this was the last thing on her mind as she needed to escape before her other two captors had returned. She finally found the exit door and yanked it open.

But her relief was short-lived when she hit into a hard chest. She found herself thrown back into the warehouse again.

Chapter 38

"Not so soon, Tia Ma'am!"

It was Jai and he had a gun pointing at her.

"Any last minute prayers, Tia?" he laughed derisively.

"Don't do this, Jai..." she pleaded.

"Why, Tia? Do you know how long I have been waiting to see this day? Do you?" he lashed out.

"You don't need to do this, Jai!" she said softly. Somewhere in the recesses of her memory she remembered that he had a mother. But she was not sure. "What about your mother? Think about her, Jai..."

"Did you think of her when you fired me? Did you?" he cried. "I was out of job for a long time as no one was ready to hire me after that black spot in my career. Do you know how much it broke her heart!?"

"What do you think you're doing?" asked a cold voice from behind.

They hadn't noticed Yuvi who had walked quietly from behind.

"What do you think? We can't afford to take all the time in the world, Yuvi...it's now or never!"

"Let me decide that. Now hand over the gun to me," said Yuvi in a steely voice.

"She got to you, Yuvi. I can see it in your eyes. She talked you into this..."

"Stop talking rubbish and hand over the gun..."

"Then what?" Jai shouted. "What's your plan, Yuvi? You think she will marry you and walk into the sunset! Wake up, Yuvi! She knows everything now...the fact that you had her sister killed as well as all the fraud you committed in the company. She will skin you alive with all the charges dumped at you, Yuvi!"

Tia could see the nervous tick on the side of his forehead as Yuvi approached Jai determinedly.

"Yuvi, we can't afford to lose time arguing over this. Get away from me!" Jai turned sideways to point his gun at Tia but Yuvi dashed at that moment to grab his gun. Tia felt the shot whiz past her ears and she was shaken as it missed her by only a few centimetres.

"You are under arrest!"

All three turned to see that they were no longer alone. Tia almost cried with relief to see that it was Regan accompanied by two other policemen. They were pointing their guns at Jai and Yuvi while behind them stood Ron and Dhruv. Their eyes were watchful and tense as they darted glances between her and her two captors.

"Put your gun down and raise your hands," ordered Regan. "Come on, both of you!"

Yuvi and Jai looked watchful and undecided as the seconds ticked by. Jai kept backing off while still having his gun pointed at the police.

"Come on, put down the gun," shouted Regan "and raise your hands!"

Yuvi raised his hands slowly but Jai looked mutinous and almost frustrated as he refused to put down his gun.

Regan and both the police officers slowly moved closer, as Jai kept backing off and refusing to show any signs of surrender.

Before anybody could gauge what was happening he saw him pushing Yuvi off and grabbing Tia while holding her at gunpoint.

"Back off," he threatened, "or she is dead."

Regan and the officers looked at each other undecided as Jai took hold of Tia and moved her backwards with him.

"Put down your guns or I will kill her!" He screamed at them and pushed the revolver right into her head.

"Okay...okay...calm down!" Regan pacified as he looked at the other two officers and nodded his head.

All the three officers slowly lowered their guns to the ground when Jai screamed again, "Come on, do it fast!"

As soon as the officers lowered their guns on the floor, Tia felt his grip slacken a bit and she instantly hit her elbow into his ribs. This caught him unawares and Tia quickly lifted her arms to grab at his gun. But Jai shoved her off violently and she felt thrown against the wall behind her. He aimed his gun directly at her ribcage and aimed shots one after another. Tia closed her eyes to block off the intensity of the bullets. Surprisingly she felt nothing except for a loud cry in her ears. When she opened her eyes she saw Regan and the officers grabbing Jai. They handcuffed him immediately while lying next to them was Yuvi drenched in the pool of his own blood. His eyes were glazed over as he lay unconscious.

Her trembling body felt lifeless and she was about to collapse when she felt the warmth of Ron's arms around her.

"Oh, Tia!" He squeezed her tight. "I almost lost you!"

Tia grabbed him tighter and let all her fears dissolve into the comfort of his arms. Tears ran down her eyes as her body shook with the aftershocks. Ron petted her back soothingly and softly murmured, "It's okay...it's all over..."

When she quietened down, she saw the ambulance had arrived. Yuvi was being pulled up on a stretcher by a few nurses and doctors.

"He saved you...," whispered Ron softly.

Tia quietly nodded her head.

Regan came over after a few minutes and said, "The doctor would like to run a quick check-up on you, Tia. You are bleeding all over. We have Jai arrested but Yuvi has been declared dead."

Tia just nodded her head, too tired to react. She was made to rest at the hospital for the night with Ron and Krystal taking care of her needs.

Nysa arrived within seconds of the doctors dressing Tia's wounds with medicine and bandages. Her face was awash with tears as she flung herself at Tia and held her tight. "I am so sorry..." she sobbed through her muffled words. "I don't know what would I have done if anything happened to you, Podgy...please forgive me..."

Her eyes were swollen and red with tears as she looked at her sister. Her face looking pained and filled with immense regret.

"You know I have always loved you no matter what," said Tia as she too cried in relief. Relief that she had found her sister back. This life was no life without her sister by her side, she realized. "It was just circumstances that made us do what we did. Please do not say sorry. I would have done the same were I in your position, Nysa." Her eyes fleeted to Ron unknowingly and he had a slight smile on his face.

"I regret that I didn't take time to understand what was really wrong or why you felt like the way you did. I should have done that. Maybe I could have tackled this mess better," her sister sobbed in a guilt-stricken voice.

Tia hugged her sister and she felt as if she was the older one instead of her. "I have my sister with me, that's all that matters to me now. Fate gave me the most priceless gift and I feel I'm the luckiest person alive all because of you."

Everyone came one after another – Dev, Maya, and Uncle Neal, all distraught with worry. Her niece, Alisha, broke down at the sight of her, just like Nysa, and she had a hard time consoling her. Jeff too made his way to the hospital and ruffled her hair without saying a word.

The next day, Regan reported that Chandru was under custody though he was being given medical aid on account of being hit hard on the head. "Chandru's arrest might just help shed a light to some of our other unsolved rape and murder cases closely related to necrophilia."

Tia shuddered at that. "How did you know where to find me?" she asked curiously.

"Actually that was due to the genius of Dhruv," said Ron as he nodded towards Dhruv, sitting next to Regan.

Dhruv almost blushed; which was so unlike him, thought Tia, amazed.

"Yuvi! Who would have thought he could go this far!" said Ron, his voice incredulous.

"I swear! I've known Yuvi since he was a kid." Regan sighed. "He had sufficient alibis too on the day of Rianna's murder, so we never got a whiff of where the wind was blowing."

"But when I think back to our time in school, and after I put two and two together, I felt that it wasn't so odd and strange after all. So I decided to follow Dhruv's intuition," said Ron, darting his glance from one to the other. "We were also short of time and couldn't afford to take any chances. Dhruv and I searched for Yuvi in his house, office and all the likely places. When we didn't find him, we hitched out a plan to call him to his house on the pretext that the police wanted to talk to him. And then we followed him as unobtrusively as possible."

"Oh," said Tia. "But Dhruv, what caused you to be suspicious of Yuvi? Never in my wildest dreams, did I think it could be him."

"Actually, it was the letter you showed to me. The one with Wicca symbols that you thought I had written to Rianna. I found similar letters in a cabinet while searching for a software CD. That cabinet was lying in an unused office cabin previously occupied by Yuvi. There were many letters in the same format kept inside a box. It was a tiny box, untidy and lost amongst a heap of files in the cabinet. They were all unsigned like the one you had except for the love messages and Wicca symbols. Most importantly, one of them was signed in Yuvi's hand at the bottom. It really shook me. That was enough proof but I decided to find out more about those letters from the best person I knew and that was our Wicca practitioner, Tara Mehta. Tara told me that the letters were made of special paper and were from her store. The symbols and the paper had a special love spell infused in them for young lovers. In course of our conversation I also discovered that Yuvi was her nephew."

"Yes, Yuvi mentioned that Tara Mehta was his aunt," said Tia, still in shock.

"Yes," said Dhruv and he laughed. "It zapped me too."

Tia nodded her head slowly.

"Yuvi's dad was her cousin, it seems. She was impressed that her nephew had used some of her tools for his love life. She winked at me and spoke fondly of her nephew. What a successful man he was, she said proudly. But when it came to love, even a man like him came to her, she boasted."

"Whew!" exclaimed Tia, shaking her head. Ron and Regan looked equally bemused by Dhruv's account.

"From then on I started keeping an eye on Yuvi. I checked the history of some of my old Infosoft chats with Rianna as I vaguely recalled her talking about her uncle's partner's son. I didn't know Yuvi at all then. And there, in one of the chat conversations Rianna sounded puzzled. She was discussing with me whether she could trust Yuvi regarding his handling of her uncle's company account. So my suspicion grew even stronger and I was a little apprehensive when he got close to you."

"Okay, that's why I found you peeping over my hedges, is it?" Tia smiled in understanding.

"Well, yes..."

"What about the masked man at the office? Who was he?" she asked.

"Yes, Jai confessed that he was Yuvi's man and he wanted to kidnap you that day itself. He didn't mean to harm you but was pushed to do so by your resistance and impressive self-defence. Since it wasn't a success, Yuvi decided to take the matter in his own hands," said Regan.

"I see..."

"I am surprised there are no broken bones, Tia, after all you had to go through with that monster – Chandru," said Regan.

"I just got lucky I would say."

"No, Tia, we caught some of the action on the CCTV camera of the warehouse. There were quite a few punches you packed. I am truly impressed!" Regan raised his eyebrows in admiration.

"That was all because of Nysa's efforts of dragging me to the taekwondo classes after school," she said with a blush. Nysa beamed from the corner of the room.

"Ron, you better not heckle your future wife too much," teased Dhruv.

"I am very generous with tips on how to handle a martial artist, especially when she is your wife," said Jeff as he winked meaningfully and everyone in the room laughed. In the next couple of minutes, Ron was the target of all their puns but he sportingly took it all in.

Chapter 39

Once Tia was back home, everyone took great care of her. Her brother and sister-in-law cooked many healthy meals for her. There were guests pouring all the time with Krystal and Nysa being frequent visitors. And then there was Ron of course. He took utmost care and was solicitous of her every need. Tia found it so good to be back with him and love him without any guilt hovering like a dagger between them. For the first time she could love him with no conditions or doubts whatsoever. It was a very happy time for them except for the dreams she had in the night that still didn't stop. Rianna apparently still didn't want to see her with Ron and on the third night she had the goriest dream ever.

Tia dreamt that she was enjoying a quiet dinner with Rianna and Ron. They all looked happy as they sat eating and chatting about their happy times together. Suddenly Tia saw herself looking very evil as she exchanged a conspiratorial smile with Ron. Ron looked evil too as he acknowledged her nod and his eyes glinted with depraved excitement. Suddenly he grabbed Rianna's throat and started choking her. Rianna turned to her for help, screaming, "Help me Tia, he will kill me!"

At that moment Tia saw herself taking a knife from her pocket and stabbing Rianna several times while she twisted and jerked in pain. Tia screamed and woke up and Ron was immediately at her side. He held her tight while she slowly calmed down and then quietly put her back to bed again.

Early the next morning, Krystal called up.

"Tia, Mira has scheduled a meeting today with Sushma Ahuja, the paranormal investigator, to come and meet you at your house. Is that okay with you?"

"Yes! She called at the right time, actually. I really need to see her now."

"Strange but Mira sounded excited today saying Sushma already knew that she would be called soon for a haunting in this area."

"Whoa!" said Tia, amazed, as she hung up.

"Who was that?" asked Ron.

"Would you believe it if I said I have invited a paranormal investigator? You could also call her a ghost hunter."

"A ghost hunter?" he asked puzzled. "I did see something regarding it on some TV channel – maybe the Discovery channel or some similar channel..."

"Yes, they help in clearing bad energy or ghosts from haunted places," she said as she locked her arms around his neck and gazed into his eyes. "Are you surprised?"

Tia laughed when he feigned defeat and said, "Nothing amazes me where you are concerned. I am signed in for life, aren't I?"

He kissed her deeply like a thirsty man who'd finally found the oasis he had been looking for.

They were interrupted by the doorbell. It was Krystal and Mira with two other women. One of them was Sushma Ahuja.

"Hello, dear," said Sushma. "As Mira might have already told you, I am what everyone calls a paranormal investigator or a ghost hunter. But I prefer to call myself a spiritual healer as I rescue spirits who are lost in this earthly realm. These spirits are trapped within a thin line between the earth and the spiritual plane. I help them cross over to the other side or reach the light which some also call heaven. I cleanse the place haunted by them by clearing their energy and helping them with a smooth transition to the other side. I heal them of their pain and unresolved issues. Hence, I and many in our field are also known as the spiritual healers."

She had long, thick hair and deeply kohled eyes. She looked motherly and made everyone feel at ease. Her assistant, Isha, however looked very young, somewhere close to Tia's age. Sushma asked Tia not to divulge anything till she got a feel of the place.

Sushma, Isha and Mira started walking around her apartment, murmuring and exchanging notes while Tia, Krystal and Ron waited in the living room. Nysa also joined them a couple of minutes later. She had shown a keen interest to join them when Tia informed her about who she had invited. She, however, took it all with a pinch of salt. It was really hard for her to believe in stuff like this.

After a while, Sushma and Mira asked permission to visit Dev and Maya's apartment too. Tia looked at Nysa, unsure. She didn't know what her brother would say to all of this. But when they went up, Maya was more than glad. She had felt some paranormal activity in the ground floor for a long time now but as time went by, she ignored it as it didn't bring any negative effect on them or bother them anyway. Another reason as to why Maya had given up trying to figure it out was, she said, because Dev had often ridiculed her doubts as superstition. Luckily this time Dev too had a change of opinion. He admitted that after the recent occurrences in his youngest sister's life, he didn't know what to believe anymore.

"There are no signs of a haunting in the first and second floors, so let's go downstairs," said Sushma after a while.

Dev, Maya and Alisha also gathered in Tia's living room with Nysa, Tia, Krystal and Ron. The psychics sat separately at the dining table as they wanted to discuss a few things alone before resuming their work. Sushma and her team then came back to the living room and to discuss their findings with all of them.

"A few days ago, I had an amazing premonition about a female in the spirit world, haunting mostly the ground floor of a three-storied building. I also got something related to sisters, or sisterly love you can say...and most importantly a murder – if you don't mind my being open about this," said Sushma.

They all exchanged surprised glances while Mira shrugged her shoulders and said, "I didn't say anything!"

"Actually, even before a client calls me about a case, few days prior to that, I will get some premonitions about the place where there is a haunting," Sushma explained.

"Okay," said Tia.

"Do you find things being displaced in the house, often?" Sushma asked.

Alisha nodded her head vigorously to that along with Tia.

"What about the tap opening in a bathroom downstairs?"

"That too!" chorused both Alisha and Tia together.

"I too have come across that phenomenon whenever I have been downstairs to dust or clean a room," said Maya slowly.

"Also a blast of cold or warm air for no reason?" asked Isha.

"Yes, that too!" said Tia quickly.

"A feeling that someone is watching you..." asked Sushma.

"Yes, I have felt that often during my sleepovers here," said Krystal.

"A feeling that it is a female...?" Isha asked, looking at Krystal.

Krystal looked at Tia and then turned back and said, "Absolutely."

"Lots of dreams about one person, a person from this family who is no more...sometimes intense and gory?" asked Sushma.

"Yes, but not gory," said Alisha in a rush. "Sad maybe at times but not gory, definitely!"

"Yes, Alisha and I have often dreamt about someone that we lost. But whereas mine has been sometimes gory, hers hasn't been so," said Tia.

The psychics got up after a while and resumed their investigation as they walked from room to room. Sushma asked Tia to accompany them for queries they might have. So she followed them while the rest stayed back in the living room.

"It feels a bit funny here," said Isha who went pale as soon as she stood near the window of Tia's bedroom.

"Yes, I feel a bit weird too...some kind of sinking feeling in my stomach," agreed Sushma.

"I can feel a change in temperature here...almost cold...," said Mira.

"Yes, as if somebody is standing here....Do you feel sickly?" asked Sushma suddenly.

"Yes, I feel sick...and almost dizzy...with this spirit," said Isha.

Sushma walked closer to Mira and focused her pendulum at that very spot. "Let us know who you are...reveal yourself to us..." she said in a deep authoritative voice.

The pendulum started to swing rapidly at that moment.

"She is here...she is here," whispered Mira.

"I can see a lady walking that way," said Isha.

"Oh!" exclaimed Tia.

"Clairvoyantly I mean...I saw a vision walking that side...it's the spirit..." answered Isha at Tia's bewildered expression.

"Where?" asked Sushma.

Sushma took the pendulum and followed Isha to Tia's study room.

"I felt a light touch on my back!" Sushma sounded excited as she walked towards the bookshelf. She pointed to the book shelf and said, "It feels like this spirit loves this place and it brings her good memories, especially because of all the photographs lined in this area..."

"Now she is going out of the study and walking towards the dining area," said Isha as they all walked out.

"She tilted the photo frame hanging on the wall," said Isha while pointing towards the wall next to the dining table.

"The photo frame is of Rianna," said Tia, bemused. "I have often found it tilted slightly for no reason, after I'd come home in the evenings from office."

"Hmm...." Isha looked around speculatively.

Sushma called out loud, "Can you give us some signs that you are here with us?"

At that moment the lights in the living room blinked four to five times.

Everyone in the room looked at each other amazed.

"Can you make a sound?" asked Sushma again.

Almost immediately, the wind chimes near the window began to ring continuously for a while.

"Do you want our help?" asked Sushma to no one in particular.

"I think so," Isha confirmed after a while. "She needs our help."

"Gosh," said Mira, "I feel this spirit is upset about something."

"Yes, I get a feeling of being upset...very angry about something...over here."

"Where?" asked Isha

"Near this designer wooden shelf," said Sushma.

Isha walked towards the wooden shelf near the dining table and rubbed her chin thoughtfully.

"Yes, I can see her clairvoyantly," said Sushma. "She says, 'she won't listen to me'."

"Who?" asked Isha.

"She says, 'Tia won't listen to me!'" said Sushma with a startled look.

There was a sharp intake of breath as everyone looked mesmerized.

"What could be the reason?" Isha looked vaguely at the shelf. "Oh, she is pointing to that photograph!"

"Yes, she points to this photograph and angrily says, 'Tia won't listen to me!'" said Sushma, "and she shakes her head desperately."

They were shocked to see that it was the photograph of none other than Ron.

"Does that make sense?" asked Sushma. "She says again while shaking her head repeatedly, 'I told Tia not to trust him but she won't listen to me!'"

"Yes, she says Tia needs help," said Isha in a worried voice. "She shakes her head in worry..."

"The accident...she says...Tia had an accident last May...I need to help her," said Sushma, her eyes agog and she looked at no one in particular. In fact both the paranormal investigators seemed to be talking and listening to someone around them who was not visible to the naked eye.

"She says Ron wants to kill her," said Isha.

"Yes, I can explain that," said Tia slowly. She went on to explain the psychics the details of Rianna's death and how Rianna had thought Yuvi to be Ron at the time of her death.

"Okay," said Sushma, as she looked around analytically with half-closed eyes. "She is confused and thinks Ron was responsible for her death. She also wants to protect you, Tia, lest you go through the same ordeal. Her confusion over her death as well as her love for you has her trapped here on this earthly plane. We need to get her to the light and help her transition to the other side. For that we have to create a virtual psychic doorway for her to cross the other side. So, first we need to cleanse all the rooms with sage and seal it so that her spirit cannot escape there. Then we need to send her healing energy from all of us so that she can move peacefully to the spirit world. Alright?"

Sushma lighted up sage and went from room to room, filling it with its essence and chanting a prayer repeatedly everywhere she went, "I fill this room with love and light to keep everyone here safe, day and night. God send your angels here to guard every door. Dear Father, send your healing energy and protection on this family so that it is guarded by your divine light forever and ever. So mote it be."

Sushma sat along with Isha and meditated for a while in the dining area while the others waited in silence.

"Rianna," said Sushma aloud, "there has been a misunderstanding here. It wasn't Ron that was responsible for your death. It was three very bad men. Two of them, Jai Biswas and Chandru Thakur, are in police custody now; while the third one, Yuvi Raval, is in the court of God for justice to work itself out. You need to forgive and get over these vengeful feelings for Ron as he was no way responsible for your death."

Sushma then came out of her meditative state and turned towards them. "Now, Tia and Krystal, we need your help to send Rianna into the spirit world. Please hold hands with Mira and Isha. We will all join hands now and stand in a circle."

All five - Mira, Isha, Sushma, Krystal and Tia stood in a circle and joined hands.

"We will invite the spirit to stand in the circle of light between us. Krystal, Tia – imagine that inside your head there is a bowl of light which will flow through your head, then your neck, your body, your legs till it reaches your feet. Imagine that the stream of light is growing roots deep into the ground. This will ground you to this earthly plane and keep you safe from anything that might be negative or dark energy. And nothing will happen to any of us. So start imagining a circle of light growing inside this circle. A circle of light that goes into a swirling tunnel. Can you focus, Tia and Krystal?"

"Yes, I can see a circle of light between us," said Tia.

"Me too. A circle of light forms a swirling tunnel between us," confirmed Krystal.

"Isha is going to get Rianna to walk into that beautiful divine light totally protecting everyone of us...so focus on that light...please focus on that light. Mira?"

"Yes, I can see the huge tunnel of light coming under Isha's arms."

"Concentrate so that we can make Rianna turn around and come forward," said Isha. "Come forward Rianna, come towards the light...Tia, Krystal, tell her..."

"Rianna, walk towards the light," said Tia

"Move towards the light, Rianna," urged Krystal.

"Focus so that Isha can turn her around and make her walk to the light," said Sushma.

"Gosh! Tia, don't waver," said Isha in an alarmed voice. "I can feel you sway...you are going back to the last memory of Rianna...don't do that, Tia! It will weaken the spirit."

"I can sense Rianna going through that painful time at her death too," said Mira worriedly.

"Rianna, you need to get away from your last memory...you are just a few steps away from home...so don't let that memory stop you dear," said Isha.

"Tia, can you tell Rianna to move forwards to the light please, because your voice is not reaching her," said Sushma.

"Go towards the light, Rianna...," said Tia.

"Tia, raise your energy please," said Isha in a plea. "Come off from that dark place...the spirit needs higher positive energy from you to help her move towards the light..."

"I am trying...my heart's racing," said Tia as her voice shook.

"No, Tia," said Sushma in an agonized whisper, "don't go to that memory pleaseee..."

"I am not able to get past it...there's panic in my heart...I can see those images of that brute Chandru...raping her...beating her..."

"It will stop her from going to the other side Tia, focus honey, focus," coaxed Sushma.

"Rianna, forget that last memory...aahh...getting pain in my body, my chest..." said Isha as her face grimaced in pain.

"Tell her to take it off," commanded Sushma.

"Take off that pain, Rianna," said Isha "Gosh! I can feel her pain...her final earth bound moments...she is feeling intense pain...aaah...it's hurting..."

"No, Isha," said Sushma in a firm voice, "that will stop her...move her away from that energy...tell her to take it off!"

"Take it off, Rianna...take it off," commanded Isha, "ouch...there is too much pain..."

"That is the point of death for the spirit, Isha! Tell her to take it off," said Sushma in a pleading voice.

"Aahh..." Isha squirmed in pain. "Oh God..."

"Take some deep breaths," commanded Sushma, "tell me it's going."

"Oh, Lord Krishna...," Isha squirmed.

"Tell her to take it off, Isha..."

"I think...I think we just need to get her in the light...," said Isha breathlessly.

"Yes? Ok...Tia, please tell her to walk forwards...towards the light please..." Sushma urged.

"Walk forwards to the light, Rianna," said Tia.

"I can see a woman spirit coming from the other side," said Isha, almost in relief, "an older woman."

"Yes, it's a mother figure...," said Sushma.

"It's their mom...Rianna and Tia's mom," confirmed Mira.

"Yes, she is walking towards Rianna," said Sushma excitedly.

"We are taking her through now...let's raise our energy levels...focus on that tunnel of light waiting for her...concentrate so that we can take her through...focus so that we can aid her walk to her mother," said Isha.

"Can she see the light?" asked Sushma.

"Yes...yes!" said Isha.

"Yes!" said Sushma.

"She is going right through towards her mother and getting hold of her hand...totally through to the other side with her mother...she has reached her mother...excellent!" said Isha.

"She's okay now," Sushma breathed a sigh of relief. "It's confirmed!"

"Good! Good! She's gone through," said Mira excitedly.

"Everyone help seal the door of the tunnel now...seal the door now with white light...seal it...so that she cannot come back," said Sushma.

"Doubly seal it," said Isha in a stronger voice.

"Are you alright?" asked Sushma.

"Yes," said Tia with a feeling of lightness. "Yes!"

"Yes, she has crossed over the other side," said Sushma as she hugged

Tia who was in tears.

"My heart's just slowed right down." Tia laughed, her face filled with wonder.

"Gosh! That was very, very painful!" said Isha with a relief.

"Are you feeling okay now?" Sushma asked her assistant in concern.

"Yes...but I need to sit down...gosh this was one of the hardest...but we managed to do it!" Isha's eyes squeezed shut for a second. "Sorry, Tia, if I squeezed your hand too hard."

"No, no..."

"I feel so happy...feel like laughing or something." Krystal swung around her arms joyously in the empty air.

"That's because of the release of blocked energy...the whole atmosphere around will lift now," said Sushma.

"Yes, I can feel it....everything is tingling – my face, my hands." Krystal moved her fingers softly over her arms.

Everyone was intensely moved by the experience as they hugged each other and wiped out silent tears. Nysa and Alisha hugged Tia as they stood in a circle and they all had a moving moment between them. Dev kissed the top of Tia's head as he murmured, "I am sorry for the lack of understanding from my side, Tia."

Tia knew her brother was not a man of many words and what little he said went a long way. She hugged him back as she felt comforted by his acceptance; the warmth of his love flowing through her.

"Tia, I am glad you did this for all of us. We are all healed in many ways," said Maya as she hugged her sister-in-law.

"Your sister, Rianna, is at peace now...and in a really good place," assured Isha.

"That was really moving," said Nysa, her tears refusing to stop somehow.

"Did Grandma come through to take Rianna Aunty?" asked Alisha.

"Yes, sweetheart. It seems your grandmother has been trying to get Rianna to the other side for a long time now. Finally she could do it," said Sushma with a smile. "Let's have a celebration now and we will discuss it over coffee!"

Tia and Krystal served everyone with coffee while they got pizza delivered from the Dominos restaurant nearby.

"Does anyone have a ring of Rianna, a fish ring studded with coral stones that she might have worn during her death?"

"Yes," said Maya. "Before her final rites, the police officer, Regan, handed me the ring and I kept it in her bedroom cupboard...Tia, maybe you can check?"

Tia found the fish ring from the drawer of the cupboard and handed it over to Sushma. "So that's how Rianna's spirit was brought back to the house," said Sushma.

"But, Sushma, there wasn't much of a paranormal activity when I first came back home three years ago," said Tia. "Yes, there was a feeling of being watched by someone or a whiff of Rianna's favourite perfume but after a while I got used to it and didn't think much. I thought maybe it was my mind playing tricks on me and left it at that. It was only from around last May everything got more intense."

"Did you have an accident last May, Tia?"

"Yes, I did."

"That's when Rianna started getting worried about you. Just as in life, so after death, she was a peaceful ghost, though somewhat troubled. Kind of minded her own business, you can say. She was confused regarding her killer during the time of her death. This confusion kept her lost in the earthly realm. She kept wandering, lost and confused, her soul seeking redemption for the injustice meted out to her. When she sensed you to be in a similar danger, her worry for you caused her to seek your attention by hook or crook. She tried to reach for you through dreams mostly. Later, she tried to get more and more physical by moving things around."

"Yes, Tia," said Krystal, her voice excited as comprehension dawned on her. "And after Ron came in your life, you started getting even more dream warnings against him."

"That's right. After Ron came in my life, the dreams got more frequent," said Tia slowly as the missing pieces of the puzzle finally fitted in.

"Right! Rianna's worries were magnified even more now because the very person she thought had caused her death was back in your life this time. So she kept sending you warnings and messages to break off with him," said Sushma.

"But Sushma, being a ghost why wasn't Rianna aware of the truth since spirits can see things which we can't?" asked Nysa, her voice laced with curiosity. "I mean our Mom knew everything, right?"

"That's because your mother is on a higher spiritual plane and has more awareness and light," said Sushma. "The earth-bound spirits are weak and are lost in a dark place. Sometimes they can be very negative too. Hence they need our energy or any higher form of energy to become aware and cross over to the other side. Once on the other side they have more awareness and foresight and often become our spirit guides too. Just like your mother is Tia's spirit guide now."

Tia looked at Ron, who kissed the top of her head with immense relief. He was so grateful that the nightmare was all over and he could finally be with the love of his life.

"But now she knows everything," said Tia with a smile. A sense of bliss engulfed her mind and soul at the thought that her sister was finally at peace.

Epilogue

"They look so good together, don't they?" asked Rianna.

"Yes, they do!" Pooja sighed happily as they looked down at the grand luncheon arranged by her son, Dev. Everybody was there – Mrs Bailey, Mrs Garg, Neal, Tia, Ron, Krystal, Nina, Nysa, Jeff, Ryan, Nina, Dhruv, Ness, Maya, Tasha, Regan, Lina, Donna, Alisha and Lola. Dev had decorated his garden with a beautiful *shamiana** of floral patterns.

"I think Dev should have arranged for a nice music band too, tch tch tch," said Kunal Arya, Rianna's dad. He shook his head disappointedly.

"Kunal, you need to keep in mind the expenses too!" said Pooja Arya, her left eyebrow raised in protest.

Kunal Arya simply shrugged his shoulders. "It's just a pinch in his pocket. My son's doing quite well for himself."

His voice had a hint of pride as he looked down fondly at his family.

"Dad, Mom's right! Dev's not a spendthrift like you!" Rianna laughed.

"Ok, you mom and daughter take one side. No business for me here," he said and started walking away down the beautiful flower lined path.

"Dad!"

"Got to check on my fishes, you ladies carry on with your gossip!" Her father winked and laughed as one of his friends joined him.

"His friends are waiting for him...men talk...let him go."

Rianna shook her head as she turned back towards the beautiful sight below her.

"I gave them a hard time," she said, with deep regret in her voice.

"Darling, you didn't know! You were trapped too. All that matters is now they are all happy, including you!"

"I guess you are right, Mom..."

"And Tia needed to heal too. She wasn't getting over losing us...she had to move on. Your release was like a cathartic experience for her. She is happy now and will continue with her life lessons. God always has a plan for all of us..."

"I can't wait to meet her and Nysa again...will we meet again in another lifetime?"

"Yes, in every life time. You are soul sisters."

"Will Tia manage on her own? She appears so vulnerable at times...my little baby sister, I worry about her."

"You can talk to her anytime you want. She will need you again from time to time...especially during her weakest moments. Your strength will keep pushing her forward, empowering her always through every moment in her life."

"And Dev? Will I meet him too?"

"Yes, Rianna. As a soul family we are connected through many lifetimes," said Pooja in a reassuring tone.

"Nysa was* always the most independent and the strongest amongst us all. A happy-go-lucky girl – always made us laugh. But Dev, maybe because of the age gap, was closer to me than Nysa or Tia. He immersed himself in his work after he lost us and became distant with both of them."

"It's his soul's journey, darling, and he has to make the best of it. You can't do anything except give him love and good energy from afar," said her Mom in a consoling voice.

Rianna sighed happily.

"I have never been so happy, Mom."

"Come, Aadi's waiting for you," said Pooja, her voice soft and gentle.

"Aadi! Mom, what are you saying!?!"

Her mom beckoned the handsome man waiting for them. Aadi, with whom she had parted so many years ago, stood there with his hand extended towards her. It all felt like only yesterday as Rianna walked into his loving arms. His embrace made her feel at peace. She turned to the dazzling light shining at her from a little distance away. She was finally home.

Shamiana - A marquee; a decorative Indian ceremonial tent shelter, commonly used for outdoor parties, marriages, feasts etc.

~The End~

ABOUT THE AUTHOR

Pratibha R DH is the author of the children book series, *Magical Ventures of Loli and Lenny*, and a suspense romance novelette, *Redemption*. Besides being able to manifest her love for writing through her career as an IT content specialist, she also blogs on topics such as mindfulness, spirituality, personal growth, writing and intentional living.

These days her mantra for living an empowered life comprises a one-hour daily pack of yoga, meditation and morning pages. She loves to spend time with her family and generally be outdoors, taking a walk or simply spending time with nature. Music, swimming, dance and reading are her other passions. She lives in India with her husband and two young sons.